Matsdotter and Adrastus

WHEN A HUMAN FALLS IN LOVE WITH AN ARCHDEMON

AELINA ISAACS

NESHAMA PUBLISHING

Contents

Dedication
For the people with gaps in their memories and holes in their hearts; our trauma doesn't own us, but one day we will own it. Together.

Before Reading

This is an adult fantasy novel with queer characters who swear, smoke, and get tattoos. Several of the characters live with mental illness, and one of the main characters receives therapy and takes medication.

There is discussion regarding a previous prolonged domestic abuse situation, which included grooming and homelessness. Other things to be aware of include stalking, gore and violence, discrimination, dead naming, and death. There is off-page implied sex work, and brief on-page sexual assault. There is a brief, off-page instance of police brutality that is discussed. Lastly, there are on-page sex scenes.

I want to emphasize that this is a feel good story focusing on characters who are healing, and battling the demons of their past, and there's so much pining that it hurts. I have included a comprehensive character guide in the back, and it may contain spoilers.

Enjoy,
Aelina

Gods of the Nether Isles

Creator Gods

Hizoh: God of Dusk

Ogmes: God of Dawn

Typhine: Goddess of the Moons

Ulena: Goddess of the Sun

Caretaker Gods

Awah: Lust

Artune: Hope

Ben: Family

Da'haut: Knowledge

Dinphine: Magic

Emolite: Laborers

Kiroli: Fertility

Loborn: Arts

Nicen: Souls and the Underworld

Mithys: Logic

Mishlat: Companions

Ryvara: Trickery

Soleyar: Luck
Xvaldin: Music
Ylos: Love
Yrlan: Judgment

Watch Your Language

The 'Old Common' used in the book is based on the Hebrew language, and some meanings have been adjusted to fit the story.

Abracadabri: The magickal force of the universe, passively used by magickal creatures and can be actively tapped into by witches, considered a type of potential energy. Also means 'to create.'

Bashert: A term used to describe the spiritual union between archcelestials.

Gehenna: Hell

Isa: Salvation

Khawbar: An internal spirit inside shedim that awakens only when bonding to another soul.

Krav Maga: A type of martial arts.

Levaya: Funeral

L'chaim: To Life

Ob: Spirit of the Dead

Polinya: A flowering plant native to Jaqul, commonly used to treat sepsis and clear toxins from the blood.

Sha'mayim: Heaven

Schlemiel: Idiot

Sheol: The Underworld, where the righteous and unright-eous go while awaiting reincarnation.

Shomer: Guardian

Tchotchke: Little Thing

Yom Tov: Holiday, Festival, or Celebration. In this case Yom Tov Ogmes is the Festival of Ogmes.

Also, the celestial nobility use a naming system that refers to a person by their lineage.

Bat: Daughter of

Ben: Son of

Xir: Child of

Who Goes There?

In addition to the usual elves, dragons and centaurs, there are a few homebrew magickal races in this world. Here are the basics and their rarity in regards to Levena's population. Rarity will differ depending on region, and some are only referenced.

Behema: A general term for animalistic shifter races, defined by their ability to shift at will regardless of the lunar cycle. Most behema choose to live in their shifted form which can range from mostly humanoid to complete animal. Common.

Draconian: Dragons in their humanoid forms, characterized by their vertical pupils. It is uncommon for most Draconians to live in highly populated areas. Uncommon.

Dybbuk: A type of malicious spirit that feeds on a soul while possessing their body with such ability they often go unnoticed. When the soul has been devoured the Dybbuk must move to a new host body, living or dead with a trapped soul. It is considered 'contagious' as it can efficiently invade a body. Rare.

Gadol: A humanoid race that is born in the same form as Humans but grow exponentially after puberty, reaching heights up to thirty feet tall. Rare.

Golem: An undead race that can vary widely in appearance but is characterized by the lack of a beating heart, common form is similar to Humans. Common.

Katan: A short-statured, humanoid race ranging up to four feet in height, with slightly pointed ears. For every fifty male births a female is born, making this race slightly uncommon.

Khatool: An animalistic shifter race defined by their feline characteristics and dislike for the cold. Rare.

Krakeni: A semi-aquatic race with eight to eighteen tentacles, able to dwell on land for short periods of time with misting. Common.

Malakim: A celestial race of angelic origins, characterized by their feather-type wings, their influence over the shedim race and passive magickal ability to sense good. Uncommon.

Mayimet: An aquatic race characterized by the need to always be submerged, their massive size, and cannibalistic nature. Rarity unknown as they are deep sea creatures. Rare.

Pitriyot: A humanoid race characterized by mycological features, such as an ability to asexually reproduce, fungi-like skin that bruises easily, and an umbrella-like head. Uncommon.

Qieren: A humanoid race characterized by their colorful skin tone, at least one set of horns on their head, and a prehensile tail. Common.

Selth: A humanoid race characterized by a star shaped array of prehensile tentacles protecting their mouth and lack of pupil, possessing completely black eyes. Uncommon.

Shafan: A humanoid race with rabbit-like characteristics, such as the snout, strong hindlegs, fur, and elongated ears. Rare.

Shedim: A celestial race of demonic origins, characterized by three different wing types, their influence over the malakim race, and passive magickal ability to sense evil. Uncommon. The three basic types of Shedim are based on affinity.

- **Esh**: Shedim with an affinity for fire, physical features include leather wings, horns, and a spearpoint tail. Common type shedim.

- **Mayim**: Shedim with an affinity for water physical features include crystal scales, fins, and a paddle-like tail. Common type shedim.

- **Jinni**: Shedim with an affinity for abracadabri, physical features differ due to shapeshifting abilities. Rare type shedim.

Tannin: A shifter race with draconian characteristics, lacking the ability to shift to full dragon form. Their shifted form is humanoid in appearance with iridescent scales, a full snout, tail and leather-type wings. Common.

Tzipor: A humanoid race with bird-like characteristics such as talons, a beak, and wings. Uncommon.

Where Are We?

Spire of Agia
Tower of Min
Levena
Dimshear
Mythaven
Brinecliff
Faygale
Wildemont
The Nether Isles
Kilbrook
Northgrave
Obelisk of Gia
West Shire
Finnas
Rosevein
Dridale
Jaqul
Pearlholde

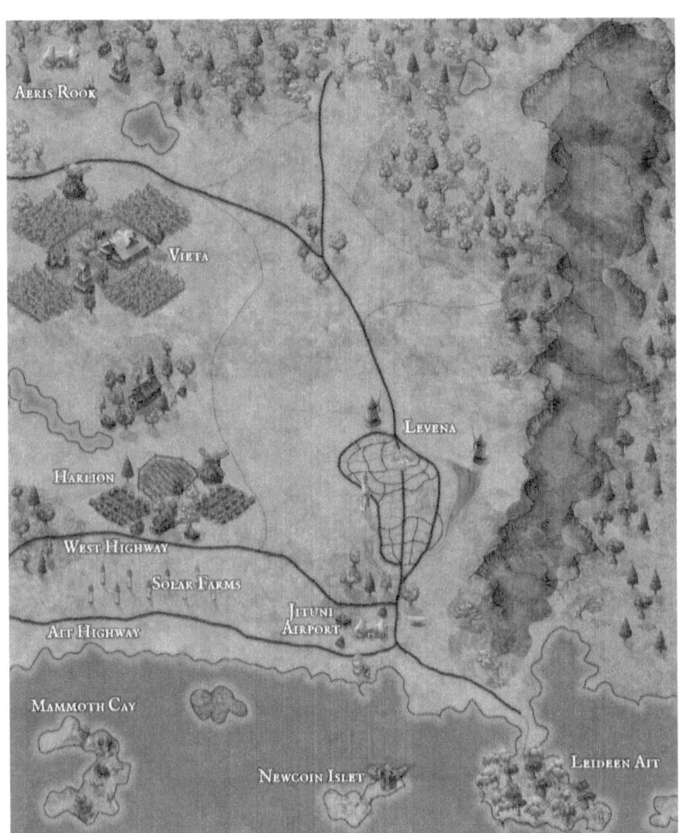

Aeris Rook
Vieta
Harlion
West Highway
Solar Farms
Ait Highway
Mammoth Cay
Levena
Jituni Airport
Newcoin Islet
Leidren Ait

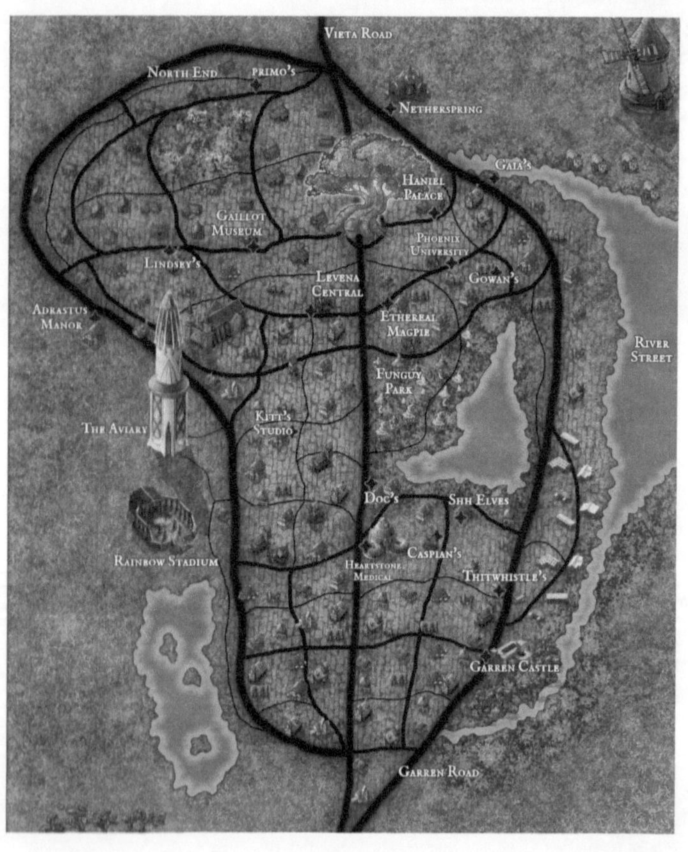

VIETA ROAD
NORTH END
PRIMO'S
NETHERSPRING
GAIA'S
HANIEL PALACE
GAILLOT MUSEUM
PHOENIX UNIVERSITY
LINDSEY'S
LEVENA CENTRAL
GOWAN'S
ADRASTUS MANOR
ETHEREAL MAGPIE
RIVER STREET
FUNGUY PARK
THE AVIARY
KITT'S STUDIO
DOC'S
SHH ELVES
RAINBOW STADIUM
CASPIAN'S
HEARTSTONE MEDICAL
THITWHISTLE'S
GARREN CASTLE
GARREN ROAD

Prologue

To be honest, I don't know where this story truly begins, or why I'm the one that was chosen to begin it. Lochian says it's obvious why, but I'm not so sure. Sure, I'm a writer, but that doesn't automatically make me an expert on our experiences. The letters help, I suppose.

You see, we've been writing to you. Wow, it's been … years, now. Anyways, the letters became a collection of stories. Chronicles of our time spent waiting for you.

It's easier to absorb everything that way, I think.

So here it is. The story of us, ready for your perusal. It's all true, and perhaps more detailed than need be, but every bit is important. And our story is first, apparently. Which brings me back to my original point.

Where do you begin?

How do you skim through the memories of your life and say, *'Yes, here it is, the moment when my life truly began.'*

Ah, well.

In my case, you have to understand something about me.

For most of my life, I ached for a friend. A genuine, true friend. I begged for one. Allowed myself to be treated terribly in exchange for false words. Beautiful lies sung by a person who said I was everything, but they *treated* me like I was nothing. There's a difference between words and actions, and it's been said actions speak loudest, but oh how I scavenged for those words.

I doted. I praised. I covered up the damage. I *worshiped*.

All for someone who never cared for me. Not really.

And the thing is, now that I have people who *do* truly love me, because I have found not one friend, but many, I've never been more terrified in my life. Life is a fragile thing, easily uprooted. You never know just how far one's roots go, and what—or who—else they may be entangled with until they're torn from the ground and exposed for all the world to see.

What would I do to keep that from happening?

What are the limits to love?

Because if I endured all of that pain and humiliation for the benefit of someone who treated me so poorly, it's not hard to imagine what I would do for someone who actually deserved it.

With this in mind, I think I know where to start, now.

In the dead of winter on a Tuesday night, an old classmate of mine holds a bag of frozen peas to my cheek. It's the first time we've seen each other in years, and we aren't even close. Not really. We went to the same university and maybe ate lunch together a few times, but that's it. We ran in different circles. I graduated ahead of her, and everyone else. Again.

But that didn't stop her from choke slamming my boyfriend against the floor on a snowy, technicolor night.

River pulled me into a putrid alcove near the bathrooms, the floor slick with vomit from the last person who took shelter there. There was a little stone ledge in there, dusted with the ashes of who knows what. Given the neon yellow particulate that accompanied the soot, I had a pretty good idea.

River trapped my hands on the ledge with his own, thrust against my back despite my protests. There were people lined up in the hallway to the bathrooms, right outside the alcove. We were separate from the bottom feeders of Levena, but no less private. I ~~should~~

I broke free from his grip and told him no, not here. That I wanted to go home. He backhanded me, rings shredding my eye and cheek. No one else cared, they never did. The place was a run down bar in the northeastern part of Levena that I hated, but River loved it because he could be himself there. I'm sure you can already infer that he's the type of man that always gets what he wants. And there, he wasn't an uncommon type of folk.

But not that night. That night an elf and a *qieren* were on a mission, searching for a regular in the bar for reasons I didn't come to learn until later. The couple were walking past the alcove when River struck me. The *qieren*, purple skinned with fearsome horns, tore through the line to the bathroom. She cleared the way for her elven companion who snatched River by the back of his neck. I was terrified for the seemingly delicate blonde, but she dragged him out into the hallway just fine.

And to my complete shock, the elf lifted him up like it was childsplay. River fiercely clawed at her arm, and she slammed him down into the old planking which shattered upon impact.

After knocking him out cold, the elf wiped her hands off on a gorgeous sheer black dress, then offered it to me. It was then I recognized her.

"Lindsey?" I asked, voice trembling. I was so cold, and covered in so much filth I didn't dare soil her. All I wanted was to go home, but I didn't know where that was anymore.

"Yeah, kid. Come on, let's get you fixed up."

The *qieren* stood protectively in front of us, arms crossed and tail snapping dangerously at those passing by. She was dressed just as beautifully, both of them wore short dresses and tall heels, their lethal beauty able to wound even the strongest of hearts.

And something in me said, 'enough.'

It said, 'take the goddamn help.'

It said, 'run.'

And I did.

They brought me back to the place that had been my house for the past eight months. It was a home to me, once. As I rescued my backpack from the closet and efficiently packed it, running through a plan I'd crafted again and again during the precious hours of night, the fact that this place was more prison than home became more clear than ever. Lindsey insisted on bringing only what I needed or was sentimental, anything else can be replaced.

Wordlessly, I did as she said in fear of telling her never mind. That I don't need help.

But I didn't.

It took me less than four minutes to fill the backpack. A few changes of clothes, my notebooks once buried under the bed, and the contents of a shoebox once hidden behind a paint can in the little cupboard under the stairs, is all I brought with me. Lindsey brought me back to her place, which brings us to now.

Peas on the face.

The *qieren*, Kitt, paces the den as she talks on the phone. She's dressed in jeans and a sweater now, as is Lindsey. When Kitt mentions a healer, I shake my head. An action I immediately regret. After holding back a groan, I say, "I don't need a doctor. It's just—"

Lindsey rolls her eyes, readjusting the frozen peas. "Your face is split open, sweet cheeks. Do you feel like explaining that, the other cuts from those damned rings, and the bruise covering half your face? Besides, I said healer, not doctor. Don't worry, it's all under the radar."

I swallow. "Do you—do you know a witch?"

Lindsey gives me a flat look. "Several. Is that a problem?"

"No, I just ... I haven't met a witch before." I admit.

"Oh, well—"

A knock rattles the front door three times in quick succession. Everyone in the room freezes, but my heart doesn't get the memo. It drowns out all noise, throbbing in my ears. It screams, 'run run run,' but I can't move. I watch Kitt pocket her phone and move towards the door.

Lindsey sets the peas on the cushion between us and stands up, fists clenching at her sides. Kitt reaches behind a towering plant in a vase beside the door frame, then pulls out a baseball bat inscribed with runes and embedded with massive spikes.

"What the fuck ..." I whisper, not meaning to have said it all.

"Go in the bedroom," Lindsey says, but I can't move.

Kitt looks through the peep-hole, then back at us with confusion pinching her features. "Either of you know a wolf *behema*?"

I shake my head, and Lindsey does too.

Then the *qieren* grins, accepting the challenge of unannounced strangers like a long lost chest of precious treasure.

She opens the door, twirling the bat around like a baton. Kitt cheerily says, "Evening. Anything I can help you with?"

From my vantage point on the couch, all I can see is a lumbering figure on the other side of the threshold, partially hidden by the *qieren*. After a tense moment the person asks, "Are you Kitt Meissa?"

Lindsey gives me one last look, then leaves me to join Kitt's side. Kitt tilts her head. "Who's asking?"

"I am Dr. Atthias, and I work at Heartstone Medical, in the psychiatry unit. I was under the impression that you are Arlo Rook's power of attorney?"

The silence is so damn thick that I could choke on it. Lindsey gently takes the bat from Kitt, startling her. Kitt glances between Lindsey and the *behema* a few times, then asks, "Do you have some kind of identification?" A moment passes, then she adds, "Alright, come in. Where is Dr. Kensworth?"

Half-shifted, the *behema* gives me a cursory glance upon entering, then shifts their attention to Kitt. They say, "I apologize for intruding upon you so late, but this matter is urgent and I felt it should be discussed in person, without Dr. Kensworth. I will be blunt with you, Ms. Meissa, you have been lied to. Mr. Rook is not refusing your visits, he's been in solitary confinement for over thirty days now. Through my colleague's findings and my own, we have found that not only is Dr. Kenswoth discriminating against Mr. Rook for his being a witch, but others in the unit as well.

"His 'treatments' are torture at best, and I'm afraid he's being allowed to do so, the corruption goes all the way to the top. We have been working to help him and the others trapped there, but we've met a wall, one that is about to have me fired. So, I come directly to you in fear of this all being buried further, or worse, the witches themselves. You must withdraw him from the program immediately, before it's too late. Here, I have a copy of Mr. Rook's records that's available to the rest of us, and Dr. Kensworth's copy which is ... much more extensive, and graphic. There are photos—"

"I've heard enough. Bring me to him. Now," Kitt says, and the atmosphere quakes beneath her demand. I've no idea who they're talking about, but it's clear he's important to her. My broken heart aches with festering jealousy. To have someone care about me that much. Then again, I did, and I just ran away from him.

River loves me. I know this. But he's like a child who loves so hard that he breaks the bones of all his favorite pets.

Lindsey's already started to gather up their boots and bags, and the bat. After a minute she ties her hair back, coming over to me while Kitt and the doctor talk. She kneels beside my place on the couch. "We'll be back. The spare bedroom is there, and it has its own bathroom. You live here now. Eat, sleep, shower. Do whatever you like. I'll lock the door behind us. There's wards, too. *No one* will be able to get in. You are safe here, okay? Don't be stupid and leave."

A small laugh tumbles out of me, unbidden. I look away, wiping at my eyes. "Okay." I nod, then look back at her. "Okay. Thank you, Lindsey. I'll make it up to you. I can pay you, I—"

"Don't worry about that right now." Lindsey shakes her head, then stands and gently ruffles my hair. "Try to get some sleep."

I quickly look over at Kitt, but she's rifling through the folder. The *behema* stands beside her, hands behind their back and ears flat against their head. I shift my attention back to Lindsey. "Good luck. I hope your friend's okay."

Lindsey winks. "He will be. Those bastards that were supposed to be taking care of him? They're done. We protect our own around here, Quentin."

I smile and nod, then watch her go.

They all leave, and when the door shuts, it clicks four times despite the fact there's only two locks, one deadbolt and one in the handle itself.

I sit there for a long time, wondering how I got here, and if I'm truly going to stay.

If such a thing as true friends is possible.

I think we both know how that turned out.

January

THE NEW TOWN TIMES

NEW YEAR, NEW PROBLEMS

A recent investigation by an independent group, Normals for Justice, reveals that the number of unregistered witches are much higher than originally reported. Levena residents are calling for stricter registration reform, and for a formal census to be mounted and fines increased for failure to register.

Carina Wells, local resident, and vice- president of the Levena Central Board, points to this discovery as proof that exposure to general magickal education is detrimental to young children, and can cause a sudden and otherwise avoidable case of witchery.

FALL QUAKES TIED TO MYSTERIOUS IMMORTAL'S APPEARNCE

Regional geologists and meterologists team up to solve a millenia old mystery. (cont. on pg.8)

GAILLOT MUSUEM'S YULETIDE GALA A SUCCESS

Newly renamed Gaillot Museum surpassed their fundraising goal; plans underway to begin construction on a children's museum in the spring, complete with an afterschool program. (cont. on pg. 6)

DANIEL KAVELLI; DOOM OR DESTINY OF INHERITED SOLAR TECH EMPIRE?

Who is the man without his father's shadow? (cont. on pg. 3)

I Know

Elochian
Levena
9621 A.C

An Archangel of Love and a Witch of Death walk into The Ethereal Magpie, searching for the Archdemon of Anxiety who owns it. It sounds like a bad joke, but no.

It's just my life.

I am close friends with Arlo, the only Hedge Witch in Levena. I'm acquainted with Tobias Daemarrel, a recently discovered archangel, through Arlo and his friends. There is no logical reason for me to be afraid of either of them. No, it's the potential trouble they bring *with* them.

Trapped behind the serving counter, I step backwards as they approach. Tobias leads the way like a man on a mission, and my back meets the wall. All six of his wings are visible. Great rose feathers hug tight to his back, with even the smallest ones the length of my arm. While conversation doesn't cease, the bar's collective attention shifts to Tobias.

Those in Tobias and Arlo's way part without a word. The place is loaded with angels, and I wonder if they intentionally chose to visit on *Malakim* Monday. The celestials present make themselves visible to Tobias, angel and demon both. Posturing, hoping to be seen, but at a distance.

But the new *archmalakim* isn't looking at anyone else. He only has eyes for me. It's the first time we've seen each other since he sang a song of love and intoxicated my entire bar, resulting in what's sure to be Levena's biggest baby boom yet. That's more of a witch thing than an archangel thing, because life has a good sense of humor like that.

I inhale sharply, forcing myself to remain still. Gossip has run thick since his first arrival. The Archangel of Levena, finally revealing himself and intoxicating everyone in a five block radius. I wasn't immune to his magick, quite the opposite, but it wasn't his power that disabled me.

It was his proclamation of, '*Here I am. Your Other Half. I am ready.*'

Now, he didn't actually *say* these things, but it was spoken on a soul to soul level. In response, mine broke down and cried. In relief, and in fear. The fear of the unknown is always there, but there is so *much* unknown with Tobias.

Archangels and archdemons are designed to function as one, as *bashert*. A singular unit for the celestials to anchor their power to. A guiding demon for the angels, and a guiding angel for the demons. Without this universal anchor, celestials cannot function. An ankle weight of a parting gift from our godly parents, to keep us from becoming too much like them.

But I've been on my own, bearing the entire bodily weight of all the celestials in the Northern Regions. No archangel has led the Haniel Clan since before my birth, and as such all the celestials look to the Adrastus family, demons and angels alike. Whatever Tobias has done all these years has shielded him from me perfectly, and I would be a hypocrite to call him out on hiding from his duties.

Then again, if I hadn't been so stretched thin my entire life, would things have turned out differently for me?

For Bartholomew?

And now, months after Tobias revealed himself, he's showing up out of the blue. Not once has he asked to help, to become involved with our people. My demons are suffering from celestial sickness, and there's only one reason why. Only one solution. I've called him a few times to no avail, and when it became clear that Tobias had no intention to assume his place, I stopped. I've wanted to try again this past week, but his silence was crippling.

I haven't mentioned my frustrations to Arlo, not wanting to put him in the middle, but it appears Tobias has done that already.

When the pair finally sit down on the other side of the bar, my irritation is well on its way to dancing with anxiety. The bartender, Lucas, smoothly avoids the disturbance and efficiently distracts the patrons from our stare down. I ensure all people see is a blank face, not wanting to let on my annoyance. I casually lean against the counter beside the liquor wall, arms crossed.

Arlo's intense stare cuts right through me, but I ignore it. I ignore the stare of every godsdamned person currently staring at us. I focus on Tobias, who stares down at his fingers tightly knitted on the marble bar counter before him.

I don't speak first.

Tobias breathes, and when he exhales, his wings loosen from his shoulders. He lifts his head and looks me square in the eyes. His are dull and tired, the once bright pink dulled to something bordering on gray, which confirms my suspicion. He wants something.

He says, "Elochian, it's good to see you. Is there any chance we could talk? Privately?"

"I'm fine here, if it's all the same to you."

"Loch," Arlo says.

I glare at him. "Why are you here? Not that I'm not happy to see you."

He smirks, breaking the tension in the air without my consent. "You're never happy to see me. I'm moral support."

I sigh, rubbing at my temple. A lock of unbound hair finds its way around my finger, and I gently tug on it as I think. I glance at Michael sitting at the nearest end of the bar, appearing to all the world like a simple human having a drink. They are far more than that, though. Michael takes a sip of his drink, then taps the counter's surface twice before setting his glass down.

He approves of whatever this is, despite the fact I don't.

But I have a duty, one that is more important than my frustration. I owe it to my people to listen to what Tobias has to say. Maybe he's ready to take his place, and I can't be the person who stands in his way, even if it took him a while to get there.

I straighten, leaving the safety of the counter in one swift movement. "Meet me in my office," I tell Tobias. I turn away without gaining an answer, escaping through the galley kitchen hidden at the other end of the bar. The narrow, open archway is curtained by ivy hanging from the ceiling. *Shedim* stop what they're doing to mark an '*A*' over their heart when I pass through.

I say nothing, keeping my head held high. I've learned by now that telling them to treat me like one of them is futile, and it distresses those ranked lower than me. The gold in my face highlights the would be lie, and all six of my wings frame the deceit like a saccharine masterpiece.

Michael meets me at the door on the other side of the galley. He's dressed in an all black suit and no tie, golden hair shaved close to his head. Simple diamond studs line their ears, narrowing as the jewelry reaches the sharp points. Their irises are jet black. In no matter what form they take, Michael is sophisticated and practical, and the decorative spirals of silver tattooed on both sides of their pale neck carry over as well. The color denotes ranking, whilst the design itself proclaims his loyalty. To me, and to me only.

It's a heavy thing, the weight of someone's life. Especially when I've shattered one before, and so easily. Michael has been Bartholomew's replacement, my *shomer*, for over a hundred years, dutiful and kind. However, I'm helpless to think of him as anything but that.

A replacement.

Michael bows his head when I join him. "Sir."

I return the show of respect, then gesture for him to lead the way to my office. When they do, I ask, "When was the last time my office was swept?"

"Annie just finished, Sir. Mr. Rook may have called ahead of time."

"Oh, so he warns you." I grumble, tugging on the end of a thin braid.

Michael chuckles, glancing sideways at me. "Sir, may I make a suggestion?"

"No."

"Of course, Sir."

I glare at him. "That was a joke, Michael. You know how I feel about your suggestions."

They smile. "And I maintain my position that you should not heed my counsel more than your own. With that being said, it is my belief that the archangel needs guidance, and it's not an easy thing to ask for."

I laugh, but there's no joy in it. "And I'm the one to provide it? I can barely stand on my own two feet."

We're close to my office now, and he looks at the closed door. "If not you, then who?"

I stop walking. "He has people. Doesn't he?"

"*Does* he? He's married to a half *katan*, there are no angels in his life now, and we have no evidence to suggest if he had a proper upbringing. Not to mention the only demons around him are his own children.

I rub my temple. "I hate it when you make sense." I shake my head, then peek at Michael. "It's ... they came alone?"

"Yes?" Michael tilts his head. "Were you expecting someone?"

"No, of course not. Stop looking at me like that." I wave him off, stepping past him to enter my office.

"Of course, Sir." Michael follows me in, shutting the door.

When he does, wards hum into place, keeping us safe from things like eavesdroppers, or a nuclear bomb. I take a seat behind a meticulously organized desk, breathing easier as my fingers brush against the old wood. Arlo paces along one side of the room before a lit hearth, while Tobias sits utterly still on the other side of my desk in one of two leather chairs. Michael settles behind me, quiet and focused.

Tobias glances back at Arlo, then to me. With a trembling hand, he tucks damp pink hair behind his ear. He says, "Thank you for seeing me. I—I don't know what to say, Elochian. How to start."

"We could start with why you've been ignoring my phone calls."

Tobias sighs, bowing his head. He whispers, "I'm scared. Ever since that night, things have been ... more. It's hard to explain. But it's *physically* hurting me. I can feel hundreds—if not thousands, of people now. I've never felt that, it's like my mind was full of cotton before. I think it's my fault. You see, I'm an Empath. I do nothing *but* feel.

"All I wanted was to live alone, like I have my entire life, and feel nothing but my own existence. People are so complicated, and hard to take. *Physically*. Some people hurt to simply be around. But then Cas came along, and everything changed. I have a family now, friends. And I decided maybe I didn't *have* to shut everyone out. But I didn't understand the consequences. I didn't—*don't*—know what it means to be an archangel. I didn't know people would need me so *strongly*, and that I could feel them if I just opened my heart. But you do, don't you? I can feel you, most of all."

I come around the desk and kneel before Tobias, itching to reach out and cup his wet cheeks. Tentatively, I take his hand instead. My fingers slide against his, and he gasps, eyes slamming shut. "It's quiet. You made it quiet."

Something settles in my heart, like a cornerstone of my foundation has found its place. I stare at him, in awe and confusion. "I'm your Other Half," I whisper. How can he not know?

Tobias shakes his head. Through hot, choking sobs, he manages, "I want to help you, Elochian. But Gods, tell me there's a way to make it like this again. I feel like I'm going crazy."

My wings stretch, confident in their movements as they reach around my body to partially hide the both of us. I whisper, "I will help you, but I won't lie and say it'll be easy. Taking your place, that is. You could still run, but it would hurt, for a while. It's like ... you are bonded to your children, yes?"

Tobias nods slowly, and my hand pulls away from his. He's stopped actively crying, but tears still overflow his bloodshot eyes.

"It's like that, but on a grander scale. All this time, the demons of the Northern Region have been without a 'parent.' An anchor, or a magnet, for their soul. We gain strength and power from them, and they do from us. It's a give and take, and the bonds are strengthened by time and nurturing, but they form on their own. It's probably why you aren't feeling well, you weren't prepared.

I lower my voice, feeling weighed down by all of this. "Celestials aren't a species designed to live independently. But, it is possible. Now that bonds have been formed between you and those in Levena, you will have to sever them, if it is your wish to leave."

Tobias stares at me, and in the time it takes him to answer, I do my best to shield myself from him. I don't want to influence his answer. Even though I desperately want him to say yes. Yes, I'll help you. Yes, you won't be alone.

Tobias says, "If not me, then who?"

"I don't know," I whisper. "Tobias ... did you truly not know what you are to our people? To me?"

Bitterly, he says, "I'm an anomaly. A witch, and an archangel. My parents didn't interact with society, or me. I've been alone. I don't know how to handle this, Elochian. I—"

"You don't have to be. *We* don't have to be. I'll help you. We're stronger together."

"Okay."

"Okay?"

He shrugs, sniffing. "Okay. I'll do it. I'll try, anyway."

I take his hands, squeezing gently. "That's all we can do."

"Thank you, Elochian. Thank you."

Tobias recomposes himself, and I slowly stand from my kneeling position. I look towards Arlo, who's finally shifted his attention from the fire and quit his pacing. He nods once, clearly pleased. "Good. Now that that's settled, it's my turn."

"I thought you were moral support," I ask, crossing my arms.

"Yes, well. I'm needy, what can I say."

I sigh, gesturing for him to take the empty seat beside Tobias. I retreat to my own seat on the other side, feeling exceptionally drained. Centering Tobias took more out of me than I expected. By the time I plop down, Arlo has finally settled into a chair. He removes his hat and lays it over a gently bouncing knee, then rakes a hand through his knotted hair.

"What did you find this time?" I ask, already having guessed what Arlo needs my help with. What he always needs my help with, these days. It's a distinct feeling, being needed. He *can* function without me. I know this. But friends help each other. I know this, as well. I'm just not used to being on the giving side.

I'm the one always needing it.

Arlo says, "The gravestone." The hairs on the back of my neck stand up. Bartholomew's headstone flashes through my mind. Gently, Arlo adds, "The gravestone we found during the game. The neighbor to the one in your painting."

"Oh. What about it?"

"It's changed."

"How?" I lean ahead in my seat, elbows resting on the desk between us.

Arlo focuses on his hat, fiddling with a loose string on the brim. He says, "It's not chipped away anymore. The ... name. It's all there." He reaches into his jeans pocket, pulling out a phone. He taps the screen a few times, then places it between us. A projection cuts into life, depicting the headstone in question.

It reads, '*In Remembrance of Thatcher Levena Gaillot, founder of what is formerly known as Min Isle and will henceforth be known as Levena in honor of the man who endlessly put others first.*

Savior of over 300 Min residents during the Fire of 38' which burned Min Isle to the ground.

While others fell in the flames, he perpetually put himself in danger time and time again, not stopping until he brought everyone to the river, to safety, until he succumbed to his injuries and was taken by the flames.

He was a friend to all those he met, endlessly loyal and an instrumental figure in what Levena has become today.

Thank you for watching over us from wherever you are now, for your continued protection from beyond the grave. We will strive to live like you did and never forget your kindness.

Rest in Peace, Thatch.'

"Oh," I say, numbed by too many emotions to name.

Arlo swallows, then dims the screen. He leaves the phone on my desk, looking at it like it might bite him. Shakily, he says, "There's nothing in the libraries, or the bookstores, or the museum, on Min Isle. *Still.* But I thought maybe you ... that someone here could be old enough. '38, I don't know what the millennia is, but—"

"Arlo ..." I begin softly, and he rears back as if I'd slapped him. I soldier on, strengthening my tone. "*Malakim* and *shedim* weren't around here before Levena was anything else but Levena. Besides, the oldest person *I* know besides my aunt is Dusan, I've told you this."

Arlo exhales heavily, snatching his hat from his knee. He slides it back on and goes to stand, but freezes when I ask, "What's going on with Leon?"

Tobias grips his armrests, attention locking onto Arlo. Like he wants to know the answer, too.

Like a child caught lying about their chores, Arlo says, "He hasn't materialized yet. I've exorcized a few ghosts in his employ, but that's it. I'm keeping an eye on things, Elochian. He's just quiet right now."

"I'm not implying you're doing otherwise, Arlo. I know that you want to do right by Thatch, we all do. But right now, I think we have other things to worry about. I know you don't think the AWO and NOJ are connected with his rise, but the AWO at the very least was a big supporter of—"

Arlo stands in a rush. "I *know*, Elochian. I was there. There's nothing I can do about Leon until he shows his face, until then I'm going to focus on what matters. Bringing Thatch home. If we can just figure out who he was, we can—"

"We can what? Know how old he was exactly? Know who his first boyfriend was? You're not going to find out his secrets and how he was cursed in *books*, Arlo. We've done nothing but scour the earth for evidence of the past, and I'm not saying we shouldn't, but when the future is trying to kill us it may be time to put the past away, for now."

To my surprise, Arlo doesn't hit me. He doesn't take off. He simply drops his head in his hands, and cries. I glance back at Michael, who stares back at me with a flat expression. I look at Tobias, who barely seems to be holding on to the fragile newfound peace I gave him. I stand, and slowly come 'round the desk.

I reach for him, but stop when he says, "It's only been two months. I thought it would take longer for everyone to give up."

I whisper, "No one is giving up, Arlo."

"They want to. And I can't blame them. Everyone is ... they have their own lives." He scrubs at his face before lifting his magick infused gaze to me. "I can't stop thinking about him. It feels like life has gone on like nothing happened, and that it's also stopped entirely. I miss him so much it hurts, Loch. Do you—" He grimaces, abruptly cutting off.

With great caution, I take his hand, because that's the only thing I can do. I can't bring Thatch back, and what can I say? Arlo doesn't want a positive or cheerful sentiment, he just wants his person, and he hasn't had time to grieve the sudden loss of him. The world won't allow it.

I whisper, "I know, Arlo. I know what that feels like."

I stare out the window, wallowing in the numbness spreading throughout my forehead. I breathe, chest heavy, and do my best to think of nothing else but the car window against my skin. The town car is dimly lit, and for a rare moment, it's only us and the night sky somewhat visible through the lightly frosted window. We pass by The Cromaeris, which is beautiful yet eerie. The temple's vibrant stained glass windows are always illuminated, and the depictions of the Creator Gods seem to loom over this side of Levena.

Michael waits until we're a few minutes away from the manor before disrupting the quiet. "You made many promises tonight, Sir."

I shift my attention to my bodyguard in the driver's seat. "If I remember correctly, you are the one who suggested the angel needs guidance. I offered it, and now you're questioning me?"

"I do not disagree at all, but I'm merely curious how you'll go about it. Your days are thin as it is."

"I'll extend my office hours, and ... I'll work on Mondays. Lucas has been asking for more hours anyways. On Fridays, I'll make time for Tobias until I can get in touch with Andromeda. She's been filling his role for some time now, and I'm sure she'll be happy to help. The Elders will have to deal with not having twenty-four seven access to me for a little while."

Michael says nothing.

I glance at them. He stares at me, a tiny smile on his face. There's a betraying crease between their brows, though. Michael says, "I think what you're doing is admirable. For both Tobias and Arlo. But don't hurt yourself, Elochian. Your rest days are in place for a reason."

"Then I give you full permission to baby me and say 'I told you so' on the day I inevitably crack. I don't do anything on rest days anyway."

Michael sighs, fondly exasperated. "As long as I have your permission."

I chuckle. The town car comes to a stop before the electrified gates to Adrastus Manor, and after a moment they swing inwards and allow us to pass through. You would think the place is a prison by the way it's fortified and protected, kept under constant surveillance and staffed at all times. Michael eases down the drive, passing by fallow fields and dark greenhouses. The evergreen hedges are sculpted into perfect depictions of my parents and other legacies, their green leaves steadfast against the winter. Everything else is veiled by the night.

The vehicle comes to a stop directly before the front doors of Adrastus House, which are protected by a stone overhang. Michael gets out of the car first, then comes around and opens my door for me. I step out, inhaling fresh, crisp air. When I exhale, it's like the estate and all those present exhale as one. I'm not at ease until I'm home, and that restlessness spreads throughout the clan if I'm not careful. The hearts of all those present in the manor reach towards mine. In the space of one more breath, my spirit briefly greets theirs and says goodnight, then I close my heart off from those around me.

I lift my face to the sky, memorizing the stars again for a quick moment. When was the last time I simply stared up at the sky, without glass separating it from me?

Michael follows my upwards stare, brow quirked. "Looking for something?"

I sigh, giving them a tight smile. "No. Just looking."

He escorts me inside, through wide halls decorated with crimson wallpaper that's older than I am. Old school iron candelabras and grand masterpieces encased in golden frames take place every eight feet or so, but the corridors always feel so empty to me. Quiet classical music plays on a distant record player, accompanied by the soft murmur of the night dwelling *shedim* of the house. Thankfully, my aunt is a day dweller like myself, which means I get to continue avoiding her for the rest of the night.

When we reach the northern staircase which leads to my personal wing of the manor, Michael bows their head. He says, "I will see you in the morning. Still on with Kavelli?"

I give him a grim smile. "Oh yes, bright and early."

Michael commits the mark of Adrastus over his heart, and my smile fades as the moment is overlaid with a distant memory that never blurs. Bartholomew committing that same action for the first time.

And the last.

"Good night, Michael." I dip my head, then turn away from my *shomer*.

I climb the stairs, palm floating over the old cherry banister that needs to be refinished. All the intricate wood trim in the estate's construction is cherry, from the baseboards to the cornices. I'm told it was my mother's favorite, something about the warmth in the color. I find comfort in the grain as well, but I don't know if it has anything to do with the color.

By the time I make it to the landing of the fourth level, my legs are shaky and my heart is pissed. On the levels beneath me are the apartments of my family and inner circle which are all family friends that I inherited, all of whom are old enough to be my parents. The servant's quarters are on the first and top floors, while everyone else in the Adrastus Clan lives in one of the ten annexes.

I follow the east corridor, passing by closed doors which lack knobs. Every step towards my bedroom is exhausting, but inch by inch, I manage to make it to the last door. I place my palm upon the wood, and within a moment the knots and grain alights a soft orange before the door groans inwards.

I step inside in a hurry, haunted by memories of Bartholomew nipping at my heels. The door shuts behind me, and the moment it does I begin to strip. Every light in the place is out, but moonlight creeps in through the tall, narrow windows which line the western wall. My wool overcoat lands over the back of a couch, my shirts litter the floor like bread crumbs, and my pants fall into a puddle at the end of my bed.

I brace myself using the cherry footboard, back cracking while I arch my spine and stretch my wings out to their full potential. Muscles and bones cry out in protest, unhappy with today's treatment. Every day's treatment, I should say. Some people clench their jaw or grit their teeth, but my tension lies in my wings. Constantly prepared for a fight and rigid for seemingly no reason at all. Often, the more I try to relax them, the more they tense.

I spend ten minutes stretching out my body, moving on from my wings to my arms, then my back and legs. I roll my neck out, then reach down and snag my phone and the rest of my paraphernalia out of my pants. I set my canvas satchel on the end table which keeps my side of the bed company, then my cumbersome key ring and phone. I hold my wallet in both hands, thumb running over the worn leather. With a heavy exhalation, I open it up and take a quick look at the picture tucked inside.

I promptly shut it, then gently set it down beside the rest of my things.

I collapse on the bed, pristinely made bedding and all, and groan into the mattress. I close my eyes, unwilling to move a single muscle. I'll fall asleep just like this. I don't care.

Except, hours pass, and I don't sleep.

I end up under the covers. Back on top of the covers. Lying on my right side. Lying on my left. Tucking my knees into my chest. Resting in a partially kneeling position. Now that I'm ready for bed, clearly exhausted, my mind won't shut the fuck up. I'm mentally planning out every aspect of tomorrow, preparing for every angle of every meeting and every escape plan. Plans Bs and Cs are a constant must.

Eventually, I wave the white flag and reach for my phone. Usually I try not to use it before bed, but at this point I need something to distract myself from the growing irritation skewering my tired brain. The latest comic is probably out, I'll—

Quentin wrote to me an hour ago.

Dot (2:35 AM): but what if it's not true love what if he's a stepping stone there are people who need that not everyone's first is their last

Dot (2:36 AM): oh no. sorry I didn't mean to send that to you! don't worry, I'll still be up with bells on and coffee waiting.

I laugh quietly, and leave him a message to wake up to.

Me (3:27 AM): It's alright, I don't mind. I hope you were able to work through this latest tangle. I won't be able to come by in the morning, but eat a muffin for me.

I pause, considering. Should I tell him I'll miss him?
I close my eyes, enduring the sudden gut punch.
I miss him.
Now.

Basic Physics

Quentin

"It's for the good of the kids. Surely you can understand, Mr. Matsdotter. It's integral to your position to keep them safe, is it not? We're all on the same side, I assure you."

I straighten the stack of papers once more, their edges tap against my desk with controlled force. With a calm I most certainly do not feel, I say, "Please, Mrs. Wells. Your fear is misplaced. I can not, and *will* not, sign your petition. You do realize that I am friends with several witches who also happen to be instrumental figures in Levena and the farthest thing from dangerous?"

My archnemesis rests a hand over her heart, disturbing the white ruffles of her blouse. Her whole ensemble is all the latest fashion, but far too dramatic and impractical for elementary school. Her exaggerated collar is high, brushing against the tips of her pointed ears adorned with rows of pearls. Several layers of pearl necklaces rest on the outside of her silken blouse, which is buttoned all the way up her throat.

"I am aware, which is why I am so worried about *you*. You are too close to the problem to see them for what they truly are. Your *friends* are danger incarnate, and you must not be complacent. I implore you to—"

I stand abruptly, chair scraping against harsh silence. Every single one of my students watch the stand-off taking place over my desk, but I don't shift my attention from Carina, not willing to show weakness. "Leave my classroom. *Now.* If you wish to harass me about this matter further, have the decency to do so in private, not in front of the children," I whisper harshly, throwing her own sentiment back at her.

Carina straightens impossibly further, her posture already painfully perfect. Her painted nails dig into her palm, and several wisps of teal have escaped from her tightly wound bun. After a tense moment, she says, "Good *day*, Mr. Matsdotter."

Carina turns on a heel, spine rigid and long elven ears flattened against her skull. Her stilettos dominate the moment, stabbing my heart with each clack towards the door. She tears the door open and pauses. Carina sweeps her attention over the classroom, settling on me last. She says, "Enjoy your time together. While it lasts."

Carina softly shuts the door behind her, and I barely hide my flinch. I'd rather if she'd just slammed the damn thing. I readjust my glasses and stare at the door for a moment, recomposing myself. Then, I walk around my desk and stand tall, facing a class of extremely curious fourth graders.

I clap my hands together, sweat trickling down my spine. "I apologize for the interruption. Ah ... do we need to extend homeroom for a few minutes? Or is everyone ready?"

The children look between each other, then back to me. There's a lot of shrugging, and a few nos. The bell went off five minutes ago, but Carina wouldn't stop shoving that damned petition in my face. Add that to the brewing snowstorm disrupting our normal routine, and you have a morning of pure chaos. A vampire in the back raises her hand, and I internally sigh. Here it comes.

"Stella?"

Stella lowers her hand, tossing her long hair over her shoulder, which is hidden beneath five layer of clothing. "Is Mrs. Wells the reason why we're *still* learning about the scientific method instead of magick? I thought we were supposed to start the next unit after break, but we're still doing the same thing."

Straight A, meticulous students are a double-edged sword.

I run a hand through my damp and knotted hair, the snowflakes have long melted and frizzed it all up. With careful precision, I say, "As I said yesterday, there is some debate regarding the curriculum. It's out of my hands at the moment, but I've made some changes and we now have a direction. Today we will be learning about something new. Something called force."

Collective groans break out, and I hold my hands up. "Alright, alright, none of that. It'll be fun, I promise." I circle around to the white board behind my desk with renewed vigor. "Open up your books to page 42." I snatch up a marker and make sure to take my time as I write out, *'Forces of the Universe. Soul. Spirit. Body. Abracadabri.'*

I circle this last word. "Can anyone tell me what this means?"

One of Stella's neighbors, Peter, says, "To create. But isn't that just another word for magick?"

I grin. "Not necessarily. Now, there's a difference between active and potential force, yes? Keep that in mind. *Abracadabri* is the force that gives life to magickal creatures, and yes, it has the potential to create. But it can't do it on its own. Think of *abracadabri* as a living thing that's got to hitch a ride any time it needs to get anything done. It's a symbiotic relationship, and for those of you who were sleeping in Mrs. Pointe's class last week, that's a relationship that benefits both parties. Magick is the name of what happens when *abracadabri* is actively put into use."

An orc named Lily, Stella's rival, raises a hand. They ask, "Why does something like *abracadabri* need a tool to work? If it's so powerful, why isn't it everywhere?"

"It *is* everywhere. It's in the trolley you take to school, enchanted for good luck by those who rode it earlier in the day. It's inside the people that you know, and love. *Abracadabri* is too powerful to exist on its own. It's like ... you know how in the spring when you're trying to water the garden, and the hose can get kinked? And for the first few moments after you straighten it out, the pressure is too much, too powerful. It'll kill the plants, tear the leaves off."

"And that's why we have witches. To make sure the hose doesn't get kinked," Stella says. Lily throws a glare her way, pissed she took their answer.

"Exactly."

Nolan, an avian *behema,* says, "But isn't that stealing from magickal creatures? What if there's not enough *abracadabri* to go around? My Da says that witches use magick for *everything,* and there's not going to be enough left for us. That's why I can't shift right." The gray feathers around his humanoid neck ruffle.

"No, no. That's not how it works. But that's a very good question. *Abracadabri* is an unlimited force. Same as gravity or atmospheric pressure, it's always there. Even if we had a billion shifters and a billion witches, there'd still be enough. Although I think the earth might get a bit wobbly, that's a lot of people."

Gentle laughter ensues, and I give the kids a wink before turning back to the whiteboard.

I allow a fraction of a smile to come through.

I'm only teaching basic physics.

Lochian (3:27 AM): It's alright, I don't mind. I hope you were able to work through this latest tangle. I won't be able to come by in the morning, but eat a muffin for me. I miss you.

I sigh, cradling my phone in my hands. I stare at his message for the twentieth time this morning. I haven't written him back. What the hell else can I say after accidentally texting him my notes?

He misses me.

What does that mean?

Does he *miss* me miss me? Or is he just saying that because it's socially acceptable to tell a friend you miss them after your daily breakfasts have slowly become non-existent? I know he's busy, he essentially runs part of Levena for fuck's sake, but for the first month after Thatch left he was at the cafe *every* morning.

And every morning we would have coffee and breakfast together. It was unexpected and unplanned, but it became something that I could count on. Oftentimes, we would sit and say nothing at all. Simply wake up and clear the sleep from our eyes together, and those were the days I liked best.

But things got chaotic. There was Felix's birthday, then Caspian's, then Yuletide. Celestials are becoming sick and unstable, keeping Elochian busy and me worried. What if he's next? There've been magickal 'accidents' lately too, which are flooding the hospital. While my specialty lies in Spirit Meta-physics, doctors called for *my* advice in the beginning.

But there's nothing *I* can do except explain the problem.

It's why Cas has been working from home, because not even Tobias is immune to whatever's happening. He seems to be enduring the worst of it, actually. Unfortunately, it's all fuel for the 'Normal' sentiment poisoning the town. Not to mention the disruption caused by Thatch's departure, and all the change that came with it. Change is a beautiful thing, but boy does it piss some people off. They're screaming for normal, when such a thing doesn't even exist.

So yes, Elochian has been distant. We haven't seen each other in ... oh fuck, it's been nearly a week now. I miss him, but then again, I always miss him. I'm greedy for every scrap of friendship he has to offer. I *still* can't believe I accidentally sent him my notes last night, or this morning, whenever the fuck it was. I expected him to tease me about it, but he didn't. He seemed ... *happy* to get my message. Or maybe I'm reading into it too much. I do that sometimes, which is why I like using emojis.

Maybe I should write to him first more often. But on purpose this time.

The staff room is full. Frantic conversation wars with the TV relaying the latest storm warning, and the murmur of a coffee maker as it prepares yet another pot. I wrinkle my nose at the burnt smelling shit in a disposable moss cup on the table beside me, and the people crowding our corner of the room. I've been here for nearly a year, but I manage to keep to myself.

Mostly. Leroy never gave me an option.

Over a mouthful of iron gray tusks, Leroy leans over the table and says, "Pretty sure we'll be all going home early. Have you seen it outside lately?"

I stare at him, vaguely gesturing to the flurries that have evolved to a full blown snowstorm outside the staff room windows. The weather can't make up its mind; one minute it's lightly snowing, then ten minutes later it's a blizzard that spits a foot on the ground before turning back again in twenty minutes. Levena is known for its bitterly cold and near intolerable winters, but even this storm is out of the ordinary.

I slip my phone in my pocket with my other hand. "Obviously."

Leroy runs a hand through his neat and trim dark brown hair, unable to veil his pleased grin. He finds great joy in my irritable moods. "Who pissed in your wheaties?"

I groan, slouching in my chair. "It's pointless. Why they're so concerned with saving snow days for the *end* of the year is beyond me. They're called snow days for a *reason*. I could be curled up in bed right now, but instead I've got fucking Carina up my ass within the first ten minutes of morning bell."

Leroy blinks. "Wow. Did not expect all of that word vomit." He feigns wiping something off his taut button up shirt, grimacing the entire time. He looks around before whispering, "She paid me a nice little visit this morning too. Let me know how *optional* she thinks woodworking is."

Hesitantly, I say, "You didn't ...."

Now it's Leroy's turn to give me a death glare. "Of course I didn't fucking sign it. My uncle's a witch. If you ask me, it's only a matter of time before the rest of these fuckers realize how much of a lunatic she is. Just because we don't like something, doesn't mean we should stop learning about it."

I pick up my disposable moss cup and toast him, which prompts Leroy to do the same to me. I take a long swig of the bitter shit otherwise known as coffee, wishing I had picked up a cup from the cafe on the way out this morning. It felt wrong, though. For the past couple of weeks, I've kept myself busy and out of the cafe, and away from professionally made coffees that always hit the spot.

Thinking about the cafe leads to thoughts about Arlo, and how wrung out he's been. Before he disappeared, Thatch essentially gifted Arlo all of his investments, properties, and businesses. So not only is Arlo insanely rich now, but he has a say in more than a good portion of Levena's economy, which has pissed off a lot of people. Thankfully everything mostly runs itself, designed for Thatch's long periods of absence, but it's a lot to settle into. Especially when Arlo's priorities lie in research, not management.

Not to mention the hell his kids are giving him.

Felix and Silas go to school at the castle, where Felix can finish out his school year and Silas can get in a few months before it ends. But lately Felix's growing magick has been misfiring, closely tied with his emotions. Tobias had been mentoring him, but that fell apart before Yuletide, around the time Tobias started getting sick. And Silas, he's slowly coming out of his shell, but trust doesn't come easy with him.

I blink, recalling what we were talking about. Leaning closer to Leroy, I whisper, "I'm worried that it won't be a matter of time. Did you see how many names she's got on that thing? Mrs. White's on there."

"No," Leroy protests, dark eyes shining beneath the fluorescent bulbs above us.

I shake my head. "I saw it. And Bob Kenc."

Leroy stares into his coffee. "I didn't pin either of them as anti-witch."

"I guess you don't know, until you do."

We sit there in melancholic, but companionable silence. Eventually, the loudspeaker system kicks on with an irritating beep. Principal Nelson announces, "Levena Central will be dismissed at 11:45 AM today. Those who walk or bike to school are urged to take the buses, as conditions are currently severe. If any staff or students are in need of alternate transportation, please visit the main office."

I groan in relief, content to let everyone else filter out before I even think about moving. "Thank Gods. Do you need a ride?"

Leroy tilts his head. "You don't drive."

I laugh. "No, but I'd walk you home."

"Ass." Leroy laughs. "Nah, I'll take the bus. What about you, you're really going to walk in that?" He gestures to windows, or rather the snow pummeling the glass.

I shrug. "Why not? It's just snow."

My phone vibrates in my pocket and I shamelessly take it out. I wince at the nearly dead battery. Whoops.

Arlo (Group Text, 10:43 AM): If anyone's out and about today, Shh called and they have a new order in for me. There's cake in it for whoever brings them over. No special trips though, I hear traffic and trolleys are having a time of it. Sidewalks aren't bad.

Caspian's read it. And Elochian. That's it so far. It's Tuesday, which means Cas is probably at home with the kids. Kitt's working, and Lindsey too. Elochian ... I think he has office hours today, so he probably won't show up. But there's a chance.

Getting out of my seat, I wink at Leroy. "I think I'm going to walk."

Leroy shakes his head. "Crazy fucker."

I rush back to my abandoned classroom. I don't have any students this period, and after the next, which is a study hall, all I need to do is switch my flats for boots and throw on my coat. I don't have any work to bring home, considering I didn't give any and there was no test today. I don't believe in homework, another 'flaw' that sets my co-workers and I apart. Kids have enough going on at home to worry about school. We get everything done in class, and their scores are all in the upper percentiles, proving that the way I do things works.

When I reach for the door, I find that it's already cracked open. I pause, head tilted. I ... I think I was the last one out, but I definitely would've shut it. I don't ever lock my door, but it's either shut or open, nothing in between. Hesitantly, I push the door open and step inside the classroom.

It's empty. The children's desks are arranged the same, and my desk is as much of an organized chaos as it was before. My chair hasn't moved, and the drawers are still locked. I keep all my valuables on me, but I keep completed work and certain necessities in my desk in case the students need them. Fourth grade is a time of change for many, after all. The basket of snacks appears to be missing a few things, but I wouldn't be surprised if a few kids grabbed something on the way out, an extra snack comes in handy for later in the day.

I don't know why it takes me so long to see it, but when I do, the whole world drops from beneath me. A scream catches in my throat, and my bad knee buckles. I grip the edge of my desk for support, accidentally shoving the basket of food to the ground. Scrawled across the breadth of the whiteboard in a disgustingly familiar hue that reeks of rotted fruit, are four words.

'I miss you, Glimmer'

The clock ticks, and besides my heart it's the loudest thing in the room. With shaking hands and nausea burning my gut, I push away from the desk and steady myself. I take out my phone and painstakingly take a picture of the message. The moment it's done, I rush over to the sink along the left side of the classroom. I yank hemp towels from the dispenser, and water splatters everywhere as I desperately hurry to wet them. Upon approaching the whiteboard, I falter.

Beside the dry erase markers, is a tube of lipstick.

Color, Mulberry Dreams. Brand, Glimmer Cosmetics.

The period bell rings, scaring the shit out of me. I hurriedly scrub at the lipstick marring my whiteboard, but it's a challenge as the stuff is beeswax based, well known for its endurance. Hot, furious tears blur my vision, and I wipe at my eyes with my sleeve. I sniff, anger and fear building as I burn through towel after towel.

When I'm finished, the message is gone. But the board is no longer white. Instead, it's a sickening deep purple that borders on crimson.

"Shit," I whisper.

"Mr. Matsdotter?" A student asks, one of many who have stopped just inside the door, bearing witness to the beginning of the end for me. "What happened to the board?"

I turn on my heel, swiping up the lipstick tube as I do. "I, ah, used the wrong marker by accident. Why don't you take a seat? You'll all be going home soon, so let's take it easy."

"You don't want us to work?" Another one asks.

I press my fingers to my forehead. It's only a study hall, not an actual class. I just have to make it through this, then I can leave.

"You can if you'd like," I say, then wave to a row of computers in the back of the room. "Computers are free this period."

A few whoops break out, followed by several cheers of, 'Thanks Mr. M!'

It takes all my strength to sit down in my chair with poise instead of collapsing, but I manage it. Hands in my lap and out of sight, I open my right one to reveal the lipstick tube. Why? After all this time, why has he come for me?

I've expected River to hunt me down. I've prepared for it, but over time I've become lazy. Too relaxed. Too happy. I thought that I had gotten away with a new life, but I was wrong. He knows where I work, he probably knows where I live. Oh Gods, what if he's at home, waiting for me?

I pocket the lipstick, then take out my phone. It's dead.

Great.

A Fucking Archdemon

Elochian

I sit at the head of a table, surrounded by demons. My wings are bound with black leather straps to keep them from full view, one of the many shining examples of ancient etiquette in Adrastus Manor.

It's been described to me like this. To other *shedim*, I'm a beacon that's hard to look at but not impossible. But when my wings are out, it's like staring directly into the sun. But I'm not allowed to spell them away, because they're far too precious for that.

To the others, I'm one step away from being a God myself.

When in reality, I'm one step away from another mental breakdown.

I'm able to control the trembling in my hands this morning, which is a bonus. Michael sits at my right, dressed in a fine black suit that matches my own, albeit simpler. They're in their clan guise, taking the form of an *esh shedim* with curling black horns and a corkscrew tail. This is the form Michael takes when in the manor, or conducting business that doesn't require anonymity.

My guardian and next of kin Tisha *xir* Adrastus, sits at my left. Dressed to kill in an onyx dress with crimson beaded embroidery that takes shape as enormous flowers over her right shoulder and left hip, she manages to make me feel inferior by simply breathing. Her hair is deep red at the roots, fading to a neon pink at teased ends which rest over the bridge of her sharp nose, hiding eyes that are as red as her lipstick. Her skin is lighter than mine, and I've been told more than once that she's a mirror of my mother.

Gilla Priess, my assistant, sits at my aunt's left. Gilla is part ally and part spy, something we've both come to terms with. Tisha appointed all of my staff when I was young, and they haven't changed. Well, mostly. Anytime I've minorly hinted at a change of staff, I'm deemed ungrateful. It's not that those in my employ are incompetent, but they've been working for me for over a *century*.

And then there's the monster in the room.

Daniel Kavelli sits across from me, flanked by a bodyguard and a *shedim* woman I don't recognize. He doesn't bother to introduce either, and after niceties have been displaced, which are minimal on his end, I ask, "How can I help you, Mr. Kavelli?"

Kavelli smirks and leans back in his chair, curling his teal mustache around a finger like a cheap villain as he contemplates me. The fact that he resents me is no great secret. Our fathers were good friends long before either of us were born, and when we were *very* young, so were we. And then everything became a competition to Daniel, one I was born to win, and he to lose.

His father passed this last Harvest, leaving a hole in my heart. Samson Kavelli treated me like a son, taking pity upon me at having lost my parents so young. No doubt more fuel for Daniel's burning hatred for me. Samson's entire solar battery empire was left to his only son, and my grief has been put to the back burner in order to deal with Daniel's latest plans.

Like the words cost him greatly, Daniel says, "You misunderstand me, my Lord. I'm here to help you."

I tilt my head. "Is that so?"

A delicate hand falls from his face. His pale white eyes brighten, like the sun glaring off a frozen pond. Long tresses of turquoise fall forward, framing his face which possesses the same kind of generic saccharine beauty all demons have. Two thin, long horns embedded with opal-like gemstones curl forward from his forehead. Every inch of him is a beautiful lie, and while he might be able to fool most people, he can't fool me. His aura is similar to Michael's in one way, and in one way only.

He's a *jinni*.

We haven't interacted much over the last few decades. His father gave up trying to tame him, and Daniel made it his life's mission to avoid responsibility, disappearing for decades. But now he's like a tiger, finally jumping out of the thicket. He's put in the work since taking up his new role, far too much if you ask me. He does nothing but push the limits of his business, and my patience. I think Samson would be rolling in his grave if he saw how his son treats those he works with, and those he deems beneath him.

Kavelli says, "Yes, my Lord. You see, I've discovered a way to revive the dead after the initial three month period. Not only that, but I can restore their bodies completely. They will not become *golem*, but whatever race they were before they died."

I stiffen, experiencing Michael's surprise alongside my own. Usually our emotions are two separate entities, but in extreme situations they can meld, a sort of communication that can be useful at times, but is usually intrusive.

Tisha shifts her attention from Kavelli to me, and I give her a minute nod. *Technically*, this is her jurisdiction. Levena is her playground, but the land it rests upon is mine, as is the rest of the Northern Region. In a soft voice that dares you to misjudge it, Tisha addresses Kavelli. "That is a breach of Byinger's First Law. If it were not morally reprehensible, it is also impossible."

Kavelli bristles, eyes darting between Tisha and me. "My Lady, we all know Byinger's laws are archaic, and they do not properly address the facets of modern civilization."

Her lips thin, and I suppress a flinch despite the fact her displeasure isn't aimed at me. "I did not realize fifty years was archaic."

Kavelli laughs, and the faux charm of it grates my nerves. "Fifty years ago solar batteries were in their infancy, back then no one thought it could efficiently power a light bulb, let alone whole cities. Technology evolves far quicker than humanity does."

A part of me wants to point out the hypocrisy in his words. Fifty years ago, he thought solar batteries would be his father's downfall, and he tried with all his might to shift the business to something 'not doomed to fail.' Now he's inherited all the success his father worked for.

When Tisha opens her mouth, I beat her to it. Quietly, I ask, "What do solar batteries have to do with raising the dead?"

Dismissing Tisha with a cool, pleased look, Kavelli crosses one leg over the other and says, "It's all highly classified, but I can say that there was an unfortunate accident involved which led to this discovery. I can assure you, it works." Kavelli's next words are razor sharp, precise. "Is there no one you wish to bring back, my Lord? Time is no limit. We merely need the remains."

"And your proof?" I ask, and the room holds its breath. Let him think I'm considering it. Show me your cards.

The woman at his side stands, then bows at the waist. She's porcelain white and built like a boxer, with jet black hair cut into a bob that hangs just below her ears. She's a lower demon, but her spirit is strong. She says, "My Lord, I am Tina Lakai. I died twelve years ago, and my parents volunteered my body for Mr. Kavelli's program."

I swallow thick emotion. There's no lie in her words, and her voice isn't hollow. It's soft, but strong and ... *appreciative*. I try to speak, but I can't. For a small, small moment, I believe him. I believe him, and even worse, I think about it.

Michael stands abruptly. "I believe it's time for you to leave, Mr. Kavelli."

I raise my hand, which startles Michael. Tisha scowls, but I ignore her and lean forward, engaging in this duel that Kavelli's taunting me with. "What do you want?"

"*Sir—*"

I flash Michael a deadly glare, and the lights in the room darken. "Sit. Down."

He immediately complies, but rage is written all over his face. Tisha is equally furious, but says nothing. She will later, but one of her few stellar qualities is that she doesn't undermine me in public. Tina sits down while I shift my attention back to Kavelli, who's happier than a pig in shit. I gesture for him to continue.

He says, "Simple. Cut ties with Arlo Rook, and all businesses he's associated with."

I allow ten good, long seconds to pass. Long enough for Kavelli to think he's won. Then I stand, and the candelabras flicker and sputter until hundreds of tiny fires go out all at once. Snow thrashes the stained glass windows of the meeting hall, which bends red hues onto our untouched plates of brunch. I reach back, fingers brushing against the metal clasps cinching leather straps in place.

Meticulously, I release my wings. The moment the leather straps fall away, I feel like I can breathe easier. All six of them stretch out to their full length, and I call upon my essence as I do so. I'm not a witch, but I *am* a fucking archdemon. A wave of cold darkness finishes off the light in the room, leaving it dark to the human eye. To a demon's eye, however, I'm a bomb of blinding energy.

Tisha inhales sharply, nostrils flaring as she bows her head. Michael averts his gaze as well. They are somewhat used to my energy, but not like this. Kavelli's companions hiss like a cat tossed into water, covering their faces with their hands.

Kavelli himself, however, continues to stare at me. His eyes water, and his sclera becomes bloodstricken as I speak.

"I will say this once, and only once. The Adrastus Clan is a friend and ally to witches, and I do not associate or do business with anyone who disagrees with that. You are to cease and desist this criminal work of yours, and your business is thereby under investigation until further notice. Byinger's Laws are in place for a reason, and only a sick narcissist would break them. Now, get the fuck out of my house."

I abruptly withdraw my power, which causes Kavelli's bodyguard to retch. Kavelli wastes no time doing as I say, stomping out of my office. Tina trails after him, but stops at the door and glances back at me. I catch a glimpse of a sad smile before she disappears after her comrades. That smile unnerves me more than the rest of the encounter.

I lean forward, bracing my palms on the table. My chest heaves, and my bones feel hollow and achy. Like I've been running in a snowstorm. I shift my attention to the windows and the hellscape outside them, then back down to my hands. No one says a word until the front door echoes in the distance, then Tisha sighs.

"He needs to be eliminated."

Michael stands. "I agree. Sir, I don't understand why you indulged him. He's a monster, surely you could feel it. I know that you—"

I lift my head just enough to lock eyes with my guardian. "Know your place, Michael. My personal affairs have nothing to do with this situation, considering I was never actually interested in saying yes. I merely needed him to talk. Of course he's a monster, but he's … there's more to this."

I shift my gaze to Tisha. "I want our best covert investigators on this. Better yet, put McCullough on point. Get me a full background check on Tina Lakai, if that's who she really is. I want a complete inventory of Kavelli's stock, warehouse locations, and interviews with his engineers. And a temporary cease and desist for *all* his operations."

Tisha stands. "As you wish, although the cease and desist will cause problems."

I hum. "Pay the laborers and engineers out of the union account. Everyone else can fuck off."

My aunt evaluates me. "Do not let your personal issues cloud your judgment, Elochian."

"I just—"

"I'm not talking about *that*. Michael is right, you should not have let him leave here alive. We don't need him, Samson should never have allowed his son to inherit such an influential power. You are well within your rights to consolidate his assets into the Adrastus Clan. You know as well as I do that woman was unnatural, you could have taken him right here and now, interrogated them both."

I grit my teeth. "I want to find out how far the cancer goes before I take what's above ground. I promise you, this is *not* personal. The NOJ already calls us a conglomerate, if I assume his assets it will only lend truth to their claims. Besides, we aren't equipped to operate a solar empire at this moment."

Tisha hums. "If you say so."

My phone vibrates in my pocket, and my heart drops. That isn't a usual reaction for me, not regarding my phone. I quickly retrieve it and check my messages, finding a group text from Arlo. I breathe a sigh of relief, unsure where the sudden anxiety came from.

A checkmark beside Quentin's name appears beneath the message, and Caspian's.

Tisha clears her throat, and I look up. "Yes?"

"Do you need anything else?"

"Do you know if there were any school closings today?" I ask, surprising her.

"I ... I can check."

"Yes, three of them have announced early closure, including Levena Central," Michael says, phone in hand.

I nod. "Good. Clear my schedule for the day, Tisha."

"But the Donahue family is expecting you this afternoon, and the Lincolns."

"Are you saying that you, Sovereign of Levena, can't handle planning a confirmation and funeral?"

Tisha tsks. "You know that's not the case. I'm saying that the people miss you. You can't keep canceling on them. They need to see their Lord, and not from afar. Especially with the NOJ trying to turn public opinion against us, as you say. Levena has forgotten why they need us, and we need them."

I sigh, rubbing my temple. "I can't do this right now. Can we talk about it later?"

"Fine. Sunday?"

"Sunday."

Tisha leaves, and after the door shuts behind her, Michael takes a knee before me. His wings make an appearance, ushered in by a soft black glow and the intensifying, familiar fragrance of brimstone. Great sinewy wings stretch until the horned tips rest on the floor on either side of Michael. He tilts his head to the side, exposing his neck. They are utterly and completely at my mercy, committing one of the most vulnerable and submissive acts a celestial can do.

Quietly, but with great conviction, Michael says, "I apologize for my behavior, my Lord. I have disrespected you."

I rest my hand on his neck, directly over his pulse. "You are forgiven, Michael. Stand." I swallow thick emotion. "Please."

Michael shakes their head. "You forgive too easily."

"That is for me to decide, not you. *Stand*." I remove my hand from their neck, and Michael does as I ask. He stands over me, unsure. "I need you to trust me, Michael. Trust that I know my limits, and that I can accomplish great things despite them. Trust that I have a conscience, and that I am doing my best to leave the past behind. I admit that I ... I know it is strange for us, to be bonded as we are so late in life, and that I may sometimes begrudge you for being someone that you're not, but I am doing my best to overcome that."

Michael nods, contemplating for a moment before they answer. With a tentative smile, they say, "I'm thankful that you chose me."

I bow my head. "I am too."

I stand outside *Shh* Elves in ankle deep snow, wings dusted in nature's own frozen glitter. The damn stuff comes down in sheets, sneaking past my overcoat's upturned collar. The snow itself is small and fluffy, but there's so *much* of it. It's not a full frontal assault like it was earlier, but annoying enough. I scowl at my boots, like it's their fault I'm in this situation. I sigh, and the air numbs my lungs. Despite the cold, I feel like I can *breathe* out here.

Michael stands with me in a human male form. It's still obvious that the person at my side is a bodyguard of some sort, despite the fact he's dressed down in a crisp sweater and trousers, a scarf curled around his neck which hides the silver markings. He leans against a nearby lamppost, arms crossed and attention cast down the street.

I cast my gaze to the right, searching the wet and empty streets for anyone else who decided to brave the weather. The roads are heated, but that doesn't make going out any easier, and they only fight the snow until a certain point. The sidewalks are a mess with people tossing snow this way and that, chatting with all those who will listen about how *pretty* it is.

This is ridiculous, I'm likely the only one who decided to come, and now I'm standing here in the beginning of a snowstorm waiting for no one like an idiot.

I turn my attention in the opposite direction and reach into my coat's pocket for my phone. Upon locking eyes with a familiar face, I nearly crush my phone in an attempt to keep it from being tossed to the ground. Quentin waves to me with a gloved hand, jogging down the wet street itself instead of dodging business owners and residents clearing out their places. My heart leaps upon seeing his boots slap against the road doing its best to fight the storm.

What if it's not thawed all the way? What if the temperature dropped and there's black ice forming? What if someone tosses a shovelful of snow into the road, and there's rocks in it and they hit Quentin and—

He makes it to my side and I swallow the emotion built up in my throat, attempting to choke me out. "Be *careful*." I snap, then stiffen against the realization of what I've done. My wings tremble finely and I grit my teeth against the sensation.

Quentin scratches at his chest, glancing back at the way he came. "The road's better than the sidewalk." He smiles. "Don't worry, I'm pretty good on my feet. Hey, Michael. He making you brave the weather?"

Michael chuckles, straightening from the lamppost. "Something like that. Sent home early, hm?"

Quentin shrugs. "Yeah, I don't even know why they bothered."

"I wasn't *worried,* by the way. It would just be an inconvenience if you broke your neck on such an *important* day, that's all."

Quentin laughs, adjusting his wood frame glasses. He usually wears a different pair everyday, but it seems like this pair is the only one I see him in anymore. Then again, we haven't seen each other in awhile. He says, "Right. I think it's just us. Arlo's at Thitwhistle's with the boys, they didn't bother going to school, and everyone else is busy."

"Oh. Well, why are we still standing out here?"

"Because you're afraid I'm going to break my ankle and turn into a damsel in distress." Quentin's smile fades a little, and while he seems to be teasing, maybe there's a certain ... truth being pushed forth, or offered between the lines. Then again, overthinking is my job.

"If anyone's the damsel here, it's Elochian," Michael says, winking at Quentin.

I roll my eyes. "Why must you two get on so well? I'm leaving you both."

I lead the way into *Shh* Elves, followed by Quentin and Michael. Michael slips by me and discreetly sweeps the place visually, assessing potential targets as he approaches the serving counter. Only three other people are in the cafe area, singularly occupying tables with a coffee or book, or both.

Quentin quietly asks, "Lochian, could I get your coat?"

"Hm?" I blink out of my fugue, looking over to find Quentin's hands hovering over my shoulders, his cheeks burned from the wind. "Oh, yes. Thank you."

"Where'd you go?" Quentin chuckles, and stained fingers take a gentle hold of my overcoat. They're long and careful, and I find myself fixating on the dye tainting his fingertips, making it look like he's been playing in blood. He slides the thick black wool from my shoulders, all without actually touching me.

"Everywhere and nowhere," I whisper, body electrified by his proximity and aura.

He's the aftermath of a storm, the wet grass and hesitant birdsong. The first rays of sun breaking through the clouds. For a moment, I can understand my demons and their inability to fully look at me without being blinded. Quentin doesn't blind me, though. Simply consumes me. Entrances me into a constant state of joy and wonder.

He laughs. "Bit early to go everywhere, hm?" With my jacket in hand, he gestures to the coat rack, but I shake my head. Quentin shrugs, draping my coat over his arm. "Want a drink?"

"No, thank you," I say absently. "What happened to your hands?"

A look of surprise crosses Quentin's face, then he visibly pales and looks down to his hands. "Oh, shit. It's ... I tried washing it off but it left ... left a stain. On me."

Avoiding my eyes, he offers me back my jacket, which I take. "Quentin?"

He fidgets with his glasses, then shoves his hand into his pants pocket. "It's just, ah ... marker. Had a problem with the whiteboard today. Sorry, I didn't think about it."

"Oh I could give two shits about this." I hold up the coat. "I was just curious." I study him for a moment, searching for evidence of whatever's caused him to react so strongly. Was it me? Did I say something wrong? Maybe I shouldn't have commented on it. No, it's not *that* out of the ordinary to ask someone why their hands are stained.

Quentin rubs the back of his neck with his free hand. "Could I ah ... use your phone? Mine died, and I need to call Arlo."

"Of course it did," I say dryly, offering him my phone.

That seems to clear away some of his nervous energy, and he scowls at me. "The charger got unplugged from the wall last night. Somehow. I *did* plug it in."

I chuckle. "Right. You know, I think I am in the mood for something warm."

Quentin brightens, cold fingers brushing against mine as he finally takes my phone. "The cider here is pretty good."

I fight to keep my breathing even. "Perfect."

Quentin gestures to a small area in the corner, outside the bathrooms. "I'll be real quick."

"Okay."

He stares at me, and I stare at him.

"What?" I ask quietly, feeling the most seen that I have all day. Exposed.

"N–nothing. I'll be right back." He scurries away and I watch him go, listening to his heart speed up as he dials a number.

A few moments later Michael joins my side, his own drink in hand. He glances between Quentin and me. "Everything alright?"

I hold my jacket to my chest, watching Quentin run a hand through his hair over and over as he talks. "I'm not sure."

Because he's a *dick*, Michael says, "Well, I'm glad that you took the day off. To rest, and all. Not because you want to turn that frown upside down."

I glare at him. "Took you long enough."

Michael grins, then takes a sip of his coffee. "Yes, well. Now that my duty here is complete, I'm going to find a seat. They're bringing the books out for us."

I'm relieved that the tension between us has disappeared, but confusion takes over. "Books?"

He gives me a flat look. "Yes. Books. The ones Mr. Rook requested that you pick up for him. The original purpose of our trip?"

"You don't need to be such an ass." I mutter, face heating. "Thank you."

"Of course I don't. And you're welcome." He takes off for the table closest to the door, content to be my babysitter from a distance. I glance at Quentin one more time before conquering the business that is ordering drinks.

A Stepping Stone

Quentin

"No, there's been almost nobody in. Why? Are you expecting someone?" Arlo asks, distracted.

I rub at my forehead. "No. The opposite, actually. I ... if anyone comes by asking for me, please don't ... don't tell him anything."

Arlo is quiet for a few seconds, and when he speaks again he is deathly serious. "Are you in trouble, Q?" When it's my turn to be quiet, he says, "I've got your back, Quen. But I can't help if I don't know what's going on."

"I think ... I think I might be. But I don't know. It could be nothing."

"Well, how about we talk about it when you get back? And it makes you feel better, I can shore up the wards. Even more so if I have ... details."

A sense of false relief settles over my shoulders, temporarily relaxing my muscles. "Okay. Later. Are the roads bad?"

Arlo allows the tangent. "Yeah. But you've got a stone, right?"

"Yes, I just ... wasn't sure if Lochian might be coming. He's got Michael with him."

"Well, it's supposed to get worse before it gets better. I've got plenty of room for people to crash, and the stone's strong enough. Plus Silas has been stress baking all day, so there's plenty of comfort food."

"Okay. Thanks, Arlo."

"Anything for you, Q. Be careful."

"I will."

I hang up the phone, feeling marginally better. I've managed to come this far with only the girls knowing about my life with River, and it's not something I like to think about. Ever. I buried that time deep beneath the flesh and heart he used to bruise and break, and the shame that came with it. I don't want to tell Arlo, and I most certainly don't want Loch to know. I'm stronger now than I used to be, and I suddenly feel incredibly unsure. I can handle this on my own, can't I?

But what if I can't? What will River do when he finds me?

I shake my head, forcing myself to focus on the here and now. I run a hand through my hair, then let it slide down my chest, opposite my wildly racing heart. Fear and paranoia lingers under the surface of my skin, but I ignore it in favor of looking for Lochian. I look at the cafe counter, but he's not there. Michael's sitting by the door, sipping from a mug and watching me. When we connect gazes, they nod, then tilt their head to the right with a small smile.

I follow his movement, finding Elochian standing near the giant, arching bookcase that separates the cafe from the rows of bookshelves. His translucent jewel wings finished with those pretty gold and black swirls slowly open and close. His long, sleek hair is cast over his left shoulder, blocking his face from view. I like it when his hair is down, it reminds me of spilled ink. There's always a few tiny braids intermingled into the rest though, even when it's down. The moment I see him, something settles in me. Right now, everything's okay.

My hand falls away from my chest, and my feet take over.

Despite the fact Arlo now technically owns *Shh* Elves, not much has changed. He is a distant manager and investor, allowing the establishment to run on its own, the same as Thatch did. The staff is the same, and so is the dark and eccentric decor. Enormous, intricate terrariums house *gadol* skulls, while others are home to giant snails with beautifully marked shells. I shudder at the sight of them.

There's only been one crucial difference in *Shh* Elves.

On a stretch of wall beside the bookcase is a framed photograph of Thatch, which has captured Elochian's attention. It's a candid photo of Thatch standing in the yard at Cas and Bias' house, hands in his pockets and a laugh pulling at his lips. It's from the night we all spent together, Kitt took the picture.

A small plaque rests beneath the silver frame and it reads, *'Thatcher Gaillot, also known as Thatch Phantom, has been the owner of Shh Elves for over five centuries.'*

Elochian scrutinizes the words inscribed there, then looks over his shoulder upon sensing my approach. He carries two disposable cups, the fingers of his right hand multi-task by clutching at a black paper bag, and his coat is slung over his left arm. To say he looks like a pack mule would be an understatement.

He holds out the cup that comes with the bag, his smile a tiny, shaking thing. "I haven't eaten breakfast yet, and I figured there was a good chance you haven't yet either. I got muffins for both of us. Don't feel obligated to eat, though."

"You're not wrong. Thank you." I take a sip, groaning at the warmth and taste of the heavenly apple cider. Shyly, I look up to him. "Did they have—"

Elochian smiles, and it lights up his whole face. I could stare at him forever, attempting to commit every unique facet of him to memory. The pale birthmarks on the right side of his face, extending beneath the collar of his shirt, are a vivid contrast to his soft brown skin. I'm pretty convinced it's his soulmark, and I wonder if any of our witch friends have seen it glow, what color it could be. Then again, with these freshly enchanted glasses of mine, I should be able to see soulmarks glow now. The golden lines inscribed across the high points of his cheeks. His nose, a strong curve that I want to trace my finger down, and then down to his thin lips, settling in the place small, but deep dimples form. He says, "Banana with chocolate chips? Yes."

An uncalled for surge of affection comes upon me, and I fight the urge to run away from it. "You're the best."

His cheeks darken, and he shifts his gaze elsewhere. "I don't know about that. What did Arlo have to say? It looks like his books are ready."

"Books? Oh, right." I hand Elochian back his phone, glancing over at Michael who gives us a little wave. "Are you in a hurry? Maybe we could ... eat together? It's been awhile."

Elochian's quiet smile stretches into an unrestrained grin, and it warms me up more than the cider ever could. "I'd like that. But let's go back here."

We walk through the archway side by side and pass through the main aisles in the same fashion. Elochian seems to be on the hunt, so I follow him until he picks a seemingly random reading nook. The small space is curtained off with peacock blue drapes, hiding bench seats separated by a worn table, and a narrow window which provides a splendid view of nothing but snow.

We sit across from each other, and thankfully Elochian wastes no time unveiling breakfast. Or lunch. I blink a few times. "What time is it?"

"One twenty-five. Or one thirty," Elochian says without looking at his phone. He offers both muffins to me, and I take the one in his right hand.

"Really? It doesn't feel that late. And you didn't even look."

Elochian gives me one of his signature dry glares. "It's a superpower," he says seriously, then bites into his muffin. I'm temporarily distracted by his fangs elongating as his mouth widens, and I abruptly drag my attention to my own food.

It's not a secret that demons have fangs, but Elochian's always kept his hidden. I'm pretty sure Elochian and ... *arousal* don't mix. But they were definitely elongated, and it's just us ...

I bite into my own muffin and glance at him again. The sight of incisors half the length of my pinky, but just as wide, pierce into the center of his muffin.

I spiral into a choking fit.

"Quentin?" Elochian stills, staring at me with alarm. His fangs recede, and his right one nicks his bottom lip as it does.

I trade food for cider and hold up a hand to settle him, or his wings, more-like. "Fine. W–wrong hole." His eyes track my face, and I don't know whether to point out the pinprick of blood on his lips. I don't think he realized they were out, and I don't want to embarrass him. "Really, I'm alright."

"O—kay."

We eat in somewhat content silence after that, but my mind is a vicious whirlwind. Is Elochian attracted to me? Did he ... see someone else before coming to meet me? I don't know how their fangs works *exactly*, only that *shedim* venom's main purpose is to act as an aphrodisiac for mating, and that they can be triggered by arousal. Do they remain distended after sex, or ... dentist appointments? I'm really hoping he had a dentist appointment before this, not sex.

After finishing my muffin, I take a long drink of my cider to drown my thoughts. When I finish, I find Elochian watching me with rapt intensity, his body practically frozen. I tilt my head, irrationally worried that he heard my internal battle. "What?"

Umber eyes transfixed on me, he slowly leans forward and wipes the corner of my mouth with his thumb. Air catches in my throat, which startles Elochian from his daze. "You had chocolate on your face." He leans back, wiping his hand off on his pants.

Distantly, I think of how much a waste of that was.

"Oh. Thanks."

"How ... how is your writing going?" Elochian starts off slow, recomposing himself by the end of his question. In a more teasing tone, he says, "Your message was exceptionally interesting. I thought you were working on a holiday romance or something."

I wave him off, cheeks flushed. Right. Romance. Just the thing I'm trying to get *off* my mind.

"I am ... but that's not what I was working on last night. I was rambling, and it was late. I'm not sure if any of it will be any good." I take another sip of my cider, which does nothing to calm the jittery feeling in my heart. When Elochian doesn't say anything, only stares at me expectantly, I hedge. "It's ... different. From what I normally write."

He leans ahead once more, elbows resting on the table. His cup is centered between his loosely clasped hands, which are at the perfect halfway point between him and me. The candles in the antler chandelier situated above us flicker, illuminating the golden lines embedded into Elochian's cheekbones, and a certain look to his eyes that I don't see very often. I don't have a name for it, but I wish that I did.

My own hands are inches from his, and my fingertips gently drum the table in a familiar pattern. My cup of cider rests off to the side, forgotten. When did that happen?

He says, "Tell me."

My fingers pause their drumming, and I take a moment to breathe.

Elochian Adrastus' full attention is all encompassing. Something I secretly wish for, and can never handle when I have it.

I exhale, mentally preparing to word vomit and doing my best to prevent it.

With much more shyness than I would have if I were telling Elochian the plot to my usual books, I say, "Most people don't have a great whirlwind romance that's an end all, be all. Or maybe they did, in the beginning, but for one reason or another it didn't work out. But that doesn't ... that doesn't make those relationships less important. A person's first may not be their last, but that doesn't take away from the impact of that first love."

"Like a stepping stone," Elochian says, not breaking eye contact with me once. Artune, he's so intense.

"Right, yeah. That's the bit I was working on last night. I don't have all the pieces, just a vague idea. A character, kind of. I don't know, I think we need more stories that focus on the big picture. The stepping stones, and the person they bring you to."

Elochian smiles, then looks away. The movement hollows me out, and I have no idea why. When he turns his attention back to me, that safety guard is back. He's still friendly, but there's

... I don't know, distance. He says, "I like it. I think you're onto something."

And then he changes everything. His fingers twitch, and his black painted nails trace against the back of my own fingers.

Breathlessly, I ask, "You think so?"

"You always are. Why stop trusting your gut now? It's a different audience, but why not?"

"Why not ... right."

In a moment of rare courage, I slide my fingers in the precious space between his. Elochian's breathing is the loudest thing in the room, second only to my racing heart. His eyes fixate on our hands, but they jump to mine when I whisper, "I missed you, too."

"What?" He asks, fingers tightening, locking mine into place. For the first time in over a week, I feel truly grounded again.

"First thing this morning, or whenever it was, you said you missed me. I missed you, too. I didn't realize how much I'd gotten used to seeing you in the morning, until you weren't there anymore."

"I ... I feel that way, too." Elochian steals a deep breath from the intimate space between us. There's only the softly glowing candelabra overhead, the snow trapped against the window, and the old table between us. The curtains hide us from the rest of the place, and I've never been more certain that this is the time. A vague sort of desperation alights my nerves, like this might be the only chance I'll ever have to tell Lochian how I feel.

"Lochian, I care about you, and there's something I want to ask you—"

"Quentin, I—"

Michael parts the curtains, startling both of us. Elochian's hand jerks away from mine, and for a moment mine remains outstretched, reaching for him. Stiffly, Michael says, "I apologize Sir, but there's a problem. Code Green."

Elochian sighs, then stands and straightens the sleeves of his shirt, a move that would be much more impressive if it were a suit instead of a cashmere sweater. "I'm surprised we had this long. I'll be right there, give us a moment, please."

"Of course," Michael says, then takes off.

"You're leaving?" I ask, standing with shaky knees. I feel robbed, empty. Cold.

Elochian takes a step towards me. "I'm afraid so. But Misfits Night is in a few days, I'll see you then. I promise."

Then, he surprises me.

He reaches forward, and his fingertips skim the side of my throat. He leans in, and I'm helpless to do anything but allow him to gently pull me closer. Elochian Adrastus kisses my cheek, then leaves me behind without a word.

And I'm left all alone. I reach up, touching the fleeting kiss on my cheek with lipstick stained fingers.

I land at home with a heavy thud, the books piled in my arms nearly crash onto the floor but I manage to keep them safe. I'm assaulted by the scent of chocolate, vanilla, and strawberry all at once. A scream is the next to register, along with metallic clanking and crying. Arlo's voice is louder than everything else, calm and even, infused with a certain type of magick that always makes my knees go weak.

"Breathe, Felix, breathe. I'm right here."

Felix kneels on the floor beside the pastry case, hands over his ears and pain written all over his face. Through my enchanted glasses, I watch Felix's aura as it pulsates in starburst fashion, its colors a mixture of blinding pink and a contrasting dark blue. Pans full of steaming cakes swirl around him and Arlo like a tornado. Arlo kneels with Felix, hands resting on his shoulders.

I wonder what it feels like to be a witch and to be so close to such an obvious source of power. Not that Arlo knows what Felix is, or if he does suspect Felix's a reservoir, he hasn't said anything. Perhaps he feels the same way I do. Acknowledging what Felix is can only bring about his doom.

Silas is nowhere to be seen, and neither are any patrons. I stand stock still until Felix's attack passes, which only takes a couple more minutes. My arms ache by the time all the pans crash to the ground, throwing cake and crumbs everywhere.

Felix crumples to the side and Arlo catches him, immediately sweeping the boy close to his chest. He stands effortlessly, looking at me with exhaustion bruising his eyes. "Can you go check on Silas? I think he's in the kitchen. I'll be right back, taking him up."

I nod, saving my questions for later. I set the pile of books down on a random table and do as he says, moving quickly. When I near the kitchen, I slow down, listening for any telltale signs of Silas in distress. When I push the swinging door inwards, I find Silas pacing back and forth. He barely looks at me, and certainly doesn't stop. His belt chains swing against his thighs, and a silver necklace rattles against the front of his hoodie.

"I'm fine." His shoulders rise to his ears. "I'm fine," he says again, half as convincing as the first time.

"Okay. Do you want me to go?"

He stops pacing, turning silent and still for a moment. His hands remain deep in his pockets, and his black outfit is covered in flour and who knows what else. "He passed out, didn't he?" He grits out.

"He did."

Silas groans, taking back off again at a furious pace. "One minute everything was fine, we were just standing there, waiting, talking. And the next minute, everything metal in the kitchen started flying towards us. He ran out in a panic, which made it all worse, everything started coming out of the ovens, hot as fuck. That's when I started yelling, which made it worse. I couldn't help it. I tried." He hums loudly, tearing a hand out of his pocket to skate through his hair. A sharp flash of cool blue light overtakes his face, then disappears just as quickly as it came.

"It'll get better," I say, and even I can hear the lie. If I'm right, it won't get better. Not at all. "It's growing pains."

"Everyone's saying that isn't *actually* making it better. I know what growing pains are, *I've* had them. Arlo's had them. This is not that, but everyone is choosing to go with the easiest explanation, and it's *Felix* who's suffering for it." He thrusts a hand in my direction, towards the door.

"Silas, we aren't going to let anything—"

He sighs with such exasperation it could blow me over, then brushes past me and takes off. The door swings harshly in his wake, and I feel utterly useless. I give him a few minutes to retreat, then go out into the cafe. I check the sign, finding that it's been flipped to closed, then set to work on cleaning up the cake catastrophe.

Except, there's no mess. The dirty pans are neatly stacked on the counter, and all the crumbs and dislodged pieces of food have found their way into the trash can. Must be Silas couldn't help himself, his magick hates clutter. I carry the dirty pans into the kitchen and fill up the sink, then begin the mind numbing process of washing dishes. After the day I've had, mind numbing is a welcome thing.

To be honest, I agree with Silas. Tobias isn't able to mentor Felix anymore, and there's only so much Arlo can do. But what else is there? Arlo asked me to speak with Arche regarding Felix, and I've passed on message after message, but the astrophysicist has ignored them all. He's the only witch in Levena known to have more than one specialty, and I've been trying to think of how to broach the subject of mentoring Felix, but when you're approaching someone who distrusts people on a general basis anyway, it makes the whole thing difficult. The thing is, Arlo actually knows him, but the whole 'mutually being traumatized by Leon' thing keeps them from talking, apparently. Arlo's shut out everyone else who went through what he did, except for Tobias. Even that development is recent, though.

My mind wanders away from that problem, moving right on to the next.

What was Elochian going to say? Quentin, I want you to get the hell away from me? Quentin, I think you're great but you're being weird and this isn't something I want with you?

Quentin ... I like you, too?

It feels like he does. He seems to genuinely enjoy being with me. Despite the fact we haven't seen each other a whole lot lately, today it was like no time's passed at all. I sigh, drying my hands. I've got no shot with him, and it's probably for the best that we were interrupted. He can be with anyone he wants, and I'm just a boring human with a teaching degree.

I leave the kitchen in favor of the cafe, dimming lights as I go. I brew a small pot of coffee, losing myself to time and thoughts while I wait. I pour it into a mug I choose at random and load it with sugar, then investigate the books that Arlo had me deliver.

I was so clusterfucked before that I didn't paid any attention to what they were. Could be anything with the way his mind's been running lately, grasping for straws. I take a seat at the table I had unloaded my cargo unto, then take a thin book from the top of the stack. *Ancient Architecture of the Northern Region.*

I set it aside, then take another that's much heavier. *Ancient Gods of Min.*

I tilt my head at that. There's Min Temple up north in the frigid, near inhospitable steppe that only the most devout of religious nuts endure to complete pilgrimage. Thanks to Thatch's grave, we now know of a Min Isle, but only in name. I've never heard of a place described as simply Min. I open the book, studying what's inside. Most of it I've read before, references to the Creator Gods and their children, the Caretakers, but I stumble upon a couple of sections that are new to me.

Creation in Waves

It is common knowledge that each of the Caretakers were allowed to create their own children, but what many people do not know is they were limited to their regions of influence. The duty of the Caretakers is to tend to the universe, each from their respective places of birth. The only time Caretakers are able to leave their regions and associate with one another are during the spring equinox. Let's take a closer look at the waves of creation, starting with the one that started it all.

The Wave of the Creators, *also known as the First Wave, created what are known as the **Ancient Races.***

Typhine created the Elves in Mythhaven, the Mayimet in the southern region, the exact origin unknown, and the Titans in the seas.

Ulena created the Shaddai in Agia, the Dragons in Dridale, and the Gadol along the northern coast of Min.

Hizoh created the Pitriyot in Gia, the Treants in Rosevein, and the Fae in Faygale.

Ogmes created the Behema in the middle region, their exact origin unknown, the Orcs in Kilbrook, and the Shafan in Jaqul.

The Creators in the First Wave were global, to say the least. ***The Caretaker's Wave*** *was more extensive, despite the location restrictions, and created the beginning of the world as we know it. The races from this time period are referred to as the **Primeval Races.***

Malakim were created in Brinecliff, by Ylos.

Shedim were created in Brinecliff, by Mithys.

Katan were created in Northgrave, by Mishlat.

Centaurs were created in the Mid-Southern region, exact origin unknown, by Emolite.

Vampires were created in Dimshear, by Awah.

Krakeni were created in the seas near Kilbrook, by Kiroli.

Merfae were created in Pearlholde, by Ryvara.

Qieren were created in West Shire, by Soleyar.

Khatool were created in the Southern Region, exact origin unknown, by Artune.

Tzipor were created in the Southern Region, exact origin unknown, by Yrlan.

*Last, but not least, is the **Third Wave**, which has led to the creation of the **Modern Races.***

Sirens were created in the Faygale Bay, by Loborn.

Tannin were created in the Southern Region, exact origin unknown, by Nicen.

Faun were created in the Min Region, exact origin unknown, by Da'haut.

Humans were created in the Min Region, exact origin unknown, by Dinphine.

Selth were created in Northgrave, by Xvaldin.

What we can take from this information is that Da'haut and Dinphine are Caretakers of Min. Some scholars contest that Brinecliff and Mythhaven were once part of Min, also known as the Northern Region, which would include Ylos, Mishlat, and Awah as Caretakers of the land. They cite local ancient maps as proof, but each map has the Min Border in a different place from the other.

God Pairings

During the spring equinox, the Caretakers were known to visit each other, partaking in romantic and platonic relations to celebrate. It is a topic of debate whether a Fourth Wave of Creation will be a result of this, but many scholars believe the Gods do not possess bodies capable of birth, and their methods of creation are far different from our own. The following romantic pairings are speculation based on cultural legends.

Ryvara + Soleyar
Xvaldin + Artune + Loborn
Kiroli + Nicen
Da'haut + Dinphine
Ylos + Mishlat
Yrlan + Mithys+ Awah + Emolite

I'm deep in the book by the time Arlo joins me with his own cup of coffee in hand. He sits beside me, leaning back in his chair and closing his eyes. For a moment he just sits there, one hand balled up into a fist in his lap, the other holds onto his mug for dear life. Thatch's cup. I continue reading, not feeling the urge to add more chaos to his mind right now. My knee aches, and I rub at it with my free hand.

This is how we spend most evenings. Sitting together and reading. Conspiring. Theorizing. Usually the boys are with us. On Misfit Nights everyone is here, socializing and researching in equal measures. There's never anything else but this. I love it. This place, this people. Everything has been going so well, and being with Elochian, romantic or not, has made me feel settled in a way that I haven't in years. I've deceived myself into thinking I can have all of it without repercussions.

The smart thing to do would be to run. To leave without telling anyone, and never come back. I've done it twice, and I could do it again. I could work anywhere.

But I've never left behind people who loved me. I don't know if I could.

"Thank you, for the coffee. And the books. And ... for everything, Q. I don't think I tell you enough how much I appreciate you."

I lift my head, looking over at Arlo. He watches me, his gaze tired instead of sharp. I slide my glasses up my nose. "You don't need to do that. I know. Do you ... need to talk?"

He takes off his beanie and rests it on his knee, then takes a sip of his coffee. Quietly, he says, "No. Not right now."

I nod. "Okay."

We sit there in companionable silence, watching the heavy snowfall and the exceptionally quiet world darken a shade at a time. The days are short, night creeps onto the scene at around four in the evening now, and it doesn't get light until almost nine in the morning. Winter always makes me feel a certain type of way, and after spending these months with Arlo, I can say it seems to make him feel the same.

Despite the fact Witch House is perfectly liveable and practically all of their things are there, Arlo and the boys stay here most of the time. If I'm not working, I'm usually at home, and there hasn't been time for social meetups besides the weekly one, which happens here. I can't … I don't remember the last time Arlo left the cafe. He does all his business from home, and the new glass case which is usually full of witch things, from charms to medicines, potions to enchantments, is nearly empty.

He had shifted around the cashier's area and put it not far from the pastry case, so you could easily look into both. I thought his hedge business was doing well since he gave it a physical storefront, but maybe it's doing too well, and he needs to get back in the kitchen now that he's using up his reserves. But that would require time, time he would rather dedicate elsewhere.

After a bit, I test the waters. I shut the religious text, then poke at the book on architecture. "This seems interesting."

Arlo sets his coffee down on the table, then rubs his temple. "Yeah. I was curious what Levena used to look like, what the houses would have looked like. I thought it might've been a lead to Old Levena, or Min Isle … whatever it was."

"Interesting. I've been going through this." I hold up the Ancient Gods book. "Nothing about Thatch, but there's a lot of talk about the Caretaker Gods, where they lived and who they loved. Did you know that Min Temple is almost eight thousand years old? It's one of the first in the Northern Region, and still the largest. Also, I think Min is the name used to describe the

Northern Region, which might have been bigger back then. Here, look."

Arlo slowly takes the book from me, eyes tainted with a green tinge. "Really? Do you think ... do you think Thatch was ever there? At the Temple?"

I shrug. "I don't know, I don't know why he would be. He was kind of an atheist, wasn't he?"

Arlo chuckles, and even though it's not a real laugh, I take the small victory. "He believed in them, just didn't like them." Arlo's face falters, and he sets the book down. "I was so excited for these, and now ..." He shakes his head. "You know where I was during Felix's attack?"

I wince. "Buried in the nest?"

"Exactly. Literally trapped beneath all that shit." He gestures to the booth that we all once shared, but now it's a mountain of books, boxes of paperwork, and to put it nicely, crap. You can't even see the table anymore. "I know I've got my head in the sand. But I can't—to stop looking feels like I'm breaking a promise. I don't know what to do."

I rest a hand on his arm. "I can't honestly say what I would do if I were you. He was my friend, too, Arlo. But I know juggling all these new businesses of yours, worrying about Felix, worrying about Leon, it's a lot. No one's saying you have to stop looking, but ... I don't know. I don't know what to say, because I don't think I could stop."

Arlo sniffs, wiping at his eyes. He lays his hand over mine and leans over, resting his head on my shoulder. He whispers, "Thank you for being honest. Loch told me last night that I'm being an idiot."

"If you went to him for advice, it's because you knew he was going to call you an idiot and wanted him to."

Arlo sits up and stares at me. Something like faint amusement crosses his features. "Well, aren't you a know-it-all."

I laugh. "You know it's true."

He shrugs. "I guess so. Are you going to tell me what's going on with this trouble of yours?"

I stiffen. It's a quick thing, but Arlo catches it before I can relax. "No. It's nothing."

"Didn't sound like nothing earlier."

"I thought it was something, but it's not. If it does become something, I'll let you know."

He stares at me for a moment, and when I don't crack, he goes on. "You better. Also, that was really fucking confusing and my brain hurts. I think I'm going to check on Felix and turn in. Silas probably won't come out of his room for the rest of the night, he's another one who's pissed at me." Arlo sighs, sliding his beanie back on. "I already closed up, but—"

The bells chime. Arlo mutters, "But I didn't lock the door yet." Raising his voice, he calls, "We're closed!"

A man steps inside, perhaps my height, but much thinner. He wears an eyepatch, a leather jacket not dissimilar to Arlo's. He has snow-filled brunette curls which go well past his shoulders. He looks like a character from a book cover, not an actual person. Despite Arlo's words, the man walks towards us.

We stand, meeting the man halfway across the cafe. He says, "I know, but I'm not here for coffee. I was wondering if I could have a moment of your time, I'm Finnegan. Finnegan Wroughtfern."

"The journalist," Arlo says dryly, crossing his arms.

"And the chief editor of the Radickal Magickal Gazette, a lesser known newspaper with more truth than you'll find in today's tabloids. I'm doing a piece on Thatch Phantom, and I was hoping for an interview with you."

Arlo's eyes flash green, and I mentally begin the countdown before he fries the guy. I stay quiet, more curious than anything. Why did this guy pick *today* of all days? The storm was supposed to get better, sure, but it definitely didn't. It's a nightmare out there.

Arlo says, "I see. As I said, we're not open, and I am not in the mood for interrogation. Good evening, *sir*."

Finnegan looks to me for help, and I say, "Nope."

He looks back to Arlo, resolve straightening his spine. "Please don't misunderstand. I'm not here to talk about the Game, but rather the man behind it."

"And still, I am not interested."

Finnegan reaches into his coat pocket. "Even if I were to tell you Nightingale sent me?" He retrieves a large black card and holds it up, revealing detailed golden linework that shines beneath the dim lights. It's hard to tell from here, but I think the design is a skull with a bird sitting atop it. I've never heard of this 'Nightingale,' but it's clear by Arlo's stiff posture that he has.

Finally, and with a bit of rasp, he asks, "And what business do they have with someone like you?"

Finnegan shrugs, offering the card to Arlo. "A personal investment, we'll say. Regardless of whether you want to meet with me, they want to meet with you."

Arlo narrows his eyes, and his aura crackles as he steps forward to take the card. "I'll think about it. As for you, my answer has not changed."

Finnegan nods once. "It seems we have reached an impasse, then. Thank you for your time, Mr. Rook, and I apologize for bothering you."

Arlo says nothing.

The man turns to leave and an urge to speak up washes over me. I look between the man's retreating back and Arlo, but no words come to fruition. This isn't my decision. Isn't my business, really, but here I am, right in the middle of it.

But Finnegan says what I can't.

He stops at the door, hand coming to a rest on the knob. He looks back at us and says, "I believe we have an obligation to right history, Mr. Rook. I know enough of Mr. Phantom to know that he is owed that, and there is no one better than you to tell his story. You can keep it to yourself if you'd like, but this is history in the making. Someone *will* fill in the blanks, but the question is; will it be the truth?"

A flash of ozone and green rushes the atmosphere, then dissipates just as quickly as it came. The bell chimes, and I turn to Arlo. "Arlo, I—"

He's already gone.

I sigh, then lock the front door. A seconds long hum settles into the bones of the house, then the wards click as audibly as the metal lock itself.

Safe.

Ready To Move On

Elochian

I sit in my nest, pills heavy on my stomach. I twirl loose hair around my finger, staring at the moonlit world outside my bedroom window. The snow abruptly stopped at midnight, but my mind won't follow the trend. My phone continues to vibrate almost constantly despite the time, but none of the notifications are from the person I want to hear from the most.

I don't even know why I'm fixating on him. I needed Michael to rescue me from a heartfelt confession for Mithys' sake. There's no such thing as a code green, only a coward of an archdemon. I'm a shame to my race. To humanity. To Quentin. He deserves better than someone who runs away from the prospect of anything that shifts the paradigm.

What would I have said?

Quentin, I care for you too, but I'm broken and a terrible person.

Quentin, I'm nothing but my legacy, and any life spent with me will be boring. *I'm* boring.

Quentin, I'm unsure how to love again, and I'm afraid you'll break what remains of me.

Even touching his hand felt like a betrayal, but it also felt like … everything.

For the first time in so long, I—I wanted to kiss someone. I've never really thought about it before, what it would be like to kiss him. Now, all I can think about is the way his lips twist in a wry smile, holding back the words, '*I told you so,*' because he's too nice to ever utter them.

The way his lips part, allowing nervous laughter to spill forth.

The way he whispers my name any time he says it. Lochian. *Lochian, I care about you.*

A dull, quiet warmth blooms in my core. Not the all con-suming, heated lust from the days before staying sane became a priority. Regardless, it's more than I've felt in a long, *long* time. I glance at the distant bedroom door, despite the fact it's locked and my room is empty. At the thought of taking advantage of this opportunity, icy anxiety rushes up my spine, spreading throughout my limbs.

Instead of pursuing the rare arousal, I lay on my side in my nest of moss, sticks, blanket, and glittering scales. I hoped that if I slept in my nest tonight, I would have a better chance of falling asleep. But the warmth intensifies to a low burn that I find hard to ignore.

I wrap my wings around myself, and try to sleep.

I don't experience any more *issues* until the day I'm scheduled to meet Tobias, which is coincidentally the same day I'll be seeing Quentin again. It's alarming and uncomfortable, to say the least. I lay in the nest, begrudgingly making a mental note to speak with Doc. Arlo and I are on different medications, but I wonder if he goes through this. It would be comforting to know I'm not the only one under distress. Logically, I know that I'm not. But friends are a greater comfort than statistics.

I roll over, groaning as my partially hard shaft rubs against the mattress. Overwhelming, electric heat flares in every nerve, and I try not to think.

I try not to think of why this might be happening after years and *years* of not feeling this way about anyone else except for Bartholomew.

I close my eyes, try not to think, and take hold of myself.

A small gasp escapes me. My balls rise in response to the coolness of my palm, and I shiver as my fingers curl. I search for a distant, but no less strong, memory of Bartholomew in my arms, and me in his. It's one I hold onto dearly during these rare times I'm overcome with the urge to release, which has since been ... I don't even know how long.

But with a shock that shoots right to my groin and gums, it's not Bartholomew's face that comes to mind.

It's Quentin's.

A white hot burst of lust barrels throughout my body, burning out my veins and awakening every muscle. My teeth scrape against my bottom lip, but the throbbing ache in my gums as they grow is greater than the pain of a pierced lip. My heart beats out of rhythm for a moment, then staggers back into place.

Quicker than the all consuming burn, a heavy, damp blanket of shame settles throughout, snuffing out any traces of the fire.

I laugh, and it claws and tears as it escapes.

The moment I chase hope, my past yanks it away.

A couple hours later, I wait for Tobias in the northern den of my apartment. It's private, comfortable, and quiet. Despite the fact our meeting is private, the Manor is brimming with activity. The fact we're meeting at all is a source of great joy for the estate, one that is contagious. I'm curled up on an ottoman near the lit hearth, sipping on spiked cider. Lips and nose buried in the collar of my turtleneck, I stare into the low flames, twirling my hair around my finger.

For the third time this morning, Michael says, "Sir."

I shoot the *jinni* a glare. They're seated behind a desk, glasses perched on their nose as they goes through my correspondence. He's dressed in the same black suit he's usually in, a contrast to my disheveled look.

"For the *last* time, nothing's wrong."

Michael snorts, going back to his work. "Right. So you're fire breathing for no reason at all."

"Fire breathing?"

"Yes. Fire breathing. All that huffing and puffing you're do-ing could burn down a house."

I roll my eyes and take a long sip of my drink. It warms my chest as it goes down, and the anxiety thrumming on my brain dulls to a low roar. I sense an incoming presence that can only be Tobias, a soul that's brighter than all the rest on the ethereal map laid out in my head. He ascends the stairs at the heart of the main house.

While I wait, I take out my phone and check it. Plenty of messages from Andromeda, the council, and the investigators on Kavelli's case. Nothing from Quentin, or anyone else impor-tant, for that matter.

Should I say something?

'Hey, I know I ran out on you earlier this week and disappeared off the face of the earth, again, but I'm really looking forward to seeing you tonight? But not in a romantic way, just a platonic way, because apparently you give me boners which stress me out and I'm ruined.'

Yeah, probably not any of that.

Instead of writing to him, I quickly send Doc a message before I can lose my nerve.

Me (10:30 AM): Hi Doc. I need an appointment that's sooner than our other one.

I sit there, zoning out on the words, and am startled when there's a knock on the door. I stand and call out, "Come in."

Annie steps inside and promptly performs the mark of Adrastus, head bowed. She does not speak due to a Vow of Silence that she made well before joining Clan Adrastus, something that is common for the more pious celestials. Using sign language, she announces, "Sir, Lord Daemarrel is here."

She steps out of the way, and Tobias enters the room. His eyes are wide, and his hair is clean and unbound. His wings are spelled away, and I quickly bury the jealousy that comes whenever I see a celestial with hidden wings.

"Thank you, Annie. I can take it from here." I bow my head to her, and she leaves. She is no-nonsense and straight to the point, which is what I like about her.

"Tobias, I'm glad you came." I offer my hand to Tobias, and he shakes it firmly. He still looks like shit, but not so defeated. I gesture towards the hearth. "Please, come take a seat by the fire. I hear it's mighty cold out there today."

"Thank you. It is, all that snow we got is frozen solid now. Pretty, but a nuisance."

I settle back into the chair I was occupying before, and Tobias takes up the one beside me. Michael is there within moments with a plate of small egg pies, and he sets it down on the end table between us without a sound, along with a silver platter complete with a small kettle and a delicate porcelain cup. "Tea?" He asks Tobias.

"Oh, I can—"

But Michael's already pouring the tea, and I hide my smile behind my cider. After taking a sip, I say, "First lesson. Save your breath. Demons *and* angels are insufferable when it comes to things like this."

Michael gives me a flat look, returning the kettle to its place on the platter. "You would starve without me." He offers the cup of tea to Tobias, who takes it with a smile and a small 'thank you.'

"This is true. Thank you, Michael."

Michael nods, then returns to his workspace. Tobias looks between me and him. I nod to the *jinni*. "Michael is my *shomer*. Do you know what that is?"

Tobias winces. "Other than the literal definition, which I'm not sure applies here. He's your protector?"

"Guardian, would be more accurate. All Arches have one, it is an old tradition that dates back to the very first pair. You will have one, eventually. Usually, Arches are bonded with a newborn *shomer* at birth to form the strongest bond possible, and are assigned a temporary one in the meantime. A mentor to the budding protege. *Shomer* not only keep us safe from danger, but from ourselves. Michael is right, I would most likely starve without him force feeding me. Or making sure I take my medications. You get the gist."

"That's amazing, and also ... intrusive."

I shrug. "Not really."

"So … you grew up together?"

I swallow, looking away. "Ah, no. We have been bonded for about a hundred years now. Like I said, the bond usually takes place at birth, but it can happen later on, as will be the case for you."

Tobias makes a face. "I don't think I need one. No offense, Michael."

Michael chuckles, but says nothing.

I turn my attention back to Tobias. "Tobias … you realize that everything is going to change, right? You may not think so now, but you will need a *shomer* to keep you and your family safe, and to help you do your duty."

Tobias takes a sip of his tea, then sets the cup down on the table. He sits back in his chair, drawing his knees up to his chest. I nearly smile at how informal he is, and he doesn't even realize it. It's a relief, one that seems to settle the house as well as me. He quietly asks, "Safe from what? I'm not naive, but who would want to hurt an Arch if they're so good?"

"You are about to inherit an aristocracy that has been running since before either of us were born, and the influence and power that comes with it is astronomical. You will be supporting the care and education programs in Levena, the *malakim* families and their well-being. You will be an anchor to the demon's power, and their life force, like I am for your angels. Such power can be transferred to a celestial of lower status, through death and defeat. Kill the Arch, and you take everything they have. But it dies there, as stolen power cannot be inherited."

Tobias is quiet for a long time. He stares into the fire, and I wonder if I've scared him off. He asks, "That's what happened to your first *shomer*, isn't it? Someone tried to kill you?"

In a shuddering exhale, I say, "Yes. It was a long time ago."

Tobias watches me, expectant. I owe it to Tobias, to my other half, to this angel who is being so mercilessly dumped into the harshness of our world, to tell him my story. I know this, but it has been so long since I've spoken aloud the intricacies of my nightmares. I take comfort in watching the flames as I begin, unable to look at Tobias or Michael as I retell about the worst day of my life.

"I was poisoned twice that year. It was untraceable, the culprit unknown. My aunt practically kept me imprisoned in this house, I couldn't even go outside onto the estate grounds. I hated it so much. I was young, and believe it or not, I liked going out on the town, talking with people. Being *in* life instead of ruling over it. It was different back then, solar technology was a new and theorized concept, just coming into its own. There was so much new and unknown at the time."

"One night I snuck out of the manor. It was the Day of Artune, and I—I was looking forward to taking Bartholomew to the festival, had been all year. He protested, but in the end, what could he do? He accompanied me, and kept me safe. To this day I still don't know how he knew, but there was—" I clear my throat and lean ahead, resting my elbows on my knees.

"There was a shot. I didn't even hear it, I don't think anyone did but him. One second we were sitting together on a bench, watching the lover's dance that had just wrung us of breath moments before. And then the next, I—I was on the ground, with Bartholomew on top of me. He was heavy, and I was so confused, my head hurt from where it hit the stone, but most of all, I was scared. In the beat of a heart I knew, because I could feel it. The absence of him. I had never felt it before."

I fall silent and numb. The world does as well, grieving for the person that my mistakes so grievously punished. I have never admitted my part in things to anyone before. Not Michael, not Doc, not Arlo.

After some time, I slowly turn in my seat and look up at Michael. At some point during my story they came and stood behind me, a silent and grounding pillar. Michael stares down at me, gaze tracking back and forth across my features. They take a knee and bow their head, placing a hand over their heart.

Tentatively, I rest a hand on the back of his neck and squeeze once, unsure what to say. Unsure what he's trying to say. Quietly, I settle on, "I won't put you in harm's way, Michael. I won't make the same mistake twice."

Michael lifts their head, eyes wet as they stare up at me. "Living your life is not a mistake, Sir."

I sniff, looking away. "Please, don't."

"My lord," Michael says, rising.

Tobias watches us, expression sad. He asks, "Who was it?"

I smile, but it's grim. "I don't know. They were never found. My life ... changed, to say the least. The opportunities to kill me were drastically cut, but there have still been attempts over the years."

"I have children, Elochian," Tobias says, not exactly accusing, but it's close.

"I know. You can still run. I ... I wouldn't blame you. I've been able to manage."

Tobias studies me. I withstand his evaluation, remaining still until he shakes his head. "No. I'm not running, not anymore. I'll do what it takes to keep them safe, even if that means bonding with a stranger. I have to ask, does the *shomer* bond ... interfere?"

I tilt my head, it takes five whole seconds for the words to click. "Oh. No. It's not a romantic bond. I've never felt a soulmate bond, but I've heard it feels much different. It will not interfere with you and Caspian at all. The same goes for the bond between you and me. That's different."

He sighs, clearly relieved. "Okay."

I rub at my temple. "I'm good friends with Lady Eilweir, the *malakim* who's been managing Clan Haniel for the past fifty years or so. She's very kind and has good judgment, she's choosing candidates for you as we speak. She's also preparing a crash course of her own for you, but I thought it best to start small, just you and I."

Tobias tilts his head. "And she's going to be fine with handing over this so-called empire to a stranger?"

Without hesitation I say, "Yes. She's hardworking and exceptionally intelligent, but this isn't what she's meant for, nor what she wants. But, as a descendant of the last archangel to watch over Levena, it's her duty. Trust me, she's very ready to move on."

"*That's* reassuring," he says on the tail end of a breathy laugh.

I laugh a little too, and when it dies I hesitantly say, "You know ... I'm curious about what Caspian thinks of all this."

Tobias rolls his eyes so hard that I have to restrain more laughter. "He was on me nonstop about getting in touch with you, which to be honest, made me not want to all the more. Not so much to take my place or anything, but he knew something happened that night which changed me, changed my place in the world. I slept for the entire next day, and ever since then I've been constantly unwell."

"And what did he say after you did? See me?"

Tobias runs a hand through his hair, sighing. "I told him everything you said. That I can cut ties and I'll feel better, eventually, or I can do what I was apparently made for. I'm not stupid, Elochian. I know that being an archangel is different from being an angel, but I didn't know the ... nature of it, I suppose. My parents were isolationists to begin with, they never agreed with the idea of celestials living with humans. 'We're Children of the Gods, for fuck's sake.' And after they realized I was *more* than them, in their eyes mind you, and a witch, it became unbearable. They were so awful, so I ... I left."

"And where did you live? Before Levena?"

Tobias blinks, then chuckles with a hollowness I'm deeply familiar with. "In the mountains, to the east of Brinecliff. I wandered for quite some time, but I didn't meet any other angels. Plenty enough demons, and they were as confused by me as I was by them. Anyways, my wandering ended in Levena. I opened the bindery, and not long after met Caspian. We made our home here."

I tilt my head. "Interesting."

He blinks. "What?"

"Well, there are archdemons in Brinecliff, Faydale, *and* Northgrave, for starters. But you were drawn *here*. I ..." A surge of emotion washes over me and I look away, blinking rapidly. It was always meant to be him. He was always meant to be mine.

Tobias whispers, "Can I ask you something?"

"Yes," I say without turning my gaze back to him.

"What did you mean about my being your other half? Because that's Cas. He's my person. But I do feel you. You're right, it's not the same, not at all. But after I saw you the other night, it was like ... it was like the first day I walked into Levena. For the first time in a long time, I felt like I could put my bags down. Do you know what I mean?"

"I do." I sigh, looking back to him. "In the past, *bashert*, which is what we are, were celestial soulmates in every sense of the word. Lovers. Lifelong companions. Enemies. Two that were One. Halves of a Whole. But over time, the dynamic changed. Celestials rebelled against this notion of a predetermined partner that is necessary for survival.

"They chose romantic partners of their volition, and instead worked with their *bashert* on a more platonic, but no less interconnected, basis. That is all you and I are. I need you, and you need me. Your people need me, and mine need you. It's a symbiotic relationship. We gain power and constitution from them, and vice-versa."

"So how have you been able to do what you do?" Tobias asks, and it's the loudest thing in the room.

"Because it's what I was raised for."

I stand outside of Thitwhistle's, bathed in a lamplight's glow. Silhouettes of my friends play on the closed curtains drawn over bizarrely placed windows. My heart rattles its cage, desperately trying to make me turn back. Michael is parked just down the street, my getaway driver for when I'm ready to flee. I told them to come in with me, but they insisted I have some 'regular person time.'

Whatever that means.

Arlo is the only person he trusts me with, which is just great because thoughts of seeing Arlo again after our weird conflict, and seeing Quentin after I ran away, are almost too much to take. And how am I supposed to act with Tobias and Caspian now? I want to simply be Elochian tonight, not the archdemon who's upending their life.

You know what, this was a bad idea. I'll just—

I turn around, nearly crashing into a draconian with visceral yellow eyes. "Shit! Dusan." I brace my hands on my knees and do my best to calm my heart.

Dusan chuckles, the sound deep and rumbling. "Good evening, Elochian. Apologies, I didn't mean to startle you. Leaving the party so soon?"

I stand, using both hands to smooth my wild hair back. I left it loose tonight, a decision I'm already regretting. "What party? There's no party."

Dusan winks at me, then reaches into her thick, insulated coat which falls around her ankles. She pulls out two small boxes, and offers me one. "You dropped this."

I take it, confused as hell. Then, I look at the small tag attached to the box via a pretty green ribbon. *Lindsey.*

"Fuck..." I mutter, then look to Dusan. "I will pay you back."

Dusan smiles. "Go on inside, and that'll be payment enough."

I raise a brow. "Why do I feel like I'm being bribed right now?"

She laughs. "Because you are."

"Fair enough." I offer my arm to her, and she takes it with a smile. "Also, how did you know I would forget?"

She shrugs. "I didn't."

"Sure. Keep your secrets then, dragon."

Dusan kisses me on the cheek and opens the door for us, since I've apparently frozen in front of it again. "Go on, dear."

"Alright, alright," I grumble, shaking off my wings before I step inside the door. A chorus of 'Hey, hello, hey!' follows, and I raise a hand in greeting. I hang up my coat on a literal coat tree, then wander over to the western hearth where Lindsey and Kitt are sitting. Tobias and Caspian are in deep conversation with Gowan and Iris further inside the cafe, and their little *shedim* run around chirping at everyone.. Arlo and Quentin are nowhere to be seen, and Silas and Felix are missing too.

The entire cafe is decorated more lavishly than it was for Felix's birthday, and another wave of gratitude washes over me. I would've felt like an idiot walking in here without Dusan's warning. The dragon seems to have no problem with interrupting conversation on the other side of the room, but I take a seat beside Lindsey on the couch.

"Happy Birthday, Lindsey. Kitty, hello."

Lindsey smiles, dazzling in a long dress woven with hundreds of glittering purple beads. "Thanks Loch, it's good to see you."

Kitty yawns, leaned back against the cushion with an arm outstretched behind Lindsey. She's dressed in a more winter appropriate getup, slim black pants and a low cut silk blouse that matches Lindsey's shirt in color. Her tail taps the floor a few times in a slow, lazy motion. "Long time no see, Loch. How's it been?"

I blow out a long breath. "Fine, busy as hell. Tonight's actually the first time I've been a real person in ages."

Kitty snorts. "You're always a real person, even when you're cooped up doing demon mumbo jumbo."

I give her a look. "I'm remembering why I missed you so much now."

She grins. "Damn right."

"How is the wedding planning coming?"

Lindsey exhales heavily. "She is the definition of bridezilla."

I raise a brow. "Really? And here I was thinking it would be you."

Lindsey scoffs. "She can't make a decision to save her life, why would this be any different? I always know exactly what I want." She takes a gentle hold of Kitt's chin, turning her face to the side so she can kiss her cheek, leaving behind a smear of plum lipstick.

"Ah, well when you put it like that. Still this summer, though?"

"Definitely, and *I* even decided on Beltane," Kitt says, winking flirtatiously at Lindsey. "It's the best time of the year for love."

My thoughts must play onto my face, because Lindsey laughs and says, "Don't worry, elves stopped throwing orgies on Beltane millennia ago. But for a wedding, might make an exception ..."

Kitt bumps her horn against Lindsey. "There are children present," she sing-songs.

"But you—"

"Are much subtler than you, my love."

"Whatever." Lindsey sighs, then directs her attention to me, turning serious. "So, have you talked to Quentin lately?"

My heart quickens. "No, not since Monday. Why?" New voices and distant footsteps come from the distant kitchen. Lindsey and Kitt exchange a look. "What?" I ask again.

Lindsey straightens a little, giving me a look I haven't seen on her before. The teasing atmosphere flips on its head, turning into something foreboding. "If you can't be bothered to talk to him, then it's not my place to tell you. All I can say is if you're gonna just be his friend, that's fine, but be his *friend*. Quit dicking him around."

Then she stands, leaving me behind in a swish of glittering purple.

I look between her retreating figure and Kitty, unsure what the hell just happened. Kitt lifts a hand, bringing her fingers close together. "She's a wee bit protective of Q, but not wrong. Get your shit together, Loch. Oh, time for cake!"

Like A Charm

Quentin

One Hour Earlier

Thunder cracks through my nightmare, blowing it apart. I sit up in a rush, cool metal in my hand and sweat trickling down my spine. After a few seconds, I recognize the furious noise for what it really is. Knocking.

I scramble out of bed and hurriedly slide my glasses on, taking the bat with me as I stumble out of my bedroom, crashing against the wall in the hallway outside my room. I groan, shoulder and knee protesting. The knocking ceases at the noise, and I consider slumping against the wall and going back to sleep. My brain hurts too much for this.

"Quentin, I know you're in there!" Lindsey calls, and I straighten from the wall with great difficulty.

"G'away! It's too early."

"I swear to Typhine if you don't open this door *right* now I'll break it down, and you know I will."

I sigh. She's right.

I trudge over to the door and adjust my glasses, then look through the peephole. Looks like Lindsey. She's scowling, providing a perfect view of her eyes. Her aura is bright green, snapping and popping at the edges.

I breathe, then physically unlock the door. I don't bring down the wards, they'll allow her in, if it's really her. The moment the mechanism clicks, Lindsey bursts into my apartment and nearly slams the door in my face.

"What's wrong?" I ask, quickly shutting the door. I blink, taking in her appearance. She's wearing a gorgeous plum dress finished with thousands of tiny beads. "Why are you ...."

Lindsey crosses her arms and taps her foot on the old floor, scowling at me. "Why am I what? Dressed up? Well, that would be because it's my birthday, and all of our friends are going to be downstairs in a couple hours. Why am I here? Because you haven't answered your phone in two days, and Arlo hasn't seen you since yesterday morning. Not that he realized it was a problem until *I* brought it up."

"Okay!" I put my hands up. "Lay off, alright? I've had a rough week, and time got away from me. I'm sorry." I try to sound genuine, but it's bitter as hell.

"What the fuck, Quen? I understand ignoring everyone else, but me? I feel like I hardly know what's going on with you anymore, as in what's *actually* going on. We don't shut each other out."

"Oh, really? You can be busy living your life, but I can't do the same? We don't live together anymore, I don't need you worrying about me."

With a completely straight face, she says, "That's kind of hard to do when you're dressed in a filthy unicorn onesie covered in cookie crumbs and salsa stains, you're only wearing one sock, and your face looks like you slept in a pile of puke."

I laugh.

She laughs.

Then, I break down and cry.

Despite the cookie crumbs, salsa stains, and wanna be puke face, Lindsey sits down beside me on the floor where I've crumpled up into a ball. "Quentin," she says quietly, cupping my cheek. "What's wrong?"

Through a break in my sobs, I whimper, "They fired me, Linds. I went to work Wednesday morning, and they wouldn't even let me in the door. I had to have a friend of mine get all my things for me, and now he's fired too. So fucking stupid." I rub at my eyes, taken aback by a new onset of tears.

Lindsey's thumb swipes through the hot mess on my cheek. "That makes no sense, you've been nothing but perfection, and your grades this year are the highest they've ever been."

I tell her about my incident with Carina, and it's then I realize I haven't told her, or any of the others about my troubles at work. When Lindsey asks why, I halfheartedly say, "There's already been so much going on."

But it's a poor excuse, judging by the glare she's giving me.

"That's not right, she has no grounds to fire you. You've done nothing wrong, and your curriculum is perfectly acceptable. It's her problem if she doesn't like witches, not yours."

"Yeah, well it is now. They've already replaced me. I don't understand it, and I don't want to complain because I'm not even a witch. I'm not the person they're targeting, just a ... bystander in their way. You know Arlo would be up in arms about it, and I can't—"

Lindsey shakes her head. "He needs to know."

"But there's already—"

She puts her hand over my mouth. "I swear to Gods if you say *one* more self-righteous thing I'm going to suffocate you." I roll my eyes, and she removes her hand. "I'll tell you what we're gonna do. You're going to peel this catastrophe off, and you're going to get your ass in the shower. You're going to put on something nice, and I'm going to raid Arlo's stores for something to fix you up. Then, we're going to go downstairs, and have fun."

"You make it sound so scary though."

"Loch's coming."

I groan, rubbing my hands over my face. "That's not helping. Things are weird, last time I saw him our hands brushed and I started to tell him how I feel, then he said my name like he was going to say something big then we were interrupted and it's driving me crazy trying to figure out what he was going to say and I feel like an idiot around him all the time and I don't know what to do with myself."

Lindsey sighs, looking up to the ceiling. "So help me ..." she mutters. "If I had a quarter for every time I had to witness the dumbest pining of my life—"

"Linds!" I whine. "What do I do?"

"Well, a good start would be to wash your cock and grab your socks."

"Wow. Stellar advice."

"Honestly? I think you need to pretend like you don't care. Quit fawning over him. Let him miss you. I think it's pretty obvious how you feel about him, and if he doesn't know that by now, then he's an idiot and you don't deserve him. You told him that you care about him?"

"That was literally the only part I got out."

She shrugs. "Only part that matters. Let's have some fun, Quen. It's been too serious around here lately, and I've been ... I don't want to sound selfish, but I've been really looking forward to tonight."

"Alright, alright. The guilt trip is a success. Help me up."

"Works like a charm."

I stand beneath the hot spray, breathing in humid mist. Lindsey is quiet, sitting on the bathroom counter. She insisted on staying until she was sure I wasn't going to hide in bed again, and this has always been our thing. Getting ready together. Except she's already put together and I feel like a drowned rat.

I wash my hair with some of the bar soap Arlo made for me, scrubbing my bare nails against my scalp. I rinse, then wash my body with the same bar. When my fingers skim over the ink in my chest, I feel more subconscious about the tattoo on my sternum than ever. It was my first one, and River paid for it. Wanted to choose the design, too. We had just started dating, and it was one of the rare times I spoke up for myself without being punished for it.

At least, not at first.

There's a quiet tap of glass against marble, but I don't think anything of it until Lindsey says, "I didn't know you were wearing lipstick again. I thought you couldn't stand the feel of it."

I freeze. "I'm not."

"Okay…" she says, letting the unsaid question hang in the air.

I finish in a hurry, and when the shower quits, Lindsey passes a towel through a crack in the curtain. I take the rough fabric with trembling fingers, wondering how the fuck I'll get through tonight. I dry off, taking comfort in how the fabric scrubs at my skin.

Maybe it's the curtain between us, or the fact that my heart is still torn open and bleeding truth, but I say, "I found it in my classroom earlier this week, before everything. I think … I think River was there."

There's another clack as the tube meets marble. "What? Did you see him? Did he hurt you?"

I wrap the towel around my waist, then comb my dripping hair back with my fingers. "No."

"How—"

I draw back the curtain. "I'd show you, but my phone is dead. He left me a message."

Her eye twitches. She doesn't jump down from the counter and begin lecturing me, only stares. After a long moment, she asks, "What do you want me to do? Arlo can help."

"No, nothing. I think he was just trying to scare me. I haven't seen him, and I haven't heard anything since then."

Lindsey turns her face to the ceiling, closing her eyes. "You can't hide inside the wards all the time."

I wince. "I know."

She's quiet for a time, and I don't dare step out of the shower. Then she opens her eyes and hops off the counter, opening her arms. I oblige her, stepping out of the shower to wrap my arms around her shoulders. I'm surprised by how much her hug settles me, and I hold her just a little bit tighter.

She says, "I won't say anything. But if things get worse, I'm tattling."

I laugh, squeezing her once more before leaning back to get a good look at her. "Thanks, Linds."

"Of course. Now, get dressed. I'll meet you downstairs." She kisses me on the cheek, then spins on her heel. Thankfully the cool blue rug is non-skid, as those stilettos of hers would be deadly on a wet tile floor.

"You're leaving?"

"I can't be late to my own party." She winks, then disappears down the hall.

"Right," I say to myself, then decide to take Lindsey's advice to the max.

Agian Snails

Elochian

The radio introduces a new song, and my wings won't stop trembling in anticipation of Quentin's arrival. Why isn't he here yet?

A raspy snicker jerks my head around. Silas stands behind me, which isn't much of a surprise except for the fact he can do it so quietly. We have a tendency to share the same isolated corner of the room, watching affairs like this from a distance. I prefer to socialize in sprints, waiting to catch those who pass by my corner of the room so I don't have to get into the thick of things.

"What are you laughing at?" I ask.

He shrugs. "You couldn't be more obvious."

I scoff. "I have no idea what you're talking about."

"Right. That's why I could eat your excess energy like cotton candy right now."

"Is that … appropriate to tell someone?"

"The truth? I think so."

"I—" Crimson flutters in the corner of my periphery, and all my thoughts clear the way for the dangerously beautiful vision that is Quentin Matsdotter.

He stands with Arlo and Felix, almost the same height as the Hedge Witch due to his heels. They're absolutely deadly, pitch black and delicate like the rest of his outfit. His form fitting pants leave little to the imagination, and his coat falls in generous ruffles past his hips.

The coat is … it's a masterpiece in its own right. Crushed red velvet that is absolutely haunting beneath the dim cafe lights. Black lace trims the piece, and the sleeves and high collar are done in a frilly and detailed fashion. His black hair is damp, smoothed against his head where it lightly curls at the back of his neck and teases layers of silver necklaces.

The worst part of it all is, he faces away from me.

"Like candy," Silas whispers.

I glare at him. He mimes eating cotton candy.

I sigh, waiting for Quentin to leave Arlo's side and come say hello. He and Arlo are fairly close, and I'm not sure if they've always been this way or if it's new. While everyone is nice, I'm definitely the newest person in the group. They all have a way with each other, an ease that I will never understand. But I don't mind standing on the shore, catching the remnants of waves as they pass.

The crowd is too dense, too far away from the door. Felix waves at Silas and me, gesturing for us to come over. "Time for cake!" He calls loud enough for us to hear, nearly having to shout.

Silas and I exchange an uneasy look, finding solidarity in the other for a moment.

"Did you make it?"

He hums. "Snowberry upside down cake? Yes."

"Well, that's worth all of the hassle. Let's go, in and out."

Silas grins. "In and out."

People shift and laughter rises through the conversation. When we join the group, Quentin is no longer at Arlo's side. What the fuck? Silas and Felix pair up, staying close to Arlo and me in the back of the group. Quentin stands on the other side of a large table with Lindsey and Kitt, but I can't focus on him long because Arlo's heavy gaze falls on me.

He says, "Loch, good to see you again."

I lift a brow. "Really?"

Kitty and Quentin lead the room in song, and Lindsey squeals with happiness.

Arlo rests a hand on my shoulder. "Really."

I exhale, upper wings shuddering as our friends sing happy birthday to Lindsey. I turn my attention back to her, quietly singing along. Lindsey grins, then quickly kisses Kitty before blowing out her candles. We don't clap or cheer for Silas' sake, but spirits are high. For a moment, it feels like everything is alright.

I'm doing what normal people do. I'm hanging out with my friends. These people who don't *have* to like me, but they do anyway.

Quentin's ignoring me.

At first, I blame it on him being caught up with Lindsey. Everyone ate cake, and they laughed and told stories while I listened. Quentin mentioned his phone being dead to Gowan, and when I had said that wasn't surprising, he only laughed and said, 'you're not wrong.'

Before I could wring more words out of him, he demanded that Lindsey dance with him. The sight of the two of them scampering off to an open section of floor on those ice thin heels was enough to give me a heart attack. So, I found refuge in my corner again, albeit at a table instead of the couch this time, and blessedly closer to the front door.

Which leads me to the next obstacle this evening.

Caspian.

He wheels up to my table, reaching out to push the chair opposite me out of the way. My body stiffens and I lean back in my own seat, one of the few in the cafe with low backs made for winged beings. I brace for brutal questions, but Caspian only asks, "How's it been, Loch?"

Surprised, I say, "Oh. Fine. Busy, as always."

"That's good." He leans closer to me. "Listen, I wanted to say thank you."

"Thank you?"

"Yes," he says, equally confused. "For helping Bias. I'm not going to pretend to know what the hell it means to be you, or him for that matter, but I do know that he's feeling better. Not just his body, but ... he's motivated. More assured. It's like the old days before ...."

On the other side of the room, Arlo offers his hand to Tobias, bowing a little at the waist. Tobias laughs, then takes Arlo's hand and is led into dance. Both their eyes glow with magick, the bright green and pink colors flicker onto the walls of the cafe as they dance. When Arlo spins Tobias, his wings unfurl.

Rose feathers sprout from his back in a great flutter that becomes part of the song itself, and those small eyes blink open as they're awakened. Some of the feathers brush against Arlo's cheek, and he laughs. Arlo's *laughing*. My heart swells at the sight of it, and Tobias' wings. But it's not from jealousy over the fact he can command them at will. Not tonight.

It's an exhalation of the soul.

With great difficulty, I tear my gaze away from my Other Half. I shift my attention to Caspian, who is for all intents and purposes dazed by his person. The admiration there is unmistakable, and I swallow guilt.

"I thought you'd hate me," I whisper.

He shakes his head, trance broken. "What for?"

"It's a big, dangerous life you're about to have, one I feel like I've guilted him into."

"Oh, I don't know about that. I think he's always been meant for more."

He glances at where Arlo and Tobias are still dancing, and joined by the others now too. Quentin twirls into Kitt, while Lindsey and Gowan dance in a way that reminds me of trees swaying in the wind, if the trees were on drugs. The pair of little *shedim* dance around Silas and Felix's feet, Silas holds Marlena's hands while Felix does the same with Zeke.

Caspian drops his voice to a whisper. "And I think Leon did too. I ... I keep waiting for the bastard to come for him again. Arlo's warded the house and he's doing his best, but he can't be everywhere at once. This *shomer* thing, how much longer will it be?"

I nod sagely. "Andromeda is finalizing the candidates, they should be ready for the Trials by next weekend."

"Good. You'll be there when he chooses, right? Not that I don't trust his judgment, but." He shrugs. "You know how this all works, we don't."

I blink. "Oh. I can. But I trust Andromeda, otherwise I would never turn over your family's safety to her, and it will be good for Tobias to be with other angels."

Caspian leans closer over the table. "Please, Loch. It would mean a lot to me."

I bow my head, feeling oddly touched. "Of course."

He grins, leaning back in his chair. "So, any good gossip from the bar lately?"

I blink at the rapid change in topic, but when I notice Tobias approaching, I catch on. "You're worse than an old hen, quit projecting."

"Of course he is," Tobias says, bending down to kiss Caspian on the cheek. "That's why I love him so much."

Caspian groans, cheeks flushed. When Tobias pulls away, laughing, Caspian reaches up and tugs the archangel back down so he can kiss him on the lips.

I look away, overwhelmed.

Only to see Lindsey coming our way, hair mussed and a drink in hand. She collapses on a nearby couch, then sets down her glass on the coffee table with a bit too much force. "Fuck, I haven't danced liked that in years." She kicks off her heels, then takes a long sip.

"Q's quite the dancer, eh?" Cas remarks, smirking at her.

"That's what years of ballet gets you," Lindsey says offhandedly.

"He's a ballet dancer?" I ask.

"Well, he used to be. You didn't know that?" Lindsey asks, the accusation veiled, but there to my critical ears.

"No," I say quietly.

"Well, he was."

"Why doesn't he still dance?"

Lindsey shrugs, her smile suddenly wicked. "Guess you'll have to ask him yourself."

"No. I mean, not right now, obviously. He's dancing."

"*You* could dance," Cas says, playing devil's advocate.

I glare at him. I stand, and run away from the fear rising in my gut.

Straight for Quentin.

Quentin

Arlo bows to me. "Thanks Q, that was fun."

"You're leaving me already?" I pout, rubbing at my collarbone.

He chuckles. "I can't keep up with you. Besides, I think someone else wants a turn."

"Wh—" I turn, and am immediately arrested by Elochian's sudden proximity. He looks just as surprised as I am, but determination creases his brow.

"Quentin, could I have this dance?" He asks in a rush, hands opening and closing at his sides. His shaking wings frame his figure, catching the dim lights of the cafe.

"Oh, yes." We stare at each other for a moment, and I find myself unable to move first. "Do you ... know how to dance?"

Elochian laughs softly, and tension leaves his shoulders. Slowly, he reaches for my hand, and I oblige him. I remember to breathe, surprised when he makes me the lead. He swallows, wings trembling so intensely they sound like dead leaves in the wind. Quietly, he says, "Part of my rigorous education. I didn't know that you danced, let alone so beautifully."

I stumble, but Elochian holds me up.

"You think so?"

"... Yes, I do."

We part, and I spin Elochian.

One of his lower right wings brushes against my neck. The scales are softer than I imagined and I shiver, every nerve on high alert. When he returns to me, our bodies are closer than before. He whispers, "I care about you too, you know. I know I'm not the best at saying so, and I haven't exactly told you what your friendship means to me, but ... well, you scare me, Quentin."

"*Me*? I scare you?"

"*Yes*," he hisses, exasperated. His hand tightens around mine, and the fingers on my shoulder have slid up, fidgeting with the hair at the nape of my neck. He looks away from me, worrying his bottom lip between his teeth. No fangs today, and his birthmark doesn't glow in my presence. Part of me whispers his soulmark could be somewhere else, sometimes a birthmark really is just a birthmark.

I swallow. "I'm the least scary person there is."

He scowls at me then, and the full force of it temporarily erases everything. My thoughts, my worries. Suddenly, I realize just how much I've missed him.

"Not to me," he whispers.

"Why?"

He looks around. We're the only ones dancing now. Arlo and Dusan stand together near the coffee machines. Gowan and Iris sit with Lindsey and Kitt near the western hearth. Felix sits with Caspian and Tobias, and Silas isn't far away from them.

Loch tugs on my hair particularly hard as he twirls it around his finger, but I know he doesn't mean it. He stares at my chest, unable to meet my eyes when he says, "I'm scared of you because of how much I care about you. The last time ...."

When I'm sure he won't pick the sentence up again, I ask, "Do you know what scares me?"

"What?" He asks, blinking those lovely dark eyes at me.

I fight the urge to admit, 'losing you.'

Instead, I say, "Snails."

Elochian makes a face, nearly stumbling. "Snails?"

"Hey. Don't judge until you've been to Agia. They're slimy and sneaky there. Did you know it takes Agian snails ten minutes to cross a foot, but only thirty seconds to eat one?"

Elochian laughs. Pure laughter that overcomes him too quickly to be restrained. His fingers tighten, making every point of contact alight anew. "That's an odd thing to be afraid of."

I shrug. "Maybe to you. Will you think less of me now?"

"No, of course not."

"Then why would I think less of you?"

"I see what you're doing. I think that's an awful big leap."

"Well, I think it's odd you're convinced the past is going to repeat itself, even though I'm not him. Them? But I'm glad you told me, and now I know. Just like you know never to bring me around snails."

"Him," he says quietly, and I feel like I've mined a chunk of gold from Elochian's heart.

The music finally ends, tapering off for the first time today. We begin to separate, but our eyes never leave the other. I lift his hand and kiss his knuckles before finally releasing him. "Thank you for telling me. And the dance. I'm not going anywhere, Lochian, and I'm ... I'm glad we're friends."

If he wanted to correct me, now would be the time. Elochian's lips part, then close, and the moment passes. Kitt calls us over for gifts, giving us the opportunity to leave the awkward situation behind. Elochian stays close to my side, but we don't say anything to each other. Lindsey opens my gift first, which is a new pair of solar goggles for the spring, and next is Elochian's.

When she opens the small silver box, Lindsey busts out laughing. Kitt looks over her shoulder, then she starts laughing too. Elochian is just confused, and when I peer over at what Lindsey's got, I laugh too.

"What?" He asks me in a frantic whisper.

I lower my lips to his ear, and his lower wings tremble in response. "Did you know they were nipple rings when you got them?"

"No!" He hisses, cheeks flushed.

A nearby Dusan chuckles at the same time Arlo asks, "Is that a box of mine?"

"Mhm. They do come in handy when you're not sure what the person needs. Apparently, she needed some new jewelry," Dusan says, bemused. Elochian caves into quiet laughter, shaking his head.

"You're a real swell pal, Loch," Lindsey calls, smiling wide. She looks at me standing beside him, and winks.

After she begins tearing into something else, Dusan quietly addresses Arlo, Elochian, and myself. "It's time for me to get going."

Arlo nods. "Tomorrow, then."

"What's tomorrow?" I ask, wracking my brain for tomorrow's plans. Saturday. Not a damn thing.

Dusan gives me a wink, then slips away.

Elochian rolls his eyes. "Are all dragons so mysterious?"

Arlo laughs. "Probably so. The only other dragon I know is Josse, and he's as mysterious as they get. Anyways, she has a guest in town apparently, and they want to meet me."

"And you said yes?" Surprise colors my tone, but I can't help it. Arlo hates strangers.

Lochian chuckles at my surprise, but says nothing.

Arlo raises a brow. "I dare you to tell her no."

I shrug. "Fair enough."

"I have to get going too," Elochian says, and my heart cringes.

"Oh, alright. Be safe, okay?"

The corner of his lips twitch. "Always am. Bye, Arlo."

Arlo nods. "Loch. See you Wednesday?"

"Yes." He waves, then turns away and leaves. Simple as that. The bells chime and a gust of cold air rushes in the cafe, signaling his departure. I don't know why I was expecting more, but it felt like we had a moment, and now it's ....

Arlo whispers, "I think this is the moment you go after him."

I look up to Arlo, considering his words. I want to. Gods, do I want to.

"I don't think you're supposed to chase after the guy who just friend-zoned you." I whisper back.

Arlo shakes his head. "If you think all you are to him is a friend, then you're sorely mistaken. *Go.*"

I move.

I don't think about it. I cross the room and take hold of the cold doorknob, then expose myself to the elements. It's not currently snowing, but it did recently and the sidewalk is covered in a thin layer. Loch's already made it to the street, headed towards a parked car where I'm sure Michael waits. The intense wind cuts through my thin shirt, and I pull my jacket tighter around myself like that'll do anything.

"Lochian!" I call out.

He stops, turning on his heel. At first he looks bewildered, then furious. I walk towards him anyway, and he nearly sprints to me. I take a few steps back when he reaches me, because the wild look in his eyes is new. I don't know what it means, is he really angry with me?

I lose my footing, and my right knee buckles. I cry out and Elochian grabs my upper arms, wings stretching wide to keep him steady as he pulls me upright. They silhouette his figure, flooded by light from the half-full moons. Soft moonlight refracts through his wings and onto the snow in a kaleidoscope of colors and patterns. Some of the intricate, detailed lines tattooed onto his wings glow to life, no longer just black, but gold too.

His hands are tight on my coat sleeves, and my own have a good hold of his elbows. For once he has me in a tight, relentless grip, like he won't ever let me go, and I can't say I mind. Our bodies are pressed together, and my disbelief escapes in a singular plume of warm air which clouds in the cold between our faces.

Worry creases his brows as he berates me. "Quentin! What are you doing out here in those *things*?"

Things? Oh. The heels.

"I ... uh..."

Words. I need words.

Or maybe, I don't.

I kiss the right corner of his mouth. The pale skin there is soft and cold against my dry lips. Elochian's chest hitches, and I linger for one more moment before pulling away. I look up at him through my lashes. There's no more anger on his face, but something equally dangerous.

That's something new, too.

"I wanted to say goodnight. Properly."

I step out of Elochian's hold, and he's so stunned that his hands fall to his sides. I give him a smile, then turn away and walk back to the cafe. Everyone's faces are pressed to the main window like fish in a barrel, and they scatter upon seeing me turn back. I shake my head and rub at my chest, laughing quietly to myself.

Someone Else's Sins

Elochian

Visions of Quentin in red haunt me, and the ghost of his hands on my body won't leave me alone. It was nothing more than a dance, an embrace between two spirits ever so close, but ever so far away. Regardless, it's enough to feed the pixies eating away at my nerves, and they become fat with worry. I've tried to keep him at arms length, to be happy with what we have, but I've been so stupid. There's no way I can simply be his *friend*, not anymore.

I'm falling in love with him.

The chaos of my mind does nothing but churn over and over, but I break out of it long enough to pursue a certain line of thought that's been bugging me. Settled into my nest, I dig my phone out of the blankets and bring up a search engine. I type in Quentin's full name, and seconds pass before an entire page dedicated to him pulls up. It's been awhile since I've done this.

First and foremost is his staff page at the university, complete with an incredibly short bio. The biography says nothing of his personal life, only that he is the 'most brilliant physicist of our time' and that he specializes in Spiritual Metaphysics. I go back, parsing through references to papers he's written and studies he's conducted, and of course it's all intermingled with his erotica books.

Why he didn't choose a pen name is beyond me, and he always laughs off the question. I find nothing else, no mention of Quentin's time as a ballet dancer, or anything about his life. Nothing on his author page, which has no picture either, and he has no social media, something I'm not sure how he manages to go without. His readers seem to find his books just fine, I guess.

I lock my phone, letting it fall back into the blanket pile surrounding me. I ... know nothing about Quentin, not really. I don't know anything about his family, or his life. Then again, *is* there much to tell? He's a human who teaches physics, and spends most of his time with his friends. He doesn't exactly lead what most would call an exciting life.

I ache for someone to pour my words into, to help me break the cyclical thoughts drowning me alive. What should I do? What is the *right* thing to do?

I toss and turn until giving up on sleep entirely. With great difficulty, I extricate myself from the nest and pad over to my desk. At the very least, I can put pen to paper. And if I'm putting pen to paper, then I might as well dedicate them to someone.

Dear Thatch,

Did you know?

Did you know when you bumped into me, and ran away before I could return the book you dropped on the ground? All you left me with was a flash of red, and an erotica that terrified and intrigued me. I always wondered why you didn't want it back, why you were in such a hurry. Did you knock into me accidentally-on purpose? But why?

I read it all that night, you know. It was the filthiest thing I had ever read, but it also … it tore me apart, and stitched me back together. I had never felt so seen, so understood. How fitting that I should find myself in the monster between the pages.

I hoarded every book, every deleted scene, every short story. I devoured every word that Quentin Matsdotter ever brought to life, and in doing so I started to feel alive again. Not whole, but alive. Even so, my heart felt like a tightwire.

Quentin Matsdotter was an anonymous mystery. Always out of reach. What would I even say to the person if I met them? I had no clue, but it was a fantasy that I clung to. Something in my life that was mine, and mine alone.

Did you know that night in the bar, with colorful lights dancing in your mischievous, all knowing eyes? All I could think was, 'it's him, it's him,' when his hand slipped into mine, sweaty and real and warm. And that was all without knowing his name, who he was and how much of an impact he'd already had on my life.

He brought me to life, you know. I suspect that you do. I wonder if everything you did, or do, is accidentally-on purpose. If you know more than you let on, more than the secrets of the universe. You know us, all of us. Right down to our deepest secrets, fears, and desires.

Did you know before I did, that my heart and soul was always Quentin's?

Warmest Regards,
Elochian
1/9621

My aunt eats me alive during brunch.

She says, "Have you given much thought to a social event, Elochian?"

I sigh, tearing the crust off my jam toast. My cousins watch me with a mix of disinterest and disgust. Edward sits beside his mother, residing in the camp of disinterest. He is the oldest of her spawn and a constant reminder of what I should be. Pious, obedient, social and clever.

Everyone thinks Edward should be head of the clan, but he's the only person who doesn't say it to my face, although I know he thinks it too. It's in the way he looks down his nose at me, full of pity. We've never liked each other, but dislike would be too strong a word for us. We simply exist in this aristocratic world together, apathetic puppets on strings.

Before taking a bite of the perfect middle of my toast, I say, "Yes, I have. You were right, I need to show my face. Or part of it, at least."

Tisha tilts her head. "Oh? Do tell."

I take a long sip of my tea, which does nothing to abate my nerves. I feel restless, despite the fact I've been so sure of this idea. Voicing it aloud makes it all that much more real. I clear my throat and place my palms upon the table. "Lord Daemarrel will ascend in two months, and so we will host a masquerade ball to celebrate. Socially accept him, so to speak."

Tisha's first born daughter, Annette, claps her hands. We are the closest in age, and she's the one I get along with the most. "Please tell me they will be as colorful as the ones from when we were kids! You do remember that far back, don't you?"

My shoulders lower from my ears, just a little. "If I try hard enough, yes."

Mabel and Roque, babies of the group at only twenty, are overcome with delight and displeasure, respectively. There's never been a ball in their lifetime, and they resent me with every fiber of their being for my unorthodox and isolationist ways. Roque says, "I'll believe it when I see it."

"Oh come now Ro, it'll be fun." Mabel pretends to be on my side for once, but it's only for her own benefit.

I turn my attention back to my aunt. "Will I regret giving you free rein?"

Her smile is sharper than her fuchsia painted nails. Tisha says, "Of course, but that's to be expected."

"Right."

I push away my plate and take another sip of my cider, which is precisely when Tisha asks, "And can I assume that I will be unable to sway you from asking Mr. Matsdotter to be your companion for the festivities?"

Sputtering can not begin to describe the fit that comes over me, and the room has never felt hotter. "Well—I—what?"

Tisha's lips twitch, but her sympathetic tone puts me on defense. "Elochian. I do not care what you do in your free time, but you cannot forget who you are. You are God-Touched. You will outlive *all* of us, and he is a human. He is not an ideal partner to lead the clan. To have fun with, perhaps. But the implications of bringing him to an event like this is ... perhaps more than Mr. Matsdotter *wants* to get into. If you still wish to do so, then so be it. But think on it, for his sake."

I cannot bring myself to speak, for she has spoken aloud my greatest fears, and in a way that I would call sympathetic, if I didn't know any better.

This life of mine is too much. Too much for anyone.

I excuse myself from the table without a word. Roque makes a snide comment as I do, and Edward's voice follows me out the door. Michael shadows my step while I escape to my apartment, silent and unassuming. When we come to the bottom of the stairs leading to my quarters, he stops following me.

The break in script jolts me out of my panic spiral, and I turn to stare at him.

Michael says, "She's wrong, you know."

I shake my head. "No—"

Michael takes a step towards me, determined. "Quentin won't live as long as you, but you will live as long as he does. *You* are fortunate to live on this planet at the same time he lives his short, but no less meaningful life. *You* are fortunate to have a chance to make him happy for the rest of it. I am telling you right now, Elochian, if you let this man go, you will spend the rest of your *very* long life regretting it."

I stand there flayed open and awestruck. After a moment I quietly say, "There are times when you remind me of him, you know."

"Quentin?" Michael asks, confused.

I shake my head. "No. Bartholomew." I struggle to find air, and I have to look away from them. We stand there, surrounded by silence, black and white checkered tiles, and red velvet curtains. When I regain my courage, I say, "He was the same way. Wouldn't let me feel sorry for myself, or feel restricted by my place. He could always turn and twist situations into something good, even if I could see nothing but despair and hardship."

Michael stands a little taller, which isn't hard to do. "What do you think he'd say?"

I laugh, and it's wet and hot. It overtakes me, a storm of grief and rage and nostalgia. A thought passes that perhaps this is healing, but I don't know. I've never allowed myself to do such a thing. The empty parts of my heart have scarred over by now. Can anything grow in such a place?

"I told you. You remind me of him."

Michael bows their head. "I do my best to honor him, Sir."

"Could you ... do me a favor, Michael?"

Michael blinks. "Anything."

"I—" I close my eyes, breathing deep. Do I really want to do this? Only after I open my eyes again do I say, "I want you to look into Quentin."

Michael's face twists. "What? Why?"

I press my fingers to my temple. "I'm missing something. Please, just ... please?"

Michael sighs, shaking their head. "One invasion of privacy coming right up."

I smile weakly. "Thank you."

Coffee With Dragons

Quentin

I cling to my hot chocolate like my life depends on it. I've had three coffees this morning, and Arlo cut me off after I nearly paced a hole in the floor. After a sleepless night spent dissecting the chaos that is my life, I decided to come clean to Arlo about Carina this morning. Not because I want help with my job, but because it's proof that the anti-witch rhetoric is becoming a real threat that won't go away on its own.

The booth is cleaned out, all traces of Arlo's research nest have been moved to Witch House. We sit there together, hidden away from the rest of the cafe. Silas no longer works full time since he goes to school at the castle, so he and Felix are free to do what they like on the weekends. Today, that means playing video games until their brains become soup. Considering how stressful things have been, I don't think it's a bad thing. They need to be kids.

Arlo holds onto his mug as tightly as I do mine, and he stares at the table while he thinks. Eventually, he asks, "Do you want your job back?"

I blow out a long breath. "Yes, and no. Obviously the administration is in Carina's pocket. I don't want to work for people like that. But at the same time, I feel bad for the kids. Is this what they're going to do, fire problematic teachers first, then change the curriculum entirely? What are they trying to achieve?"

Arlo sighs, tugging at the gauge in his ear. "What a nightmare. I never went there, but back in the day I always heard good things about it. Julianna's kids go there."

"Yeah?" I smile a little at the sound of Arlo casually talking about the mayor's kids. "You know, I remember seeing you on the news, when she first called you the Defender of Levena."

He laughs bitterly. "I forget how young you are sometimes."

"Shut up." I pause, wondering if Elochian thinks I'm young. He's even older than Arlo is, although I'm not really sure how *much*. "Speaking of, do you by chance know how old Elochian is?"

Arlo's brow lifts, and the sass in it is unparalleled. "Why don't you ask him?"

"Arlo, please, for the love of Artune, help me out here."

He smiles a little. "Fine, if only because it's you. He's a hundred and seventy. Or a hundred and eighty ... I can't remember, but one of the two."

"Oh," I say faintly. "Oh."

Arlo winks at me, then goes back to drinking his coffee. I stare off into space, wondering why the fuck I like impossible men. After a moment, I return my attention to the impossible witch at my side, deciding now is as good a time as any to bring this up.

I fiddle with my glasses and say, "What if … what if you got all the witches together? Do an event or something, show Levena that you're just everyday people. It's easy to make shadows on the wall seem scary."

"An event," Arlo says flatly. "All the witches. Together."

"Why are you saying it like that?"

"Quen, Tobias and me being friends isn't normal. As a rule, witches hate each other. It was one of the biggest reasons why Leon could steal people like he did. They were scattered, easy to pick off."

"Silas and Felix don't hate each other."

Arlo gives me a look. "That's different."

"How?"

"Quentin."

"Arlo. You could get along, if you tried. Have any of you ever really tried? If Leon's back, then he's just going to do the same thing because like you said, it worked before—"

"*Quentin*," Arlo says, firmly this time. Not angry, but definitely not happy. "Maybe we all could've been friends. Before. You think *I'm* fucked up? I'm a fucking bushel of sunshine compared to some of the others. I'm not asking them for anything, they've been through enough. The last thing anybody wants is to be made a circus animal. We shouldn't have to *convince* people that we deserve to be here."

I lean back in my chair and cross my arms, looking away from Arlo. All at once I feel chastised, pissed off, and righteous. To the wall, I say, "You're right. You shouldn't. But I'll be damned if you won't let me stand by your side. And maybe if you gave other people the chance, they'd do the same. Maybe they're tired of hiding, just like you were. Like Thatch was. But how will you ever know if you don't ask?"

Arlo's hand rests on my forearm, and I look over at him. "I'll think about it."

I nod once. "Alright. I'm not ... I know I shouldn't be telling you what to do. But I am. Kind of."

He's quiet as he withdraws. He taps the table once. "Thank you."

"For?"

"Thank you for not signing the petition."

"Oh. You don't have to thank me for doing the right thing."

"Maybe not. But I am anyway. You're a good friend."

My cheeks heat. "Stop. Drink your chocolate."

Arlo grins. "While we're on the topic of good friends, how's Loch today?"

I sigh, trying to keep my disappointment at bay. "Fine. He's having family brunch today, which you know he hates."

Arlo nods. "His aunt is a fine piece of work."

"Aren't all aunts?"

"Wouldn't know. So you're going to completely skip over the swooning in the snow part?"

"I was *trying* to." I take a sip of my hot chocolate, which is more room temperature than anything. "There was no swooning, it wasn't anything. Just ... kissing a friend good night."

Arlo laughs. "Listen, I love you, but I don't think I'll be kissing you goodnight anytime soon. Come on, what did he say? Does he want to ... you know?" He gestures at me vaguely. "Actually name whatever this is between you?"

I open my mouth, but the sudden change of expression on his face stops me cold. I'm facing Arlo, who has the better view of the cafe beyond us, so I have to turn in my seat to find the cause of it. Dusan, joined by perhaps the most intimidating woman I've ever seen. Arlo stands, expression grave, and I do the same.

"Good morning, you two." Dusan gestures between the woman at her side, and us. "Arlo, Quentin. This is my mother, Idina Garren."

Idina is a tall and broad woman, with several inches on her daughter in every way. Her hair is long and stark white, some of it is restrained by tiny braids and beads, but the length of it hangs around her hips. She wears no jacket, and her dark clothes are loose and comfortable. Her eyes are the same sunshine yellow as Dusan's, but lined with far more wrinkles and twice as much wise mischief.

What strikes me the most odd about her is that she wears no jewelry. She is plain, and simple. And very, *very* old. I have never felt more human than I do looking at her. Am I supposed to bow? I feel like I should be bowing.

"How do you do, Mr. Rook?" Idina asks, her voice lilting and calm. She reaches for Arlo's hand first, and the way she moves is smooth and effeminate, intentional. Tucked under her left arm are a few old books, the pages weathered to say the least.

When Arlo's hand meets hers, he inhales sharply through his nose, then politely says, "Please, call me Arlo. Um, please, sit down." He corrals us all back to the booth. "Can I get you anything?"

Idina smiles, and it's disarmingly beautiful. "No, thank you. Perhaps after." She turns to me, shaking my hand the same way she did Arlo's. "Hello there."

"H–hi. I'm Quentin."

Her smile broadens. "Yes, I've heard about you."

At my sputtering, she winks and leaves me behind.

It goes like this. I sit beside the elderly dragon, and across from her daughter. Arlo sits beside Dusan, and across from Idina. Idina's tomes rest on the table between us all, and my fingers itch to touch them. *What has Dusan told her about me? Why is* anyone *talking about me?*

"What can I do for you?" Arlo asks.

Idina glances at Dusan. Her daughter nods in acquiescence, smiling quietly. "I am here because a couple of months ago, I regained memories of a man you know as Thatch Phantom. I, however, knew him as Thatcher Gaillot. Unfortunately, I only saw him three times in my life, but he had a lasting impact on my family, beginning with my father, and ending with Dusannara."

Arlo sucks in a breath, reaching for Dusan's hand beneath the table. *I ache to hold someone's hand, and that Elochian was here to hear this.* He's been working just as hard as Arlo, Caspian, Kitt, or anyone else on this, and I feel like this is a moment. A breakthrough on the tip of a tongue.

Idina rests a hand on her stack of books. "The morning after I dreamt of Thatcher, I received the call from Dusannara explaining what had happened. Naturally, I searched our familial archives for anything that might not have been there before, potentially veiled by the Gods. But I found nothing.

"I let it be, as much as I hated to, until I heard that his gravestone had been uncovered. And I wondered then if history is being revealed in stages, by accident or design I haven't quite figured out yet. Regardless, I looked again, and this is what I found. You may have them, but might I suggest preparing yourself before reading."

"Prepare myself?" Arlo asks hoarsely.

Idina smiles, gaze shifting to her hand on the books for a moment. When she looks back to Arlo, she says, "They are mostly love letters, games and such of the like, between my father, Henix, and Thatcher. There are some diary entries of Thatcher's as well, both before my father's arrival and after. They were lovers for a short time, until he died."

"Your father?" I ask.

Idina blinks at me. "No. Thatcher. He died in the fire which transformed Min Isle to Levena. As you've guessed, they renamed the town in his honor."

"But he didn't die. He can't die," Arlo says.

"He can't now, but he most certainly did. My father led the memorial, and commissioned his headstone. He found the ... well. He found what remained of Thatcher. There are even accounts here from some of the people he saved."

I rub my chin, whispering. "Resurrection? I don't think there are any accounts of a God returning a person's entire spirit, not just the soul, which is definitely what would've happened. His body had the ..." My theory breaks off, and I wince at the memory of Thatch's body wrought with burns and scars. I gently add, "He has the scars to prove it."

Idina nods approvingly. "Quite, but if he works for the Gods, so to say, then it's possible. But why use the same body, is what I wonder."

"And he told Arlo he's ten thousand years old, which is a lot longer than—when did this happen? We have '38, but not the millennia." I ask quickly, mind working faster than my mouth.

"The fire of Min happened in 6038," Idina says.

"Oh," I say, blinking rapidly. "That's only three thousand years ago. And we have evidence of him existing in 5012. That ... doesn't make sense."

Idina shrugs. "I'm surprised you think time is a linear thing."

"They knew who saved them, at the time," Arlo says, speaking up for the first time. It takes me a moment to backtrack and catch on, but not Dusan.

She pats Arlo's hand. "It would appear that his memory, and all these documents, began to fade about a month after the fire. But he was given a proper goodbye, yes."

Arlo swallows, throat clicking. He stares at the books like they might bite him. "How old was he? Was he born there?"

Idina laughs, pushing the books towards Arlo. "Read, dear boy."

He leans back and shakes his head. "Not now. I'd rather fall apart in private if it's all the same to you."

The elder dragon softens. "Would you rather I tell you about the first time I met him?"

Arlo huffs out a small laugh, then wipes at his eyes. "I'd like that."

"Alright then. Firstly, I must say that after the fire, the town was rebuilt and centered around the castle. It was the site of the first library in Levena, run by my grandfather, Bailey, and Thatcher. Sadly, Bailey did not survive the fire." Idina pauses for a moment, her expression solemn. "But I digress. Thatcher first arrived at the castle when I was eleven years old, and I dare say it might have been his first time seeing my father again.

"He knocked on the door and I answered, as I had a bad habit of doing for anyone and everyone. He was windswept and confused, and I think I broke him, if I'm being honest. My father was there a moment later, sweeping me into his arms. Thatcher had said, 'Ah, hello. I—I think I have the wrong place. I was looking for the bookstore that used to be in through here.'

"And I could feel my father's rapidly beating heart when he said, '*Oh.*' He laughed quietly, which was to say quite loudly as he was a big man. He said, *It hasn't stood for years, it fell during a fire we had, and I ... it was my father's, and I didn't have it in me to keep it going without him.*' He stopped, surprised at himself, and asked, *'Did you ... my apologies, have we met before?'* Thatcher of course was devastated. He said, *'N—no. I'm sorry to bother you. Have a good day.*' Then he ran off, and I didn't see him again for nearly three thousand years."

I sniff. "What. The. Fuck. Did you think that would make him feel better?" I throw a hand in Arlo's direction. His face is tucked into the crook of Dusan's shoulder, and she pets his hair.

Idina laughs. Actually laughs. "No, I didn't. But I can't tell this next part without telling the first part, which is depressing, I know. Look through the storm clouds for the sun and all that. As I said, I didn't see him again for three thousand years, which is when this one was born." She smiles proudly at Dusan. "He helped deliver her. I understand that he later bought that very same hospital, which I can't help feeling sentimental over, although I'm sure it has nothing to do with me."

"That's why you've always remembered him," Arlo says to Dusan, sitting up suddenly. "He has literally been watching out for you since ... always."

"I know," she says, and her voice cracks on the two words. "I never thought to include my mother in my investigations, if only because I didn't know they—*we*—are connected so deeply, and that I always forgot him so quickly after he departed."

Now, it should be said that I do my best to maintain a mask of seriousness in times like this. But the sudden force of my next thought and the blunt truth of it knocks words and giggles out of my throat before I can stop them.

"Because Thatch was basically your grandfather."

By the time my hands fly up to my mouth, all three of my companions have broken into fits of laughter.

What else can you do?

A short time later, I search for something with caffeine. When I'm a few steps away from the booth, I slip my phone out of my pocket. After joining the end of a long line, I check it. Leroy texted me. He was fired only a couple of days after I was, and all he did was refuse to sign the petition. Rumor has it there's six more faculty on Carina's shit list, and I'm kind of disappointed there's not more.

Leroy (10:37 AM): did you make it out of bed today?
Me (11:10 AM): dressed, over caffeinated, and in public as we speak. You?

Elochian sent a message as well, only four words.

Lochian (9:58 AM): can boredom kill you?
Me (11:11 AM): it's the leading cause of death among my college students

I chuckle, stuffing my phone away after I send the message. The laughter fades as I think about Thursday. I'm nothing more than a night professor, teaching those who are failing their regular classes, or close to it. Sure, by the time I'm done with them they actually understand—better yet, *want* to understand—the metaphysics of our world.

I clench my fists at the realization that really, Eduardo *can't* do anything to me. My seat on the board is an inherited thing, and not even the president of the university would dare piss off the woman who once sat in it. This thin immunity does not bring me the relief it should. I'd rather have a shield of my own making. He is the only person in Levena who knows my true identity, besides River.

When I step up to the counter, I'm surprised to find Idina at my side. I hurriedly look between her, and the opposite side of the cafe where our nook hides.

The elder dragon smiles at me. "Don't worry, I was only standing with you the whole time."

"Um." I shake my head, then gesture for her to order first, unable to come up with any words. She orders two hot black teas and a box of assorted pastries, while I order coffee for Arlo and a spiced latte myself. Idina pays for everything, glaring at me when I try. I dumbly follow her over to the pick-up line. If you had told me this morning that I'd be having coffee with dragons, the key here being more than one, I would've thought you were mad.

She peeks into Arlo's witch case and nonchalantly says, "You know, if anyone can figure out this business, it's you."

"Me? What do you mean?"

She hums, watching the baristas work. "You're clever, I can see it. And brave enough to break walls."

I rub the back of my neck. "Yeah, well. I was fired for doing just that."

"Perhaps it was to pave the way for something else. You teach at the university, do you not? Speak the truth there."

"Ma'am, I know you're a very ol—*wise* being, but the all-knowing thing is a bit creepy if you ask me."

Idina laughs, and we move ahead in line. "Dusannara is proud of her life, and the people in it. You understand that you are part of her clutch, yes? The same as Arlo and the others."

I clear my throat. "I ... I did not know that. I'm not like Arlo and Kit, and Cas. She raised them. Don't get me wrong, Dusan has always been kind to me, but I'm not ... it's not the same."

Idina shrugs. "Agree to disagree, my dear."

"Can I ask you something?"

"Hmm?"

"Why don't you live here?"

"Ah."

Our order is called and Idina is slow as she takes the box, leaving the drink carrier for me. We begin to wander back to our people, but Idina pauses about halfway there, occupying a somewhat secluded area near the hearth. "You see, when the celestials moved in, Adriel and I thought it best if we ... moved on. Dusannara was adamantly set against it, and accused us both of cowardice. Which in hindsight, I think may be true. How differently things would have been if we stayed. Picked a side."

"A ... side? I'm not following. Why would you leave because of angels and demons?"

Idina levels me a heavy look. "Do not let today's modernity and false pretense of civility fool you. Celestials are monsters, through and through. There are not many things that dragons are afraid of, but hell hath no fury like an archcelestial scorned."

I sputter, anger and confusion rising. "B–but you're a dragon. Everything is afraid of you." I clamp my mouth shut, but the damage is done. Idina sighs, dropping her gaze to the box in her hands. "I'm sorry, that was—I shouldn't have said that."

"Do you want to know how the fire started?" She asks quietly.

I blink, not at all expecting that. The macabre side of me overtakes the polite side, and I say, "Yes."

Without looking up from the box, Idina says, "There were no witches back then. There were only the Descendants of Dinphine, which is what my father was. Those given magick were given a singular purpose, to serve the Goddess that gave it to them. But my father left the temple, left his Goddess, and chose his own father. He made his own path, he was happy. But the temple would not have it, and they came for him.

"They came for Henix in the dead of night, and when they tried to take him, my grandfather pleaded. He begged. They shot him with what would've been a fatal orb of magick, had he been human. It forced the change, and triggered his primal instincts to protect what was his. He saved Henix, yes. But his life, and the village ... Thatcher, it was all collateral damage."

Idina lifts her eyes to mine, and a chill runs down my spine. "Boy. Listen to me when I tell you, when a beast like *that* is afraid of something, you damn better run away. It's only a matter of time before monsters snap, and it's always worse when they're trying their damndest not to."

I straighten my shoulders, not daring to disengage from our battle of the wills. Quietly, I say, "I'm sorry that happened to your family, but I think you're wrong. The angels and demons of Levena are no monsters."

Idina's lips quirk. "For your sake, I hope I am."

Measure Up

Elochian

On Wednesday morning I sit across from Doc, engaged in a battle of the minds. There's no snow today, and the sun illuminates their jewel toned office through partially curtained windows. They work from home, and the comfort of the place is unparalleled. Doc is dressed better than I am, wearing a fine plaid skirt and an emerald blouse. A small tussle of damp peppered curls rests between their perked ears, and their nails are painted dark green. They play queen's pawn, and I counter.

"I don't think my meds are working."

Without looking up from the pieces, Doc says, "Oh? Your levels are good, and to be frank you haven't had an attack in several months."

I swallow, throat clicking. "No, it's not that."

Doc finally moves their bishop. "Given that's the—"

"I can get hard again. Sometimes." I blurt out, fixing my gaze on the pieces, cheeks burning. Doc remains silent while I make my next move. "I thought I'd see if I could ... you know. But it was a disaster."

Doc leans back, considering me. "I imagine it was quite confusing. If I may ask, was it a physical, or mental block?"

"Mental," I say, glancing up at them.

Doc watches me, calm and easy. "It could be that your body has adjusted to the dose, given you haven't increased in awhile. These things are known to happen. Is there anyone you're fancying? Or was it a ... surprise, of sorts? I was under the impression you didn't experience attraction."

I'm quiet for four more turns, and Doc allows me to be. Eventually, I whisper, "I'm becoming attracted to Quentin, I think. It's not all the time, but sometimes I look at him, or think about him, and it's like ... I don't know. But when I tried to—you know—I thought of Bartholomew. Or started to, then the guilt, Doc. It was everywhere, suffocating me. He's been on my mind constantly lately, and I miss him."

"Quentin, or Bartholomew?"

"*Both*. I miss Bartholomew, and I feel like I'm betraying him. I've been waking to the feeling of blood on my hands again. I'm scared all the time, and this stuff with the NOJ is making it worse. And ... I find comfort in Quentin, I do. I feel protective of him, and I—I kissed him on the cheek, which started this whole mess. And even if it wasn't for my personal baggage, I'm an archdemon. My life is one constant hell, I'm always busy. Absent. I have nothing to offer but my wealth, and Quentin doesn't care about that."

"I think Bartholomew would be disappointed in you." Doc speaks aloud my greatest worry, and I rear back as if their words have fangs and claws. "He gave his life for you, which is as I understand it, the greatest honor for a *shomer*. He did not do so lightly, and he did not do it so you would live alone and unhappy."

Doc moves their queen. "I think the real question is, how long will you punish yourself for someone else's sins?"

"I'm not—"

"And by extension, you're punishing Quentin. Whether you want him to or not, he cares about you, so don't use him as an excuse. He is an adult who makes his own choices, as are you."

I take their queen. "And what if he leaves me? Or dies?"

"You'll live on, just as you always have."

The thought of a world without Quentin cripples me, and we spend the rest of the appointment in silence. Doc is good like that.

Until the end, when they say, "You know, Elochian. There's no harm in caring for yourself. No harm in where your thoughts wander, they are yours alone. I think it'd be good for you to practice, per say, and relearn your body."

I groan. "Are you telling me to go fuck myself?"

Doc sighs, pinching the bridge of their snout. "Gods, sometimes you're worse than Arlo."

I'm not in the mood for painting today, so Arlo and I lay on the floor of our usual studio and stare up at the ceiling. The easels haven't been moved from the edge of the room since the last time I felt like painting, which was before Thatch left, and the stacks of canvases beside them remain untouched.

Arlo doesn't mind, and I think he needs this quiet as much as I do, sometimes.

I'm the first to break the silence that fell after our initial greetings.

"How's things?"

Arlo turns his head, staring at me oddly. "How's *things*? Are you … small talking me right now, Loch?"

I roll my eyes. "I hear it's what normal people do."

Arlo chuckles, turning his attention back to the ceiling. "Fine, I guess. Can't sleep, but that's my own fault."

"Reading?"

"Yeah. The journals are … they make me feel small. Like a blip in Thatch's life. I already knew that, but … they really loved each other. Henix and Thatch, I mean. Levena was so different. *He* was so different. Less afraid." Arlo sighs. "How could I ever measure up to a love like that? You saw the letters."

I nod, although Arlo's not looking at me. Late Sunday night he sent all of us pictures of the more important, and less personal, letters, but even those were tinged with such fondness for not only the land, but the people in it. They left each other love notes using codes, desecrating religious texts to do so. Even through pictures sent in a group text, I could almost see Levena as it was, and see Thatch as a young man with his first love.

Carefully, I say, "Quentin said something to me the other day that I keep thinking about. Sometimes, people are like stepping stones. Sometimes, things don't work out, but that doesn't mean the love you shared with a person is any less for it. They were just … a part of the journey that takes you to the person that *is* the end all be all. You weren't the stepping stone, Arlo. You're his soulmate."

Arlo is quiet for a long time, and when he sniffles I rest my hand beside his. "You're not a stepping stone, either. Not to him."

I inhale sharply, his words are like a kick to the ribs. I ignore his sentiment, switching the topic to something even *more* uncomfortable. "Can I ask you something?"

"Hm?"

"Do you ... your medicine. Are there any side effects for you?"

Arlo turns his head towards me, but I keep my gaze pinned on the ceiling. "Why?"

"I'm having trouble. I talked to Doc about it, and they say it's normal for people to ... *adjust*, after being on their meds for awhile. I know we take different things, but I know a lot of things like that affect—uh. Ability." I scratch at my temple. "To perform, specifically."

"Oh." Arlo hums. "I had that in the beginning, yeah. But honestly sex was the last thing on my mind, especially with myself." He holds up a hand, wiggling his fingers. I smirk as it falls back down beside mine. "Or anyone else. But that kind of went away. It takes me a little longer to finish now, I think. But it didn't, uh—" He clears his throat. "It didn't get in the way."

I finally glance over at him, smiling a little. "Thank you for telling me. It helps, I think."

"Do you ... I mean, are you ..." Arlo trails off.

I roll my eyes, then tell him the same thing I told Doc, more or less. In a whisper, I add one crucial detail. "I'm thinking about courting him, Arlo."

"You mean you're not already doing that?"

"No." I glare at him, and he chuckles.

"You know, I don't think it will be a deal breaker for him if you guys don't have sex, Loch. You sound like you're having a panic attack just thinking about it. Just be honest with him. You being able to ... *perform* as you say, doesn't automatically mean you *have* to do it, you know?"

My heart catches at the memory of him swaying in my arms, our bodies pressed together, and I sigh. "But what if *it* is a deal breaker? Quentin is a ... he's a very sensual being."

"Let me ask you another question. Are you sexually attracted to Quentin?"

I sit up abruptly, curling in on the soft flare of heat in my stomach. My wings flutter annoyingly, filling the room with their incessant chatter. "I might be. I don't know."

Arlo sits up too, but much slower. He says, "There are still things that you can do that doesn't involve ..." He scrubs a hand down his face. "I can't believe I'm giving you the sex talk right now."

I bark out a laugh, which draws one from him too. "I don't *need* the sex talk. But I'm open to ... different perspectives."

"Alright, alright. I need a brush in hand for this." Arlo pushes off the floor with a groan, then pulls an easel into the center of the room. My fingers twitch, and I stand too. Wordlessly, I drag over my own easel and fetch a canvas. Arlo puts on his usual playlist, then casts the room in a familiar illusion.

The shoreline on Leideen Ait, specifically, the view from Thatch's beach.

Later, after we've thoroughly embarrassed ourselves, Arlo says, "By the way, I've gotta postpone Misfits Night this week." He exhales a long, dramatic sigh. "The boys and I are officially moving out of Thitwhistle's."

I deflate. "Oh? Why?"

He shrugs. "It's time."

I don't know what makes me push it, but I ask, "But why now?"

Arlo tilts his head, staring at me for a moment before answering. "I ... I feel him the most there, at the cottage, and it hurt too much to be there without him. I think I'm ready now, though. It feels wrong to not take what he's given me."

"He's given you a lot of assets, to say the least."

"I'm not talking about the money. I feel like he's given me my life—no. He's given me my heart back. You know? And I'm just—" He waves a hand in the air. "Moping. The boys deserve better."

I delicately swipe my watery crimson stained brush over my canvas, then stand back and reevaluate. Not bright enough. "No one blames you for it."

"I know."

We paint in relative silence after that, and I fail to bury my disappointment over Friday being canceled. Not only because I won't be seeing Quentin, but I've grown fond of the others as well. Kitt doesn't work at the bar anymore, but she was a great help while she was there, and I enjoyed seeing her. I was planning on talking to Arlo then about my next problem, but if I won't be seeing him ....

"Hey, Arlo."

"Yeah?"

"Have you talked to Gaia lately?"

"No ..." The trepidation in his voice has me dancing around the subject, but I still have some bravery left over.

"Do you think that you could arrange a meeting with her? For me? I have some questions, and she's the only necromancer in Levena."

Arlo peers around his canvas to stare at me. I stare back. He asks, "Questions about what?"

"There's someone in my clan who says they can bypass the *golem* state using solar batteries, even if the bodies have long been dead."

He snorts, but doesn't turn back to his painting. "That's not possible."

"It is. I saw the proof with my own eyes," I say, because I believe it. Tina felt *wrong*. Her heart beats, yes, but her aura was off. Oppressive. I play my last card, one I've only recently discovered was in my deck.

"I've learned that this person is the founder of the NOJ, but the name he uses there is different from what most people know him as. He demanded that I cut ties with you, and according to my sources, he's using the celestial sickness as reason to push Arches out of Levena. There's a major power play coming, and I can't help but feel this experiment of his is only a small part of it. I need to get ahead of it, and I can't do it alone. I know things are sore between you two, but please. I'm asking as a friend."

Arlo groans. "Fine. No guarantees, though. Now, tell me more about this dickhead."

I set my brush down. "There's not much to say. He's come into a substantial amount of wealth and resources, and he has a grudge against me. To be fair, I think it would be anyone in my position, but still. He's a shapeshifter, and I meant that literally and otherwise. He knows how to make anyone like him."

"Damn."

"Damn indeed."

Arlo hesitantly asks, "You remember that reporter who came to see me?"

"Yes."

Arlo tugs on the gauge in his ear as he comes around his painting. "Cas thinks we should talk to him, and as much as I hate to say it, I think he's right."

I meet him in the space between canvases. "And what makes you think you can trust him? I thought he was hell spawn or something like that."

Arlo laughs. "I did not call him hell spawn."

"You certainly implied it."

"Yeah, well. That was until I talked to his mother, and I can trust her, as much as I hate to admit it."

"You ... talked to his mother? What'd you do, tattle on him like a child? Who is she?"

"No!" Arlo lowers his voice, even though we're alone. "His mother is the Nightingale."

"As in ... the *mob* boss?"

Arlo waves a hand. "You know, some people call you a mob boss too."

I scoff. "There is a big difference between my estate and her ... *operation*."

"Either way, she vouched for Finnegan. Said, and I quote, *'the only reason he's got a damn newspaper is because I paid for it, and do you think I'd waste my money on something futile?'*"

I wince. "And I thought she was crotchety a decade ago."

"Me too."

"So she wasn't pissed that the first time you've reached out since the Taking was for advice?"

Arlo glares at me. "You are *on* my case today, aren't you?"

"Next week I'll be quieter than a mouse. Enjoy it while it lasts."

He shakes his head and sighs. "I didn't reach out to her, she used Finnegan as a means to set up a meeting with me. She's concerned about the witches in Levena, she says they need someone to look up to, someone to guide them. She doesn't really care about the article, but she agrees with her son. She thinks it'll help. What ... what do you think? Should I do it?"

"I do," I say immediately, surprising him and myself. Quietly, I add, "I saw Thatch too, Arlo. He was a tangled thread in my life that I could never figure out, and that hasn't stopped just because I know the *name* of the thread now. I think we owe it to people like me. Like us. Like him. It's not just his history, but ours too."

Arlo sniffs, turning his gaze away. "Thank you, for being honest."

"I'll remind you that you said that. And don't mention me in the interview, please. I'd rather keep Tish off my case, thank you very much."

He gives me a small smile before we disperse, cleaning up our mess. We take turns rinsing our brushes in the sink, leaving our canvases on the easels to dry until next time.

When we gather up our coats, Arlo says, "It freaked me out, seeing her again, but it was also ... it felt right. Talking to her felt like talking to Quentin. He thinks I need to unite the witches."

I hum. "He's got a point."

Arlo shoves at my shoulder. "Yeah, well. If the mob boss is the nicest of the group, we've got our work cut out for us."

"We?"

"*Yeah*, we. There's no way I'm doing this alone, and since you're peer pressuring me, that's like signing up for the job. Same for Q."

I bump his shoulder with my own. "Okay. I can do that."

Transcript

TRUTH AND TRAGEDY

Transcript Excerpt from Interview #578

1/7/9621

Wroughtfern: And why do you think these personal journals have suddenly appeared?

Rook: Personally, I think it's a matter of

time. Thatcher's story takes place over millennia, and it won't be fully realized in a day, a week, or even a month. I think we will be discovering these bits of his life for a long time, and perhaps the universe is parsing out these clues until we're ready for them.

Wroughtfern: And what about you two? Will you parse out your findings, or share them with the community?

Daemarrel: Everything we've discovered thus far has been donated to the Gaillot Museum, including the journals. They include Levena's history after all, and its origins as a place formerly known as Min Isle.

Wroughtfern: Of course. I did visit the new exhibit during the Yuletide social, and it was impressive then. I can only imagine what it looks like now. Kitt Meissa is the Director there, she's on your team, correct?

Daemarrel: Yes, she is dedicated to providing the community with the correct facts regarding their history, and of the man who affected so many lives in Levena. It's important to know where we came from, and the mistakes we made.

Wroughtfern: Mistakes?

...

Rook: He's referencing the Fire of Min Isle, which occurred due to an attempted abduction by the Descendants of Dinphine. They sought to restrain and control magick, and those given it. People who were able to manipulate *abracadabri* back then were not known as witches, simply Descendants. It was a different time, and their attitudes regarding magick had a lifelong impact.

Wroughtfern: And yet, here we are with another group, two in fact, seeking to restrain the rights of those different from the everyday person.

Rook: And yet, here we are again.

More The Merrier

Quentin
Two Weeks After The Article

I'm being watched.

When you're lecturing fifty people, that's to be expected. But there's a certain stare that's heavier than all the rest. Hair raising and unnerving. I can't pinpoint where it's coming from, who the intruder is. The feeling intensifies every time I turn back to my chalkboard, and I've never felt more on display than I do right now. Stripped bare and inspected.

Chalk dusts my thighs where I constantly wipe them. Sweat dampens the back of my shirt. The thick burgundy fabric is rolled up to my elbows, and I had to undo one of the top buttons. When I finish writing the tail end of a paragraph, I turn back to the auditorium full of bleary eyed students. I sweep my gaze over them as I speak, searching for the culprit.

"Minerva specifically addresses the differences between soul and spirit, while Dushinger focuses on the quantitative *abra-*

cadabri pull a soul has, dependent on their physical state. While we should take care to look at these with a modern perspective, there is—"

Words catch in my throat as my eyes fall on a person in the back row, swaddled in a parka and darkness. My heart jolts in my chest, and I start again.

"There is solid weight in both their works, and they are crucial to understanding Spiritual Metaphysics. But even I can admit that the topic is dense, to say the least. So we'll take our time with it. Are there any questions?"

A student in the front raises a hand, and I nod. "Isn't Dushinger's work moot now? I thought it was determined that he was wrong."

I shrug. "Depends on how you look at it. He thought spirits had a stronger pull on the universe than souls because a corporeal body demands it. But we now know that it's because souls actually form a feedback loop with the physical world. Yes, they take more from the universe, but they give back exponentially as a spirit. As a soul, they only take enough *abracadabri* to exist.

"But anyways, the point is, he wasn't completely wrong. Spirits do have a stronger pull than souls, but not for the reason he thought. Science is constantly disproving or expanding on common held truths, which is why it's important to keep an open mind. To the past, and to the present."

My watch buzzes and I briefly check it, then turn my attention back to the class. "Alright, that's enough for tonight. Remember, you've got *two* whole weeks for the Minerva vs. Dushinger paper, don't wait until the last minute. Also, I've extended my office hours, and they're posted on my door. If you need help, *ask*."

Fifty people slip into motion at once, and I lose precious seconds answering brief questions. After, I march up the steps and meet an archdemon on the uppermost row of the auditorium. I chuckle under my breath, shaking my head as I come face to face with him. A knee length, black parka surrounds his figure, wings and all. All of his hair is swept back, restrained by a black beanie. He even painted over the gold in his cheekbones.

But his eyes are what get me. He could set the world on fire with just one look.

"I swear to Mithys, if you laugh."

I chew on my bottom lip. "I'm not, I swear. How long have you been brooding up here? And what's with the parachute?"

"You know, I was going to pay you a compliment, but I'm taking it back."

I chuckle. "Okay, seriously. Why didn't you tell me you were coming?"

He glances at the podium. Most of the room has cleared out, but a few people glance our way as they pack up. A human woman occupies the desk Elochian once did, tapping her pencil on its surface and oblivious to the end of class, lost to the music blaring from her earbuds.

Elochian turns his attention back to me, and that rare predatory glint is back. "I wanted to surprise you. Besides, I didn't want you putting on airs just for me." He smiles. "You can tell that you really love this stuff. Soul particles."

"I do." I look away, rubbing at my collarbone. "Um, I was actually planning on meeting someone after this."

"Who?" Elochian asks, and the word is like a magnet. I meet his gaze, having to fight laughter at the sight of him scowling again in that damn parka. I don't fight the urge to tease him, though.

"I'd invite you along, but I'm not sure if you can walk in that thing."

"I can walk just fine."

"Okay, okay. I'm going to see Archeon Mochizuki. That astrophysicist I told you about?"

"The Teleth."

"Yeah. Did Arlo tell you about Felix?"

Elochian deflates a little. "He did. Does he know you're doing this?"

"Not *today*, specifically ... do you want to come with me?"

He sighs. "Well, I was hoping to see your office, but another time, maybe. Let's go antagonize a witch. That's always fun."

I blink. See my office? Does he actually mean see my office, or *see* my office? No, he can't be suggesting that. I don't see a tip of fang anywhere, and I'm starting to wonder if I imagined that whole deal. But there was a pinprick of blood on his lip, before. I wouldn't have imagined that, I'm not that weird.

"Um ... right. Yes. Let's do that," I say.

The woman practically twirls out of her chair as she stands. A cacophony of patchwork colors make up her outfit, which extends to her wrists and beneath calf-length boots. She sidles up to Elochian and says, "You would never know that the same person who wrote *Adventures of a Spice Trader* can preach physics like it's poetry. We need to stalk you more often, Quen."

Oh. I cover my mouth in attempts to stifle my laughter. Elochian lightly backhands Michael in the stomach, cheeks flushed and eyes narrowed. "*Michael.*"

"Right. Not stalking. Admiring from afar without first notifying said person of interest." Michael tosses long, rust red curls over their shoulder, giving me a wink.

I shrug. "You're always welcome to not stalk me."

Elochian groans. "Again, I ask. Why must you two get on so well?"

Elochian figures it out about five minutes into our walk. Everything is a journey on Scarlet University grounds. Thankfully, a glass corridor connects the steel physics building to the stone astronomy tower. This little hall always makes me stop and take a moment to observe the physical metaphor of old science versus new. A neutral bridge between two different worlds.

At least, that's what I tell myself.

"He doesn't know we're coming, does he?" Elochian asks dryly, perched on a generous window ledge. Michael stands beside him, amused by my pacing.

"Not *exactly*. But, I have it on good authority that he is up there today. And, I have a secret weapon."

Elochian raises a brow. "A secret weapon?"

"Yes, I—"

An angel opens the glass door that leads to the base of the astronomy tower, wasting no time upon seeing me. The *malakim* gathers me into a fierce hug, taking my feet off the ground. His endless snow white hair falls over my back, and his thick arms wrap around my shoulders. "Quentin! You came."

We separate, and I grin at Dante. "It's good to see you too." I gesture towards Michael and Elochian, which makes my mind blank for a moment. Elochian's parka is now draped over Michael's arm, and all six of his wings are spread wide like a damn peacock. "Uh ... Dante, these are my friends, Elochian and Michael."

Dante bows at the waist to Elochian, and when he stands he marks an '*A*' over his heart. I tilt my head at that, but say nothing as he shakes Elochian's hand, then Michael's. Dante says, "The more the merrier. Come, let's go bother Arche."

Dante leads the way through glass doors and up spiraling steps, the stone worn smooth by centuries of trespassers. I walk with Dante, catching up on the latest news. He's one of those people who is nice to everybody, all the time. Constantly smiling and laughing, a total extrovert. Nobody understands why he is Archeon's best (and perhaps only) friend, but Dante makes it a point to let everyone know that yes, he is the witch's *best* friend.

When I first started here, Dante was the one who gave me a tour, helped me settle in. I had thought he was interested in me, given his tendency to make you feel like the center of the world every time he speaks to you, but that's just Dante. In the short time I've known him, he's never been with anyone, and that's the way he likes it.

At one point I look back and find Michael with a shit-eating grin, while Elochian looks fit to murder somebody. "You alright?" I ask in a whisper.

"Fine."

Michael pats him on the shoulder. "He's fine."

"O—kay."

As we near the uppermost level, classical music makes itself known, intensifying with every wrap around the tower. Dante winks at me. "That's a good sign."

"Blowing out his eardrums is a *good* thing?"

"Oh yes. Now remember what I told you."

I nod hesitantly. "You really think I have a shot?"

Dante rests a large hand on my head, ruffling my hair. "If anyone does, it's you."

"Okay." I straighten and his hand falls to my cheek, gently patting once before withdrawing completely. I look back to Michael and Elochian. "Ready?"

"Yup," Michael says, a hand on the back of Elochian's collar. Elochian avoids my eyes.

I put my confusion on the back burner for now, then wade into the belly of the beast.

To say the astronomy lab is breathtaking would be an understatement. The stones here are painted twilight blue, and detailed with various different constellations. The distant ceiling is a near invisible glass shield which keeps out the elements and provides the telescope with an unobstructed view of the night sky, which is brilliant on this cold snap of an evening. The telescope dominating the center of the lab is the size of a small house, loosely surrounded by multiple levels of metal scaffolding so the scope can rotate and change position.

On the northern side of the room is a series of control panels interrupted by two enormous work desks, and a wall of monitors and screens. Archeon sits there with his back to us, and smoke silhouettes his figure. He calls, "There is no possible way you went to the cafeteria and back already."

Dante winks at me again, then steps away from the stone landing and onto black and white tiles. He says, "You're right. I decided I needed to stop enabling you, or you'll never learn to bring your own dinner. Or lunch. Or anything that resembles food."

Archeon exhales a stream of smoke, stubbing out his cigarette. He spins around in his chair with a retort on his open lips, but abruptly stands when he realizes he's got company. He glowers at Dante with crimson eyes, hardly paying the rest of us any real attention. "*Dante.*"

"*Arche.*"

I step past Dante and press a hand to my chest. "My apologies, Professor Mochizuki. I was under the impression you knew I was coming. I'm—"

"Quentin Matsdotter. I know who you are, and I'm not interested in whatever it is you're selling." Archeon cuts a gloved hand through the air, drawing attention to his pale fingertips, the nails painted black. The black leather of his fingerless gloves matches the x-shaped harness across his chest.

Beneath the harness is a long sleeve, the thick white fabric rolled up to his elbows and partially undone to reveal the hollow of his throat. His pants are tighter than hell, and his well polished wingtip shoes look like they cost more than my apartment. His blue-black hair is as finished as the rest of him, shaved on the sides and only long enough on the top to do a fancy little combover thing.

"Oh, I'm not selling anything. I just need a consultation."

"A consultation," Archeon repeats flatly. "At eight o'clock on a Thursday night."

"Well, to be fair, it'd be more appropriate timing if you accepted visitors during office hours. I *suppose* I could ask Dishaw instead, but—"

Archeon's gaze sharpens. "He's a fucking crackpot." He lights up another cigarette, harsh attention sliding to Elochian standing beside me. "And with such a noble audience, to boot."

I lift my chin, adjusting my glasses. "These are my friends, Elochian and Michael, and I'd appreciate it if you treated them as such."

Elochian inclines his head, and Michael waves from behind him.

Archeon smirks, exposing the hint of a vampiric fang. "Very well. Come in, then. If nothing else, this will be interesting."

Michael moves away from Elochian's inner bubble, chatting up Dante like they're old friends. Before I can move, Elochian takes my elbow. He whispers, "Do you want me to talk to him with you, or would you rather speak in private?"

"Oh." I shake my head. "I guess I just figured you'd be with me. Unless that's too much—"

"No, it's not," he says immediately, wings tense.

"Are you okay, Elochian? Have I done something to upset you?"

His grip on my elbow softens. "No, you haven't." His gaze flickers to Dante, then back to me. It finally clicks then, and I smile. I don't call him out on it, but I happily carry the knowledge that Elochian is jealous. Over me.

"Alright. Let's do this."

Archeon is sprawled out in the seat he was in before, cigarette dangling between his lips. He gestures to two rolling chairs a little ways down the stretch of control panels from him. Michael and Dante have busied themselves with deep conversation, so I take a seat and give Archeon my full attention.

Archeon looks me up and down, sizing me up. He takes a long drag off his cigarette, then blows the smoke into the air above us instead of into my face. I appreciate the gesture, and I hate that I still love the smell of those damn things.

"What do you want?" He asks, his tone different from before, like he's truly listening.

"Honestly? Your help."

"And what could somebody like you want from someone like me?"

I avoid the dig. "I'm not the person who needs help. My friend is. He has a son, and I believe ..." I glance at Elochian before I reveal my theory. Archeon leans forward in his seat, oblivious to a line of ash falling from his cigarette.

Quietly, I say, "I think he's an *abracadabri* reservoir. He's come into his power early, and it's too much, too fast. It's only been two months, and he already possesses multiple abilities, including Teleth skills. My friend is finding it hard to give him the proper mentorship he needs, and I thought maybe you could help him learn how to control it."

"Ah. A witch consultation." Archeon inhales deeply. He pointedly looks down at himself, then at me. "You want me, the university shut in." He lifts his cigarette burned down to the filter. "The chain smoking lunatic, to teach a kid."

Elochian scoffs. "And I'm certified. Your point?"

The corner of Archeon's thin lips lifts, and he pauses for a moment before saying, "My point is, I don't like kids. Kids don't like me. Find your help elsewhere."

"Felix isn't a kid," I say, and both men stare at me. "What I *mean* to say is, Felix may look like a kid, but he isn't one. I suspect he hasn't been one in a long time, not really. He's kind of like you and me."

"You don't know anything about me."

"I know that everyone thinks you're something that you're not. Not really. You've seen some shit, and your way of dealing with it is different from most people's. But it's not bad, and it doesn't hurt anyone. Except maybe yourself, but … I wouldn't have come if I didn't think it was important. He nearly set the place on fire the other day."

Archeon frowns. "I thought you said he has telepathic abilities."

"He does, but appliances tend to suffer greatly around him. Ovens included."

"And what is the basis for your reservoir theory?"

"Besides an educated guess based on a textbook example, I've observed his aura. He possesses a wealth of pure *abracdabri* force, and I'm afraid he'll … I'm afraid he'll be targeted if he can't hide it better. I don't want him to go through what you and the other witches did."

Archeon flinches, turning away. He stares into the beyond, and contemplates. Elochian and I exchange a look, and his gaze is heavier than before. He's heard my transgressions, what does he think of me now? Until this moment, I thought I was doing Arlo a kindness. Why bother him with my theories until I had more solid proof?

But I should've told him. He should be here now.

Archeon stands, butting his long ago burnt out cigarette in an ashtray. "And if I say yes? What are you offering me?"

I follow his lead, straightening my jacket as I stand. "Tenure."

Archeon's eyes widen a fraction, flaring bright red, but his face remains placid. "Fuck off. That's not a real offer. Diaz regrets the day I signed my employment contract, he'll never give it to me. I've been rejected twice, as *you* well know."

I stare at him, ignoring his dramatics. No one likes the fact a supposed nobody has a seat on the Board of Directors to the most prestigious university in the north. Eduardo is the only reason why Archeon hasn't lost his job entirely. The astrophysicist is obsessed with the moons, which are derivative and a drain on funds, according to most of the board, and not what Archeon promised he would focus his research on.

He is the world's leading expert on multi-dimensional theory, uncharted and exciting waters that Archeon abandoned for reasons he won't name. He refuses to teach face to face, and he drives off every intern that *does* sign up to work with him. Eduardo thinks his phase with the moons will pass, and is happy to wait it out. The general consensus is Eduardo is as mad as Archeon is, but of course no one says it to *his* face.

"I will give you a personal letter of recommendation, and a guarantee that the board will vote in your favor, if you hold up your end of the deal. Train Felix. Help him. Mentor him." And because I feel like the moment calls for it, I reach into my pocket and take out a packet of gum. I offer it to him and say, "And trade this in for cigarettes while you're with him."

Archeon scowls at me, but takes the pack of gum. He says, "I'm not agreeing to anything."

"But you'll meet him?"

Archeon sighs, lighting the pack of gum on fire before dropping it to the ground. "I'll meet him."

Elochian insists on giving me a ride home.

Even as I'm sliding into his backseat, he says, "Three degrees, Quentin. Three. And it's pitch black out!" He shakes his head and goes on, dropping his lecture to a mutter as he buckles up beside me. "Honestly, walking home in the dead of night."

"It's nine o'clock, sunshine. Not exactly the dead of night." I chuckle, resting my elbow against the cold, thick glass of the window. Only a seat separates Elochian from me, and his upper left wing brushes against my neck as he settles. It takes everything in me not to gasp at the soft caress.

Michael shifts the towncar into gear, now in their *shedim* form and quiet. Elochian, however, is all restless energy. "I am anything *but* fucking sunshine. And it's dark enough to be dangerous."

I laugh, and my head bumps against the headrest. "Oh, no. It's official. You're my sunshine." I swallow my fear and soldier on through the thick air between us, grateful for the cool glass against my skin. Without looking at him straight on, I say, "I mean, that's what friends do, isn't it? Give each other nicknames they hate?"

Elochian hums, fingers tapping his knee. "Dot."

"Dot?" I ask, scandalized. "Do explain!"

His wing flutters against my neck as he shrugs. "Everyone else calls you Quen, or Q. It's my nickname for you." Elochian pauses, and his fingers slowly inch towards mine. "Only mine," he whispers.

"I like that," I say quietly, reaching towards him in that same unsure manner.

Unsure what is happening, how much of this push and pull is real or imagined between us. His fingers curl around mine, firm and unrelenting. I release a long, slow breath through my nose, and my mind clears.

"Quentin, how were you able to make that promise to Archeon?" Elochian asks, and I find myself unable to lie to him.

"Oh, um ... Eduardo—Mr. Diaz—he's a good friend of the family, and he owes me a favor. It's not really a big deal."

"I see," Elochian says, and I can tell he wants to ask more about it, but he doesn't. He adds, "Well, I'm glad that he agreed."

"Me too."

We spend the rest of the ride like that, quiet and bridged by only our fingertips, afraid to forge a connection any stronger than that. But why?

Why am I holding back?

The first thought is immediate, like a slap to the face. River.

He's still after me, evident by the gift I found today in my office. The strip of candid photo booth pictures burns a hole in my inner jacket pocket, threatening to alight my heart, and Elochian in the process. Even if the threat of my ex didn't hang like a noose, I can't help but feel like this thing between us is just as I said. Imagined. One sided, and Elochian is too nice to turn me down outright.

When we near the end of Syorini Road, where the vehicular streets give way to pedestrian ones. My hand retreats from Elochian's, or rather, attempts to, but the archdemon holds firm. "Elochian, I—"

"We have never been friends, Quentin."

"What?" I ask, completely thrown.

With his free hand he unbuckles, then shifts closer to me. He takes both my hands in his, and I'm paralyzed with trepidation and hope, helpless to do anything as his trembling upper wings form a partial shield around us.

Elochian whispers, "You have always been more than that to me. When I first laid eyes on you, I knew I had to find a way into your orbit. If I could just breathe the same air as you, spend every free moment that I had with you, then the ache in my chest might lessen. When I'm not with you, I miss you. When we're together, I want all your attention. And while I may not be very good at this, I do think you feel the same way."

"I do. More than anything." I rasp. "But I thought … I don't know, I thought you weren't ready. That you didn't want … more. With me."

Elochian looks down to our joined hands and his lower wings shake, sounding like dead leaves in the wind. "I have only been selfish once in my life. Only once did I lay claim to something, *someone,* as mine, and mine alone. It brought about the happiest time of my life, and I have suffered for it ever since. I've been afraid, so afraid, that the past will repeat itself. But I've come to the realization; that's okay."

"What is?" I ask, cautious.

"To be afraid. I'd rather be terrified and able to call you mine, then be terrified and alone. And if you'll have me as I am, cowardice and all, then I'd very much like to court you, Quentin Matsdotter. It will be slow, and awkward, and I'll make you regret every moment of it."

I laugh, and it's only then that I realize tears have welled up in my throat. I scrub at my eyes with the back of my free hand. "I would have it no other way."

The car comes to a stop and he takes my hand, cool lips brushing against my knuckles when he kisses away the remnants of my tears. Against wet skin, he whispers, "Be patient with me."

I wrap my arms around his neck, perfectly aligning our bodies despite his ridiculous parka and my own heavy overcoat. I rest my head on his shoulder, and Elochian's hands hover at my sides for only a second before he hugs me back.

I murmur, "You may have all of my time, and all of my heart." His wings stop trembling, and pride takes root in my chest. We part, and through a smile I say, "Goodnight, sunshine."

He smiles back. "Goodnight, Dot."

When I grab the door handle, I say, "Goodnight to you too, Michael."

Elochian jumps at his bodyguard's name, like he'd forgotten we had company that entire time. Michael winks at me in the rearview mirror. Between one blink and the next, there's a flash of difference in their features, a new form I haven't seen yet. But then it's gone, and he says, "Goodnight, Quentin. Safe travels."

I step out of the car and watch it pull away, feeling bereft already.

I walk the short few minutes home, wondering how long it will take for my good fortune to turn around and bite me in the ass. I try not to dwell on it. Elochian wants me to be *his*. I have been waiting for this moment for so long, and now that it's here, I'm supposed to just ... go home?

I check my phone real quick, ignoring the group messages in favor of rushing a message to Lindsey.

Me (9:18 PM): I think Elochian and I are boyfriends now.

After I put my phone away and continue walking, I wonder about that word. Boyfriends. Do demons say boyfriends? Or is there a more antiquated or primal word, like intended, or mate? I didn't really clarify that part. I guess it doesn't really matter.

The night is cold and dark, but the lampposts along the streets are soft beacons in the night. A couple of them have fliers for this week's joint NOJ and AWO banquet, which I tear down on my way past. If Levena was a pile of kindling, Finnegan's article was lighter fuel.

And yet, the town isn't burning. It's tense, and sides are forming, but there's been no explosion. Not yet.

I bury my hands in my pockets, and in my right one I fidget with Archeon's card.

All I have to do is give Arlo the card, and tell him Archeon is willing to help. No big deal. And maybe mention that his son is a magickal power plant and that I might've suspected it the whole time, and then told someone else first. No big deal.

When I make it to Thitwhistle's, my heart sinks a little. I've grown accustomed to someone being awake and the lights on downstairs, but I'm the only one living there now. During the day there's always people, but not at night. Arlo and the boys moved into Witch House last weekend, and it's weird not seeing them everyday. I didn't realize *how* weird until faced with the physical proof of it. Is it possible to ache for a best friend like you would a lover?

I use the back door, which drops you off right at the staircase leading to the apartments. When I take hold of the knob and slide in my key, the wards hum in recognition. My phone vibrates, and before heading inside I check it. There's a couple messages in the group chat, one from Arlo, and something from an unknown number with an attachment.

What the fuck ...?

I open the message, finding not just one picture, but many. Me and Elochian waiting for the towncar outside the university. The towncar, and its plates, as we drive away. Me getting out of the car, two perspectives as I look both ways down the street.

Me, standing at the back door with my phone in my hand.

My head jerks up and I search my immediate surroundings. No one in plain sight, but that same feeling is back. It wasn't just Elochian watching me earlier in class. I'm being hunted.

I rush inside and lock the door behind me, ensuring that the wards go up. I do my best to control my breathing, but my chest heaves. I back away from the door, keeping it in my sights. My knee aches with a new wave of pain, and I crumple into a pile of adrenaline and fear.

I'm so fucked.

The curtains over the hall window are partially drawn. I stare at them, willing myself to get up and draw them closed. To hide. The wards keep the windows locked, but what if he breaks the glass? Will they cover the gap?

I struggle to my feet, remaining slightly hunched over as I do. I take a step towards the window. A figure comes into view, taking up the entirety of the narrow gap between curtains. My breath hitches, and I freeze.

A pale hand rests on the glass.

And at that moment, my phone rings.

Slowly, I take it out of my pocket, and answer it.

"Tell me everything! I need details, Q—"

"H–help," I whisper, then try to collect as much air into my lungs as I can. I don't quite shout, but it's a close thing. "Help."

The hand retreats, but my fear doesn't abate.

"What's going on?"

I try to mirror her focused calm, but each word I manage tears hysteria from my heart. "He's outside. He followed me home. He's outside. He's going to kill me, Linds. He's going to—"

"Don't move, and don't take the wards down. We'll be right there, stay on the phone."

I take in a deep, shuddering breath. I can still feel him out there. Prowling. Hunting. Every fiber in me demands to run and hide, but I don't. I slump against the wall and stay on the phone with Lindsey until she has to hang up in order to Travel.

I hold my phone in my hands, staring at the message Elochian sent me while I was on the phone.

Lochian (9:23 PM): I'd like to take you out for breakfast tomorrow, if that's okay.

I put my head in my hands, and cry.

Arlo, Lindsey, Kitt, and Caspian all arrive at the same time. Lindsey calls, "Quentin!" and my name is followed by thundering footsteps.

Lindsey finds me in the same position I've been stuck in. Knees tucked into my chest, using the wall and floor as a grounding point. When she sees me, she stops running. She slowly approaches, crouching down to my level. "Quentin, are you hurt?"

I shake my head, disturbing the sweat ridden hair stuck to my forehead.

Lindsey reaches for me, then stops. "Breathe, Quen."

"W–what?" I look at her, confused. I am breathing. Shallow and slow, but it's to keep me safe. Keep me hidden.

"You're shaking. Go on, let it out."

"O–oh." I exhale, broken and wet.

I do my best to take in a deep breath, but it breaks into a vicious sob. Lindsey gently takes me into her arms, holding me against her chest. She pets my hair, moving it away from my face. The creak of wood across the hall notifies me of Caspian's presence, but I can't pay him any mind right now.

The back door opens, and I startle at the sound. Lindsey holds me closer. "It's just Arlo and Kitt, they were scouting the outside."

Arlo kneels beside us and rests a hand on my back, rubbing in slow and small circles. "They're gone," he whispers. The tension rolls off him in waves, and I don't need my glasses to know his aura is nothing but well restrained rage.

"H–he'll be back. I d–don't want to l–leave, b–but I w–will—"

"You're not going anywhere," Arlo says firmly. "You are my brother. My family, and no one fucks with family."

And that makes it all so much worse, and better.

After a little while, once I've shed all my adrenaline and panic through tears and snot, Lindsey and Arlo help me up off the floor. My knees are weak, but I manage to stand on my own. Kitt and Cas are by the window, staring intensely at the glass, or through it, I can't really tell.

"What is it?" Arlo asks.

Cas holds up a fingertip smudged with sickly purple. "Lipstick, on the inside of the glass."

"That's impossible," Arlo says, looking at me. "That wasn't there before, right?"

I shake my head. "It wasn't. That's his ... *thing*. You'll see."

Kitt peers out the window one last time, then comes over and gives me a hug. "It'll be okay, Quentin."

I nod against her shoulder, sniffing. After we pull away, I make sure to look at everyone as I say, "I don't want Elochian to know."

Silence falls for a few seconds before Arlo breaks it. "We could use his help, Q, and I think he would want to know."

"It's not his business!" I snap, then flinch away from my own words. I scrub a hand over my face. "Please, I don't ... I don't want him to think of me like this."

"Like what?" Caspian asks, bewildered.

"It's—!" I bury the truth and partially turn away from them all, crossing my arms over my chest.

Lindsey rests a hand on my back. "Okay. We won't tell him. Unless we need to."

I nod quickly. "Thank you."

Kitt crowds my other side. "Let's go have a cup of tea, and we'll talk about it. Lindsey said there's pictures we need to see?"

I swallow past a lump in my throat and say, "Okay."

We settle into our booth, Cas transfers from his wheelchair to the cushioned bench seat with Arlo, while Kitt and Lindsey squish on either side of me. I always feel at peace in this spot in the world, and it's nothing to do with Arlo's enchantments. There have been nothing but happy memories grown here.

Until now, that is.

My nerves calm somewhat as we sit in silence. The others are patient, but expectant. Arlo takes a small pouch out of an inner pocket of his leather jacket, revealing a small glass pipe and a jar of broken up herbs from its depths. He packs it, glancing up at me every now and then. Lindsey's fingers are entwined with mine, and Kitt rests a firm but gentle hand on the back of my neck.

After a few more moments, the bowl is packed. Arlo hands it to me first, and after I take a hit, I pass the bowl off to Kitt, then offer my phone to Lindsey. My hands are shaking too badly to work the buttons, and I can't bring myself to look at the picture right now. I don't need to, anyway. It's burned into my mind.

Lindsey steals a deep breath, going through my phone one-handed. I wonder if she'll ever let me out of her sight now. She finds the picture, and her face pinches as she hands the phone off to Arlo. He studies my phone and hits the pipe, expression blank. When he passes the phone and pipe to Caspian, he takes off his beanie and rakes a hand through his hair.

Then he fixes me with a hard stare. I swallow, anticipating a lecture.

Instead, he offers me his hand. I have to cross my arms a bit to hold both his and Lindsey's, but I make do. I feel like a twisted up, burnt pretzel, both inside and out. And because I'm human, my stomach chooses that moment to remind me that I never ate dinner. I push away the hunger pang, and when it's clear that no one is going to break the silence, I begin in less than a whisper.

"We met when I was in boarding school, back home. He was older than me, but I didn't care. My family ... well. I didn't have any friends, not even at home. But River was always there for me. We weren't i–intimate, not at first. He wanted to wait. He was always there, always watching, even when I was at school. At the time, I ... I thought it was nice, having a protector. Someone that *cared* enough to want to keep me safe.

"Then everything changed. M–my dad died. I graduated school early, and moved right in with River. My mother … oh, she was furious, and it was the first time I had ever provoked emotion from her. It was addictive. So I did everything River told me to. We made such a mess of that place, and I made sure everyone knew how much of a failure her son was. But eventually, it escalated further than I was comfortable with. The things River wanted me to do …"

Arlo never looks away from me, and I can't bear to look at anyone else.

"I didn't want to," I whisper. "For the first time, I said no. And for the first time, I saw River for who he truly was. But it was too late. My entire life revolved around him, and I had nowhere to go. I couldn't go home, and all my friends were his friends. I didn't have a job, or a car. River took care of everything, even though he hardly worked himself. I never understood that part."

I close my eyes, needing a moment.

Kitt's nails scratch against my scalp. Lindsey's thumb traces over my veins. Magick leeches from Arlo's skin into mine, soft and warm. I feel Caspian too, even though we're not touching.

Caspian asks, "What did you do?"

I open my eyes, focusing on him. He looks at me differently, like I'm one of his children. It hurts and heals. Do they all see me as a child, because I'm so much younger? Arlo called me brother, but does he mean it?

Venom creeps into my voice when I say, "I ran away. I broke into the cas—my mother's house. My room was packed away, all my posters, all my things … I had to go searching in the basement, but I found my stuff. It all fit in one big box, she must've thrown a lot away, but not at all of it. My dad had left me a, um … a secret rainy day fund, of sorts. He knew I would leave one day, just maybe not for the reasons I did. Thankfully it was still there, hidden in my favorite book. That was the only thing I took with me when I came here, to Levena."

"I thought you were from here," Arlo says. His hand sparks against mine, but it doesn't hurt. "I had no idea. *How* old were you?"

"That's what everyone thinks." I shrug, which is hard to do given my crossed arms. "I graduated when I was sixteen."

Absolute, crystal clear, silence.

Kitt says, "Gods, Quentin." She rubs a horn against my shoulder. "You weren't much older than that when we found you."

I give her a dry look. "I was twenty-one."

"So he followed you, and tormented you for … years," Lindsey's whisper trails off, and my stomach twists.

"Yeah." I laugh darkly. "One day in Basic Physics, he sat right down next to me like nothing happened at all. He convinced me that he'd changed, that he was better. Me, being the stupid idiot I was, believed him. I was so fucking lonely, and I believed him. All his pretty words." I shake my head, like that'll do anything to combat the rising nausea. "It lasted for one year. Long enough for me to let my guard down."

I release my friend's hands, my own are sweaty. I go to adjust my glasses, belatedly remembering they're not there. Caspian reaches into his shirt pocket, pulling them out. He hands them to me, and I nod in thanks.

"Can I ask you something?"

I nod again.

Slowly, Caspian says, "So, you left him and moved in with Lindsey, right? Why didn't you run again? Living in the same town as him … I mean, if he's still fixated on you, this was bound to happen."

"It's not his fault, Cas," Lindsey snaps.

Caspian rolls his eyes at her. "That's not what I'm saying."

"Really? Because it sounds like it." Kitt adds, fingers tightening on my neck.

All the while, Arlo watches me.

"I trusted her," I whisper, which stops the bickering. Attention bouncing between my friends, I say, "She promised to keep me safe, and for the first time in a long time, I felt like I could trust someone. I don't know why. I almost did run."

"And you still can, Q," Lindsey says. "All of us, we can keep you safe. But the only way we can do that is if we work together."

Caspian smiles, and I wonder if his previous question was intentional. Like he knew what my answer was going to be. Him and Arlo both are manipulative bastards when it comes to getting you to admit heartfelt truths.

"Quentin, what race is River?" Arlo asks suddenly. "Is he human?"

I nod. "Yeah, he is."

"Is he a witch?"

"Um, no. Nothing special. Just a human."

Caspian says, "Humans *are* special. Just not that particular one."

"Yeah, well. I'm going to die *way* before any of you, so sorry if I don't think so." I bite out, then duck my head. "Sorry, I don't know where that came from. I'm tired."

Lindsey rubs a circle between my shoulder blades, and no one speaks. What is there to say? It's true.

After a tense moment, Arlo asks, "Are you sure, Q? I thought I felt—no. Not thought. Whoever was here, was definitely a witch."

I blink at him. "I don't think so. If he was, I don't know how he would've hidden it from me. We were together all the time."

Arlo's face shudders as if I'd slapped him. Looking away from me, he says, "You'd be surprised."

February

Lecture Of A Lifetime

Elochian

I jolt out of sleep and straight into panic.

I sit up, head on a swivel as I survey my bedroom. It's empty, and early morning light filters through the windows. I tuck an errant lock of hair behind my ear, debating on whether to call out to Michael. His bedroom neighbors mine, a door adjoins them in case of an emergency. It's the same room Bartholomew used, and I haven't been in there in years.

I decide not to bother him, since there's clearly nothing wrong. I dig around the blankets in my nest until I find my phone, hoping that Quentin wrote me back sometime during the night. It's not odd for him to take long to reply, considering that his phone is dead most of the time. But there's nothing. Not from him, anyway.

Buried in the emails and texts from those in Clan Adrastus is a message from Arlo.

Arlo (4:53 AM): Gaia agreed to meet with me, but it has to be this morning. Meet me at Thitwhistle's at eight.

I squint, making sure that I'm seeing the time right. Why the hell was he up so early? It's only a little after six now, but I'm completely awake. I have a council meeting this afternoon, but if we're quick I should make it back in time.

Who am I kidding? I'm going to be with Arlo, of course I'll be late.

I sit in the booth at Thitwhistle's, wondering why the fuck it's so busy. Sure, it's early morning on a Friday, but still. There's something in the air, like unsettled chaos and an abundance of cinnamon. Small bouquets of dried basil, rosemary, and crocus hang from the support beams, while white and green candles decorate every nook and cranny. There's more bread than pastries being served this morning, and I indulged in a slice of cinnamon date bread earlier. Ally and Olly are excellent bakers, and the bread was almost as good as Silas'.

Just don't ask me which one is which.

My text message to Quentin is still unread, and I have half a mind to go upstairs and knock on his door. The urge is strong and unsettling, and I have to remind myself that people sleep in sometimes. That doesn't mean anything is wrong.

When Arlo walks into the main room, the atmosphere quickly shifts, like a collective relaxing of the shoulders and exhalations of long held air. It reminds me how the estate reacts when I come home. He says hello to people as he passes through, kind but clearly on a mission. After the fourth time he says, '*chag sameach*,' I realize why it's so busy. It's Imbolc.

Arlo's birthday.

I stand, holding onto my apple cider for dear life as he joins me. He's dressed for business today, all boots and leather. A ring of green encircles his golden irises, signaling that his magick is either primed or in use. "Hey, Loch. Thanks for coming on such short notice."

"Of course. Thanks for doing this, and on your birthday, no less." I gesture to the cafe. "It looks good in here. Happy Birthday, you old witch."

"Thanks." Arlo smiles, but it doesn't reach his illuminated eyes. "It's no problem, but we better get going." He leads me to the front door, which confuses me. Both Arlo and Quentin's stones are keyed for travel in and out of the bookshop.

We step outside, and I have to shield my eyes while they adjust. The sunlight is hot and blinding, ricocheting off frozen piles of snow littering the town. It's almost enough to ward off the bone deep chill the air carries. Michael waits just down the street in the towncar, and I send them a quick text as I walk beside Arlo.

"Felt like going for a walk?" I ask.

Arlo says nothing for a block. Gaia's place is at the opposite end of River Street, a jaunt even in the summertime. He casually glances around, quiet as he says, "My wards were compromised last night. No traveling until I get it figured out. I think bending the space like that provides a ... window of opportunity."

My heart picks up the pace, as do my feet. "Someone tried to break in? To the Castle, or Thitwhistle's? The island?"

"Thitwhistles," he says, scanning the streetsides.

"Is Quentin alright? Was he home?"

Arlo doesn't look at me when he says, "He's fine. But it was a long night, I think he'll probably be sleeping awhile."

I stop walking. "Arlo," I say, commanding his attention. He stops and stares at me. "He's okay?"

Arlo breathes deep, and the seconds-long pause before he says, "Yes," is everything. "Yes, he's okay."

"Who was it? AWO? Leon?"

"I don't know."

"Arlo."

"*Elochian*, I really don't know! All that was left behind was traces of magick. Whoever it was, they're a witch. That much I do know."

I open my hands, willing my elongated nails to retract. They protest for a moment before obeying. "Okay. I can send you Lurin. And Kellan. They're both excellent trackers, I can—"

Arlo shakes his head. "No, Loch."

I stare at him, bewildered. "What? Why?"

"I want to keep this low for now. We don't need to make ourselves a bigger target than we already are."

"But—"

"Elochian, I appreciate it, but please. Trust me. Can you do that?"

I glare at him. "Of course I do. But you're being an idiot."

"Your ball."

"*What*?"

Arlo rolls his eyes, and I've never wanted to punch him more. He steps closer to me, lowering his voice. "I want to use your ball as an excuse to get all the witches together. On the one hand it'll appease the community and show them we're nothing to be afraid of. On the other hand, all the witches will be together, including me. This person we're dealing with is a showman, they're toying with–"

Arlo's brows pinch, and the pause is nearly imperceptible, but there all the same.

"Me. With us. This is a perfect opportunity for them to make a move. But we'll be ready, and a part of that is we need them to think they have the advantage. Okay?"

I sigh. "I really want to punch you right now."

He smiles a little. "Go for it, but it'll hurt. I've had worse gifts."

Reluctantly, I nod to the street and we continue walking. We avoid the detour that is Market Street and continue down Garren Road. An enclosed trolley goes by, its lights dim beneath the overwhelming sun. I mutter, "A party full of angels, demons, and witches. *That's* not a recipe for disaster or anything."

"Oh come on. You and Quentin have done nothing but give me the unity speech."

"Yeah, I like giving advice, not taking it."

Arlo hums. "You're going to ask him as your date, right?"

"Should I?"

"I swear to the fucking Gods ..." Arlo scrubs a hand down his face.

I ignore his exasperation, losing myself to thought as I study the frozen, small lake in Funguy Park as we walk by. People skate upon it, from young to old, human to demon. Families and couples, loners and friends. At the narrow northern tip of the lake, a mass of kids have claimed the area for hockey. An adolescent werewolf swipes at the contested puck with their full force, and it crashes into the net which billows from the impact.

Parents, guardians, and friends cheer from the sidelines. I wonder if Quentin ever dreamed of being there, on the sidelines watching his own child. The thought of that child not being *ours* slaps me across the face, harder than the icy breeze nipping at my cheeks.

As we near Gowan's block, I say, "My aunt … made some very good points."

Arlo stares at me, and the look on his face makes me want to laugh. "Since when did you listen to her?"

I pull my scarf up over my face. "Since she pointed out that Quentin's a human, and I'm an archdemon. She basically told me I need to stop playing around and find a partner that is part of the clan."

Arlo studies his feet as he walks. Eventually, he says, "Quentin said something to me last night that I've been thinking a lot about."

"What's that?"

His face pinches. "That humans aren't special, and he's going to die before any of us. I think … I think we haven't been very considerate. I don't know."

"Michael said … Michael said that I need to make the most of Quentin's life, *because* of that fact. He thinks I'm wasting time, dithering like I am."

Arlo chuckles hollowly. "I think he's the one you should be listening to."

We let the conversation die, and after a few minutes I ask, "So, what's Kitt and Cas planning for you? I haven't heard anything yet."

He lifts a shoulder. "Dunno. No one's said anything to me about it either. Everyone's pretty busy, and I'd rather it not be a big deal anyway. Maybe the boys and I will have a movie night or something. They're both on an old film kick."

"Oh," I say, surprised. I'll have to see if Quentin will want to visit the island later on with me.

Gaia Lichin's home straddles the land between Garren Road and River Street. When the underwater neighborhood was con-structed, my engineers were sought out in regards to keeping the waterway and its inhabitants warm all year round. A low fog hangs over the street, hugging the stilts holding up the structures resting over the still waters. Some homes, like Gaia's, rest on the edge of water, giving them access to both worlds. The majority of the residents live under the water, however.

It's easy for people to forget that River Street spills underneath Levena as well, a subterranean and accessible network for amphibious folk to use and live in. Funguy's pond was left out of the heating system, but Syorini Lake across town is warmed, a fact that the merfolk greatly appreciate.

Given Levena's bitter winters, the entire thing was a challenge to say the least. It was also Bartholomew's passion project. As a demon of *mayim* descent, he loved the water. It could be thirty below and he'd be begging me to join him in the water. I'd always say, *'Yes, the water's warm, but what about the air? I'll freeze when I get out.'*

And he would say, *'Come on, Key. That's part of the fun, you've got to enjoy the warmth while it lasts, then run like hell when it's time to get out.'*

I joined him in the water every time. I always froze my ass off afterwards, but he made it worth it.

Arlo stands beside me, breathing like he ran a marathon. The stilted house is nondescript and plain, a stone rectangle with square windows lining the walls every six feet or so. Manufactured comes to mind, but the extra touches wipe that thought away. The back of the house is hard to see, but there's a ... step of sorts, where a good section of the building rests partially underwater. The stilts are thick pillars of stone as opposed to a wooden construction, built to last a lifetime.

Bone chimes rattle softly in the breeze, tapping against the white washed stones marking the front corners of the house. Runes decorate the black door frame, and a bell hangs high above it, too high for most people to reach. When it's clear Arlo can't take another step, I close the distance and bring my fist to old wood painted dark green.

A moment later, the necromancer opens the door.

Gaia squints at me, black eyes narrowing as fresh daylight assaults her. "Oh, Mr. Adrastus." She looks over my shoulder, at Arlo standing in the street. Her face softens, an expression I did not anticipate. "Arlo. Please, come in."

I bow my head. "Good morning, Miss Lichin. Thank you for meeting with us."

"Well, it's about time, isn't it?" She steps back, gesturing inside with a black tentacle mottled with neon pink and stormy white. "Come on in. *Chag sameach* to both of you."

"Blessed Imbolc." I nod, stepping past her. She is twice my size, both in height and width, larger than the average *krakeni*. Her home is similar to Julian's, all smooth polished stone and moss furnishings. Julian is actually a close friend of Gaia's, but I didn't feel right asking my DJ to set me up with the necromancer.

I can see three statues of Kiroli from here, another surprise. The Goddess of Fertility is the patron of *krakeni*, an ironic turn of events in Gaia's necromantic case. Then again, Kiroli's lover was the God of the Underworld, so there's that.

After we both pass over the threshold, Gaia shuts the door. With all the genuine warmth in the world, she says, "Arlo, I'm glad you're here."

He tugs at the gauge in his ear, gaze skittering between her and the floor. "You are?"

Gaia smiles, folding her tentacles over her chest. A short pink dress laced with white hangs off one shoulder, and the length of it falls at her knees. Cords of leather laden with shells and teeth hang around her neck. Silver rings inlaid with crystals cover the tips of her tentacles like bracelets. Her nostrils flare, wrinkling her flat nose.

"Oh, yes. You see, we need your help."

The open foyer is humid and cool, no doubt recently misted, but a flash of hot fear overcomes me at that statement.

"Who—" We begin to say, and are promptly interrupted by new arrivals.

An elf and a *golem* steps into the northern end of the foyer, where the room spills into a kitchen that reminds me of Arlo's witch kitchen. Arlo looks as if he might throw up. He swallows, tense and quiet. Absolutely confused, I join his side, providing what comfort I can.

The elf is tall and thick with muscle, their skin darker than the depths of the sea. Their long, black hair has an undershave on the sides, revealing spiraling tattoos on their skull. They wear an obnoxiously green windbreaker, and crystalline wyvern sits on their shoulder, seeming to glare at Arlo like their master does.

The *golem* was elven in their previous life. Despite the silk cloth tied over their eyes and wild rainbow mohawk, it's clear they are related to Windbreaker. Their skin is the same shade, albeit dry and brittle, and their face has the same sharp, dangerous edge to it. Congealed, black blood leaks from their right nostril, teasing at their cracked lips.

I have no idea what kind of familiar stands at their side. The size of a large dog, but with hooves and brown fur, the legs striped black and white. Not to mention the long neck that comes up to the *golem's* shoulder, complete with a deer-like head and dual protuberances reminiscent of horns, but not quite.

"I should blow up your liver right now, you fucking asshole," the elf says.

Arlo winces, looking askance to Gaia. The *krakeni* smiles at him. "I'm not the only one who wanted an audience with the impossible to reach Hedge Witch."

"You *do* realize he owns a shop twenty minutes south of here?" I snap. "It's not that hard to find him."

The elf turns their feral gaze on me, and I force myself not to shrink under it. I am an archdemon. I *am* an archdemon. They say, "Stay out of it, my *Lord*."

Arlo scowls. "Hey, don't talk to him like that. Your problem is with me, not him."

"Then he shouldn't be nosing into things he knows nothing of."

The *golem* says, "Demi, that's no way to ask for help. Remember why we're here."

Windbreaker huffs, but I don't miss the way their anger softens. "Fine."

Gaia smiles, revealing rows of blunt teeth. "Good. Now, let's have some tea and get down to business."

I sit at a round table with four witches, feeling anxious and relaxed all at once. Half a dozen candles burn in glass pillars, each one recessed into the table at different depths. The tension between the four is palpable, but warm water laps at my bare feet, distracting me from the drama. It's been so long since I was in contact with the river. It's almost like coming home.

Gaia clears her throat, breaking the silence that's fallen since brief introductions for my sake. She waves a tentacle in Demeter's direction. "I believe we should begin with you two, as I feel your matter is most pressing. But we're going to keep this respectful. This is neutral ground, you hear?"

Arlo nods, as does Demeter and aer companion. It irritates me that Gaia deems their matter more important when she has no idea why *we're* here, but I say nothing.

Demeter exhales a long breath, then focuses on Arlo with something akin to barely pieced together apathy. "Dimitri's *ob* is coming apart. Ne's fading more and more each day, and we can't figure out why. The others say it's time, but it's only been ..." Demeter's gaze skitters to the *golem* at aer side, then back to Arlo. "It's only been eight years."

Dimitri raises a hand, giving it a little shake. "I can speak for myself, Demi."

Demeter glares at Dimitri. "If you call me that *one* more time."

Dimitri shakes nems head, jutting a thumb at Demeter. "Aer's just worried, don't let aer bitchiness fool you." Black blood spills from a corner of nems lips. Ne frowns, turning away. Demeter offers nem a napkin from aer jacket pocket, thin brows pulled together. After wiping away the blood, Dimitri says, "Okay, maybe you can do the talking."

But Demeter doesn't say anything. Aer looks at Gaia askance, then to Arlo.

Arlo says, "*Obs* aren't really my expertise, but I can take a look. But you are right, it's too early for it to unravel."

"You're still able to slip through the Veil then?" Gaia asks, leaning forward. A slick tentacle rises, framing her face.

He blinks. "Yes? Why?"

Gaia and Demeter exchange a look, then the *krakeni* continues. "I haven't been able to open a door into the Veil since

Samhain. I've suspected there is something amiss with the Veil itself, but if you can still access it ... maybe not. Maybe it's me."

Arlo shrugs. "Well, I haven't *actually* stepped into it since ... about a week before that, now that I think about it. I'll take a look now, if that's alright with you, Dimitri." Arlo barely looks at Demeter or Dimitri when talking, but especially Dimitri. I'm curious as to what happened between them, but I won't be finding out right now.

I raise a hand. "I'm not sure what an *ob* is, but is shifting into the Veil right now a good idea? What if Le—"

"Do *not* speak his name," Demeter hisses, and my wings rise at the venom in aer tone.

"What if Leon, what?" Dimitri asks. Demeter shoves out of aer chair, taking to pacing. Dimitri sighs, fidgeting with a loose string on nems sleeve. "A name is a name, Demi. We're not doing ourselves any favors by being afraid of it."

"It's not the name I'm afraid of! It's like you've completely forgotten what he—" Demeter cuts off in an abrupt whine. By the way the others react, what I'm missing has become crystal clear. All four of these witches share something in common.

Trauma at the hands of Leon.

Quietly, Dimitri says, "You don't have to fight for me, or even with me, nib. But please, stop holding me back. I know damn well what Leonadias did, and I want him to pay for it. But I can't do that by hiding, or pretending that it didn't happen."

Demeter comes to a stop behind Dimitri. Ae rests aer hands on Dimitri's shoulders, squeezing tight. Dimitri reaches up, holding one of aer hands in nems. Demeter says, "I'm not going anywhere, *schlemiel.*"

Dimitri grins, revealing blood stained, perfect teeth. "I know."

"I'm sorry," Arlo blurts out. "I know it sounds cheap, and it's too late, but I truly am. I wish that I could've been what you needed, after. I wish that I was there for you."

Demeter stares at Arlo, and Dimitri smiles a little at him. Demeter says, "It *is* too late, and we're not the only ones who needed you. We looked up to you, Rook, those who fought with you." Ae gestures to Gaia, then places a hand over aer heart. "Those who survived with you. And then you just ... disappeared. Do you know what Levena did with us? The survivors?"

Arlo shakes his head, hands clenched into fists in his lap.

"They put us in a cozy, abandoned part of town, and forgot about us. We had nothing. Nowhere to go. Can't get registered, because it costs a fortune, or our lives were erased by fucking—" Demeter hesitates, cooling down. "By fucking Leon. Dimitri and I, we don't exist on paper. We've been forgotten, by Levena, and by you."

"I didn't mean to."

"Bullshit, you just didn't need us anymore. Your happy little band all survived, got married and had kids. Hell, you own half of Levena now! What would you want with—"

"I was dying!" Arlo braces his elbows on the table and hides his face in his hands. I watch him breathe, and reach over to rest my hand in the middle of his back. After a moment, his hands fall from his face to the table, palm down. He says, "Every day I fought, and every day, I lost. I kept losing, and losing, and losing, until finally I was nothing more than a fucked up, toxic mess. And then, I lost the war. I lost the war against myself, and I truly died.

"My—my best friend saved me. If she hadn't found me, then I wouldn't be here right now at all. So yes, I forgot about you, but to be fair I forgot about everyone else too, even myself. I could have done better, I *should* have. But I want to help, and I can now. We don't have to be friends, you don't have to like me. But please, let me help."

I breathe, trying to keep my own heart steady through a sentiment that I relate to so, *so* much. I rub Arlo's back, focusing on Gaia's smile full of fondness and pride, the lines softening around Demeter's eyes and mouth. Dimitri's raspy chuckle is the final weight, bringing me back down to normal. Ne says, "Try arguing with that, nib."

"Fuck you," Demeter says, and that's that. Neither of them accept or deny Arlo's words, but if the broken tension is anything to go by, it's a step in the right direction.

Gaia says, "Thank you for your honesty, Arlo. Perhaps one day, you can speak to the others. I know Bud misses you, and Eleanor."

Arlo nods, still not quite meeting her eyes yet. "Okay, yeah. Of course."

"This is great and all, but we're getting off track," Demeter says. "Can you check or not, Rook?"

"Hold on," Gaia says. "Not to be crass, but why are you here, Elochian?"

Without preamble, I say, "There is a *shedim* in my clan who claims that he can raise the dead."

"I haven't heard of another necromancer rising," Gaia says, tentacles agitated.

"That's because he isn't one. He brought a woman to my office who died long ago, claiming to have raised her using solar batteries. She was completely restored. Not a *golem*, but not ... what she was before, either. I've no idea how, only that she was dead, and her family gave consent. Regardless, it's clear to me that he broke Byinger's first law, at the very least.

"Who is it?" Gaia asks, sounding like a stereotypical, scary necromancer for the first time. "Have you prosecuted him?"

"No. His team has intercepted every charge I've brought against him, and the judge agrees with them. Since her family gave consent, they feel no laws have been broken. And there is no law saying a necromancer *has* to be the one to return a spirit."

"That's bullshit," Demeter says. "You are the literal king of demons!"

"Even kings answer to someone," Dimitri says, but it doesn't feel like a save.

"I don't even know how you would use solar power to create an *ob*. That doesn't make any sense ..." Gaia says, shifting her attention to Arlo. "Unless ... oh, unless." She laughs, but it's empty. "He's not using solar power to create an *ob*. He's using it to cut into the Veil and force his way in. But how can he manipulate the threads?" She murmurs, tapping her chin.

"But the living can't enter the Veil," Arlo says, subdued and far off.

Gaia looks at me. "He's not a *golem* himself?"

"No ... I'm sorry, what's an *ob*?"

"Elochian, are you familiar with the necromantic process? You mentioned Byinger's law."

I raise a hand, tipping it side to side. "A little. You reform a person's spirit by pulling their soul and bodily energies together, right?"

Gaia nods. "Yes, in a way. I like to think of it as stitching, or weaving, and it must take place in the Veil. The thread I use, and resulting patchwork, we'll say, is the *ob*. In more plain terms, it's the same as a spirit, but in a different state. We call it the spirit of the dead. The *ob* remains intact for about a hundred and fifty years, and when it's time for a soul to pass, the body begins to degrade, like Dimitri has."

I think on that for a moment, wondering if Quentin is familiar with the concept. It's in his realm of study, after all. I ask, "So, what is the difference between you and Arlo, then?"

"I can only step just inside the Veil, so I have to be in physical proximity to the deceased or passing person. It's like holding back a rubber band, and if I stay in there too long, it'll snap. Arlo can travel the Other Side freely, but he cannot weave an *ob*. He can also interact with souls long since gone, while I can only interact with spirits in the process of passing. The people I help must have a body to return to, while Arlo works ... the other way."

I lean back in my seat. "Interesting. I never knew that."

Gaia presses her tentacles to her temple. "Indeed." She studies me a moment longer, then gestures to Arlo. "Okay, go on. But be careful."

Arlo nods, swallowing. "Are you ready, Dimitri?"

"You're all acting as if going to croak," Dimitri says, leaning back against Demeter.

"Your dead guy jokes will never be funny," Demeter mutters.

Arlo stands, water sloshing around his ankles. Demeter holds Dimitri tight to aer stomach, closing aer eyes. Oh, we're doing this right here, right now. I place my hands on the table, unsure what to do with myself. I look over at Gaia, but she only has eyes for Arlo.

The Hedge Witch reaches up, brushing his fingers along the tattoos on his neck. The lines alight a bright green, casting light onto the smooth stone walls of Gaia's watery den. He raises his hands before him, moving them in that strange way that he does when he's doing Big Magick. His lips silently move, and a temporary moment of stillness overcomes him.

Arlo brings his palms together before moving them forward, like he's parting water, or a curtain. He inhales sharply, and the candles sputter. His hands tremble, then shake. When his entire body begins to convulse, frozen in place, I stand in a rush.

Gaia takes my arm, tentacles wrapping around my wrist. "Don't. Something's wrong," she says. "Dimitri, can you feel him?"

Dimitri shakes nems head. "No."

A flashbang overtakes the room, exploding outwards from Arlo's collapsing figure. I rush forward and catch him before he smashes his head and drowns. His weight nearly crushes me, but Demeter is there seconds later. Together, we haul an unconscious Arlo into the dry den and lay him on what may be a loveseat for Gaia, but for Arlo it's a full length couch.

"What happened?" I ask breathlessly, staring down at Arlo now damp from sweat and water. He's breathing, so that's a good thing.

Gaia shakes her head. "Nicen is blocking us from the Veil. We've angered him."

I give her a weary look. "I hate to be that person, but I don't think the Gods care what you two are up to." I pause. "But you might be right. Wrong, but right."

"What the *gehenna* are you talking about, your lordship?" Demeter asks.

"We haven't angered Nicen, but Daniel might have. The problem demon. Could his dealings be connected with this ... block?"

"That's a possibility," Gaia murmurs.

Arlo stirs on the couch, eyes moving beneath his lids and fingers twitching. I kneel beside him, resting a gentle hand on his shoulder. "Arlo, you alright?"

He groans. "Oh, sure. Fuckin' dandy."

I roll my eyes. "He's swearing, so that's a good sign."

"It's him," Arlo says, slowly opening his eyes. He stares past me, unseeing, and it chills me to my bones. "There's nothing but ghosts and lost souls over there, all Leon's. He's claimed the Veil as his. It's ... it's only a matter of time before he breaks through. I don't know why he hasn't yet."

Thick, horrid silence follows his words. Oh. Not Daniel, then. Dimitri takes Demeter's hand, skin cracking as ne squeezes tight. Gaia covers her face, exhaling long and slow. My fists open and close, and I think; Quentin. I need to keep him safe. I need to keep him close.

I need him.

Arlo says, "I—I need to leave. I need my boys." He tries to sit up, but his eyes roll and a moan punches out of his gut. I rest a hand on his shoulder, using my other to dig out my phone and text Michael.

"Easy, take it easy. You're no good to them passed out."

"Arlo?" Dimitri asks, and it's quiet, unsure. We both look at nem, watching as nems throat fractures along the surface. "I don't blame you for what happened to me. You did the best that you could, and you brought me home to my nib. But we can't let it happen again. We can't let anyone else get hurt like we did."

Demeter quietly says, "Nem's right."

Arlo's eyes close, and his throat clicks. "I don't know if I can do it again," he whispers.

"Hey." I shake Arlo's shoulder. He blinks at me, confused and tired. His eyes are wet with the threat of tears. "Alone? No. I don't think that you could. But you're not alone, okay? No one wants you to be a martyr, but a leader? We could use one of those."

Arlo laughs, then covers his eyes and breaks down.

I hold his hand as he cries, and our newfound companions form a semi-circle of sorts around us, standing guard. I think about Thatch, wondering if he can hear Arlo from wherever he is.

We leave with the promise of Gaia, Demeter, and Dimitri's assistance. All three were extended invitations to Witch House, and the ball. I told them to invite any and all witches that were interested. Arlo is silent the entire car ride to the castle, and I wait in the car with Michael while he makes the trek down the castle's driveway.

"What happened?" Michael asks the moment Arlo steps out of the car.

I tell them, sparing no details. It only hinders their job, not knowing everything they possibly can. His hands tighten around the steering wheel as the tale takes a turn, and their form changes from human to *shedim* as I finish.

"I find it awfully funny that Leon has claimed the Veil, so to speak, and our dear Daniel is able to cut into it without consequence," Michael says, low and deadly.

"There's definitely something there, but what? Is Daniel a liaison of his? A solider, a spy? Is he turning the dead for Leon's benefit?"

"Where is Leon buried?"

"I think Arlo cremated him, that's why he hasn't materialized yet, he needs a corporeal body."

"Which requires a contract," Michael says.

I nod, wondering how they know this.

Michael doesn't relax, and I don't either. Obviously Leon doesn't *need* a body to fuck everything up, but it would be infinitely worse if he did. Michael glances at the castle, then back to me. Hesitantly, they say, "I finally found something on Quentin."

"What?"

Michael hums, pulling their phone out of their breast pocket. They offer it to me. "Unlock it. It's all there. Be warned, it is … graphic."

I do as he says, full of trepidation. Waiting on the other side of a dim screen is a series of photos, each one depicting someone in critical condition, unrecognizable. "What … what am I looking at? Who is this?" Silence follows my question, and when I look up I find Michael staring straight ahead, gripping the steering wheel so hard his knuckles blanch. Again, I ask, "Michael. Who is this?"

Rage and terror races down my spine, because deep down, I know.

But I have to be sure.

Michael clears his throat, but he doesn't release the wheel. "I wasn't able to find anything old on Quentin, he was a ghost before moving to Levena. I wasn't sure if he danced in Levena, or somewhere else, but I figured that was my best lead, short of having a chat with Mr. Diaz. I visited three different studios, and the last ballet master finally knew who I was talking about. But … they knew him as someone else. The name he went by then is the same one he was admitted under. It was widely accepted as an accident, but the ballet master felt differently."

I haven't moved past the pictures. I sit there, quiet and motionless as I stare at the parts of Quentin's swollen, bruised face not captured by bandages. What the hell kind of accident would cause this?

"His name—"

I practically throw Michael's phone back at him. "No. Don't. I—I shouldn't have done this. I don't want to know."

Michael nods once, and silence chokes us both out.

Only when Arlo comes back into view, clearly pissed off and without the boys, do I quietly ask, "Do you think it was? An accident?"

Michael turns in his seat, staring at me dead on. "No."

Arlo opens the door and slides into the seat beside me with a great huff. That must be the fire breathing that Michael was talking about. "Silas left early, apparently. He is home, so there's that. I'm traveling back to deliver the lecture of a lifetime, but I wanted to check in with you. Can you come to the house tonight?"

"What a day to play hooky," I mutter, rubbing at my temple. "I suppose so. Why?"

Arlo braces his hands on his knees, staring at them resolutely. A travel stone rests between his palm and knee, one I haven't seen before. "I've been waiting, hoping that it wouldn't come to this. But I can see now how stupid I've been. It's time to get everyone on the same page. I— I have a plan. Or the beginning of one. But I need your help." He looks at me then, lips latching onto a grim smile. "Please."

Unintentionally, my professional mask falls into place. "I will be there. Text me, let me know what you need. I have a few visits I need to make first."

Arlo nods, face drawn and tired. "Thank you."

In a rush of cold wind and a flash of green, Arlo disappears from the towncar.

Michael says, "I was not aware of any plans this afternoon, Sir."

"I'd like to visit him, if you don't mind."

"I see." Michael dips his chin. "As you wish, Sir."

Michael won't let me out of his sight now, but I can't blame him. He stands a respectable distance away, but his presence here is undeniable. It feels like as much of a betrayal as the sentiment I'm about to spill onto the snow veiling Bartholomew's grave. I haven't been back here since the Game, a fact that has been gnawing away at me. I like to visit every month.

My knees are numb, so I bury my palms in the snow to regain that feeling of seeping, glacial pain. It's the least I can do.

"I have so much to say, and I don't know where to start. I don't even know if you can hear me, but I like to think that you can. Arlo says it's possible, and he hasn't led me astray. Alright, look, I'm just going to say it. I'm seeing someone."

Tears splash onto the snow. I wince, burrowing my nails deeper into the cold blanket covering my love. "The thing is, the more my heart opens to him, the more I feel you. But at the same time, I feel like I'm forgetting you. Your voice—" I choke on a sob, but I don't stop. I can't.

"I know that it was big and loud, full of light, but I can't remember the cadence to it, or what my name sounded like on your lips. And I—I like the way Quentin says my name. Lochian. I like the way he fiddles with his glasses when he's nervous, or the way his eyes light up when he goes on a tangent about something he loves. But most of all, I love the way he treats me like I matter because I simply exist, not because of who I am to others.

"So I guess what I'm trying to say is ... I need to let you go, and I think that I might be ready. You will always live within my heart, and when my time comes, I will search for you. I pray that perhaps by then, I will have found forgiveness in myself, and you."

I pull my hands out of the snow and try to steal a great gasp of air. I become entranced by the rolling blankets of gray above us, wasn't the sky clear before? The naked branches of the trees embracing the cemetery scratch at the clouds, trembling and swaying in the vengeful gusts. I find myself swaying too, back and forth, back and forth.

My heart claws at my ribs, and a moan escapes me at the intense, nauseating dizziness following closely on the heels of panic.

And then, I see him.

A hawk watches me from the lower limb of an old oak. The size of it is near impossible, its yellow feet could easily crush my skull. Its plumage is mostly brown and white, except for its tail. Each pink feather is complete with black bands near the tips. The bird tilts his head, watching me with big, amber eyes.

"I love you," I whisper.

The hawk spreads its wings and takes to the sky, crying out into the wind as it passes overhead. Tears spill down my face, unwilling to be restrained this time. Silently, Michael takes a knee beside me long enough to pull me into his arms. He carries me back to the towncar, then sits in the back and holds me until the storm passes.

Wayward Witches

Quentin

I awake to the biggest grump of all grumps tugging on my ear.

I shield my head with a pillow. "No, you can't make me! It's too early."

The old barn owl chirrups, pecking at my fingertips.

I groan, the sound muffled. "I don't want to."

Bosko pinches my side, which finally does the trick. I practically jump out of bed, cursing the entire way. "Ah, fine! I'm awake. You are the *worst* babysitter."

Bosko stares at me with a *'does it look like I care?'* look.

I stare back.

He wins.

I rub my hand over my face, wiping the sleep from my eyes. "I didn't think this was part of your job description." I reach for my phone, and Bosko continues to judge me. When I see the time, I sigh. "Okay, maybe it is. Almost four o'clock. I thought

Arlo would be ..." I fall silent as I check my messages, and a chill overcomes me.

Arlo (2:59 PM): come to witch house when you wake up and pack a bag. use the new stone on the kitchen counter to travel and do it outside the wards.

Linds (3:00 PM): Hey, did you get a message from Arlo? He wants us to meet at his house for some emergency? Let me know if you need a ride, I'm going to get Kitt.

Elochian (3:19 PM): Hello Quentin, this is Michael. Elochian isn't feeling well and cannot attend the meeting, but he trusts Tobias to act in his stead. I have already spoken with Arlo regarding the specifics, but I wanted to let you know on a personal level. Be safe.

Kitty (3:23 PM): We're on our way.

I set my phone down and rest my hands on my hips. "Wow. Okay." I look at Bosko. "Don't suppose you know what's going on."

He blinks, one eye closing before the other. Bosko opens his wings, then takes off through my open bedroom door. Arlo must have left that open last night. When I fell asleep he was still here, sitting beside my bed. Even with the front door locked, I feel more vulnerable with the bedroom door open.

"Right." I get to work packing a bag, and it feels like returning to my childhood home. Hollow and cold.

Kitt is quiet most of the drive, even more so than Lindsey and me. It's not often that Kitt takes out her old truck, but I always love riding in it. It's a brilliant apple red with thick white wall tires, built to trek over mountains. The old steam engine was replaced with solar, and the spacious inside is restored, supple leather.

But the joy I usually find in the truck is absent today. My stomach anchors me to the seat, nothing but dead weight. I stare out the window, watching Bosko as he flies overhead. I feel bad as he endures the wind, and I hope that the storm holds off until we get to the island.

I ended up packing two duffel bags, one for clothes, the other for my laptop and writing materials. I've done nothing but eat, sleep, and write lately, except for the one day a week I teach. There's no way I'm leaving behind one of the few things that gives me sanity, even if the only problems I'm solving are fictional ones. My bags ride in the seat beside me, and I absently fiddle with the handle of one.

I already miss my apartment. It felt like home right from the first night I stayed there, and that feeling has only grown as I've made it *mine*. I've never had that before. I don't want to stay at Arlo's. I don't want to keep hiding.

I sit up straighter in my seat, palming the new travel stone in my jeans pocket. Why did Arlo leave me a new one? For a second, I think about going back home. Forgetting all this.

I think about many things, actually. The what ifs build up in my head in anticipation of this meeting. But most of all, I think about Elochian. What is he doing right now? What does he think about, when he thinks of me? *Does* he think of me? Is he okay?

And before I know it, we're there. Kitt parks on the mainland side of the landbridge, a short distance from a protective grove of trees. Staring straight out the windshield, she whispers, "I won't lose him again. I can't."

"Hey." Lindsey reaches over and takes her hand. "It's going to be okay."

Kitt shakes her head. "How can you say that? You know what this is, right? He's calling us all over to listen to this big spiel on how he's going to fix everything, and he'll just smooth over some minor details like him being a martyr or something stupid like that. He can't—" Her anger dissolves, making way for whispering truth. "He can't die again."

Lindsey pulls Kitt closer to her, their bodies are awkwardly separated by the middle console but they make do. With her free hand, Lindsey reaches up and wraps her fingers around the base of Kitt's horn. She says, "So we don't let him. Okay? But give him a chance. If he was going to do something like that, he wouldn't have invited us over to tell us about it, don't you think?

"She's got a point," I say quietly. When Kitt glares at me, I shrug. "Let's hear him out."

Kitt rolls her eyes. "Let's hear him out, they say. Alright, fine. But if I need help strong-arming him, you better believe that I'm calling on you two."

"Sounds fair to me," Lindsey says. Kitt sighs, then rubs her horn against Lindsey's forehead. Lindsey's hand falls away, and she smiles enough for all three of us.

I agree, and the three of us get out of the car. We make the trek to the cottage side by side, and no one comments on the fact my bags are still in the truck. The landbridge is cleared of snow, and the river runs freely a good distance out, but it's frozen along the banks. The receding sun threatens the bruised horizon, but it's not even though it's not even five yet.

Winter is my least favorite of the seasons, but it's more toler-able here than back west. There you're stuck inside for months on end, the days dark and a hundred degrees below zero. Why people decided to populate Agia is beyond me, but that's humanity I suppose. Tell someone they can't do something, and watch what happens. At least there's snow and partial sun here, making the bitter and short days worth it.

When we make it to the house, we find everyone except for Arlo waiting in the glitter dusted dining hall. Arlo bought a new table, and seeing how there weren't many chairs to begin with, he commissioned a full set, ten fit for winged beings, and ten with highbacks. Caspian sits at the head of the eighteen foot table in a highback chair, his wheelchair within arm's length. Tobias sits at his right in a low backed chair, his wings spread out in a relaxed position behind him. They break their quiet conversation at our arrival, nodding in acknowledgement.

Finnegan sits at Caspian's right, his hands neatly folded in his lap and a manila folder on the table in front of him. He nods to us, then turns his attention to Dusan.

Gowan sits across from him, lost in thought as thorns grow and recede along her cheeks. She doesn't seem to notice us, or anyone else, for that fact.

Doc quietly keeps her company, and they fidget with a massive stack of papers before them. They nod at us and smile tightly.

And last, but not least, are the dragons. Dusan and Idina sit beside Finnegan, poised and beautiful as they leaf through one of the books they gifted Arlo, a personal journal he decided to keep. Finnegan watches as they flip through the pages, his curiosity evident.

A banner hangs in the archway separating the kitchen from the enormous dining hall, a bright and colorful thing that seeps glitter onto everyone in a twenty foot radius. *'Happy Birthday Dad'* is written in a beautiful, glitter-blanketed script, and my heart stumbles.

I forgot that it's Arlo's birthday.

By the way Kitt's tail stops swishing back and forth when she looks at the message, I suspect that she did too. Lindsey rests a hand on her shoulder, silently urging her on. Kitt doesn't move, only asks, "Where's Arlo?"

Caspian gives her a dry look. "Said he needed some air."

Quickly, I say, "I'll go get him."

Kitt raises an eyebrow, and her tail does that snappy thing it does. After a hard moment, she says, "Make it quick."

I dart out of the house before conversation begins again. Air comes much easier after I step outside, burning my lungs as I suck it in. I don't know why I feel like this. It's only a missed birthday, it's not a big deal. What am I even upset about?

Is this what Elochian feels like when he has a hard time? Like he's suffocating?

I focus on the snow my boots crunch through as I walk, the frozen air sawing in and out of my lungs. The willows are heavy with snow, and the brush rows and fallen logs are frosted with mounds of powder. By the time I make it to Thatch's beach, I feel somewhat better. Arlo studies the river with his back to me. His aura is calm and content instead of the usual grief and chaos I find when he's out here.

Bosko rests on the witch's shoulder, his feathers fluffed up and beak hidden in his breast. Arlo wears a thick isle-knit sweater and jeans, both tainted with silver glitter. His curls lift in the temperamental gusts, and as I step up beside him, I notice a new handsome dusting of dark hair along his jaw.

When he notices I'm staring at him, he tilts his head. "What?"

I chuckle, gesturing to his outfit. "Just admiring your pizazz."

He scoffs. "*Pizazz*? I call it biological warfare."

"O—kay, but seriously. What the fuck's going on?"

Arlo shakes his head, sighing. "Um, well. I had a meeting with Gaia this morning, and it … went good, and bad. So I went to get Silas, only to find he's not at the castle. So I get back home, all pissed off, only to find Felix and Silas covered in glitter and glue, with a cake in the oven to boot. They wanted to surprise me. Felix pretended to be sick so he could stay home and decorate." He glances over at me, a green twinkle in his otherwise golden eyes. "He called me Dad. Felix did, I mean."

I smile. "Aw, Arlo. That must feel good. Also, Happy Birthday."

"Thank you. I know I need to go back. I just … I needed a minute." He turns to go, but I take his arm. He looks down at my hand, confused.

I let him go. "I have something to tell you, Arlo, and I don't think it can wait. I should've told you sooner, I know … but I didn't."

"Okay," he says slowly. "What's going on?"

I exhale a big breath. "I … I think I know what's going on with Felix."

He looks at me, confused. "With Felix? What do you mean?"

I tell him my theory about Felix, and my meeting with Archeon. The longer I talk, the deeper his frown becomes. When I'm finished, he says nothing. He turns his hard stare back out to the water. After a few minutes, actual *minutes*, of unbearable silence, I say, "I didn't know how to tell you, and I didn't even know if I was right. But it's a good thing that Archeon agreed to help, right?"

Evenly, but with just as much passion as if he'd yelled, he says, "You should've told me sooner. I could've—I would've kept them home. He's a target, and I've just provoked the person who wants to hurt me more than anything else in life, or death, for that matter. I can't—what do I do? Hide him here?"

"You provoked Leon when you killed him eight years ago."

Arlo glares at me. "Not helping."

"Well, it's true. Just because you've been hiding and biding your time doesn't mean he has. You're right, I should've told you, but I— I kind of thought you knew, too. Did you not even suspect? He's so powerful, Arlo. But ... the Castle *is* safe. It's under your protection. Don't take that away from him, he's already had so much taken."

"I know, but ..." Arlo rubs the back of his neck, dropping his head. He whispers, "I'm so scared, Quentin. I barely kept myself alive last time, and people were lost because of me. How can I keep everyone safe? Keep the kids safe? Loch says I'm not alone, but he doesn't get it. You said it yourself, Leon has been after me. Maybe—"

"Don't you *dare* finish that sentence. You know that's not the answer. You'd give yourself up, and he'd still kill us all."

"You're right. You're right."

"I may not understand, but I *am* here for you. We all are."

"I know." He slings an arm around my shoulder, giving me a half hug. "What I did to deserve you, I have no idea. Thank you for asking Arche for help. Thank you for being there for me."

I smile at him. "Of course." My smile fades, and I clear my throat. "Have you heard from Elochian? Michael said he wasn't able to come."

"He came with me to Gaia's this morning, I think the whole ordeal there probably took a lot out of him. I know he wanted to be here, that he wanted to be here with you."

I nod, chewing on my bottom lip.

"What?"

I shake my head. "He said all these things to me last night, Arlo. Such beautiful and promising things. But I'm so messed up in my head, and I can't help but wonder ..." I trail off, my heart heavy and cold.

Arlo allows a few moments to pass, and when it's obvious I'm not going to spill any more truths, he says, "Be patient with him."

I shoot him a look. "I can be patient. It's not that. It's just—I told myself I wouldn't do this again. Fall so fast, and for pretty words."

A sad smile plays at Arlo's lips, and he rests a hand on my shoulder. "Loch's not the same as anyone else you've been with, and you know that. You told him you were in it for the long haul, can't back out now."

"I don't *want* to back out."

"Then what *do* you want?"

I grumble and take off my glasses, scrubbing at my face with my free hand.

"What's that?" Arlo asks.

Glasses in hand, I cut through the air. "I want to spend every day with him! I want to be there when he gets home at the end of a long day. I want him to be there when I need to soundboard ideas. I want to wake up beside him, and stay in bed with him all day. I want him to want me half as much as I do him, because I'm tired of being the guy who makes a fool of himself over some guy who doesn't even love me back. Some guy who doles out words of affection and his attention like it's a reward I have to earn!"

Arlo pulls me into a deep, brutal hug. One of his hands tugs on my hair, gentle but unyielding. He shakes me a little and says, "*Stop* it. Stop it right now. Elochian is not River. And you are not the same person that you once were, either. You don't deserve what happened to you, but regardless of that fact it *did* change you. You are loyal, steadfast, and outspoken. I feel sorry for any man who dares to wrong you, Quentin Matsdotter, but I don't believe Elochian will *ever* be one of them."

I grip handfuls of his jacket and bury my face in his chest, unable to say anything in fear of breaking apart further. The wind thrashes us we hold onto the other, becoming colder and colder by the minute. Before pulling away from Arlo's warmth, I whisper, "Will I ever be able to trust my gut again?"

Arlo rests his chin on my head. "Yes. I think you will. Until then, I'll be here."

Despite my protests, Arlo insists that I sit with him at the head of the table. I feel like I'm sitting in Thatch's chair, occupying the space that should be his. If not him, then Caspian, or Kitt. Sitting beside him, staring at all of our friends gathered around the table, the weight of the past few months we've spent together is more present than ever. He's my best friend, and I know now that I'm his, too.

Besides, if I didn't sit with Arlo, who would?

Kitt has Lindsey.

Caspian has Tobias.

Doc? Gowan? The dragons?

Finnegan is ... he's not a friend, but the ease at which he interacts with those gathered suggests he could be. He has a habit of staring at Arlo, which makes me settle in my place a little bit easier. This is my place, not his.

Arlo clears his throat and stands, bracing his hands on the table. He says, "I'm not sure how to start. I guess when it comes right down to it, I need help. I've asked you because you're my friends, my family, and I want to keep you safe. But I can't—it can't be like last time. It was my own fault, I know, but not this time. This time, we're going to stand together. But you have a choice, so if for any reason you don't want to be part of this, please tell me now. I understand."

"And what is *this* exactly, Arlo?" Finnegan asks, even though he knows damn why we're here. Leave it to reporters to be dramatic.

Arlo straightens, crossing his arms over his chest. "A rebellion. The uprising of the AWO and NOJ happening at the same time as Leon's return is no coincidence. I think Leon has a puppet in at least one of the groups, and he's using them to do his dirty work. Earlier today, I stepped into the Veil and found Leon there. He could have had me then, but he let me go. He's waiting for something.

"I don't know why, but we needed to be prepared for him to make a move at any moment. It's time for me—for *us*, to take him seriously. I cannot fight on two fronts, hell I'm not sure if I can even fight on one. There are so many spirits gathered on his side, and so many people afraid of us, of witches. So, I think the best course of action is to divide and conquer. Which is where you all come in."

Idina asks, "And how are you so sure that he has an insider in one of these hate groups, other than the 'coincidence' of it?"

Arlo glances at me, uncertain. I tilt my head, confused.

He says, "I *don't* know if he's in one of them for sure, but I do know he *is* possessing a willing body, and he's in Levena. They broke through my wards last night. I don't know who, exactly, it's too early to tell, but it was his magick signature, without a doubt. If we don't find Leon before this becomes a late stage possession, it'll be tricky to exorcize him. Early on, the original soul still inhabits the body, and the malevolent soul resides in the Veil, feeding on the person's spirit like a parasite. Over time, they completely eat away their host. When the original spirit is gone, the invader can fully break free from the Veil and have total autonomy, with a stitched together soul of sorts."

I stare up at Arlo, shell shocked. "Arlo—are you—" I close my mouth, unsure what the fuck to say.

He stares down at me, and nods.

Tobias begins speaking, but I can't hear him. I stare down at my hands clutching my shaking knees. That's how Arlo's wards were broken. By the only person stronger than Arlo, the only person that knows Arlo more intimately than anyone else in this dimension.

That's why he asked so many times about River being a witch.

He isn't one, but the ghost possessing him is. Leon, the fabled Witch Killer, is possessing the most evil man I have ever met. How does that even *work*?

I want to ask, but now isn't the time. The time would have been back on the beach, when we were alone. Did he wait because of how I kept Felix from him? Or did he forget?

Arlo's hand rests on my shoulder, and he squeezes gently as he talks. I sigh, uncurling my fingers, and focus on breathing. No, he didn't mean to hurt me.

But it still does. Hurt, that is.

Arlo releases me and turns away from the table, picking up a big box on the floor. He hefts it onto the table. "This brings me to my next point. I have built an armory, or the beginnings of one, anyway. I've imbued spells into items tailored specifically to each of you, and there's enough one way travel stones for everyone. They're linked to bring you to the island, in case of emergency."

"You have an armory," Kitt says flatly, staring at the box suspiciously. "In there."

Opening the top flaps, Arlo asks, "Quentin, could you help me?"

On shaky knees, I rise from my chair and join him. He takes out a small sack tied off with hemp string, finished with a small wooden tag. It's heavy, and I wonder how something so small could hold so much life saving potential. The first one is for Caspian, and I pass it down the line. Only once everyone has a bag in front of them, including our surprise guests, does Arlo set the box aside and sit down. I do the same, fiddling with the string on my own bag.

He's already given me two different travel stones, the first one destroyed and the second one a solid weight in my pocket. And now a third? Not to mention the necklace he gave me ages ago, which is supposed to ward off bad intent. I chuckle a little to myself. Could use a recharge.

Arlo says, "Alright, this stuff is for emergencies, and I *can* make more, but it's time consuming, not to mention draining. We can discuss the contents on a one on one basis afterwards."

"This is why your Hedge inventory has been running low," I say, thinking of Arlo's booth back at the cafe. What I don't say aloud is, *'this is why you've been so tired. It wasn't the stress and lack of sleep, or not only that.'*

He nods. "My magick is needed elsewhere, so my business isn't going to be a focus anymore."

"But what about the people who rely on your charms? Like Ren?" Gowan asks, her quiet finally broken.

"I will make time for my regulars, but that's it." Arlo shrugs, gaze downcast. "It's alright. I haven't had great business lately anyway."

Silence descends, and uneasy looks are shared across the table.

Gowan clears her throat. "I want to be part of this, Arlo, and I'll do what I can, but Iris and me ..." She dips her head and flowers bloom across her crown, pale leaves unfurl along with them. She looks back up, granting us with a shy smile. "We're starting a family. In twelve months, there will be little fae in the world."

The room shifts from tense, cautious hope, to surprised joy. Congratulations shower Gowan, in the form of words and hugs. I find myself in the hugging department, and when I pull away from her, my eyes are wet with happiness and worry.

"I'm so happy for you," I whisper.

"Thanks, Q." She holds me close, and only flowers cover her exposed skin, not thorns.

Arlo takes advantage of the break in conversation, temporarily leaving the room. He comes back with an enormous cake missing a few slices, then goes back for plates and silverware. Quietly, he doles out the cake once inscribed with the words, '*Happy Birthday Dad,*' to everyone gathered. When Arlo gives Gowan her piece, he says, "I'm happy for you, Flowers. We'll talk after, okay?"

I'm temporarily distracted from the moment by my vibrating phone. I take it out of my pocket, and smile a little at the message waiting for me.

Elochian (6:02 PM): Are you okay? Are you with Arlo?
Me (6:03pm): Yes and yes. Are you okay?

Finnegan pokes at his cake. He says, "You know, if you truly want to reunite the witches, then you need to start in the End. The witches need more help than most, which isn't a bad thing, but Nightingale just doesn't have enough resources for everyone."

"What do you suggest?" Arlo asks, taking his seat once more, sans cake.

Finnegan shrugs. "Shelter, for starters. They're the first to be turned down if any of the supported housing units open up. Which is a big if. Once people get into those places, they usually don't leave. Witches are seen to have advantages other people don't, which in the community's eyes, makes them less deserving of assistance programs. And this isn't doesn't even touch on the mental health services they require, or unregistered witches that can't get any formal assistance. They are the Nightingale's priority, but even she can admit it's not enough."

Gowan says, "It sounds like you two are close."

Finnegan snorts. "I would hope so. She's my mother."

Nauseating jealousy forces me to put my fork down, the once luxurious chocolate cake and peanut butter frosting now sour. How nice it must be to be friends with your mother. I say, "Blood doesn't mean anything."

A tense pause follows, then Finnegan simply shrugs it off. "True."

"Well, you did want to help wayward witches, Lo," Caspian says, cleaving through the tension.

"But how many are there?" Kitt asks, glancing between Finnegan and Arlo. "Probably way more than you can fit here."

"Unregistered? It's hard to say, at least a hundred that I'm aware of. There's twenty I can think of that would do well here, and you already know a few of them. The rest need more help than even you can give, I think. But the others, they would be a valuable asset to your community."

Arlo frowns at the word 'asset.'

Doc taps a claw on the table. They say, "Perhaps you could connect me with your Nightingale. I am happy to help in any capacity, pro bono."

Finnegan considers the *behema*, then nods. "I will."

To Arlo, Doc says, "I have news. Should I start?"

"Of course. Go ahead."

Doc sighs, readjusting their papers. "I'm afraid that Otolon has broken out of confinement, and Dean disappeared from the hospital without a trace. Nim notified me of both counts and has been keeping their ear to the ground, but they haven't heard or seen any evidence of either of them thus far. However, I think it's safe Leon has successfully procured, and hidden them."

Arlo freezes, and Kitt mirrors his stillness.

"Who are they?" I ask, but the question is overrun by Kitt's.

Kitt asks, "When? When did this happen?"

Doc's lips curl back from their teeth. "I only found out this morning, but I believe the break outs simultaneously took place last night."

"When someone with Leon's energy was poking around the cafe ..." I say, trailing off. "So who are they?"

When Arlo doesn't speak, transfixed by his hands curled into fists in his lap, Caspian carefully answers me. "All of Leon's allies are dead, except for Dean and Otolon. Dean was his right hand man, did all his dirty work. Otolon was ... he was the scientist, the one who figured out how to use witch's blood. Dean surrendered on claims of insanity, and Otolon was put into executive confinement. The only way Otolon could've gotten out was if someone *let* him out, same for Dean."

Arlo gestures to Cas abruptly. "How soon before we can build?"

Caspian stares at Arlo for a moment with an 'are you serious' glare, then goes through his papers on the table. He holds one up, looking closer at what I realize are blueprints. "I don't know, another month or five, at least. It's not just expanding the house, you're going to need places for all the familiars." He glances at Finnegan, then back to Arlo. "You're seriously considering this? Inviting twenty strangers to come live with you?"

Finnegan raises a hand. "I wouldn't recommend anyone unsafe, if that makes you feel better, Arlo."

Oh, we're on a first name basis now?

I scoff. "Even if they're the best people in the world, throwing twenty witches together and expecting their spirits to co-exist peacefully is wishful thinking."

Everyone looks at me. Now I've done it.

"What do you mean?" Tobias asks.

"That's—just—a lot of magick under one roof. You've seen—" I glance around the room, making sure there's no sign of Felix around. He and Silas have a penchant for eavesdropping. "You've seen how Felix's magick reacts with those around him. It's unstable because he's young, but magick can be unstable for other reasons, too. Stress. And I'm sorry, but if I was one of those witches and was given a brand new, fancy place to live, I'd still be stressed. Traumatized. It's a lot to go through, to process. Multiply that experience by twenty, and it's going to be too much."

"That's a good point," Tobias says. "But you don't have to do all twenty at once, and if you do decide to do this, you could do interviews or something of the sort. In my opinion, besides the fact that it's the right thing to do, it could make this place impenetrable."

"In time, the land here could become a reservoir," Idina says, looking at me curiously. "Isn't that right, Mr. Matsdotter?"

"Y—yes. With enough witches residing on it, for a long enough period of time. I—I don't know how long that would be, though." I duck my head, unable to meet her intense gaze. Does she know there's *already* a reservoir here, hopefully sleeping upstairs?

"I want to talk to them, if nothing else, Finnegan," Arlo says. "My plan is to connect with as many witches as possible, invite them to the island for a feast where they can be themselves. And then, if they are open to it, I want to invite them to Elochian's ball. He's already given me permission, and is gathering witches of the demon persuasion. We want to make a peaceful, united front to show that we aren't afraid, and that we belong. So, with that being said, Tobias, are you able to do the same with the angels, search for any witches that might be interested?"

Tobias nods. "The *shomer* ceremony is coming up, I'll be meeting Andromeda in person and can talk to her about it."

Arlo bows his head. "Thank you. Dusan, do you think you can talk to Josse?"

Dusan chuckles quietly. "You think because I'm a dragon, that old lizard will let me in that clocktower of his?"

"No, but I have a friend that can get you in. His droid was manufactured by Josse a few decades back, and is the only person I know that Josse will see. Then, you just need him to listen."

Idina smiles. "Josse and I were good friends back in the day. I'll go with her."

"Thank you," Arlo says, sounding more tired than ever.

It goes like this.

Lindey is in charge of tracing Daniel Kavelli's finances, along with Carina Wells, who unsurprisingly happens to be the leader of the AWO.

When Arlo didn't give Kitt a job, she proposed a new exhibition at the museum focusing on the Descendants of Dinphine, the original witches, using Thatch's journals to tie it together. Surprisingly, Arlo gave her permission. I suspect the love letters between Thatch and Henix won't be a part of that exhibit.

Caspian is in charge of preparing the house, drafting plans and arranging the labor. Arlo said even if we don't accept new witches, he wants to have enough room to house as many of us as possible, in case of a lockdown or something. I do think he's already made up his mind about the witches. He did long ago when Thatch planted the seed.

A home for lost witches, so no one would have to go through what Arlo did.

Tobias and Elochian will be gathering allies in their clans, and investigating potential leads on any celestial AWO and NOJ supporters to watch out for. They will provide safe haven for witches in either the Manor or the Palace, for now. According to Tobias, Elochian seemed worried and excited when he was talking about breaking tradition, inviting witches into his manor. Tobias certainly seemed to be excited, and less nervous about ruling the angels than he was before.

Dusan and Idina will meet with Josse, and Idina mentioned that she may speak with her tribe back home. The thought of an entire flock of dragons coming to aid our cause is amazing, and terrifying all at the same time. Idina took great interest in Kitt's plan, and offered to collaborate with her on the project when she returned.

'My family was there, after all.'

Doc offered to investigate the missing doctor, a task Arlo gratefully laid at their feet. Despite the fact I wasn't the one experimented on, a chill runs down my spine at the idea of a madman like that running free. Especially if he's reunited with Leon.

Finnegan will continue to work as a liaison for the Nightingale, and the witches in the North End. I volunteered to go with him and talk with witches since I'm familiar with that part of town, but Arlo said no.

"I need you here, Quentin."

"For what? Everyone else has a job but me."

We huddle on the couch, our bones slowly being warmed by the fire. Everyone else has gone home, except for Kitt and Lindsey who I last saw talking to Finnegan in the dining room. They're waiting for me, but I don't know why Finnegan is still here.

Arlo sighs. "Because I do."

"That makes no sense."

"I—I just need help around here. With the boys."

"No you don't."

"But I do. Silas wants to start a band, and Felix wants a garden. I'm going to be busy preparing, and school will be over soon. I need someone I trust to watch over them."

"We are *literally* fighting your archnemesis, who may or may not be possessing my evil ex-boyfriend, and you want me to babysit."

"Yes."

I throw my hands up, slumping back against the couch. "You are impossible."

"Does that mean you'll do it?"

I grumble for a minute. I know what he's doing. To him, I'm a weak, powerless human. I'm a walking kick me sign, all I've done is bring trouble to our doorstep. Best to just shove me away and hide me. My thoughts drift to the bags he gave everyone, the time and energy he spent—*spends*—in keeping us all safe. Maybe for a little while, I'll make his job easier. For now.

Pretending to still be put out, I say, "Be your nanny? I guess so, but I have conditions. I'm not living here."

Arlo's lip quirks, but he says nothing.

"I'm not running anymore. I've come too far."

"Okay." Arlo smiles, pulling me into a hug. "Okay. Thank you, Q." Before pulling away, he shakily asks, "Can I ask you for one more favor?"

"Sure."

"Can you stay here tonight? Please? I already made up the guest bedroom, and Felix is really excited to see you. And I think Silas was planning on making pancakes. I can—"

I pull back, giving him a smile. "Yeah Arlo, I'll stay. My bags are packed anyway."

"What? But, you said—"

I shrug. "I didn't know I was done running, until I did it again."

Sweet, Secret Relief

Elochian

Wind tainted with ice shreds my cheeks and tangles my hair. Begrudgingly, I glance over at Michael. He walks with his hands in his pockets, not a care in the world. When he catches me looking, he smirks.

"Cold, Sir?"

"Get it over with."

"Hm?"

"You were right."

"I said no such thing, Sir. I merely suggested that heading out during a freak storm might not be pleasant, especially when Mr. Matsdotter is clearly safe."

"There we go, that's the warm condescension I was looking for." A few paces after the midpoint of the landbridge, I add, "I just need to see him for myself. I had—I didn't sleep well."

Becoming more serious, Michael asks, "Have the terrors returned, Sir?"

I focus on the ice patches ahead, thick in the well trodden valleys of the road. "It was a new one," I say carefully. "Everything was different, and it was—it was Quentin instead. The end result was the same, I—" I suck in a breath, unable to fully voice the horror that was Quentin's mangled body in my hands.

The worst part of it was his smile, bloody and genuine. With broken, jagged fingers, he caressed my face and told me he loved me.

Michael says, "We're here."

I look up, squinting through the ice and wind. We've long since cleared the initial tree line, and are now face to face with the cottage hosting lit candles in its numerous windows. Bosko flies overhead, then disappears into the trees. Michael rests a hand on my shoulder, and I look over at him.

We stare at each other, speaking without words.

Him, promising unending loyalty and a desire to not only keep me safe, but Quentin too. Whether it's because of who Quentin is to me, or the fact he cares for the man on a personal level, I can feel it. He thinks of Quentin as ours.

And then there's me, finally making a godsdamned decision.

The front door opens, interrupting us. Quentin stands there, dressed in fine slacks and a thick turtleneck. The cuffs of the billowing sleeves are pushed up to his elbows, and his fingers are dusted in white. His hair is wet, combed back in that way that makes him look professional. He's got his wood framed glasses on again, and for some reason that thought replays in my head.

He breaks into a smile upon seeing me, overwhelming every thought and worry. He moves towards me, and I lurch forward in response. We meet in the middle, and it's so effortless the way his arms settle around my neck, mine around his waist. Air escapes me in a harsh exhalation, but I don't care. I hold him tight, lifting him off the ground a little with the force of my relief.

"Lochian," he murmurs against my shoulder.

"I have a question for you Quentin, and I need to ask you now." I blurt out, pulling back far enough to see his face. Hair and ice blows in front of my eyes, but I can't let him go. Not yet.

He blinks, eyes wide. "Oh. Okay."

"I'm throwing a masquerade ball next month. For Tobias. Well, partly for Tobias, but the point is, I was wondering if you might want to go. With me."

Quentin inhales sharply, lips parting.

Quickly, I add, "As my date. It would be very proper and public, and with guaranteed bouts of societal torture. Everyone will want to know who you are. I've never ... I've never had a public relationship. But I would like to. With you."

He stares at me. "But we haven't ..." He trails off, opting for a soft smile instead. "Yes. I would love that."

"Quentin ... you can be honest with me."

He shrugs, cheeks darkening. "Alright ... I'm not sure how I feel about that, considering we haven't been on an actual date yet. Don't get me wrong, I love the time we spend together back at the cafe, but I don't know if I would consider any of it a ... romantic date."

"Oh," I say, taken aback for a moment. I shake my head, laughing at myself. "If I could borrow some of your honesty, I have to admit that to me, our time together is—I don't view it as platonic." I run my hands down his arms, and my fingers slide against his. When he squeezes once, snaring me, I have to remember to breathe.

I whisper, "Dot, this here ... it sets me on fire. Dancing with you? It is only by Soleyar's favor that I didn't burn up into nothing more than ash and teeth. I haven't felt this in a long, *long* time. I don't know what to do with it. With *you*."

"Oh. Lochian, I'm not ..." He clears his throat, glancing around. We're alone, accompanied only by a crystal dusted forest. Michael must have gone inside, they're nowhere to be seen. Quentin licks his lips, and I'm distracted by how dry they are. "This is new to me, too. I'm not used to being with someone who—well, I'm just used to being wanted for other things. *That* being the focus."

"Sex?"

He nods quickly. "To be clear, that's not what I'm asking of you. I—I need to relearn a lot of things. I've never really, uh ... been in a good relationship, one could say." He winces, looking away. At the pinched look on his face, my wings go very, very still. I stare at this beautiful, wonderful man, wondering how such a thing is possible. Who could ever mistreat him?

Who indeed?

Instead of leading him further into bad memories, I bring him back to the moment. To us. I lift his hands to my lips, pressing a gentle kiss to the knuckles of each one. In a whisper, I admit a secret to him, and myself. "I think I want you to. Ask me. Not today, but someday. But it might not be off the table for me, as long as it's not off the table for you."

A chuckle bubbles in my throat at Quentin's stunned expression, but I don't allow it to surface. He shakes his head a little, staring at his knuckles. "I ... yes. Not off the table for me, either. But I'm still yours, Lochian. Either way."

His eyes rise to my lips, and my heart stalls.

I try to force it into motion. I can do this. I can. I'm ready.

But he pulls back, keeping one of my hands firmly captured in his. He nods to the house and says, "Come on, I'm surprised you haven't started freaking out about my wet hair yet."

"Well, now that you mention it." I chuckle, ignoring the sweet, secret relief calming my panicked heart. "You'll catch a cold like that, you know."

"There it is." He laughs, tugging me towards the house. Before we cross the threshold, he stops abruptly and leans close to my side, dropping his voice to a whisper. "Um, be mindful of Silas, 'kay?"

"Is he alright?"

Quentin nods quickly. "Yeah, fine. Come on. Have you eaten?"

We step into the witch's house, and I sigh. There's something about Arlo's innermost wards that make you feel like you've just come home after a long day on the road. The entire island is warded, but the house even more so. Altogether they are ten times more powerful than the shields surrounding the cafe, and I wonder how Arlo does it. Where does his power come from? How is he so *endless*?

"Lochian?" Quentin asks, brows furrowed.

"Hm? Oh, um—"

"He had more important things to do than eat this morning, dear Quentin," Michael says, passing into the big den just before we do. They balance four plates of pancakes, somehow managing to serve them up on the coffee table without a fuss. He straightens, planting his hands on his hips. He scrutinizes Quentin and me. "And what's your excuse?"

Quentin laughs. "You're nosy, aren't you? If you must know, I was inspiring the next generation. Thanks for ratting me out, *Arlo*."

The witch laughs, putting his hands up. "I ratted out myself, who do you think the fourth plate is for?"

"Keeps it from getting wasted." Silas grumbles, sitting beside Arlo on the big couch. His usually wild hair is braided away from his face, although the plaits are sleep worn and some white tendrils have escaped from them. Hypertrophic burn scars cover the right half of his face, and his throat is more of the same but deeper, more vicious. His eyebrow and eyelashes are missing on that side, but they are whiter than snow on the left, same as his hair.

None of us really know Silas' background, except for maybe Arlo, but he hasn't shared any details. This, however, sheds some light on things.

What surprises me more than anything is that he's wearing one of Thatch's hoodies. I can *feel* the remnants of the immortal's energy in the threads. It's a little big on the kid, the hems on the sleeves are tattered and worn, but it fits him in a way I don't think it could anyone else.

"It wasn't going to get *wasted*, you know I eat breakfast late," Arlo says, taking his plate.

"It's good manners to eat when someone's cooked for you," Felix quietly adds, curled up on the other side of Arlo, his knees drawn up to his chest.

"Couldn't have said it better myself." Michael sits down on the little couch like he owns the place, on the end closest to Felix. The two couches form an L of sorts, sharing a long slab of wood which serves as an industrial style coffee table.

Quentin gives me a quick, chastised grin before sitting down beside Michael, pulling me down with him. Reluctantly, and with a little frown that I adore, Quentin releases my hand. He offers me my plate before taking his own. While his are drowned in syrup, my own are thoroughly buttered and dusted with a hint of powdered sugar. Arlo's are smeared with butter and peanut butter, a dripping mess.

I bite back a little smile, glancing over at Michael. He winks at me, then goes back to eating his own breakfast. Or snack, more like. Michael dutifully eats oatmeal and fruit every morning, well before I'm even awake. He points a forkful at Silas and asks, "Where'd you learn to cook like this?"

Silas shrugs, staring resolutely at his plate. "Dunno. Experimented a lot with what there was in the cupboards. When I was younger."

"Think you'll make a career out of it?"

Silas lifts a shoulder again. "I don't think so."

"Fair enough," Michael says, and the conversation rolls further into something like normalcy.

We talk about small things.

The glittery remnants of the previous day which hide in every nook and cranny of the house, something Arlo will be cleaning for months. Quentin's knee presses against mine.

Bosko's bad habit of bringing dead mice inside. My traitorous hair falls down in the small space between his elbow and mine, which bump and collide as we eat.

Felix's desire to start a garden in the spring, he wants to be able to personally stock Arlo's new hedge kitchen. Quentin has a cold, he sniffles and steals air through his mouth between bites.

I set my plate down and lean back as far as my wings will allow. Carefully, and ever so slowly, I rest my hand above the small of his back and below his shoulder blades. Neutral ground. His muscles tense under my fingers as they fan out, then relax when my palm settles against his spine.

Both kids tease Quentin about his travel chalk, which he used on the new board in the kitchen. We skip around the Big Things. Arlo and I talked for a long time before I came over. In between assuring me that Quentin was safe, he filled me in on last night's events. The roles everyone is to play. Quentin's revelation about Felix, and Archeon.

Lastly, he asked for advice about inviting unregistered witches into his home.

I told him every witch off the streets was one less that Leon could steal, torture, and twist. I also told him if he wouldn't do it, I would. I would break the rules, and invite witches into Adrastus Manor. Tobias's quick agreement made me feel even more secure about my decision.

I was never taken. I was never targeted. But my people were. The day Arlo and I met was not a happy one. I knew of him, saw him on the news. But we never actually met, not until he won and found the lost witches. Or what remained of them, that is. Twenty-six of them were demons, and fifty-nine were angels, Tobias among them. *Fifty-nine.*

I failed the celestials of Levena. The witches. I had the room. I could've sheltered them. Protected them. And I didn't, because I played it safe, and followed the rules. I listened to my aunt. Witches were deemed dangerous. Unstable. It was a risk we couldn't take. We did what we could, but it wasn't enough. To this day, there has never been a witch in Adrastus Manor.

There has *never* been a witch in Adrastus Manor.

And now I'm about to introduce witches onto its grounds, dozens of them at least. For the first time, I wonder what kind of trouble I'm brewing. Then again, change doesn't come quietly, does it?

Arlo walks me to the door. The ice storm has given way to blinding sun, which makes everything glitter and glisten.

Quentin and Michael are already outside, saying their goodbyes to each other. I watch them, lost in my thoughts. Michael gestures wildly and Quentin laughs, throwing his head back. Air catches in my lungs, and I'm reminded of the ghost of his knee against mine.

Arlo rests a hand on my shoulder. I look up at him, and he stares down at me. A moment passes, quiet and full of *something* just out of reach. Measuring each word like a grain of sand, he says, "He needs you."

"I—"

"Elochian, I need you to be the demon he needs you to be, or else—" Arlo's hand falls from my shoulder when he glances at Quentin and Michael, who are watching us now. He shakes his head, and gives me a half-smile. The look in his eyes betrays it, though. "Go on. We'll talk later."

I stare at the man for a second, then shuffle closer.

He raises a brow, thrown off guard.

Unfettered, I pull him into a hug.

It's awkward at first, then his arms wrap around my shoulders, above my wings, and he holds me tight. He laughs a little. "I think this is the first time we've done this."

"Quiet. You're ruining the moment." I squeeze around his middle. "We hugged the day after you came home from the hospital."

"Oh. Right."

He holds me just a little bit tighter, and we stay that way for a long minute. Then I let him go, and he waves halfheartedly to Michael before shutting himself inside the house. When I join them, Quentin asks, "What was that about?"

"Nothing."

Quentin and Michael exchange a look.

I groan. "He's stressed out. Isn't that what you're supposed to do when people are upset? Give them hugs?"

"That's what most people do," Michael says, leaving the, *'and you're a weirdo who doesn't do hugs,'* unsaid.

"Well, there you go."

Quentin smiles. "I'm sure it made him feel better. We did have a long night, we stayed up late doing some investigating. Finnegan has some good leads in the North End, there's a cluster of disappearances on the outskirts of the End, near Vieta Road."

"Finnegan was here? Late?"

"Because *that* was the point of that statement," Michael mutters.

Quentin frowns. "Yeah. Him and Arlo are pretty buddy-buddy, apparently."

"Double jealous," Michael adds, and we both glare at him. He laughs. "And this is when I say goodbye. Quentin, lovely to see you again."

Michael takes off in the direction of the landbridge before either of us can scold him. I sigh, rubbing my temple. "I'm sorry about him."

Quentin chuckles. "It's fine. So ..." He nudges a loose clump of snow with his boot. His hair falls over his eyes, and his cheeks are flushed against the cold. I swallow the fear rising in my throat, and reach for him.

A Careful, Tender Offering

Quentin

Elochian's cold fingers slide against my cheek, and his palm settles against my ear. The pads of his pointer and index fingers dig into my scalp, and his thumb sweeps across my temple once. His eyelashes are so long, thicker than any I've ever seen, and the tips of them turn gold under the rare sun. I find myself enraptured by them, by him.

He whispers, "I—I'd like to kiss you. Now. Would that be alright?"

I inhale sharply, and those watchful eyes darken in response. Can he hear my heart beating out of rhythm? With all my strength, I whisper back, "Y—yes, that would be alright."

Elochian nods slowly once, and he stares at me like I'm a chess board or something. He studies my eyes, my lips, and farther down to my throat before coming back again. My fingers twitch, and I take his free hand. His fingers tremble, and I steady them in mine, bringing them between us. His hair lifts on a stray breeze, and a curtain of it falls forward, blanketing our joined hands. I remain as still as I can, afraid that this moment is a dream I'll wake up from at any moment.

He leans closer, and his wings spread wide behind him. I'm distracted by them for a moment, they seem to grow not only in size, but color. Flashing through all the colors of the iridescent rainbow. The ink along his lower wings changes from black to gold in places, but I can't pay attention because he's right *there*.

I keep my eyes open as our noses brush, and Elochian does too. The aureate lines in his cheeks slash through the cold, alighting the small space between our faces. The light complexion on his face doesn't glow, but I don't care. His eyes are endless dark pools which beckon me into their syrupy depths. He exhales a shaky breath onto my lips, and for a moment we remain that way.

Breathing in the other.

His nose is cold against mine, and I find myself entering a meditative state, at peace with his face ever so close to mine. If nothing else, this moment would be enough to sustain me for the rest of my short life.

Elochian closes the distance, firmly pressing his lips against mine. For a few seconds that's all there is, mouths pressed together, lungs and hearts demanding more.

More.

Ever so slowly, I tilt my head and deepen the kiss, slotting my lips between his. Elochian releases a small sound of content, a whisper of a moan that is nearly lost to the trembling of his wings. He steals the air from my chest, and I go weak in the knees. He pulls me closer, keeping me grounded. His hand tightens around mine, whilst the other one curls into my hair. He does not offer me his tongue, and I do not seek it.

This is not a kiss of reckless abandon. It is not a kiss of desperation, or lust.

It is a kiss of promise. Of tentative hope, and the start of something new.

It is a careful, tender offering.

Elochian's lips leave mine, and his forehead rests against my own.

He says, "Oh."

I nod, chuckling breathlessly. "That was one hell of a kiss, sunshine."

He smiles, and there's a rare, wry curl to it. He leans back, rubbing my cheek. "Be ready at seven."

I blink, disoriented by the feeling of his fingers slipping from my hair and his boldness. "Tonight?"

Elochian's hand finally falls from my face, and my heart lurches in response. He says, "Yes, you made a very good point regarding our situation, and I must resolve it immediately. Unless you have plans ...?" His wings droop, and I have to fight a laugh, struck with the idea of a pouting cat.

"No, I don't have any plans. I'll be ready with bells on."

"Okay," he whispers. "Good."

I stay on the island until Archeon arrives, and even then I don't want to leave. It's not that I don't want to go home, or that I don't want to see Elochian tonight. But it's the first time I've felt protected since all this bullshit with River started, completely safe. I know I can't hide forever, but it's tempting. The gifts from Arlo are a comfort, at least.

A ring that can form a twenty-four hour shield which works against physical and magickal attacks.

A notebook that when activated, will dictate the events going on in the surrounding vicinity. It also has a code word that causes the thing to detonate. Because of course it does.

A pen charged with five offensive spells, charmed to work like a wand. It is my understanding that the attacks are similar to magick missiles, which increase in ferocity with each cast.

A small, wicked boot knife. There is no magick to it, but Arlo seemed to think having a blade on me would be a good idea. It only made me sick, but I didn't complain, considering he's right. There's a partner to the blade, one that can strap to a small holster on my thigh. Why I would need one *there* is beyond me.

And lastly, a bottle of enchanted ink, should I decide to take him up on his offer.

I stand in the hallway and watch the Rook family gathered inside the den, having done my part by making introductions. I don't know if it was because I expected Arlo and Archeon to go at it like feral cats or what, but the whole thing was kind of anti-climatic. They exchanged brooding hellos, and Arlo thanked the Teleth for coming.

Archeon had glanced at me and said, "Thank him, not me."

Now, he and Felix sit together on the big couch, while Silas and Arlo watch them from the smaller one. Archeon, or Mr. Mochizuki as Felix says, reaches into his vest pocket and retrieves a small, glass jar. He opens it, overturning its contents onto the coffee table. Seashells. Marbles. Coins. Silver beads. Wooden buttons. Tiny scraps of fabric and odd bits of thread. Teeth. Bone fragments.

Archeon wrinkles his nose, chewing his gum with renewed conviction. The other witches lean forward, curious, especially Arlo. He didn't have this when he was Felix's age, a teacher. Then again ... did he ever?

Archeon shifts his gaze to Felix, who snaps to attention. Archeon tilts his head, considering the boy. He says, "Tell me about yourself."

Felix blinks. He glances over at Arlo, who says nothing, only nods. He clears his throat, looking between Archeon and the bits on the table. "I—I can feel what other people are feeling. I can hear them, sometimes. Lately I—I've been moving stuff. Not when I mean to, though. If I try, it's—it doesn't work."

Archeon nods. "Right, but what about you?"

"Me?"

"Yes. Who are you? Who is Felix Rook?"

Felix sighs, releasing a breath bigger than he is. He's grown these past few months, both in height and meat on his bones, but he's still a kid. Quietly, he says, "I am a human. A boy. A witch. A—a son. A friend. I like plants, and video games. I'm not as brave as I'd like to be."

He reaches out to the table, then freezes, surprised at himself. Archeon gestures for him to go ahead, and he does. Felix picks up an old, worn disc that I belatedly recognize as a coin. He stares down at it, flipping it over in his fingers. "I'm powerful. I can feel it, trying to get out of my skin. It hurts sometimes, and it scares me."

I straighten from the archway I've been leaning against, stomach dropping. I haven't heard him talk like this before. Arlo takes Silas' hand, which tells me maybe he hasn't either, or he didn't expect Felix to talk about it.

Archeon picks up a tooth, studying it in the same fashion Felix does with his coin. After a moment, he asks, "Because of the pain?"

Felix looks up from his coin, enclosing it in his hand. "Pain? Pain doesn't last. Power? People with great power aren't—" His face twists, and he shakes his head. "I don't want it. I'm afraid it'll ... ruin me."

"It might." Archeon hums. "Or, it could save you. Power doesn't make you good or bad, it simply is. Given to someone with a heart like yours? I'd wager in this case it was a gift to the world, not a curse. You are the master of your magick, of your fear, of your *life*, Felix."

Felix wipes at his eyes, sniffing. He nods, but says nothing.

Archeon sets the tooth down with far more care than necessary. "I will speak no more on this for today, besides this. It is my belief the core of your problems lie in the fact your head and heart are of two different minds, and only when the fear is cleared from between them can you take hold of your magick, bend to your will. I can teach you how to manifest and direct your power, I can teach you how to shield yourself from the world and all its input, but what I *cannot* do is change what is in your heart."

He gestures to Felix's hand. "Do you know what you hold there?"

Felix shakes his head, uncurling his fingers to reveal the coin in his palm.

"Close your eyes, and listen to it."

Felix nervously glances at Arlo and Silas, which prompts Archeon to not quite startle, but it's close. Almost like he forgot we were all there. Archeon waves dismissively at Arlo, and me. "Go on. Let us work. Silas, you can stay."

Arlo's knuckles pale as he holds onto Silas' hand, but the younger witch doesn't seem bothered. Glancing between Silas and Felix, he asks, "Alright then?"

Silas shrugs, and Felix nods. Excellent communicators, these two.

We leave them be, and Arlo slides the massive doors on rails closed, providing the big den with privacy. He paces down the main hall, and I follow him. He sighs, running a hand through his hair. "That ... was not how I expected that to go."

I push my glasses farther up my nose. "Do you agree with what he said?"

He's quiet for a moment before saying, "I don't think he's wrong, and I wonder if it's my fault."

I take his hand, squeezing gently. "You're scared of someone else, not yourself."

He gives me a small, self-deprecating smile. "Who's to say I'm not?"

The cafe is the same as I left it, right down to the fear tainting the atmosphere. To say I'm disappointed is an understatement. I couldn't have this *one* thing to myself, could I? One small part of Levena that River hasn't poisoned.

For late afternoon it's busier than usual, and Helena stops me in a hurry before I can take off upstairs. She glances around before handing me a sheet of red paper covered in bold, black lettering. She says, "Some inspector came by this morning and left this on Arlo's case, I think he was hoping to seize the inventory, but it's been empty."

"Oh," I manage.

'*Due to a recent polinya outbreak, you must cease and desist all sale and manufacture of uninspected magickal items, including, but not limited to, transportation stones, potions, enchanted objects, elixirs, balms, and ink. Any and all items produced without inspection will be seized, and each one incurs a $150 fine.*'

I look up at her. "What the hell is *polinya*?"

Helena's lips push thin. "Apparently a plant, the raw pollen is poisonous to magickal creatures, and conveniently, the pollen is being found in witch establishments. It's all over the news today."

"Who brought this by?"

"A nasty older fellow. A human ..." The vampire frowns. "Bernard, that was it. Bernard Key. He wasn't too happy to find nothing to seize, and that Arlo wasn't here. You can tell he was sniffing for trouble, for a fight. I tried calling Arlo after I managed to get the old cat out of here, but no answer."

"Ah, he probably won't be in today. But I'll let him know. If anyone else bothers you, tell them to leave a card. You can always call me if you need to as well, but like you said," I nod to the empty case, "it's already empty."

"I'd rather tell them to stick it where the sun doesn't shine." Helena scoffs.

I smile in pained sympathy, then hesitantly say, "Be careful, okay?"

"Oh, Quentin." Helena pulls me into a hug, squishing me to her bosom as she plants a big kiss on my forehead. "You too."

Only when I retreat upstairs and close the apartment door behind me do I feel like I can breathe properly. I quickly research *polinya*, finding that it is a real thing, and many of the symptoms of poisoning are similar to celestial sickness. Well, *that's* not suspicious at all. I create a group message explaining the unwanted visitor and *polinya* outbreak, and send it to Arlo, Tobias, Elochian, and reluctantly, Finnegan.

After that, I do my best to push thoughts of River, shitty people, and all my other worries aside. Just for a few hours, then I can fret on my own time. I'm going on a date with Elochian, something I've *dreamed* about, but never actually entertained. I spend the afternoon cleaning up my abandoned apartment, and myself. I even remember to drink water, and I pat myself on the back.

The thing is, I have no idea where he's taking me, which makes getting ready a minor problem. For one, I can't anticipate the chances of River finding us, and for two, I have no idea what the night calls for. I eventually video call Lindsey for advice when I have a pile of outfits pared down to three.

She answers on the second ring, snuggled up on her couch with strands of Kitt's hair partially covering her cheek. Blue light dances across her tired face from the quietly chattering television. She whistles upon seeing my wet hair and bare chest, the towel wrapped around my hips. "I've told you before and I'll tell you again, if I liked dick yours would be the first one I'd jump on."

"Wow, just wow. Hello to you too."

Kitt's head tilts into view, temporarily blocking Lindsey's face. "Ooh, where you going all sexy like?"

I roll my eyes. "Shut up. I need help picking out an outfit. A date appropriate outfit."

Lindsey abruptly sits up, and Kitt releases a strained '*what the fuck,*' as she's thrown aside. "Holy Typhine, is it happening?"

I glare at her, but it's rendered useless by a small, treacherous smile. "It's happening." Lindsey squeals, and Kitt hollers her approval as she leaves the room, presumably for snacks. I laugh. "I'm glad my love life is so amusing."

"Months. Months of pain, Q."

"What are you talking about?"

"The pining!"

I shake my head. "I'm going to hang up on you."

"No you won't, you need me too much."

"Fine. Which one do you like the best?" I turn my camera around, showing her the options. Kitt's face pokes into view, licorice between her lips. She makes a face, and Lindsey blinks. I groan. "What?"

"I thought you said you were going on a date, not a royal fucking wedding," Kitt says, and Lindsey busts out laughing. My heart aches, and I realize how much I've missed the sound of it. When was the last time we hung out, just us?

"Very funny. He's an archdemon! I'm sure we'll be going somewhere fancy and formal." I give the outfits another look, and grimace. "They are pretty over the top."

"You're thinking about this too hard. Has Elochian ever dressed like that a day in his life? Does Elochian like to do fancy and formal things?" Lindsey asks, stealing a strand of licorice from Kitt.

"Well, I don't know about the first one, but the second one, no. I wish he would just tell me where we're going!"

"Nah, this is way better. We get to watch you suffer." Kitt teases, and I smile despite myself. "You know, on Lind's birthday he was practically drooling over you. Wear something like that."

"Ohh, yes. The come hither outfit," Lindsey adds. I open my mouth, and she gives me a look. "Go with the come hither outfit. And you can't deny that's what it was."

I drop the phone on my bed, giving them a good view of the ceiling. I stalk over to my closet, searching. "I'll have you know, there will be no hithering."

"Okay big man, when was the last time you had sex? Better yet, did you trim things up down there?" Kitt asks.

"It was that dancer, wasn't it? Oh, what was his name ... Elwin!" Lindsey exclaims before I can respond. "Yeah, that was before the Arlo era. Yikes."

"*Yikes*? Good one, old lady. And I did *not* have an 'Arlo era.' Besides, it's not going to be like that. We're taking things slow."

"He definitely did some grooming," Kitt mutters, and Lindsey laughs.

"I hate both of you."

I get dressed, using the time to build courage. As I fasten buttons, I clear my throat and say, "I'm thinking about telling him the truth. About what's been going on with me. About ... River."

Lindsey and Kitt fall quiet, and they stay that way until I pick up the phone. Lindsey smiles at me, but it's not as full as before. "I think you should. But tonight? Is that how you want to remember your first date with him?"

"No, I don't ... but I feel like I'm damaged goods, Linds. Shouldn't he know?"

Kitt says, "You are not damaged goods," at the same time Lindsey shouts, "Quentin!"

"It's true! I literally have a stalker, and if Arlo is to be believed, he's possessed by the actual worst person ever. What if—what if—" I can't bring myself to finish that sentence, because what *if* River finds us tonight?

"Hey!" Lindsey calls, snapping me out of it. "You are not damaged goods because someone else is a fucking evil asshole. We *all* have problems, Quentin. Elochian has problems!

Tonight isn't about that, though. Tonight is about you two, the start of something new. Michael will be with you guys, right? They will keep you safe, and tomorrow, you can tell him."

"Okay." I sniff, wiping my eyes with the back of my hand. Words fall out of me in a rush, in fear they won't make it out at all. "You're right. I don't know what I would do without you two. I miss you so much. Maybe ... can we plan a movie night together? I miss that."

Kitt smiles, and Lindsey curses me out while she wipes away her own tears. She says, "Tomorrow night. Popcorn and sprinkle chips, and all the details. Deal?"

I laugh. "Deal."

I wait outside the locked up cafe, watching the world go by. It's that time of night when the sun has retreated, but the moons haven't made an appearance yet. The vehicular section of Garren Road boasts headlights upon headlights, people moving to and from their lives in a hurry, while the pedestrians move in a slower, more intentional manner. The trolley car goes by, all string lights and gentle music from a busking musician.

It all makes for a romantic ambiance of the lamplit town, highlighting couples walking hand in hand, families making their way home together, stories of the day rolling off their tongues. Winter still has a chokehold on Levena, but there's a shift in the air, an anticipation of new growth and the desire to be outside again.

Despite all of this, my heart won't stop pounding out of my chest.

I hold on tight to the stone in my pocket, rubbing my thumb over its slightly rough surface. Ready to disappear at a moment's notice, because what *if*?

What if Elochian finds me boring?

What if he changes his mind?

What if he realizes I'm only a human, nearly a *tenth* of his age, and I don't belong in his world of age old, noble demons?

What if everything goes well, and River destroys everything?

I'm kicked out of my cyclical, acidic thoughts by the sight of Elochian striding towards me, seemingly out of nowhere. He's alone, dressed in an outfit that renders me without a heartbeat. A black, double-layered overcoat brushes against his calves, which are clad in knee-high black leather boots. The coat is hemmed with thick golden thread and amber beads that seem to emanate their own light. The embroidery continues on the high collar, the thick fabric upturned and cocooning Elochian's neck. Three layers of golden chains threaded with pearls drape over his shoulders at varying lengths, their origin hidden by the collar. More chains and pearls are hinted at beneath the overcoat, layered around his throat like necklaces, and around his waist like a loose belt.

He's done something to his hair, it falls around his shoulders and elbows in big, loose curls that shine like ink beneath the lights of the city. Gold powder dusts his eyelids in a barely there fashion, and a thin line of kohl touches the corners of his eyes, ending in a fine, upwards curl. He didn't hide the golden lines in his face, and they glow brighter as he approaches me. His wings too, they flutter and make a fuss, casting moving, luminescent rainbows on the sidewalk.

But none of this is what stops my heart.

Elochian can't stop smiling, and he doesn't look away from me to hide it.

Only when he stands before me and bows at the waist does my heart restart, kicked into action by a nervous laugh. "What are you doing?"

Elochian straightens, reaching for my hand. I offer it to him, and he kisses my wrist through a smile. When he lowers my hand from his lips, his fingers tangle with mine. He says, "Bowing to you. It's a show of respect."

"Maybe I should have asked about any weird demon dating rituals before this," I say, teasing.

He winks at me. "Too late for that now." Despite the fact he studied me every step of the way over here, his eyes roam up and down my figure. He brings the fingers of his free hand up to my throat, capturing the black lace of my collar between them. "You're incredibly handsome tonight, Quentin. I was hoping you'd wear this."

I smile, cheeks aching with it. "It's one of my favorites."

He squeezes my hand, then glances over his shoulder towards the street. "Are you ready? The next trolley will be here soon."

"Oh, is that how you got here? Where's Michael?"

"Yes, it was." He grins, leading me towards the street. "And here I am thinking you were excited to go on a date with *me*, not my bodyguard."

I roll my eyes, falling into step beside him. "Tell me he's not around here somewhere."

Elochian shrugs, then looks up to the sky. I follow his gaze, but it takes me a moment to discern what he's looking at. A few lamplights down from us, a pigeon is perched on the peak of an iron post. I look at Elochian quickly. "No way."

He laughs. "It's one of their favorite guises, believe it or not."

"That's awesome." I laugh too, and it overwhelms me for a moment. I wipe my eyes with my free hand, chuckling. "I'm never letting him live it down."

Elochian is quiet, and I look over to find him staring at me, all evidence of his good humor gone. I can't tell what he's thinking, or feeling. I wonder if I should bring up the *polinya* thing, or anything else that's beyond this moment, back in reality.

I don't. Instead, I ask, "What?"

He shakes his head, and the corner of his lip curls upwards. "Nothing. Just … this is easier than I thought it would be. It's easy to be with you."

I flush at his words, and we come upon the trolley stop where a small group of people wait. I glance sideways at him. "I think it's easy to be with you, too."

After a few minutes of small talk, the trolley arrives. We go all the way to the back, sidling up close in a booth. Its an open air one, meaning the sides of the trolley are open, allowing passengers to get on and off easily, but a few of the more accessible booths have protective bars that prevent anyone from tumbling out.

Elochian sits on the outside, taking the brunt of the chill air as our journey begins, hand still firmly in mine. He says, "It's been a long time since I've been on one of these. I forgot how much I liked it."

"They're pretty handy. I like the ones that have—" A treant duo take up the small stage area in the front of the trolley, one has a guitar and the other an accordion. I grin wide at Elochian as they begin to play. "I like the ones that have buskers. They make the ride go by faster, and usually if I'm by myself, I'll be taking notes or something, and I like to imagine it as a soundtrack. You can find inspiration everywhere on one of these things."

"What do you mean?" Elochian asks, and I find inspiration right there in his eyes, wide and eternal as they swallow the warm string lights of the trolley.

But I don't tell him that. I say, "Well, look out there."

I reach past him, pointing to Levena as it goes by, slow and easy. We've crossed into New Town, shaded by the illuminated canopy of *Etz Hayim,* surrounded by its saplings which are still twice the size of the great willows and pines at Arlo's place. The saplings have been modernized by man, the same as *Etz Hayim,* acting as apartments complexes or office buildings. A few seconds pass before Elochian turns, as if he can't bear to look away from me. Or that might just be the romantic atmosphere getting to my head.

When he finally does look, I point to the people on the rolling streets, then the cars as they pass the trolley. "All of those people have a story. They talk differently, walk differently, laugh differently. Some of them are alone, some of them have families the size of a small army. Some were born with everything, and some were born with nothing.

"And that's only the people, not to mention where they live, where they shop, where they eat. There may be layers of overlap in how people live, shades of gray that connect them, but in the end, no one experience of the world is the same. You can only take so much from books and your memory when it comes to writing, for me, anyways. You have to look out there. Be *in* the world, if you can."

He turns, staring at me with something like quiet awe. I shift in my seat, glancing at the musicians as they play a more whimsical tune. "What?"

Elochian says, "Nothing."

I push my glasses up my nose, fighting the urge to roll my eyes. "Fine, keep your secrets."

He turns away, but not before I catch a glimpse of something ... something sad?

We don't say anything for a little while after that, the air's changed. It's still comfortable, but all the things we haven't said take up the small space between us. I think about what Lindsey said, and she's probably right, but I feel like more than ever I need to come clean. When we go past the museum and hook a right past Full Moon Fields, I open my mouth.

But *Elochian* blurts out, "I think Thatch set us up."

I rub at my collarbone, blinking at him. "W—what?"

He takes a deep breath, then fully turns in his seat and takes both my hands in his. He says, "After Thatch left, I ... I remembered the first time that I saw him. It was—" He clears his throat, squeezing my hands. "It was the first anniversary of Bartholomew's death. He was my *shomer*, the one I was matched with at birth. My painting, '*Survivor's Guilt*,'it's about him. I—I wasn't in a good place, it was the first time I had left the Manor since it happened."

I absorb every emotion and sentiment he has to offer me, grateful to have earned his trust. When he falls quiet, his thumb rubs over the back of my hand, and he stares down at it. I allow him to have a moment before gently asking, "Where were you going?"

"I don't know. Anywhere but there. It had settled into my bones, that place. I didn't realize how much until I was outside its walls. I went from drowning in a sea of people, to wandering the streets, lost and alone, the first time I had been so in a year. Looking back on it now, it's a miracle I wasn't taken out immediately. It was before I had Michael, and maybe if he was there I would've been paying attention to where I was going, but I wasn't. I crashed into someone and fell on the stone. I scraped both my elbows, barely missed hitting my head. For so long, everything after that was hazy, all I was left with was a flash of red and a book. But then, I remembered.

"I remembered him running away, and I called after him. He stopped long enough to look over his shoulder, smiling. Not a big one, but a sly one that said, *'I know something you don't.'* And then he took off. I picked myself up, soaked in snow and mud, but because I'm curious, I started looking through the book, right there in the street. It was the filthiest thing I had ever read, and I couldn't believe this man would just carry around a book like that!"

"Oh," I say, cheeks heating. "Oh no."

He laughs. "Yes, it was one of yours. The first spice trader book, a signed edition, at that. I was—I don't know what I was going to do with it, certainly not keep it, but when I was finally found and dragged back home, the book had ended in my overcoat's pocket, and eventually, on my shelf, where the rest of your books ended up as well."

"Elochian, that's—I don't know what to say." I pause, waiting for a memory of my own to resurface, because a *signed* edition? But nothing comes, no hidden traces of Thatch make themselves known. Hesitantly, I ask, "Does Arlo know?"

He shakes his head. "You're the only person I've told."

"Why ... can I ask why you like them so much? My books? You're not—I mean, it doesn't seem like you'd be in it for the, uh. For the sex."

Elochian laughs, quiet but seemingly never ending. Embarrassment has no place in my heart, because that *laugh*. I want to bottle it in a jar, keep it forever. I want to keep *him* forever, or what's left of mine, that is.

"I can appreciate those parts, seeing how well-written they are," he winks, shooting an arrow through my heart, "but you're right. That's not what hooked me. It was the characters. The

... *connection*, despite everything. Despite their circumstances, despite who they were, despite what they had been through, these people were able to find love. I couldn't envision myself loving anyone else, not like I loved him, but ... what if? What if the end of my story wasn't the end? And I think Thatch knew that, he knew you were my beginning. Maybe not, but ... my life changed the day I found you."

I sniff, blinking back tears. "That was beautiful."

"And so are you," he says, releasing one of my hands in favor of cupping my cheek. He wipes away warm tears from my cheek. "So are you."

"Elochian, I—"

The intercom buzzes to life, announcing, "We have arrived at Absolute Corners, next stop; Brass Quarter." I nearly ignore it and continue with my confession, as we've stopped a few times now to let off passengers, but Elochian stands and pulls me with him.

"This is our stop."

"Here?" I ask, surprised. I'm more familiar with Absolute Corners than I care to admit, and the idea that Elochian might be too is ... worrisome.

"Yes." He steps down onto the cobblestone, helping me down beside him. I'm grateful for it, as my knee is pretty pissed off today. Besides, I'm happy to never get my hand back. My wariness must show, because Elochian starts to lead me down the street and says, "Trust me."

"I do."

His step falters for a moment, and he gives me a nervous smile. "You're going to like this place. I promise."

I chuckle, unwillingly disarmed. "I believe you."

We make our way into the outskirts of the North End, which to the naked eye is ingenious and bizarre, to say the least. Shanties line the streetsides, multi-level and architecturally impossible, all rusted metal and worn tin. Pipes snake in one building and out another, and steam engines huff great clouds into the night. When the solar revolution came, the End opted to stick with what they knew, which is why you won't find any panels or turbines here.

Droids and people spill out of dance halls, bars, and establishments that appear to the world as pretty inns, but I know better. The brothels on this side of town have dignity at least, and they treat their workers better than all the rest. I never minded this part of the End, it's the far side that haunts me.

Across from an old time theater that I always wanted to visit but never did, is a great neon sign, a purple gash across the night. It declares the steel building beneath it, untouched by the usual age-old rust, as *Primo's*. I stare at the place wistfully, but when we don't walk past it, instead coming to a stop before two wide glass doors, I can't help but smile wide at Elochian.

"This is where we're going?"

He nods, staring at the storefront. "It looks busy ... " he murmurs.

I follow his gaze through big windows to where a crowd of people are gathered on the right side of the store. I've never known Elochian to care for a crowd, or be within a hundred feet of one. He meets my eyes again and puts on a brave smile.

"You got me, right?"

I squeeze his hand. "Always, sunshine."

That makes him laugh, and his wings calm down. "Thanks, Dot." He looks down to our hands, then back up to my face. "I seem to have a problem with letting you go."

I shrug. "I don't mind."

He takes a step towards the store, then halts and looks at me askance. "Are we—shall I introduce you as my ... boyfriend?"

I've perished. Right there, absolutely done. My heart swells, and I lick my lips in an attempt to hide my smile. Gods my face hurts, have I even stopped?

"I'd like that. W–would you?"

"Yes." Elochian nods, then leads me inside without another word, oblivious to the fact I'm overrun with happiness and excitement.

When he opens the door, beautiful music and happy conversation spills over the threshold. His wings tense, but he doesn't hesitate, making a beeline for the cashier's counter at the back of the store. But I'm slow and distracted, so Elochian stops in a narrow aisle between two display cases full of vinyls, ready for perusal.

He looks around, slowly taking it in like I do. After a moment, he whispers, "It is pretty amazing, isn't it?"

"Amazing is an understatement."

To the left is a reading area, furnished with mismatched couches and chairs, accompanied by bookshelves, magazine racks, and a coffee bar. Rows upon rows of records dominate the center of the store, and the right side of the room is—oh, it's wonderful.

A small stage is nestled into the front corner, complete with a keyboard, an upright piano, a cello, a bass, and several guitars. Behind them all, an old drum set keeps watch over the small crowd at the other end of the space, some sit while others stand on the fringes. Half the instruments have companions, while the other half cry for a musician to bring forth their song, including the drum set.

And the walls, the *ceiling*. Algae bulb chandeliers hang in the open space, and between them a number of instruments dangle in various states of distress. Some are brand new, while others are no more than a loose collection of strings and wood. The less battle-weary pieces rest on the walls, and beside them are framed articles or photographs of the musicians who once played them. It's one of those places that you could visit a hundred times, and still not see everything.

"I never want to leave," I say to Elochian, and his smile widens.

"Come on, there's someone I want you to meet."

I follow him more willingly this time, but am disappointed when Elochian's hand *finally* leaves mine. A tall, thickset *shed-im* with silver skin and the eyes to match beams upon seeing Elochian, and he comes round the counter to pull him into a hug. "*Ai*, Elochian!"

Elochian freezes for a moment, then hugs him back. It goes on for a good thirty seconds before the man pulls back, smiling wide at a now blushing Elochian. "And who's this?" He reaches for me, but when our hands connect I find it's not a handshake he was after, and I receive the biggest hug I've ever had. My back cracks from my hips to my neck, and I fight a groan of relief.

I find myself smiling after my feet touch the ground, cheeks warm.

Elochian chuckles, gesturing between us. "Primo, this is my boyfriend, Quentin Matsdotter. Quentin, this is Primo."

"Oh, dear Elochian." Primo claps his hands once, his smile broad. "This is good news, how long have you two been an item?"

I share an awkward look with Elochian, who curls a lock of hair around his finger like it's his job. I say, "Tonight's our first date, actually, but we've been friends for a few months now."

Primo stares down fondly at Elochian, and something unsaid passes between them. "Well isn't that sweet." His gaze slides to me, glinting like steel. "Tell me Quentin, do you play anything?"

I shrug. "I've been known to beat the skins a time or two."

Elochian's face screws up, but Primo laughs. He says, "Is that so? Well, come on then. Let's go make some music." He slings an arm around my shoulder, ruffling my hair a little like we're old friends. I glance over my shoulder at Elochian, who hides a wide smile behind his hand.

Old and Wrinkly

I am lost in the moment.

Lost in the red and pink lights bearing down on Quentin. Lost in his hair as it tosses back and forth, and the few strands sticking to his forehead.

Lost in his whole body as he plays, like he's dancing in place. The way he throws his head back, exposing the strained tendons in his neck, and the hint of inky branches which tease the hollow of his throat.

Lost in the beat as it thuds throughout the shop, throughout my soul.

A hand rests on my shoulder, but I don't flinch. Michael whispers, "You're crying."

I wipe at my eyes with my sleeve and say nothing, only continue watching. Primo is on the cello, and I don't recognize the guitarist, pianist, or bass, but the entire group plays like they've been doing so for years. Quentin's jacket was draped over his knee at the beginning of the set, but now it's crumpled on the floor beside him. A sheer black blouse clings to his chest, and the puffy sleeves once cuffed at the wrists are now pushed up to his elbows. The frilly neckline draws attention to his Adam's apple, I've never noticed how prominent it was before until now, and I wonder what—

"Hmm." I turn away.

Michael raises a brow, hand falling from my shoulder. They're in a feminine elf form, dressed in casual clothes. "Everything alright?"

"Yes. Completely fine."

"Your—" They lean closer, whispering despite the fact the music essentially drowns all other conversation. "Your fangs."

As much as I hate to, I leave the stage area in favor of an ice cold drink. Thankfully the snack bar is empty, everyone else is watching the musicians. Last I knew, Primo doesn't play much anymore, and by the crowd's reaction, that may still be the case. His main love is the cello, but he can play anything. Or maybe it's Quentin they're all fawning over. They're all looking at him, and how could they not?

I drain a cup of water, then fill the disposable moss cup only to drain it again. I run my tongue over my teeth, and I wince upon drawing blood. They're receding, if not slowly. Michael leans against the counter beside me, facing the opposite direction. "That's new," they say.

I sigh. "Tell me something I don't know."

Michael grins at me. "I'm proud of you."

I raise a brow.

"*Not* about *that*. For bringing Quentin here. He's having fun, when was the last time you saw him like this? And reconnecting with someone from your past, I know it's been ... well, you haven't seen him in a while."

I take another sip of water, but slower this time. The music changes tune, abandoned by the drums. Hesitantly, I say, "I used to come here all the time. It was my place before it was ours, but after he died, I couldn't—it was too hard. But I think he would've wanted me to take it back."

Michael's smile softens. "And you're doing okay?"

I open my lips, then pause when I see Quentin squeezing through the crowd, waving like a madman when he sees me. I exhale, "Yes."

Quentin combs a hand through his wild hair, laughing a little upon joining us. I love his little laughs, how he can't contain the joy inside him. I don't know why, but the world stops right then for a moment. It replays in my mind, juxtapositioned by the images of him broken and bedbound, unrecognizable.

Oblivious to my plight, he restarts the world with a breathless question. "Hey, how'd I do?"

I reach for his hand, pulling him close when he obliges me. His eyes widen, and so does his smile. I whisper, "You're brilliant." I bend down, leaving a tentative kiss on his cheek. "I'm sorry I didn't stay till the end, I—I needed a moment."

"That's alright. Are you ready to go?"

I wince. "If I say yes, will you be disappointed?"

"Not at all. We can come back, right?"

I chuckle, disarmed by his eyes bigger than saucers. "Of course. Are you hungry?"

"I could eat." He shrugs, his nonchalance betrayed by the way he licks his bottom lip. He glances at Michael, and winks. "Hi."

Michael smiles, clearly pleased that Quentin recognized them despite the fact they've never used this particular form before. "Hello, Quentin."

When Quentin unfolds his jacket, I wordlessly take it from him. He bites back a smile, saying nothing as I help him into it. I turn him towards me, buttoning it to his chin. The three of us take our leave, but instead of heading east to the trolley station with us, Michael goes the opposite direction. A few short minutes after we start our walk, a pigeon flies overhead. Quentin chuckles, shaking his head. We're hand in hand again, and my heart is settled.

"How can you always tell?" I ask, looking over at him.

"Oh," he says, wrinkling his nose as he thinks. Finally, he shrugs. "I don't know. I guess if anything, it's you. There's a certain way you stand when they're next to you."

I stare at him. "How I stand."

"Yeah! I don't know." He laughs abruptly. "To be honest, it's like the stick comes out of your ass whenever he's near, and your wings don't shake as much."

I laugh too, unable to stop it. "Oh, I see how it is. You think I'm stuck up."

"Hey, I didn't say that! You're just ... there's two sides to you." He bumps my shoulder with his. "There's Lochian, then there's *Elochian*. He brings out the first one."

I bump him back. "You do too."

He winks at me. "I try."

The sign marking the trolley's stop is empty, and so is the covered bench. We take a seat, and I sigh upon meeting the warmed stone. Quentin clears his throat, then says, "So, Primo's a demon, right?"

"He is."

"But he said he's not in your clan."

I tilt my head, wondering why they were talking about the clan of all things. "He is not. When Primo moved here, he made it clear he wanted to be independent. Was the way he'd always done it, he said. To the displeasure of my council, I gave him my blessing. Back then, I lived for pissing them off. I think that's why I loved going there so much. I enjoy music, don't get me wrong, but ... I don't know, it's one of those places you go for the people, if you know what I mean. Like Thitwhistle's."

"So if you said no, what would've happened?"

"Hm. Nothing really, but I imagine his business would've been greatly impacted. Being associated with a clan can provide luck and good fortune, and it's frowned upon for celestials to go it alone, because why would you? As it is, I don't think many of the older demons visit there, but the young ones don't care so much about that kind of thing."

"Wait—how old is Primo?"

"A hundred and ... four? Somewhere in there."

"And is he young to you?"

"...Yes."

"Ah. I see."

I study him for a moment, the crease between his brows, his foot quietly bouncing. I stare at our thighs, pressed against the other and playing host to our joined hands. "Does the difference in our ages bother you?"

He looks at me, incredulous. "Doesn't it bother you?"

"No." I swallow, squeezing his hand. "The only thing that bothers me is the obvious. I ... I will outlive you, Quentin. If life has her way, I will outlive you a hundred times over."

He flinches. "And you're okay with that?"

I release his hand and wrap my arms around his shoulders. I pull him close to my chest, and he comes easily. He tips his head back, staring up at me. I whisper, "I will stay by your side as long as you will have me."

In all seriousness, he asks, "Even when I'm old and wrinkly?"

I break on a small laugh. "Especially then."

He smiles, but in a flash, nervousness takes back over. "Could we—I mean, I don't know what your plan is, but do you think we could just ... eat at my place? If that's okay with you."

I bury a spike of anxiety by kissing Quentin's forehead, soft and slow. I lean back and say, "Of course. There's a deli on the way that's open all the time, we could get something there."

Quentin hums, resting his head on my shoulder. "That sounds nice."

We wait for the trolley in content silence, and I think that I could stay pressed against Quentin like this forever. I listen to the music and hooting and hollering coming from deeper in the End, nothing more than a distant echo, and I wonder if it sounds like this every night. Admittedly, I've never been further in than Primo's, and the realization fills me with a sense of shame. There is a whole side to Levena I haven't seen, and yet I'm supposed to be protecting her, all of her.

Quentin says, "What did he look like?"

The question takes me off guard, rendering me speechless. After a few seconds of stiff silence, I lift my thigh and reach into my back pocket with my free hand, retrieving my wallet. I flip the bi-fold open one handed, revealing a worn picture on the inside. Quentin's fingers gently rest over mine, and he brings the photograph closer to his face.

We were no older than Quentin is now, River Street was at our backs and the blinding summer sun was in our faces. He preferred his *mayim* form, and was fully shifted in the picture. Smooth, jewel toned skin with thick, ruffly gills on either side of his throat. Thin, branching horns of diamond crowned his head, and they continued down his neck and spine. Only the tips of the silver *shomer* marks are visible in the picture, he was dressed in a formal outfit, the same as I. His hair was the deepest blue I had ever seen, with too much vibrant hue to be called black, and he always kept it in a tight knot at the back of his neck.

"What were you doing?" His thumb sweeps over my face in the picture. "You look so happy."

I chuckle softly, unable to help myself. "Ah, it was the day the new tunnel was built, the one that connects River Street to Syorini Lake. This was taken *before* the ceremony, which explains why I'm smiling in this one."

"I have noticed you tend to have resting bitch face when it comes to pictures," Quentin teases, then blinks up at me. "Do you ... could you tell me more about him?"

"Yes, I think I could."

Quentin falls asleep on my shoulder on the way back to his apartment, and I don't have the heart to wake him up. He snores, and it's so soft that the trolley nearly overtakes the adorable sound. I hold him close to me, fighting my own heavy lids. I focus on his scent, which isn't hard to do considering he broke into quite the sweat while playing. Tonight he reminds me of an open pasture full of wildflowers, the same bright color as his eyes. It's a welcome thought, especially as snow curls into the air around us with a vengeance. I watch the lights of the trolley play on his face, the way they skip over the bridge of his nose. It's a solid, strong line, one that appears unbroken. Gently, I trace my finger down the length of his nose, then along the place in his cheek where smiles grow. I stray towards his lips, but my hands falls before making contact.

We're in public, after all.

Tonight went so much better than I thought it would. I never expected to make it inside Primo's, and yet we stayed there for hours. Reuniting with the *shedim* injected gold into the cracks inside my heart, and so did unloading memories and sentiment into Quentin's waiting heart. I thought talking about an old partner would be … well, not a good thing to do, but Quentin seemed to truly enjoy talking about Bartholomew, and my life with him before.

And then there's the fact we're officially *boyfriends*. It feels like such a minor word for what we are, but I'm afraid calling us anything else will scare Quentin away. Tonight was our first date after all, and in the grand scheme of things, we haven't known each other that long.

I know there are things he isn't telling me. He hasn't opened up to me, not fully, but I can't blame him. On the surface, his past appears to be a bomb of trauma, so how much lays underneath? But I am a patient man, and I will be ready when he is.

When we come to our stop, he still doesn't wake. Only when I cradle him in my arms and carry him off the trolley does he stir, but that's only to nuzzle his face against my chest. Satisfaction warms my heart at the action, and I easily carry him home. Michael emerges from the shadows in his preferred male *shedim* form. He smirks upon seeing us, but says nothing.

"His keys are in his coat pocket," I whisper, and as a team we manage to make it inside Thitwhistle's without waking Quentin up. Michael locks the back door behind me, and offers to take Quentin from my arms when I shift his weight. I shake my head, so Michael wordlessly leads the way upstairs, unlocking Quentin's apartment for me.

I've been in his cozy apartment a couple of times, but never farther than the foyer which separates the kitchen and small dining area from the living room and office. He's only been in here for a few months now, but the open spaces are not without his personality.

A vintage loveseat is neatly decorated with a knitwork blanket and frilly pillows, undisturbed and picture perfect. A series of mismatched, round windows and blown up illustrations of molecules occupy the wall opposite the couch, and a television set that doesn't work. There's knobs and a screen, but plants grow out of the back of it. Deep purple begonias accompanied by ferns that frame their companions like wings.

I direct Michael to Quentin's room with a series of head nods, and he has to push on the door with some force to get it to swing inwards. For some reason the first thought I have is, *'there's a body behind that door,'* but the look on Michael's face after poking his head through the frame is nothing but fond exasperation.

"Clothes," he mouths, and I smile a little.

I've never been in Quentin's room before, and I'm surprised by the state of it. The rest of his apartment is clean, well tended to, but his bedroom is a fucking disaster zone. Clothes on the back of the chair, on the floor, blanketing his bed. His box spring rests directly on the floor, and small paper wrappers pile up on the side not pressed against the wall. Glasses half-full of water, and mugs completely drained of tea, judging by the stains, litter the nightstand.

His alarm clock is an old style radio, and it plays a soft rock song. Michael clears off the bed, effectively sweeping everything into a pile at the foot of the bed, and the mountain is tall enough to reach the mattress. Revealed beneath the mess is a pretty quilt neatly made across his bed, shocker. Michael pulls the blanket back, then moves to shut the radio off, but I shake my head. I kneel on the mattress and gently lay Quentin down, rolling him onto his side in an attempt to free my arm trapped beneath his shoulders.

When I finally break free he reaches out, latching onto my coat. "Ungh, don' go."

I chuckle breathlessly. "Were you only pretending to sleep?"

He groans. "*Please.*"

I swallow thickly, glancing over at Michael. Except he's already at the door, leaving me with a little wink and smile before disappearing. I sigh, then summon courage and carefully lay behind Quentin. I open my lips to tease him, but those soft snores start up again, and I wonder if he was only talking in his sleep.

Well, I'll only stay for a little while.

Overwhelming heat rouses me from the fog, and when I open my eyes it's only to become lost in Quentin's, which are lazily focused on me. The corner of his mouth quirks, and he pulls up the blanket between us to hide it. The thick comforter is big enough to cover us twice over, and it provides a sort of blanket wall between us. I've still got my jacket on, and so does he, although we've both lost our shoes.

He says, "You're in my bed."

"I—I didn't mean to. I'll—"

"No, it's okay." He reaches for me, taking hold of my shirt. The blanket wall collapses, pushed down by his outstretched arm. "I don't mind, is what I mean. Unless you want to go."

I reach out from beneath the blanket to run my fingers up and down his arm, from wrist to elbow. "What time is it?"

He swallows, then chuckles nervously. "Come on, isn't this your superpower?"

"Not when I first wake up."

"Fair. I have no idea, only that it's still night." He nods to the window at the head of his room. I glance over my shoulder to peek at the slightly ajar curtains presenting a sliver of the world outside. No twilight or dawn on the horizon, only pure darkness. My wings ache, and I have to shove away part of the comforter weighing them down. They stretch out, then relax once more against the bed.

"They don't glow at night," he says, followed by a curious hum.

"What?" I turn to him, only to find him falling back into sleep. In an act of pure selfishness, I gently poke his calf with my foot. I realize my boots are off, and I distantly wonder how that happened. When my sock brushes against his knee, he stirs.

"Hm?" Eyes closed, he moves to push his glasses up his nose, but I took them off earlier and put them on a pillow. He settles for swiping hair away from his eyes. It's all mussed, and damp strands stick to his forehead. His eyes blink open, showcasing pastures veiled in early morning fog. Bits of sleep dust cling to his eyelashes, and I carefully wipe it away.

"You were talking about my wings."

"Oh, yes. They're so pretty, and unique. Like a snowflake." He gasps, eyes widening. He whisper-shouts, "Elochian!"

"*What*?" I whisper back through a laugh.

"That should've been my nickname for you. You're my snowflake."

I make a face. "I'll be your sunshine all day long over that."

"That'll have to do," he says, his smile languid and peaceful.

After a moment I whisper, "I've never seen you without your glasses. Can you see me?"

"Always." He blushes, fidgeting under the blanket. "I mean, up close like this, I can."

A realization dawns on me, and I smirk. "You were watching me in my sleep."

"I was n—okay, I was. Can you blame me?"

"I suppose not." It's my turn to pull the blanket up to my face, hiding away my nervousness. "Did you have a good time tonight? Was it too much?"

"No, it was perfect, absolutely perfect." He shakes his head. "I can't believe I fell asleep. One minute I'm on the trolley with you, and the next I'm here ... with you. I thought I was dreaming, to be perfectly honest."

A huff of embarrassment disguised as a small laugh escapes me. "I'm not a dream."

Quentin lifts a shoulder, lips opening and closing a few times before he finally says, "You are to me. A very nice dream. I—it feels like this is all too good to be true. Like at any moment I'm going to wake up."

I shift a little closer to him, and my knees bump into his. "I'm not going anywhere, Quentin. I promise."

A glimmer of excitement alights his eyes, then he inhales sharply through his nose. On a breathless exhale, he quickly says, "I need to tell you something first, before you make that promise." He falls quiet, averting his eyes to the blankets between us. His fingers dance beneath the heavy fabric, his nerves evident in their tempo.

I tentatively explore the unknown, seeking him out. When my fingers brush against his, Quentin looks up at me, surprised, then curls his around mine. Quentin holds onto me unlike all the times he has before, desperate and worried, and I wonder how many ways there are to hold someone's hand, to express your feelings, your affection, only through your palm and fingers.

I say, "Quentin, I will always listen to whatever you have to say, but you do not *owe* me anything, you don't have to—"

"No, I do," he says, closing his eyes. He gives my hand a little shake. "I *really* do."

"Okay. I'm listening."

He chews on his bottom lip, then says, "You remember when I said I haven't really been in a good relationship before?"

Flashes of him in a hospital bed. Bandages soaked through. Bones. Broken, so many of them. An accident (but was it really?). With as much calm as I can muster, I say, "Yes."

He opens his eyes then. "It was ... it started when I was in school. He was a dropout, I was the gifted kid. I—I don't even remember how we met, I feel like I should, but ... maybe I blocked it out, I don't know. But we were friends for a long time before we were anything else, and I can see now that he was—" He grimaces, fingers tightening around mine.

"He was molding me into exactly what he wanted. My mother ... she had a plan for me, one I wanted no part of, and I saw him as a way out. I was graduating early, so why *couldn't* I live on my own? I ran away, and for a little while it was exactly what I wanted. He treated me like I was everything. Then ... I saw him for what he truly was. A monster."

I press a gentle kiss to his knuckles, and Quentin gives me a watery smile.

"It was too late. My mother exiled me, and I was completely dependent on him. I decided to bide my time, do what it took to make him happy until I could leave, run away again. But I—I had to do things, Lochian, things I am *still* ashamed of, things that I will never be able to forget. Believe me, I've tried. But I can still *see* them, the people, the—"

He shudders, closing his eyes. I cup his cheek, and he flinches when my skin meets his. When my hand starts to fall away, he presses his cheek to my palm, keeping his eyes firmly shut. We stay that way for a moment, and when he opens his eyes again there's resolve there.

"The point is, I ran away. Again. But this time, I fled hundreds of miles, zig-zagging my way through the country until I came here, to Levena. I had connections here, as threadbare as they were, but it was enough to start a new life. Eduardo gave me a part-time job while I attended university, and I started doing the things I loved again, and—well. He found me. Snared me with promises to do better, *be* better. And me, the idiot that I am. I believed him. Everything that happened thereafter was my own doing. A snake may shed its skin, but it's still a snake."

"You are not at fault for a predator's machinations. Even if you told him no, do you think he would've let you be? You think he would've been happy with that?"

"No, he wouldn't have."

A moment passes between us, heavy with the weight of the world.

I say, "What happened after that?"

Quentin's nostrils flare, and his heart awakens. Its wild beat entwines with my own, and their persistent thrumming is the only sound in the world. He searches my eyes for a long moment, chewing on his cheek.

"I lost my job, graduated, and ... later, by pure luck, Lindsey provided me a way out. I took it. I went back into hiding, doing my best to keep living because *damn* it I wasn't going to run away again. But I never heard from him again, never saw him, and I got ... complacent. Then, las—"

His voice cracks, but he soldiers on despite the new tears running freely down his cheek. "Last month, he came to my work. I—I didn't see him, but he left me a message. Then, he—he followed us back here one night, Elochian. He's seen me with you, and I wouldn't put it past him to hurt you because of that. He's jealous, and vindictive. Gods, I am so sorry. I should never have agreed to this, this was—"

I cover his lips with my thumb. I become temporarily overwhelmed by the knee-jerk reaction, and I clear my throat. "Don't," I whisper. "Please, don't say it was a mistake. Don't say you are a burden. If you truly wish it, I will return to arm's length, but don't push me to it in the name of protection. Haven't we done that enough?"

"Have we?" he asks, lips trembling against my thumb. "I can't lose you, Lochian."

I surge forward, crashing into him. He grunts against my mouth, and his teeth nick my upper lip as we collide in a near miss. I release his hand, wrapping my arm around the small of his back while my legs bracket his hips. A thick laugh escapes him, and his fingers stroke through my hair. I can't help but laugh a little too, and we try again.

I tilt my head, and kiss him.

He sighs, or maybe that's me. Or maybe it's the world exhaling, finally righting itself. The kiss deepens, our lips parting more with each push and pull, our bodies like the moon and the tides. He doesn't give me his tongue, seeming content with this. A thought burns in the back of my head that perhaps he'll become bored, but I smother it in another one of his tender, soft kisses.

I cinch the arm around his back tighter, bracing myself with a hand near his head, which causes his back to arch and—oh.

I break out of the moment, panting heavily.

"What's wrong?" He whispers, wiggling in my tight grip. His eyes widen, and he goes incredibly still. "I—"

"I swear to Mithys if you say 'I'm sorry,' you'll be in big trouble."

He laughs abruptly, surprised. "I see how it is."

I chuckle, shoulders relaxing a little. "There's nothing to apologize for, it's natural. I was surprised, that's all. I ... I hope you don't take my own state personally." I wince, wondering where the hell the weird spikes of arousal fueling my elongated fangs and morning wood are now. "It's ha—okay, we're not going to go with that. It's difficult for me, sometimes ..." I trail off, unsure what to say. Sorry, hope you're okay with defective equipment?

Quentin smiles. "Okay. Thank you for telling me. Do you like kissing? Is this okay?" He lifts his head a little, nudging my nose with his. "I can, erm. We can resituate, if it makes you more comfortable."

I smile, too. "Kissing is perfect. We can figure out the rest as we go, how's that?"

"I like the sound of that."

Fred And Dave

Quentin

Green light spills upwards from my phone situated between us, illuminating our battle. I study my opponent, but they give nothing away. I reach for a piece, and he smirks. It's a good move, so I go through with it. I'm used to people trying to throw me off my game, Caspian especially. He's the best out of all of us, but I manage to beat him more often than not.

Michael's smile fades, transforming into a yawn. He leans ahead and studies the board more closely. A few minutes pass before Elochian breaks the silence, exasperated. "Come on, you're drawing this out."

Michael glances at him, raising a brow. "Am I? Why don't you go on and try to beat him, then?"

Elochian sits beside Michael instead of hovering between us, crossing his legs beneath him. The rug is comfortable enough, but the little coffee table overrun by stickers separates us. I've been spoiled this morning, and I try not to think about what happens when our bubble of bliss pops.

After an *insane* makeout session, Elochian fell back asleep beside me, and later we awoke to the smell of cinnamon rolls and coffee. We waddled out in yesterday's clothes, hand in hand, and found Michael ready for the day, in different clothes and ready to go.

Michael made it clear they would've rather made breakfast than venture downstairs for it, but seeing how my cupboards are bare, that wasn't possible. I earned a scolding glare from both of them for my lack of groceries, and I can't deny that it made my heart warm a little at their concern. I didn't tell them that between the instant noodles, bread, and peanut butter, there were plenty of meals left.

And then Elochian used *my* shower, utilizing a small duffle bag that Michael procured. From where I don't know, but Michael is a magician like that. As a distraction, I asked Michael if they liked chess, which spurred our first game. I beat him twice in the time it took for Elochian to freshen up and get dressed, and this third round he's putting up a fight.

Elochian runs his hands through his hair, smoothing back the wet strands from his face as he studies the board for a moment. His fingers graze the projection of the queen, freeing her in a slow and easy gesture, a move Michael should've done four turns ago. Elochian's eyes flick up to mine. They swallow the fluorescence of the game, and seize my heart. The corner of his mouth twitches, and I grin in response.

"Okay, let's see what you got, old man."

That takes him off guard, and he laughs, hands raised. "Competitive much?"

Michael chuckles. "You should've seen how smug he was when he toppled my king. The *second* time."

I gasp, affronted. "I am not smug!"

"Then make your move, Dot," Elochian says, teasing.

"Oh, I'm making it," I say, pushing my glasses up my nose.

And so begins the first of many games of chess between Elochian and me. It's like time bends around the apartment, allowing hours upon hours to pass without interruption. Elochian beats me, then loses once before managing to get me again. Groceries arrive somewhere between our third and fourth game, surprising me.

Shame makes me go cold, and when Elochian won't take my money, he tells me it's an advance on his lessons. I tilt my head, confused. "Lessons? For what?"

He shrugs. "I haven't decided yet. You're a man of many talents, I'm sure we can think of something."

Then he *walks* away, and I'm left standing there like an idiot. Was he ... flirting? Serious? It takes a few moments for my brain to reboot, and I shake my head before helping him and Michael put things away. Both of them act like this is their place, like they've done this a million times before, and I wonder how pathetic I am that I find this ... amazing?

Michael starts on lunch, and when I protest that we just ate, they simply point at their watch. "It's two thirty."

"What? Really?"

"Really."

I look back at Elochian, who waits for me to resume the game in the living room. "You don't ... there's nowhere you need to be?"

"Except for right here, no," he says, confused. My jaw tightens, and I walk over to him. I sit down beside him instead of across, close enough that our knees are pressed together. His wings tremble, and he asks, "What's wrong?"

I take his hand, squeezing gently to assure him I'm not angry. Ashamed, yes, but not angry. I whisper, "Elochian, this is the first time we've ever hung out here. And don't you have ... I don't know, work stuff?"

He blinks at me, frowning. "I thought we were having a good time. Do you want me to go?"

"No, no. That's not—I don't want you doing *this* because you feel sorry for me."

"I *don't* feel sorry for you."

"*What*?"

"I don't feel sorry for you. I think what happened—" He glances at Michael, then back to me. Dropping his voice to a barely there whisper, he says, "What was done to you, and what you had to go through, is absolutely vile. But you didn't let it break you. Quentin, look at this place. Look at your life, your friends. *You* brought it all together despite what happened to you. That commands respect, not pity."

He takes my hand, holding tight. "Honestly? I have nothing but work for me back at the manor. I shut my phone off last night, and I'm too scared to turn it back on. I feel safe here, with you. Can we just ... can we just be, for a little while? Does there need to be a reason for that other than I want to? That I want to hide away from the world with you for a little while longer?"

I exhale, and my lungs ache with the force of the air they'd been holding. I nod quickly, running my thumb along the side of his pointer finger. "Thank you, for saying that. I'm sorry, I shouldn't have—ugh. It's like there's this little voice in the back of my head telling me all the ways this will go wrong."

Quietly, and with all seriousness, Elochian says, "I call mine Dave."

A laugh tumbles out of me. "What?"

He shrugs, cheeks darkening. "It's more fun to say things like, '*Fucking Dave,*' instead of admitting that really, you're pissed off at yourself."

I grin. "I like that. Okay. Let's call mine Fred. Fred and Dave. They can be friends."

Quentin smiles. "Okay. And if you'd like, I'll tell you that I want to be with you as many times as you like. Everyday."

"Promise?"

"Yes. I promise."

It only lasts for a few more hours. Eventually we move on from chess and squish together on the couch to watch an old movie on my laptop, which is situated on the coffee table. Michael and Elochian box me in, and it feels so *right*. I doze off a few times on Elochian's shoulder, losing only small bits of time if the movie is anything to go by.

I've seen it a million times, it's one of my favorites, but *Elochian* hasn't. I wanted to capture all his reactions, but am robbed by my nonsensical exhaustion. Despite staying up late, I *did* get some good sleep. The best I have in months, actually. Maybe my body doesn't know what to do with itself.

Nonetheless, a solid knock on the door has me jumping off the couch as if electrocuted, all whispers of sleep chased away. Before I can reach the door, Michael beats me to it. They grin at me, then look through the peephole. I glare over my shoulder at Elochian, who shrugs.

"If you can figure out how to calm down his guard dog streak, let me know."

Michael's demeanor doesn't change, but the fact that he doesn't retort puts me on high alert. He shifts his attention to Elochian. "It's your aunt, Sir."

Elochian bristles, wings opening wide. He doesn't look at me, just moves for the door, and something shifts in my heart. I put my arm out, stopping Elochian in his tracks. He blinks at me, lips parting. I raise my chin, slick back my hair, then straighten the sleeves of my shirt and the hem of my sweater vest. Michael steps aside, joining Elochian who stands a few feet behind me.

As prepared as I'll ever be, I open the door.

A demon stands on the other side of the threshold, partially hidden away by layers of black furs. A delicate, long red tail with a diamond shaped tip curls around her ankle, which is hidden away in thigh hugging black leather boots. A golden chain home to a singular pearl falls into her ample cleavage, which despite the furs, manages to be on full display. Her wings aren't visible, and neither are her horns. Lengthy nails that end in crimson points trail along a jawline that I find familiar, and cheekbones that are even more so.

My breath catches, but not at her beauty. Elochian and his aunt look far more alike than I thought they would. If I didn't know better, I'd say they were mother and son.

I bow at the waist with one hand drawn across my stomach, and the other balled into a fist at my back. After straightening, I say, "Tisha *xir* Adrastus, what a pleasure to meet you." I extend a hand to her, keeping my feet planted on this side of the doorframe. "Quentin Matsdotter, at your service."

Her red lips outlined in fine black lift upwards, a minute thing. She takes my hand, shaking it gently, as if I might break. "The pleasure is mine." Her eyes flick behind me, and her smile sharpens as she releases my hand. I fight a shiver, remaining still. "Elochian. As I said before, I don't mind what toys you keep, as long as you do your duty. Hiding away and isolating yourself is *not* that."

Elochian steps forward, joining my side. Without looking at me he takes my hand, holding tight. He says, "And as I said before, Quentin is much more than that to me. I'm allowed to have a night to myself, I—"

Without raising her voice, Tisha says, "Daniel Kavelli has cut off power to River Street due to your refusal to strike a deal. The water is dangerously close to freezing, and we have mere hours before the aquatic residents of Levena lose their homes. You humiliated the most major source of solar power in the entire region, and disappeared when the consequences came crashing down. It is time to wake up and clean up your mess, Elochian. There is a car waiting for you downstairs, and—"

"No," Elochian says, softly.

Tisha doesn't say anything for a moment. Her eyes shift to me, and although her calm expression doesn't change, it *feels* like a glare. She opens her lips, but Elochian shakes his head.

"I don't need Daniel, and I don't need you."

"Oh really?" Tisha laughs, and it claws down my spine. Elochian's fingers tighten impossibly around mine, and I return the pressure.

"Yes," Elochian says, refusing to engage with her. His wings are still when he says, "Return to the Manor, I will deal with this."

Tisha sighs. "You aren't—"

I don't really know *what* happens, but one moment there's a smug grin on Tisha's face, and the next it's slapped away. Like time has blurred around me. Wings unfold from her back, small but fierce, all red scales and black horns.

"Fine. But don't say I didn't tell you so."

She storms off down the hall, and I shut the door in her wake. Elochian immediately begins shivering, and I pull him against my chest. I rest my head on his shoulder, wrapping my arms around his lower back. I don't say anything, simply hold him. His shaky breaths wash across my neck, eventually smoothing out.

He whispers, "I have to go."

"What are you going to do?"

He leans back and tries on a smile, but it's unsure. "I don't know. I'll figure out something. Tisha's right, all the solar farms around here are Daniel's. The turbines are mine, but they aren't strong enough. I just need something to keep the street warm enough for a week, at most, while I figure this out."

I think about batteries. Energy. Magick. Magick reservoirs.

"What if—what if you asked Arlo for help? Arlo can enchant objects, and if you had enough 'batteries' you could energize the old system. But instead of solar power in the batteries, you use ... magick power."

"That's brilliant, but ... that's a lot of energy, Quentin. I don't think he can do it."

I chew on my bottom lip. "Not alone. And if Tobias helped, that would show a united front between you two. And maybe the other witches, what were their names?"

"Gaia will, she lives there. Demeter and Dimitri are ... I don't know about them. Dimitri might. If we had enough, we could do it all once, couldn't we?"

"Yes." My brain kicks into gear, imagining energy fields, potentials, the distance needed to cover. "And—oh, I hate to say this, but if Felix were there, it would empower the communal spell."

"And if we—"

Michael says, "Arlo Rook, this is Michael. We have a problem, and we need your help." Elochian and I startle at his voice, and Michael rolls his eyes. He offers the phone to Elochian. "Focus. You can talk on the way."

The necromancer's house isn't big enough for all of us, but there's no time to sit inside anyway, as much as I'd like to. The group of witches gathered outside and bundled in layers is full of faces I know, and don't. The auras are wild and primal, each one as unique as the person who owns it. Snow comes down in thick sheets, burrowing into every nook and cranny, doing its damnedest to find bare skin.

Despite the howling wind and plummeting temperatures, those present listen to Arlo with pure, unadulterated focus. He says, "Thank you all for coming. As you know, time is of the essence, but so is precision, so I'm going to go over this one more time, and quickly. Using the configurations we talked about earlier, we're going to transfer some of our magickal energy into the empty batteries supporting the heating system.

"You do not need to go into the water for this, but you *will* have to stand over each guidelight that marks them. Instead of doing this independently, we're going to do this as a group. By doing so we will be empowering each other, and hopefully prevent burnout. If you start to feel drained before the spell is complete, send out a flare before pulling out of the circle so we can prepare. Does anyone have any questions?"

Around a cigarette, Archeon asks, "Yeah, where's the name tags?"

Laughter bubbles throughout, not an effect the vampire was expecting, and he scowls through a puff of smoke. He stands apart from the rest, hiding in a trench coat and a thick scarf. I was briefly introduced to Gaia, and only through Elochian pointing them out do I now know who Demeter and Dimitri are.

Most of the new witches stand with Finnegan, each one wildly different from the last. A handsome human stands close to Finnegan, a hand stroking up and down the spine of the massive dog at his side. The fawn colored canine echoes the stature of the witch himself, but the man seems to be shy and unsure despite his size.

The siblings known as Dimitri and Demeter huddle together on the other side of the dog. Demeter's stance invites you to pick a fight, while Dimitri just seems bored. From what Elochian told me regarding his visit with them, it seems like Demeter just wants the best for Dimitri. My heart aches as I watch Demeter stand protectively with aer nibling.

I would take hatred from my siblings instead of the sheer, glacial indifference they show me. I've always told myself that I was born to the wrong parents, the wrong family. Everyone else fit in perfectly, I was the puzzle piece that wouldn't fit no matter how hard you jammed it in. It wasn't their fault.

My gaze stutters on the old *Tzipor* on the other side of Finnegan. She wears the same wry expression that I've seen on Dusan and Idina, and it's almost unsettling to be under her scrutiny. Evangeline Nightingale. Mobster or savior, depending on who you ask. And Finnegan's mother, apparently. At this point I'm going to assume he's adopted, he looks fairly human to me, but then again I've never met a *Tzipor*, maybe they have a humanoid form like celestials do.

Idina stands with the dragon and inventor known as Josse, an elderly man with the most amazing patchwork jacket I've ever seen, and old school wire-rim glasses. A patched together scarf wraps around his neck and black afro streaked with silver.

Two more witches stand apart from everyone else, one being a demon that Elochian doesn't know. I can tell that it bothers him, and I wonder how it's different from being around an unaffiliated demon like Primo. Maybe since he gave Primo permission, it's like an itch instead of a sting. I still don't really understand how he can *feel* all the celestials in Levena without—without it getting to him. Ah.

I squeeze Elochian's hand, and he returns the pressure but doesn't tear his gaze away from Tobias. *His* archangel. His words from the first night we met don't pain me like they used to, but I can't lie and say I'm not jealous of some fated connection between Tobias and Elochian, no matter how platonic it is. I'm just better at understanding it, studying the facets of my jealousy before neatly packing it into a box and shoving it in my closet.

Tobias and Arlo face all of us, their backs to the river. Tobias adamantly keeps his hands in his pockets, and his cheeks are flushed from the cold. His wings are spelled away, but his presence is undeniable. It grows every time I see him, like a physical thing that coddles you and sets you at ease, even if the man himself isn't.

Felix and Silas wait impatiently on the other side of Arlo, eager and nervous in equal measure. Arlo decided he'd rather have the boys here with him than alone at home, and he reluctantly agreed to allow them into the circle, per my suggestion. They are powerful, and this is their town, too. Arlo made them promise to pull out of the circle if needed, and they did.

Evangeline raises an elegant hand finished in talons, steadfast in the gusts barreling down on us. Arlo nods to her, and she gestures to Elochian. "Why is he here?"

Elochian inhales, but otherwise shows no outward signs of anxiety. After a nod of assent from Arlo, Elochian says, "I made a promise to keep the aquatic residents of Levena warm and safe. Instead I entrusted their safety to someone else, and in doing so I failed them." He pauses, eyes sweeping over the small crowd.

"I cannot easily remember the last time I saw so many witches in one place, and I wonder if this was his plan all along, to create a situation where you were all out in the open. You see, the person who once kept these waters warm is a known anti-witch supporter, so I'm taking no chances, and I will not allow him to harm any of you. So that is why I am here. To supervise, and direct my forces if needed."

"Are you saying there's an army of *shedim* hiding around here?" The shy human asks, fingers tightening in the bandanna around his familiar's neck. I feel like I know him, but I can't remember from where.

"Yes," Elochian says, smiling tightly.

"Peachy," The unfamiliar demon adds, staring at Elochian for a hard moment before looking away.

"Okay, let's get started," Arlo says, clapping his hands.

The witches assigned to batteries close by start walking, while those assigned farther down the street disappear with simultaneous cracks, their departure powered by one shot Travel stones. Illegal travel stones, I may add.

Elochian deflates when the attention fades. I rest my head against his arm, and he gives me a tired smile. "That was really good. Very noble-y," I say.

His brows lift. "Noble-y?"

I roll my eyes. "It's a word."

Elochian laughs abruptly. "Coming from the wordsmith himself, it must be true."

"I—"

A long and low whistle from Arlo cuts through the air like a dull blade, followed by a ground trembling hum that signals the beginning.

Elochian leans over and kisses my cheek. "It's time. Stay with Michael."

I swallow fear, clinging to him until the very last moment. "You be careful ..." I trail off, not wanting to draw attention to the obvious.

Everyone will be able to see him, plain as day.

He says, "I will."

Then his wings open and close faster than I've ever seen, curving as they work through headstrong wind and cheek biting snow. At first he rises directly upwards, then glides effortlessly towards the breadth of River Street, taking up his position as sentinel. I don't know why he insisted on surveying the area himself, he has people set up all around us and then some.

Despite the overwhelming storm clouds and lack of sun, he's like a brilliant kaleidoscope up there, complete with that beautiful amber in his wings. Michael rests a hand on my shoulder, and when I look up at him, I find he's watching Elochian too. "He'll be fine," he says, but I'm not sure if it's to me, or himself.

"I know." I rest my hand over Michael's, surprising him. He smiles down at me, and I try on a smile of my own. "He's pretty up there. It's not often his wings glow like that, hm?"

A singular crease appears between Michael's brows, and he looks up. He studies Elochian for a moment. Hesitantly, he says, "They aren't glowing, Quentin."

Elochian is now a blinding rainbow starburst intermingled with gold, and silhouetted by violent storm clouds. Tentatively,

I slide my glasses down my nose, and the glow disappears. He floats high above River Street, his wings fluttering too quickly for the human eye to follow. The binding ink whorls are nothing more than black lines, until I push my glasses back up. It's hard to tell with his wings going so damn *fast*, but I am able to catch glimpses of gold following each twist and swirl of black.

"Oh," I say, quiet and unsure. It's not his aura. His aura is a soft cloud that usually stays close to his body, always thickest around his heart. On his bad days, it's bruise blue, but most of the time it's the color of leaves in summer. Right now it's such a pale green that it's nearly white, and it floats lazily around him like an intricate spider web on water. More connections than I can count stretch in every direction, fading the farther out they go.

Idina joins us, lips parted as she watches the spectacle unfold. After a moment, she says, "I forget how much I miss him, until times like this."

The hum in the ground increases to a vibration that sets my teeth on edge, and the stones of Gaia's house moan in response. Michael shifts me behind him, a hand on my arm. He puts the river to our backs and I hold onto him, trying not to startle when a black veil embedded with galaxies and stardust ascends through a metaphysical crack in the earth, thick and billowing like an honest to Gods blanket. It grows higher, and higher.

I adjust my glasses, breathless.

Michael says, "I see it. It's not just you." He glances at Arlo, then to Elochian, and back to the veil. He whispers, "I didn't realize the circle would be so physical. And the familiars, look at them. There's no way we haven't attracted attention."

"Let them see," Idina says. "Let them see."

Bosko soars overhead, and his wingtips touched with Arlo's neon magick skim across the veil. It parts like dust, the particles are unimpeded by gravity. Small tornadoes of stars and magick spiral in his wake, and moments later four more birds follow his path, each one glowing in tune to their master's power. Small animals run across the wall, perpendicular to our position and seemingly immune to gravity as well, but the only one I recognize is Tobias' hare, Daisy. She's usually white, but her fur has turned a deeper pink than her witch's hair.

Unbidden, I ask, "What was your father's specialty?"

Idina chuckles. "Light. He was like the sun."

"Do you miss him?"

She nods. "Every day."

"My father was my best friend," I admit.

Idina smiles knowingly, watching the witches work. I shift my attention to Arlo and the boys. Silas stands at his left, and Felix at his right. Like Arlo, the boys manipulate *abracadabri* with their hands, stretching and kneading the forces of the universe into something tangible. Something good. Their backs are to me, but I sense peace from them. Ease.

It's the fluid way that they move, like the branches of a tree swaying together.

It's the tone of Silas' hums indicating he's excited, not unhappy.

It's Felix, an unending source of hope, of magick, of love. I don't need enchanted glasses to see how magnificent of a witch he already is, and everything that he will be.

It's Arlo, doing what he was always meant to do.

The intricate web of Elochian's aura has connected with the veil, lighting up the places it's attached to like the ends of a neuron. He isn't a witch, but he carries power with him all the same, boosting those around him.

And then there's me, standing on the sidelines. A human. Powerless. Useless.

What am *I* doing here?

Then it hits me.

I tell stories.

"She's right," I say, looking up at Michael. "People should be watching, and seeing what witches can do. The good they can do, and the celestials."

Michael stares down at me for a moment, expression pinched, before turning his attention to Elochian. I reach for Michael's hand, and am pleasantly surprised when he takes a firm hold of mine. Together we watch from the sidelines, hand in hand and tongues still. I don't know how long we stand there, the veil and storm has cast everything into a weird state where it could be any time, and my phone is dead. My feet begin to ache, and the cold settles deeper each minute we stand still.

About the time my knee starts to feel like rocks grinding on glass, three beams of light shoot up from the water in front of Arlo, Silas, and Felix. Green, white, and gold. It's a quick flash of a thing, followed by one right after another all around the water, as far as the eye can see. Yellow. Blue. Violet. Red. Pink. Colors I have no name for, and they make my heart sing.

"Can you see it?" I whisper.

"What?" Michael asks, tensing for an attack.

I blink away tears, laughing through the emotion building in my throat. "They did it."

We all meet at Arlo's place, and I have to wonder if the place got bigger somehow. Nineteen of us comfortably fill the downstairs, the groups and cliques easily spread out between the dining room and den. Besides Idina, Elochian, Michael, and myself, everyone present is a witch. The residual magick in the air is a heavy, palpable thing, like a weighted blanket tucked around your body. Comforting, if not a little suffocating. Most of the familiars are outside, but some of them stay close to their masters.

Elochian and I sit near the hearth in the big den, accompanied by Michael, Silas, and Felix. I'm exhausted from simply standing in the frigid air, I have no idea how Elochian is even awake right now, or the witches who performed a magick show that I'm sure was seen from space. Thankfully no one bothers me, and I'm able to be a simple observer as Arlo knits together those around him. He stands at the head of the room, a cup of coffee in hand and his focus on Josse, listening intently as the old dragon tells a story about his greatest creation, Floyd. A few newcomers listen as well, including the demon I've heard addressed as Rain.

After catching Elochian staring at her for the fifth time, I elbow him. "Lochian?"

He turns away, scratching at his temple. "Hm?"

"What's the deal?"

"Nothing."

"Obviously."

He scrutinizes me. "Were you always this sarcastic, or is this a boyfriend perk?"

Michael laughs suddenly, and I'm helpless to do anything but laugh as well. Felix shrugs and says, "He always is, Mr. Lochian."

"Now that he's got you hooked, he's going to be a delight," Silas adds dryly, tugging on the strings of his (Thatch's) hoodie.

Elochian smiles at both of them. "I see."

My cheeks burn, even after the laughter subsides. "Thanks, boys. You're some real good wingmen."

Felix yawns, resting his head on Silas' shoulder. "No problem."

Silas hums, short and low. "Go to bed if you're tired, I'm not a mattress."

"Shh," Felix says, and Silas rolls his eyes. He reaches for me, but my brain doesn't compute. Elochian understands, offering him the blanket once laid out on the cushions behind me. Silas covers Felix up, then closes his eyes and rests his head on Felix's.

Evangeline joins us, opting to sit on the little couch beside Michael. The Nightingale is beautiful, aged like fine wine with eyes and a nose sharper than knives. A dark mole resides underneath her right earlobe, and her long, silver hair is thrown over one shoulder.

The human sits beside her, still wearing his trench coat but without his canine companion. He's big and broad like Arlo, with tanned, slightly wrinkled skin and big freckles cast across his nose and cheeks. His hair isn't much longer than mine, a copper tinged brunette. I still can't put my finger on why he's so familiar.

Evangeline says, "This is a cozy gathering, isn't it?"

"It is," I agree, slightly stunned by her presence. Why do old women make me feel so flustered? Sounds like a good question for Doc.

Elochian's lips part, but Michael speaks before he can. Waving a little to the human, they say, "Hello there."

The human smiles, then immediately ducks his head and stares at his big hands fidgeting in his lap. "Hi."

"What's your name?" Michael asks.

The human glances up at me, then back down to his lap. He says, "Bud. Bud Raff."

"Come on, you'll love it. Bud's the best dancer in town."

I frown, discouraged.

"Oh come on, baby Please, for me?"

I swallow my argument, and nod. "Okay. But … after, we'll be alone, right? The only person I want to celebrate my birthday with is you."

River smiles, all teeth. It's the kind that comes before the warning. "Baby, you know I've been planning a surprise for you. Don't go ruining it." He leans down, kissing me hard enough to bruise. "I can't keep a gift to the world like you all to myself."

I stand without thinking. Elochian grasps at my sleeve, looking up at me with concern. "Bathroom. Need to use the bathroom," I say.

I slip away unimpeded after that. I tuck into the main hall, passing by Demeter and Dimitri chatting with Arche. They say hello, but I can't speak.

I disappear through the back door and carefully close it behind me, then make it around the corner of the house before bracing myself on my knees. I close my eyes, focusing on the cold cutting straight through my clothes.

The door creaks in the distance, followed by the crunch of snow, and I brace myself for Elochian's worry. I say, "I'm fine."

Silence meets me, and I look up to find Bud there, not Elochian. Staring down at his hands clasped together at chest height, he says, "I—I didn't think you remembered me, but I guess you did."

I push back nausea in order to say, "I didn't, not at first."

Bud hesitantly looks up at me, then back down at his hands. "If you're worried that I'll tell, please don't be. I—I left that life behind too."

I shake my head. "I wasn't, it just—I was surprised. I never knew you were a witch."

He nods. "That's how I power my magick, collect *abracadabri* energy, through dance. But the rest of it … I needed the money." He meets my gaze, finally holding it. "I hope that we can be friends, and if it's all the same to you, I'd rather forget about ... before. Can we do that? Can we start over? Eva says there's a chance I can live here, and I'd really like to. It's so warm, and everyone is so kind."

I study Bud, cataloging the ways he's changed. Aged. We are so different, but so alike in many ways. We're both humans, both survivors. Even then, I felt a certain kinship with him, as humiliating as our time together was. We were doing what we had to do, and in that sense, no one else will understand me like he does.

I extend my hand to him. "I'd like that."

He shakes my hand, offering a wobbly smile. "Thank you, S—"

"I don't go by that name anymore. It's Quentin now. Quentin Matsdotter." I smile back, gently releasing his hand.

"Oh," he says. "Well then, it's nice to meet you, Quentin."

"Likewise, Bud."

We small talk for a little while after that, and it calms my nerves. Reprograms my brain, associating Bud with normalcy instead of my life before. Bud gets cold and turns in, and I tell him I'll be in soon. Like clockwork, Elochian comes out mere moments after Bud goes in, as if he'd been waiting by the door. He immediately takes my hands in his, then brings them up to lips and blows on them.

"You're freezing," he says. "Are you alright?"

I pull my hands away from his, and hug him. I nod, and my cheek rubs against his neck. When his arms wrap around me, I whisper, "I'm okay."

"Quentin," Elochian says, drawing my name out. He rests a hand in my hair, the other between my shoulder blades. He doesn't ask me again, and I love him for it.

I—I love him.
I'm in love with Elochian Adrastus.

Dear Thatch,

I missed you today.

I've missed you since you left, but today was different. I wish you could've seen them, seen him. There's a new fire to Arlo's eyes, a new determination. He once told me that he does best when the world is falling apart, and today was proof of it. I don't know what that means for your future, but I do know that Arlo will never shed the armor he calls 'Hero.'

Hopefully, there won't be a need for heroes by the time you get back.

But he wasn't the only one I wish you could've seen. The look on Elochian's face when the heating system kicked back on, and the ice threatening the edges of the river began to thaw. Despite our months together, I feel like today was the first time I truly saw him. When that shadow of doubt is overturned by the fire burning within, he is truly something to behold. An archdemon of the highest caliber.

I have a feeling things are about to change, that what we did today is the start of something new. But maybe … maybe we sowed the seeds of this thing long ago, and the roots of it have finally settled, allowing a hint of life to claw through the earth, revealing a hint of what's to come.

Then again, maybe you were the one who gave us the seeds to begin with.

I know that you won't ever see this, but I've decided to start writing to you. If nothing else, it will help me keep track of the chaos that is our life.

I hope that you're doing okay.

Love, Q

2/9621

Think I Like You

Elochian

I stand before great marble statues of Gods that I should find comfort in. All my life I've been told I should be grateful for the blood that runs in my veins. I am of a *God*. I am the last living descendant of Mithys. I am the last living celestial with so much God in their body, that there's no room for the person themself.

I have never accepted my fate, never been grateful for my purpose in life. I always thought that the day it finally happened would be a somber one. Casting the white flag into the air, so to speak. But it wasn't, not at all.

I will never forget the way I felt up there, high above Levena and everyone I love. The power of the witches seemed to awaken the land, and me. The thin walls between me and the other celestials crumbled, but it wasn't overwhelming and terrifying like I thought it would be. I could feel them all, yes, but it was like ... like standing in a field, watching each individual leaf sway in the wind. Like how the Manor feels, but more.

And for a brief moment, I could see it. Mithys floating high above what was his, feeling—no. *Connecting*. Connecting with his creation, his *community*, and vowing to keep it safe, to give birth to a lineage that would be the ultimate guardians.

A lineage that ends (starts) with me.

I stare up at Mithys' figure cast in white marble, then briefly close my eyes and pray for the first time in decades. In the space between heart and mind, I whisper, '*I am honored to be your blood, and I hope you can forgive me for what I have to do. Maybe you planned it. Maybe you orphaned me intentionally, filling me with flaws, defiance, and questions. I don't know. I don't know.*'

Pebbles shift beneath my *shomer's* feet, and I open my eyes. Michael stands behind me, and Tobias and Caspian are too occupied with the statues to pay my sentimental moment any attention. We stand in the center of a solarium, a mere vestibule to Haniel Palace. I keep my chin raised and shoulders back, hands clasped tightly behind me. I'm dressed in battle armor, one of my finer suits reserved for special occasions.

Tobias choosing a *shomer* is most definitely that.

The archangel stands poised and elegant in a pantsuit that echoes the colors of his wings. His hair is free, and his feathers are still. Caspian waits on the other side of him, the most patient I've ever seen him. The sleeves of his simple dress shirt are partially rolled up his forearms, and the color matches Tobias' outfit perfectly.

Their children are with Arlo and Quentin for the day. My thoughts dwell on Quentin for hardly a moment before Caspian says, "Do you think the Gods really looked like that?"

I peer over at him. "Like what?"

He vaguely gestures to the marble statues perched throughout the barely tamed Garden of Life, planted by the last Archangel of Levena, Juniper Haniel. The solar glass protects the permanent garden from the elements, and it's like walking through a jungle instead of neat flowerbeds. Fruit and shade trees stretch towards the impossibly distant ceiling, allowing enough clearance for flight space above their canopy. While the hexagonal panels of the solarium can change color, right now they're clear, allowing a winter day's worth of rare sun to filter in.

Caspian says, "So big. And their heads, what even is that? Not to mention they are all … very naked. Did you inherit his dick too?"

Michael snickers, but wisely keeps their mouth shut.

"They are anatomically correct, yes. The Gods do not have faces, only the essence of their beings which form their 'heads,' or rather the plumes you see before you. As far as your last question, I do believe Elochian is well endowed, yes."

I sigh, already done with today. The four of us turn, finding the owner of the teasing, deep voice walking towards us. Andromeda Eilweir struts down one of the black pebbled paths cutting through the garden, flanked by a small reception of angels. Tobias looks nervous, even though he and Andromeda have spoken in missives.

Andromeda is a fierce woman, leader, and angel. Her enormous wings contrast her short stature, even the smallest of her feathers are the length of my arm. Each of them are burnt orange tipped with black. Her short hair has the same coloring, and dual lines are shaved along the sides of her temples. Her skin is pearlescent white and pink, glittering beneath the filtered sun rays.

Teeth hang alongside the silver chains in her ears, and silver studs decorate the shoulders and hips of her rose colored leather outfit. Homage to her successor, I bet. There's no doubting her bloodline, even without all the regalia. Demons collect bones the same as angels collect teeth, and many wear them.

It's an old tradition that keeps your kin close, along with the power and wisdom they once possessed. The boons are dependent on the piece, and the person they came from. There's a reason why the Adrastus Tomb is near inaccessible, unless you're a direct descendant of a person interned there. Even then, bones can only be removed with my approval.

In this regard, I am different from my kin once again. I do not wear the bones of my family.

I bow first, followed by Tobias and Caspian. Andromeda bows to me in return, but when it comes to Tobias, the angel and her entire company take a knee and bow their heads. They all lower a hand into the dirt path we stand upon, palm down. As one they say, "We ask to be in your service, Lord Tobias Jane *xir* Daemarrel, our beloved archangel of Levena and the Northern Region, as we are and all we hope to be."

Tobias' heart stutters in my eyes, and Caspian's hand captures his. I wait, trusting Tobias to do this. It is the first, and least formal, confirmation he has to deal with. Sure enough, he firmly says, "I accept you as you are, and all that you hope to be. Rise. Please."

They all rise as one, and I take in the small crowd gathered before us.

Andromeda's *shomer* and partner, Xenith, is a striking man. He stands at nearly eight feet tall, almost double his lover's height. He wears plain, revealing robes cuffed at his ankles and wrists. His wingspan is the same dark blue as his skin, but his cropped hair and sharp eyes are nothing but darkness. I have a hard time meeting his gaze, but it has nothing to do with how he looks.

Xenith was Bartholomew's soulmate.

Unlike Arlo and Thatch, most people don't find their soulmate. Or worse yet, they know exactly who they are, but they can never have them. I only knew Xenith to be Bartholomew's best friend and comrade, a fact I was always jealous of. After the *levaya*, Xenith changed everything.

"Did he know?" I asked, knees pulled up to my chest.

"No. I thought, why burden him with things we cannot change? He had you, and the clan. I have Andromeda, and the flock. There was no room for anything else." Xenith sighed, resting his head against the stone at our backs. He stared up at the stars for ages, then turned his gaze to me, wet and breaking. "I wasn't in love with him. But by Gods, did I love him. Only ... only after did I realize I could have told him."

"That you were soulmates?"

He smiled. "That too."

I recognize her entire council, one I'm nearly as intimate with as my own. We usually meet at each turn of the seasons, when the *malakim* and *sheidm* councils bring forth news of old business and requests for new business. This year's Imbolc meeting was delayed due to Tobias' ascension, and it will now take place in two weeks.

Today is an opportunity for Tobias to dip his toe in, to preemptively meet the council that will test, demand, and guide him. I've armed him with information and gossip in equal measure. Paired with his empath magick, he'll be able to sort the manipulative bastards from the celestials who actually give a damn.

Andromeda and Xenith move forward, leaving her contingency at rigid attention. Michael and Xenith exchange a silent nod of acknowledgment, then Xenith winks at me before his partner begins to speak. Andromeda says, "Lord Adrastus, it is good to see you again, it's been too long. To say that I was surprised to receive your invitation would be an understatement, but the Eilweir family will be there with bells on."

I bury my amusement at the formality, dipping my chin. "Lady Eilweir. Yes, I thought it was time the Manor saw some life, and no better time like the present. I'm glad to have at least one ally there," I say, genuinely meaning it.

Andromeda smiles at me, then turns her full attention to Tobias. She offers her hand, and Tobias shakes it firmly. "Lord Daemarrel, I'm so pleased that we're finally meeting in person."

Tobias nods, features pinched. "As am I, Lady Eilweir. May I introduce my husband, Caspian." He gestures to Caspian, who extends his hand to Andromeda.

She shakes it, bowing her head as she does. "Mr. Daemarrel, a pleasure to meet you. If you have any further questions regarding the statues, please, don't hesitate to ask. I could use an interesting twist in the day."

Caspian chuckles. "Oh, I think I like you."

Andromeda grins. "Likewise, good sir." She claps her hands together. "Now, on to business. We have less than one month until your Ascension. I was hoping to delay such a big event until you and your *shomer* bonded more, but with the celestial sickness and all it entails ..." She trails off, and we all hear what she doesn't say.

More magick accidents. More sick celestials. We've since learned about half the cases are due to this latest fuckery with the pollen, not that the news is talking about that. It's all being blamed on Tobias and I, our existence as Arches. Fucking Daniel's sudden decision to shut off the power to hundreds of Levena's most vulnerable civilians backfired, to say the least. I originally thought it was a trap, a way to bait all the witches into one place. But I truly don't think he expected them to band together like that, or he never would've offered them the chance to save the day. He's been quiet, which puts me on edge.

Tobias says, "I don't know if I'll ever be truly ready for this, but I'm ready to try."

Andromeda smiles, pleased. "Only fools feel prepared, good man. Now, have you made your decision regarding the Trial?"

Tobias nods, rose feathers shaking. "I have." He reaches into a pocket and retrieves a piece of paper, offering it to her.

She reads it, then nods. "Perfect. I will have it arranged immediately. Are you ready to meet everyone?" She gestures towards the group watching us with eager eyes and tense wings.

Tobias exchanges a look with Caspian, who nods once. The archangel says, "Yes."

One by one, Tobias' future council clasps forearms with their archangel. They tell him how long they've served the clan for. Who their kin is. Their community ties. What businesses they have their hands in. And wasn't that a nice stroke of genius with the enchanted batteries, will you patent the idea?

Petra Olan, the Director of the Levena Food Center, is the first angel to introduce herself to Caspian without being prompted. George, the Director of Levena Head Start, doesn't acknowledge Caspian at all, and he isn't the last. As time passes, Tobias becomes more clipped. I'm used to Caspian's short temper, but not Tobias' building rage. Caspian smiles quietly during the whole affair, unbothered on the outside.

It's endless. This is the part I hate most about being an Arch. The duality of people who want something from you. The constant strategizing, reading between the lines and plotting. Always plotting. The ball will be ten times worse than this. *Why am I throwing a ball again?*

Celebrating my *bashert*. Digging up gossip on Daniel. Reminding people who I am.

Quentin.

Quentin in red, dancing in Adrastus Hall, in my arms.

I shake my head, try my damnedest to focus.

After niceties have been displaced, the bulk of the group moves off the path and into a clearing which houses a pavilion temporarily dubbed as the 'observation area.' I stand with Michael, Tobias, Caspian, and Andromeda in the center of the expansive rectangle of undisturbed, lush grass. A short distance opposite us stands Ichabod, the Master of Arms, and the *shomer* candidates. All four are lined up, quiet and still.

Not one has been spoken to, or have they spoken, and they won't until the end, as is tradition. The final process of choosing a *shomer* is different for angels than it is for demons, but there are a few key similarities.

There are several competitions, each one designed to highlight desired qualities in *shomer*. A series of duels, including weapons of choice and hand to hand combat. A flight demonstration focusing on agility and speed. A stealth mission reminiscent of capture the flag. A written test based on current celestial laws, both regional and citywide. The last competition is the Trial, which is a challenge chosen by the contracting party. In this case, Tobias.

Since I was a child when my first *shomer* was chosen, my father set the Trial. Then, when it came time for me to choose a new *shomer*, I was able to pick. I was petulant and catty back then, and the Trial I chose reflected that. I quite literally sat on the floor and refused to get back up. The first person to get me off the floor without touching me, won.

The others asked. Begged. Demanded. Bribed, like one would do with a child. Michael simply stood behind me, and waited.

And waited.

And waited.

He stood there for an hour, quiet and steadfast. I could feel it, my soul entertaining the idea of this person who seemed to know exactly what I needed without saying a word. I smile a little thinking back on it, and Michael rests a hand on my shoulder. I look over at him, and he gives me a quick wink.

A soft wave of affection washes over me, and when his hand falls from my shoulder I turn my focus back to the field. The first candidate steps forward. These people have been training for this moment their entire lives, a moment that no one thought would happen. Nevertheless, the angels of Levena have treated every day as if tomorrow their leader might walk through the door. I give them the respect and attention they deserve.

Kita Lanworth. Fifth-generation descendant. 53 years old. A strong and fit specimen, her eyes are bright and temporarily bound wings well-kept. She takes her place at the corner of a twelve by twelve square. Bare toes digging into the white sand and fists raised, she faces off against her opponent.

Roland Teketo. Fifth-generation descendant. 97 years old. He's built for stealth, his bound wings are dark and fit for diving. He stands in the corner opposite her. They watch each other, bodies primed with energy and ambition.

"You can see it," Tobias whispers to me. "They want this."

"It is a celestial's highest honor to protect an Arch," I whisper back, not for the first time. Tobias opens his mouth, and I shoot him a look, stopping the self-flagellation before it begins. "Don't. Don't you dare say you're just you, that you're not worth it. Not here. Not now. To them, you are. Now act like it."

Tobias' lips close, pushing thin. His wings shudder as he turns his gaze ahead, shoulders straightening. As I shift my own attention, I catch Caspian's eye. He nods, giving me what I'm learning is his satisfied nod. I focus on the match.

Ichabod shouts, "Begin!"

They dance. Kita throws the first punch. Roland dodges, skipping backwards. They're completely different body types, but that's the point. It is unlikely you will have easy enemies in life. Kita reminds me of a day lion, full of muscle and great power that strikes in heavy bursts. Roland is quicker, his hits efficient but small. Like a valley cat that hits and runs, working best in a pack that picks off their target in tandem.

Except here, he has no backup. No pack.

Kita manages to sweep his legs out from beneath him. He falls on his back and she lunges forward, driving a knee into his throat. There's no breaking free, and Ichabod calls the match in Kita's favor. It's quick and brutal, but the pair clasp arms and bow to the other before leaving the sand.

I step forward a touch for this next pair.

Amber Mirthwood stands where Roland once did. Sixth-generation descendant. 26 years old. She was my favorite on paper. She has high scores intellectually, physically, and got into just enough trouble during training to make her interesting. She's the youngest of the group, a perspective that I think Tobias would prefer, and the council's second least favorite due to her being sixth-generation.

And then there's Charlie Crash. (Yes, that is his real, legal name.)

Sixth-generation descendant. 32 years old. He has the lowest scores intellectually, and physically due to the fact he's smaller than all the rest. I think he's rather clever though, proven by his test performances. He seems like the kind of person who solves problems better 'in the real world' as opposed to on paper. He's about the same height as Quentin, but he's wiry and thin.

He *does* have the highest flight scores of the group, and he's the fastest celestial in a hundred years. He does nothing but get into trouble and ask questions, making him the council's *least* favorite. It's the good kind of mischief, in my opinion.

He stands opposite Amber with a big grin on his face. Amber's back foot shifts, finding purchase in the sand. Her brows are set in a hard line, she is nothing but focus.

Ichabod shouts, "Begin!"

In the blink of an eye, Amber is flat on her back. Oliver stands before her, left hand outstretched, palm down. His pointer and index finger are extended, lingering in the place Amber's forehead once was. A cloud of sand surrounds them, falling to the ground in the next blink.

"Did he just ... knock her out?" Caspian asks, not to anyone in particular.

"Yes," Andromeda says. "Charlie specializes in *krav maga*. While all our students are trained in it, he is a true master of the art."

"If I moved like that, I'd be a master too," Caspian says, throwing a hand in Charlie's direction. "How is that fair? He didn't even give her a chance."

"Fair?" Andromeda tears her gaze away from Ichabod carrying Amber off the sand, and her fierceness makes me stand a little taller. "Do you think anyone attempting to kill you or your family will be *fair*? Do you want them to have a chance?"

"Well, no—"

"It's mercy," Tobias says, resting his chin on a fist while he contemplates Charlie rejoining the line.

"Indeed, my lord." Andromeda studies the archangel for a moment, then turns her gaze ahead. "I believe Charlie is so gifted in the ways of *krav maga* because of his heart, not his speed, although that may play a factor. He doesn't like to fight."

"Interesting. A *shomer* who doesn't like to fight," I murmur.

"Interesting is certainly a word used to describe Charlie Crash," Xenith says with a touch of fondness and amusement, the first words he's uttered since this whole affair has begun. They might as well have been praises from the Gods themselves, as far I'm concerned.

Hours later, I'm hungry and tired and ready to go home. On a quantitative level, the results are close, but to me it's more than winning versus losing. How did the losers lose? Was it with dignity? Were the winners smug? Flying around and beating each other up is impressive, and being able to regurgitate laws is fine, but that doesn't speak to their character.

Thankfully, all that's left is the Trial, which to be honest, I've been curious about.

A table with one chair now separates us from the prospects. Ichabod stands beside it with a large box in his hands, and he nods at Tobias. "We are ready, my Lord."

Tobias bends down and kisses Caspian on the cheek. Caspian smiles up at him, then wheels over to the table. The tires of this particular wheelchair are rugged, and they endure the grass with ease. Tobias stays by my side, hands clasped behind his back. He surveys those gathered for a moment before speaking. When the archangel does speak, it's like hearing him for the first time.

He says, "For this Trial, I ask you to play one game of chess against my champion."

Interesting. Not win against Caspian, but simply play. I doubt the wordplay was careless on Tobias' part.

Ichabod sets the box down on the table, revealing a chess board inlaid into its surface. He pulls out a drawer, and withdraws the black and white marble pieces stored inside. As he sets Caspian's white pieces up for him, Ichabod calls to the trainee currently in the lead. Roland takes a seat across from Caspian, setting up his own black pieces.

Caspian grins at him. Roland bows his head in submission, face serious.

Ichabod waits for Tobias' acquiescence, and after he nods, the Master of Arms says, "Begin."

It takes five minutes for Roland to beat Caspian.

Three minutes for Kita to beat Caspian.

Six minutes for Amber to beat Caspian.

As Charlie takes a seat, Andromeda addresses Tobias. "Interesting choice of Trial, my Lord."

Tobias smiles tightly at her. "Isn't it?"

I chuckle, shaking my head. Michael watches the next game begin, attention keen.

Two minutes into Charlie's game, he raises a hand. Ichabod comes to his side, offering the man a piece of paper and a pen. Charlie quickly writes, scowling the entire time. After he gives the paper to Ichabod for reading, Charlie stares daggers at Caspian.

Ichabod frowns as he reads the paper, glancing between it and Charlie. After a moment, he addresses Tobias. "My Lord, Charlie would like to know if his opponent is purposely—" Charlie jabs a finger at the note, thick red brows creased together. Ichabod snarls, "No, I am not reading that."

Tobias loudly says, "Go on. I'd like to hear it in his words, please."

Ichabod glances at Andromeda, an instant mistake. "You heard him," she snaps.

The Master of Arms sighs, resigned. He looks down at the note and reads aloud, "Why the fuck is he letting me win?"

Everyone shifts their attention to Tobias but Caspian and myself. Caspian's grin widens when realization dawns on Charlie's face. Clever boy. Tobias joins those at the chess table, steps slow and calculated, wings slightly open. He stands by his husband's side, and when his magick touched gaze settles on those around me, including Andromeda and her council, something settles in my chest. I dare call it pride.

Tobias says, "I believe you have all forgotten a key aspect here. I am not choosing a *shomer* for myself. I am choosing someone who will protect, guide, and watch over my *family*. Before anything, I am a father. A husband. And not one of you has addressed my partner properly. Only half of you deigned to speak to him at all, and if you did, it was a passing thought. Caspian is a regional chess champion, three times over. He *let* every single one of you win, and did so in a way that it was blatantly obvious. But not one of you questioned it, you all underestimated him."

Tobias shakes his head and fills his lungs, resting a hand on Caspian's shoulder. He softly asks, "Have you made your choice, my love?"

Caspian nods, patting Tobias' hand. "Oh yeah. We're adopting this one." He extends his other hand to Charlie. Stunned, Charlie takes it, shaking firmly. "Pack your bags, kid. You're coming home with us."

Ichabod sputters, looking to Andromeda once again. She shrugs, barely veiling a grin. "Don't look at me. He's your archangel."

George leaves the pavilion, leading a group that is as pissed off as he is. He marches right up to Tobias and says, "This is an *outrage*. Just because you do not know our ways does not mean you can shun them entirely. It is unfair to those who actually take this honor seriously. Charlie Crash is *not* an acceptable *shomer*, and you cannot just ... take him home! *This* is your home now."

Tobias' wings and aura flare out, sending a gust of wind and magick throughout the field. George stumbles backwards, and Tobias looms over him. Just shy of a shout, Tobias says, "My home is a little yellow house with white shutters, and always will be. I will be your Arch, but I will do it *my* way. I do not need to live here to do it. Now, if you'll excuse me, we are done here for today."

Tobias, Caspian, and an unsure Charlie head our way, and I've never felt more inspired. Andromeda looks over at me, pleased. "Well, it would appear we are finished here. I'm looking forward to seeing you again, Lord Adrastus." She reaches for me, and we clasp arms. "It is always an adventure with you."

I laugh quietly. "I am not adventurous. I merely know people who are."

She hums. "Agree to disagree, my Lord."

Frazzled

Quentin

Time is measured by long nights, the people I see, and the click of a lock.

Elochian visits me nearly every night now, accompanied by Michael, of course. His days are filled with archdemon things, and my own are partially spent with Silas and Felix, or my own work. Our nights together are simple, a time for us to recharge from the day and just be together. We've gone back to Primo's a couple of times, but that's all our lives have allotted time for.

No matter what we do, each night ends the same way.

Laying in bed together. Our hands clasped between us, legs entangled and lips ever so close. We talk about everything and nothing, breathing in each other's words. And then, one of us falls asleep. Most of the time I succumb first, I can't help it. But sometimes, I get the rare pleasure of watching Elochian lose his battle. I love the way his lashes flutter and quiver when his eyelids finally shutter closed. The way his fingers twitch as he falls into a deeper sleep.

The way he pulls me close to him, groaning a little when our bodies finally align.

But I haven't woken up to him in my bed again, not since our first date. It's always a note, paired with a cup of water and my phone neatly plugged into its charger. They're just little scraps of paper, nothing really, but each one hides in a box in my closet, along with Thatch's letters.

My purpose has changed in the past few weeks. I keep the boys company in the afternoons during the school week, except on Thursdays, and Archeon stays with them then. I've taken them to Primo's a few times, and I think it's now Silas' favorite place in the world.

I've certainly become close to Primo, and I've found out that his place rests on some of the oldest ground in Levena. What it was used for is a different story, though. According to my research, the End was the first separate 'neighborhood' of sorts that was built after Levena changed into Min, skipping over the roots of *Etz Hayim* to rest on the edges of a swamp. Why build there, in a time when the land was so inhospitable?

Besides playing babysitter, I'm back to teaching my Thursday nights in person, and Elochian escorts me to the university if he can manage it. I insist that I don't need his protection, but it's like talking to a brick wall when it comes to that. I can't say that I really mind, and we usually bring home food and stay up late, which I like.

And during the rest of my time, I write.

Finnegan says he's never read articles like mine before, and they're exactly what he needs. Of course they're under a pen name, but Elochian let it slip that he could tell it was me. Then I teased him for being a fanboy, and he blushed for days. He does that a lot lately.

"What're you thinking about?"

I blink away visions of Elochian's darkened cheeks and thoughts of change, turning my head towards Arlo. "Life. Everything and nothing."

"Good one." He scoffs, wiping excess ink from my forearm, which stings like a fucker. "Well, if you want to talk, I'm not busy. Just sitting here, tattooing my best friend's arm while he stares off into space."

I chuckle. "Sorry. I think this is the longest I've sat still and just ... relaxed."

Arlo laughs, dipping his needle in fresh ink. "I think some people would disagree with your method of relaxation." He introduces the needle to my skin once more, and I watch as a book's spine comes to life in a cloud of soft green magick. Kitt's studio is quiet, she's been open less lately and she doesn't live in the apartment upstairs anymore. She mostly lived with Lindsey to begin with, but she finally, and fully, moved out of the backup apartment (escape plan) around the time she proposed.

"Arlo," I say quietly.

"Yes?"

"Thank you."

He lifts the needle from my skin, blinking up at me. "Quentin, you don't need to keep thanking me for this, it's not—"

"*Yes*, I do. This is big magick, Arlo."

Arlo stares at me.

I stare at him.

He sighs. "You being safe is thanks enough. Now knock it off and leave it alone."

I smile. "Fine. Only because you asked so nicely."

Arlo winks at me, then goes back to work. He hums along to a song on the radio, something he usually does after smoking herb. The haze of our last session hangs in the air around us, a rare thing now, what with all the kids usually around. Well, maybe rare for him. After a few minutes he says, "By the way, Silas has been talking nonstop about that Primo's since you brought him by."

"Oh yeah, it's teenage musician heaven, you know. You should come check it out with us sometime. When was the last time you took a break?"

"Oh, I don't know." He laughs a little. "I consider this a break, honestly. You're easy to be with, Q. And it's so quiet."

"Giving me shit for my relaxation methods, when yours are the same." I huff, teasing.

"Hey, I said *some* people might disagree, not me."

"This is true. Um, how much longer is this going to take?"

"Eh, 'bout twenty more minutes. Why, got a hot date?"

I roll my eyes. "No, but my couch is calling my name. Lochian's got some fancy council meeting with Tobias tonight, remember?"

"Oh, that's right. Hey, did you get the picture Cas sent?"

I laugh. "Of Marlena terrorizing Charlie? Poor guy, probably not the kind of life he expected an archangel to have. I like him though."

Arlo stops tattooing for a moment, peeking up at me. "You met him?"

I swallow. "Yeah, they all came by the cafe a few days ago."

"Oh."

"You were with Finnegan," I say, instantly regretting my tone. "Looking at that complex in the End, I mean."

"Right, yeah." He shakes his head. "It's been too long since I've seen them. Maybe I'll stop there on the way home."

"I think Cas would like that. He seemed a bit frazzled."

Arlo barks out a laugh. "Frazzled? Caspian? No."

I laugh too, settling back into the comfortable fog of peace and pain. We fall quiet for a little while, simply existing together. Eventually Arlo wipes my arm one last time, then leans back and stares at his handiwork. Quietly, he asks, "What do you think?"

I lift my arm, marveling at detailed vintage book spines, sheets of parchment with tiny writing that is foreign to me, and an inkwell complete with a featherless quill. I tilt my head, staring at it. I look up to Arlo with a question on my tongue, only to find one of Bosko's feathers cradled in his hands, the bird situated on his shoulder like he'd been there the whole time.

He says, "With this, you will be able to tap into my magick. Call upon the quill and use it to keep your most precious words inside the books, or inscribe runes onto the parchment to cast your own spells. What you can do will be limited, but it's better than nothing."

"Arlo, I—I didn't realize—I'm not a witch, I can't do magick. I thought you were just giving me a storage tattoo. What if I give you a heart attack? Has this—" I drop my voice, even though we're alone. "Has this ever been done before? Is it legal?"

Arlo smiles fondly at me. "Quentin, relax. I wouldn't offer this to you if I didn't trust in you, or myself. It will hardly affect me, I promise. And the spells ... think of it as an extension of my own magick. You won't be able to do anything I can't, and like I said, it's minor stuff. Light cantrips, shields. Some charms. But you don't have to do this if you don't want—"

I slide out of the chair and wrap my arms around Arlo's shoulders in a weird, half-hug to accommodate Bosko and my freshly inked arm. I sniff, doing my best to hold back tears. I rest my head on his shoulder, soaking in the feeling of Arlo's big hand rubbing between my shoulder blades. "I do. Thank you, Arlo. Thank you."

Bosko chirrups and Arlo sighs, emptying his chest. "It's the least I can do, Quentin. Now come on, let's get you fixed up."

I lean back, sitting on the edge of the chair. I nod, wiping at my eyes. "Okay. I'm ready." I hold my arm out for him, unsure what the hell I'm getting into. I'm really doing this, aren't I?

Arlo cradles my forearm in his hand, then lays very real cream and gold feather over the inkwell embedded into my skin. It nearly covers the whole thing, and I wonder how this is going to work. He lowers his lips, hovering a mere inch or two above the feather. He fills his lungs with air, and magick I suspect by the way his eyes alight, holds it for a moment, then exhales.

Emerald, fluorescent light overtakes the feather, transforming it from reality into metaphor. Heat settles into my skin, a dull warmth that explodes like a supernova. I groan, crashing into Arlo as I curl over my arm. A hand settles on the back of my neck, squeezing tight, which keeps me from slumping forward anymore. The light dissolves into my skin, sparking as the last bits of magick break through flesh.

I breathe.

And then it's over, the pain ebbing like the tide.

Arlo holds onto me while I breathe, adjusting. There's a distinct *something* different in my body, but I can't pinpoint where or what it is. Like a fleeting itch, or the jarring sensation of hitting your funny bone. I stare down at my arm, slowly flexing my hand open and closed. There's only the subtle shift of ink on flexing skin, shiny despite the dim light filtering in through the cracks of our huddle. Bosko's feather is the only source of color in the piece, more vivid than it was in life, on the verge of unnaturally vibrant.

I close my eyes and search my body, hunting for the origin of this new feeling. I imagine holding a string in my hands, chasing its length through my limbs until reaching my chest. I stiffen and Arlo gives me space, hand falling from my neck.

I open my eyes and clear my throat, raw and aching like I've smoked a pack of cigarettes. "My heart. I can feel you there. Can you feel me?"

Arlo rests a hand over his heart, his expression soft. "Yes."

"Does it ... hurt?"

That softness breaks into a small smile. "No, not at all. Go on, do you remember what I said?"

Normally, I would draw up something clever or snappy, but I'm too overcome with emotions to find any. I nod, bringing the shaky fingers of my right hand to my left forearm. I draw a series of circles around the pile of books, clockwise twice, counter-clockwise once, then a tap in the center.

I thought I would feel it, but sound heralds my first conjuration. The rustle of pages floating through the air, the whisper of words as they promise knowledge and secrets. Light follows, transforming the black linework into bright silver intermingled with the faintest hint of green, evidence that Arlo's magick is no longer fully his, not while it's within me. The cloud of light flows down my forearm like a river, spilling into my open and waiting palm.

And finally, as the light transforms imagination into reality, I feel it. Perpetual, everlasting warmth. It starts in my arm, coursing upwards until reaching my heart where it's pumped throughout the rest of my body. I thought magick would feel unbalanced for me, wild and restless. I've felt his magick before, when using his travel stones and otherwise. I know that it's warm and comforting.

But this is different. This warmth ....

It feels like Elochian.

A weight settles into my hand, slow and easy. I blink away tears, focusing on the familiar leather bound journal in my hands. It's more detailed than the books in my tattoo are, and I don't need Arlo to tell me it's a manifestation of my deepest desire. It's not the original, I'll never get that back, but seeing such a perfect replica of my first journal mends a crack in my heart.

Arlo says, "It's beautiful, Quentin. You did so well."

I hug the journal, not caring how pathetic I look. Head bowed, I say, "My father gave it to me. I—it—my mother burnt the original years ago."

"You must miss him."

I look up at Arlo, finding only sincerity in his eyes barely alight with magick. He never had a father at all, at least I have fond memories of mine. There are so many things I want to say to him, and so many things I want to hear. I swallow, looking down at the journal. Carefully, I spread the pages.

It's untouched. There are no notes in the margins. No loopy, near indecipherable words. No crossed out ideas or circled thoughts. It's clear, ready for a new beginning.

I close the book, then repeat the process I did to conjure it in the first place. Only once it fades into ink do I feel like I can breathe properly.

"You're a natural," Arlo says.

"Sure." I smile, if only a little. I duck my head and rub at my collarbone, suddenly overcome with uncalled for loneliness. Elochian said his meeting would go late into the night, and he wouldn't be by. My heart aches at the idea of going home to an empty apartment. And it's not just him I look forward to seeing, Michael and I have become good friends. When Elochian and Michael are there, the place feels like home.

Arlo takes his phone out of his jeans pocket, then shrugs. "You know, Arche said he'd stay with the boys until nine, and we've got a few hours to kill. Feel like visiting the Magpie?"

I chuckle. "Are you asking me out for drinks, Arlo Rook?"

"Well I think this calls for celebration, don't you?" He gestures vaguely to all of me, and I laugh. He smiles, pleased.

"Well, when you put it that way."

The lights are harsher than I remember.

I sit with Arlo at the bar, spinning a glass full of amber whiskey and melting ice. It's busy, but not fully packed. I love the hanging garden, the soft emerald velvet of the stools and the kind smiles you find everywhere. For being a club, the place feels almost like … like home. Music thumps throughout the place, electrifying my chest with every beat. It's fast, made for a more sensual kind of dance. I glance over my shoulder, watching couples grind on the dance floor and singles courting potential partners. There are more angels in here than last time, I think.

I haven't been back since the last time we were all here together, and I think the same can be said for Arlo. There's reasons for both of us to avoid the bar, besides the fact our gatherings revolve around food instead of alcohol. I think for Arlo, it's memories of Thatch. For me, it's memories of shame.

"Are you alright?"

I jump at the sound of Elochian's coarse voice on the other side of the door. I groan, knocking my head back against the bathroom stall. The music I was once a part of echoes throughout the bathroom, and my ears ring from being on stage. I manage to sputter out, "F—fine. Just—ugh. Too much to drink. Go ahead, I'm oh—fuck. Okay. I'm okay."

Internally, I scream, 'I am definitely not okay. Please leave so I can calm down.'

Elochian shifts on his feet, fancy shoes scraping against even fancier tile. Strained, he says, "I can't. It's... Tobias' magick is too much."

"You're hard too?"

Absolute, dead *silence.*

Oh dear Gods. Allow me to wither and perish on the spot. Please.

"Um... no. I don't—that's not it. He's my archangel."

"Oh," I say like I completely understand, even though I don't. Tobias? An archangel? His?

My brain is a fog of lust, embarrassment, and confusion. I want (need) Elochian to go (stay). Silence filled with unsaid things and tension thicker than blood chokes me. He knows damn well what my actual problem is, and he's still just standing there! Maybe he wants...

He says, "I'm—if you—I—"

But it's too late.

The fleeting fantasy of Elochian coming into the stall and helping me out lasts for only a second. A second of that in my mind is more than enough. I cover my mouth, doing my best to suffocate the moan that escapes me.

And then another silence follows, this one a million times worse than the first.

Elochian leaves, and I slump to the floor in embarrassment.

"It feels different here," Arlo says, bringing me back to the moment. His hands are wrapped around a glass of water, and the flashing lights play in his mellow golden eyes.

I rub at my eye, smudging my glasses. "How?"

He casually glances around, and I follow his gaze. Through my glasses the world is a sea of color. Auras pale and vibrant, calm and wild, melded with others and isolated. Testing a theory, I slide my glasses down my nose a little. The incoming headache intensifies, but the auras remain. So, I can see them without the glasses, but they help with the strain.

In a low tone, Arlo says, "It's hard to explain. Places can hold power, depending on how they're treated. It feels … like the roots have gone deeper, and stronger, but there's …" he trails off, eyes settling back on me.

"Termites," I say, because I can feel it.

Arlo stares at me, expression unreadable. "Yes."

I scrub at my eyes with both hands, pushing my glasses up into my hair. "What should we do?" My palms dig deeper and deeper into my eyes, unable to soothe the burning.

Firmly, but not unkindly, Arlo says, "Quentin, look at me." My hands fall into my lap, and my glasses fall back down onto my nose, askew. Arlo fixes them for me, then rests a hand along the side of my throat. He frowns. "Are you feeling okay?"

I shake my head, and I wince against the pain ricocheting against the walls of my skull. I'm no stranger to tension headaches, but this feels like one on steroids. Is it a migraine? "No, my head. Hurts."

Arlo searches my eyes for a moment. He says, "Okay. I'll leave a message with one of Lochian's people, then we'll go back to your place."

I nod the barest amount. "Okay."

He hesitates. "Why don't you come with me?"

I glare at him. "I'll be fine. Just go."

He glances at the security guard at the other end of the bar, then back to me. "I'll be right back."

Irritated by his mothering, I pick up my glass, throwing back the now room temperature whiskey. By the time I set it down, Arlo's gone. I run a hand through my hair, unsettled and full of emotions I can't name. I can't remember the last time I felt so on edge and unmoored. Is it because of the tattoo, my unrightful claim to magick?

I tap the counter and the bartender quickly attends me, glancing in Arlo's direction as he pours another whiskey. "Trouble in paradise?" He asks, and I take him in for the first time. A demon, short in stature and his wings spelled away. His eyes are uncanny, and my heart jumps at the familiarity I find there. Not in how they look, but the focus and intent behind them. Like staring into the eyes of a predator.

"No, long day, that's all. I haven't uh … seen you here before."

The bartender chuckles, sliding my drink towards me. He rests his elbows on the counter, cupping his chin in his hands. "Figures you wouldn't remember me."

I shift in my seat, subtly leaning back. "I'm sorry, do we know each other?"

"I've worked here a few months." He titters. "I used to see you every now and again with that *witch*." He spits the word. "And all your friends. You were so pretty playing the drums, I liked hearing you. But ever since that night, it's like you disappeared. I've missed you."

I laugh nervously. "Sorry, I don't remember."

He leans closer, and every nerve in my body screams at me to *move*, but I can't. He whispers, "It's just like you, to disappear without thinking of the damage you leave behind." Color swirls in his eyes, the black giving way to toxic blue. "But I know now that it wasn't your fault. He's kept you away from me."

He cups my cheek, his hand calloused and cold. Tears well in my eyes, and I try with all my might to punch him in the face.

All I manage to do is curl my hands into fists, nails biting my palms. He brings his lips to my ear and whispers, "Don't worry baby, I'm here now. Let me take you home. Doesn't that sound nice? Haven't you missed me?"

"Y—" I choke back the word, and his hand leaves my face. In a blink, he's on this side of the counter, taking my hand in his. Does no one see him? See this? His fingers dig into the wounds that my own nails carved, and hot tears fall down my cheeks. "P—please."

He smiles. "Oh, I missed the way you beg. Come now."

He pulls, and I go (un)willingly. My feet touch down on the floor. I stagger, my gait unsteady and bones resistant to his dark magick. I open my mouth to scream Arlo's name, but nothing comes out. I can only watch on in horror as he leads me towards the back exit, unable to turn my head or look anywhere else but directly ahead.

Why does he look like that? Where is Elochian's security? Where is—

"Quentin!" A hand falls on my shoulder, yanking me backwards.

Fresh air and free will rushes me like a tidal wave. I crash against Arlo, gasping for both. "He—" I extend a shaky hand in my kidnapper's direction, but he's long gone. Anger and fear war for dominance, but I stumble through both and say, "River. H—he had me. He was t—taking me. I c—couldn't m—move."

Arlo wraps his arms around me, and we disappear right then and there. I hold on tight to him, succumbing to tears as time and space bend around us. They are not tears of fear and melancholy, though.

No, these are burning tears of rage.

Is This Okay?

Elochian

I bring my fist to Quentin's door, and hesitate. I glance at the hearth at the end of the hall separating the apartments, its ashes are long dead and cold.

I breathe, but it does nothing to calm my heart or thoughts. I shake off the trembling energy building in my wings and curse the damn things under my breath. This is all my fault, I've failed Quentin, failed Arlo. Any place of mine should be safe, and instead I allowed the fucking enemy into our midst.

'Lucas' is long gone. The bar closed early, and so far there have been no leaks regarding the security breach. Based on the quick report from Michael on the way over here, I suspected Kavelli to be the culprit. There are very few shapeshifters in Levena, and he has the most motive to hurt me. But why threaten Quentin?

And then there's the matter of what Arlo said downstairs.

"Quen is convinced that it was someone he knows, but the magick that subjugated him was Leon's, without a doubt. Illusion

work was one of Leon's specialties, which explains the disguise, but he wouldn't be able to perform magick without a body. I've suspected possession, but this is proof."

"But why him? *Why try to get to you through Quentin?" I ask, willing myself to remain in place, to hear Arlo out instead of bolting upstairs. "No offense, but you were* right *there."*

"I don't know."

The floorboard beneath me creaks, signaling that someone is on the other side of the door. Quentin throws open the door, dressed in a one piece ... pajama-type outfit with a hood pulled up over his head. The entire thing is themed to be like a unicorn with soft white fur and a golden horn, complete with a black mane and tail.

He wields a long, steel baton like he might actually know what he's doing with it, and he's not wearing his glasses. He's alert, but remnants of sleep linger in the dream dust built up in the corners of his eyes. His right cheek is flushed from laying upon it, and his dark hair is damp with sweat on that side.

"What's wrong? What's happened?" He asks, stepping forward to look past me into the hall. His knuckles whiten as he tightens his grip on the baton and the sight breaks my heart. Quentin blinks at me, finally lowering the baton. "What?"

I suddenly feel very foolish for taking so long. I step past him and he follows me in, confused. He shuts the door, setting the baton down against the wall. He opens his lips, and I kiss him. He grunts against my mouth, then chases my tongue as fervently as I do his. I take his face in my hands and breathe life and love into him, unable to find any words.

He laughs onto my lips. "I should have a near death experience every day."

"Don't say that," I whisper, kissing him lighter than before. "I'm so sorry, Quentin. Please, forgive me."

"Elochian, you're not all knowing. It's not your fault."

"But I—"

He presses a finger to my lips. "Please, just come to bed with me. I'm tired, and I want to hold you. Can we do that?" He glances at the door, hand falling to his side. "Where's Michael?"

I can't help but smile at his concern. "Arlo gave him a key for next door."

"Oh," he says, cheeks darkening. "My couch not good enough for him anymore?"

I laugh then, unable to do anything else. "Afraid not. Do you … could I stay the night, do you think? My morning is blessedly open, and I thought we could sleep in."

He grins, a blink-and-you'll-miss-it kind of smile that's as blinding as it is beautiful. He tries to play it off, but it's already ingrained into my memory. "Um, sure. Just … wait here a second, will you?"

"Alright."

Quentin takes off down the hall to his room, tail shaking behind him. I chuckle, overcome with adoration for those ridiculous pajamas and his wondrous, calming lips. Seconds later, several crashes and bangs echo throughout the apartment. Before I can ask, he calls out, "I'm fine!"

I shake my head, wondering how messy his room could've gotten since the last time I was here. It's been less than a week, but it feels like ages. I've become accustomed to him, to this place. To peace.

While the couch and immediate living space around it is neat and tidy, picture perfect one might say, the corner of the room dedicated to Quentin's desk is another story. I find myself wandering over there, peeking inside a half empty coffee mug and skimming over scraps of lined paper. Uncapped pens, and pencils with the erasers chewed off, are scattered all over the place. A long forgotten muffin hides beneath a stack of haphazardly stapled papers, and the words on them are dissected by red pen.

I lift my gaze to a corkboard on the wall behind his computer, finding maps of Levena, both old and new, and newspaper clippings. I frown, studying the almost manic hodge podge of information. I understand the articles, but why the maps? And why such old ones? I lift the corner of a piece of paper, revealing a scrap underneath covered in handwritten notes.

Timeline

5012 - Leviathan

6000 - Thatch born

6017 - Formation of Min

6038 - The fire

6049 - Idina was born

8011 - Dusan was born

8021 - Shedim Immigration

8085 - Formation of Adrastus Clan

8321 - Malakim Immigration

8502 - Formation of Haniel Clan

9100 - Dusan's parents left Levena, and Dusan opened the orphanage

9016 - First Game

9447 - Elochian's parents died

9500 - Juniper Haniel died, last archangel

9518 - Arlo was born

9538 - First time they met, beginning of Arlo's fight w/ Leon

9612 - Leon's death

9619 - Arlo's Attempt

9620 - Thatch's return

9621 - River

Quentin's footsteps sound and I casually walk back to where I was before, thoughts churning. Quentin comes out about the same time I make it there, and his bright smile falters upon seeing me. "What's wrong?" He asks.

At this moment, I don't want to talk about plans, propaganda, or mysterious maps. I don't want to ask what the timeline is about, and why it holds the intimate details of not only my life, but our friends. I simply want to hold him, and be held.

"Nothing," I lie.

Quentin stares at me for a moment, then takes my hand and leads me to his room. When we pass the threshold and I see the bed, I freeze. Quentin nervously looks between the mass of blankets and me, chewing on his bottom lip. He says, "I ... if I had known you were coming, I could've made it better. But Michael said you sleep better in a nest, so I thought I'd try to make you one here. It's—I can fix—"

"No," I say, but I have to say it twice because emotion gets in the way the first time. "No, please. This is so thoughtful of you, I love it."

Quentin's eyes flash up to mine. "Yeah? You don't think it's lame?"

"How could I think that?" I take the initiative, carefully stepping up onto the mattress and into the deep nest of blankets, pulling him with me all the while. We sit opposite each other, and when I reach for the hem of my shirt, Quentin takes a gentle hold of my wrist.

"Lochian," he says quickly, eyebrows raised in alarm. "Did I try to initiate sex or something? Do demons use nests to—Michael said—"

I laugh. "No. I—I thought we could sleep like this, if that's okay." My ears burn, and I hurriedly add, "But not entirely naked. Is that okay? Am I too much?"

"Oh," Quentin says, his panic softening into tenderness. "No, Lochian. You're never too much for me. I'd like that." He swallows, looking down at his hand wrapped around my wrist still. "Can I ... can I have a rule?"

I nod. "Of course."

"Can you not ask questions?"

Bandages. Blood. Shattered bones. Unrecognizable.

I do my best to not let any of it show, having to focus on breathing like normal people do. In. Out. Don't hyperventilate. Don't hold your breath.

I say, "Anything for you, Dot."

He smiles, relaxing a little. "In that case, can I ... help you?"

I let go of my shirt, and he releases my wrist. "Yes. Yes, you can."

Quentin shimmies closer to me, and our knees knock together. He reaches for me, trembling fingers dimly lit by the small lamp on his bedside table. The soft pads of his fingertips graze my sides when he takes hold of my shirt. Those nervous eyes lift to mine, and an unfamiliar sensation sparks deep within me.

My gums throb when he whispers, "Is there a trick to it? Your wings, I mean."

My lips part, and I shake my head.

He slowly lifts my shirt over my head. My wings, flexible and pliant, slip through the holes in the back of my shirt, their origin hidden by a folded over hem. He has to get up on his knees to fully thread the length of my wings through, and I hastily run my tongue over my teeth, testing for sharp points.

I don't cut myself, but it's close. I'll have to be careful. I'm aroused by Quentin more often in the safety of being alone than when we're actually together, and even now it's not ... I'm not burning for him sexually, or maybe my body is, I don't know. But in my mind, that's not what I want.

It's so frustrating, and I'm hopeless in trying to explain it to him. But I don't feel panicked by the thought of his expectations anymore, at least.

Quentin sits back on his heels, his hazy eyes almost owlish as they traipse over my arms, chest, and stomach. He's always looks at me like I'm something precious, like all my imperfections are something to treasure. He smiles a little, fingers rising of their own accord to trail through the thick hair on my stomach. He blinks, remembering himself, and pulls back. "You can touch me there," I whisper.

His smile returns, unsure. "Okay. Do you ..." He tugs at the zipper of his sleepsuit, looking down before gazing back up at me. He laughs nervously. "I'm only wearing boxers under this thing. Is that alright?"

"Yes." I reach for him. "May I?"

Quentin swallows, nodding. "Yes."

I fumble the first time, but quickly recover. I clasp the cool metal between my fingertips and guide the zipper down. I wonder at how simple of a thing it is, a zipper. Something I thoughtlessly use everyday, and never with the care that I do now. As the teeth separate and the furry pink of the suit slackens, inches of pale skin and ink become known. I become distracted by the masterpiece beneath the fabric, and stop at his belly button.

Quentin begins to shrug the piece off, but stops when I rest my hands on his shoulders. An entire conversation unfolds through simple touches and skittering eye contact. My fingers gently squeeze his shoulders before sliding down an inch.

'I can do that for you.'

His eyebrows lift. *'Are you sure?'*

I smile. *'Yes.'*

I shift the fabric down one sleeve at a time, marveling at his soft arms. At first I'm unsure what I'm supposed to keep quiet about, but then I see them, and another delay occurs as I try to figure out what they even are. Dozens of small burn scars, each one a perfect circle, litter the top of his shoulders from one side to the other.

Cigarette burns. He's covered in cigarette burns.

I try not to pause for too long, but the way he stiffens beneath my hands tells all. With great difficulty I shift my attention down to the enormous linework tattoo on his chest, and my mind blanks as I realize what it is, what it *truly* is. Situated just beneath his collarbone is a dark brown birthmark in the rough shape of a crescent moon. A gnarled black tree originates from the twisted roots buried in his ribcage. Its dead branches cover his pectoral, and their tips surround the birthmark, highlighting it. I'd bet anything that's his mark.

"Beautiful." I look back up to him. "You're beautiful, Quentin."

He shrugs, tension loosening from his shoulders a touch. "Well I don't know about that, but thank you."

I rest my hand on his chest, over the heart of the tree. "I mean it."

"Okay."

The fresh ink on his left forearm is protected by a square of plastic, but through the clear wrap I can see bits and pieces of the new tattoo. I think of Quentin getting this alone, and my heart hurts a little.

"I'm sorry I couldn't be there with you."

"Oh, that's okay. You were busy."

"I know, but ..." I curl forward, bringing his arm to my lips. I leave a gentle kiss on his wrist, just on the other side of the tape and plastic. "It hurt, didn't it?"

"Sometimes you have to endure a little pain before you get to the good part. Come on."

Quentin kicks off the rest of his pajamas, and I leave my trousers on. He lays back on a mound of blankets, ones I've never seen in his apartment before. I pretend to be distracted by a snarl in my hair while Quentin shifts a free blanket onto his lap, his cheeks flushed as he subtly pushes down. Then he opens his arms to me, and my heart beats faster when they carefully wrap around my lower back, pulling our bare chests together. He whispers, "Is this okay?"

And I whisper back, "Yes."

My wings stretch open, then relax on either side of us. Quentin's chest rises and falls evenly beneath me, his skin hot and a little sweaty. He asks, "Do you want me to cover you up?"

I nod, yawning. "Mhm."

I don't move as he covers us up, and a pleased hum escapes me as we settle for the last time. Quentin's breathing lulls me into that state between dreaming and awake, and I slacken in his arms. It's not the first time we've fallen asleep this way, but something about tonight is different.

Like another wall has come down between us, but I'm unsure whose it is.

Sleep takes my hand, leading me into her black velvet depths. Before I fully succumb, Quentin whispers, "Your wings are so pretty."

The Truth Stands

Quentin

Sleep eludes me, which is the only reason I'm able to answer my wailing phone before it wakes Elochian.

It's a near thing when I have to crawl out from beneath him. His light snore tapers off when our bodies separate, then starts up again by the time I snatch my phone off the nightstand. His wings rustle, sticking straight as he stretches into the place I once was. I watch, unbothered by the now vibrating phone in my hand, until his wings lazily lay back down on either side of him. For being so thin, they are incredibly warm to lay beneath.

I tip-toe out of the room, and answer the phone.

"Hello?"

"Is this Quentin Matsdotter?"

"Yes?"

"This is Officer Wells from Station 7, and I have some questions regarding Arlo Rook. Do you have knowledge of his whereabouts between 6:00 PM and midnight?"

I pull my phone away from my ear, double checking the phone number and time. The number matches the police department, but *four* in the morning? "Um, I'm sorry, what? Is he there? Has he been arrested?"

"That is correct, sir. He claims that he was with you the entirety of the evening. Is this true?"

"Y—yes, I had a tattoo appointment with him this afternoon, and after we went to get some drinks. I wasn't feeling well, so he took me home."

"And what time was this?"

"Um, I don't know. Eight?"

"And he left right after?"

"No, he—" A floorboard moans behind me, and I turn. Elochian stands in the bedroom doorway, a blanket wrapped around his shoulders and hair a tangled mess.

He quickly signs, "I have a message from Arche (moon), Arlo (owl) never came home."

I run a hand through my hair and calmly say, "No, he stayed with me. We watched a movie together, then he left a little before one."

Silence on the other end.

"Are you sure about that?"

The threat clears my fatigue, pointing out a key fact I missed. *This is Officer Wells.*

Carina's husband. He's a known AWO supporter, present at every one of his wife's rallies. But I've never talked with him, only seen him in passing or pictures, I don't know what he sounds like. It could be a different relation, or none at all. A mere coincidence.

He takes my silence as consideration. He says, "Mr. Matsdotter, you're a clever man. I don't think you visited the Magpie at all. I think you went home, parting ways with Rook after your session."

"I never said I had drinks at the Magpie."

"Clever, clever. So, what will it be?"

"And what do I get in return? Silence doesn't come for free."

He laughs, and it grates my nerves. "Ah, yes. Well, we could get you back to where you belong, teaching the little ones what is and isn't."

My knuckles ache, and the phone creaks in my hand. "What you allow me to spoon feed them, you mean. No thanks. The truth stands, I was with Arlo all night. He was never out of my sight."

Wells hums, lowering his voice until it's practically a growl. "But he was though, wasn't he? It was quick, but long enough for you to be exposed. Next time, He won't leave you behind. Next time, He will steal you away, lock you up, and throw away the key."

I can hear it, the awe and importance placed on the man who ruined my life. The man who stole my young adulthood. The man who robbed my dignity. The man who took and took and *took*, simply because he could.

The man who is hurting my friends.

"The truth stands, and so do I. Fuck you, and fuck him."

After my thumb hits the end button, I throw my phone.

I'm on the other side of the window this time.

Caspian, Lindsey, Gowan, and Felix squish around me, our noses nearly pressed to the glass. Arche, Elochian, Tobias, and Silas wait behind us, pretending to be calm. Each one's nervous ticks give them away though.

Arche chews his gum, snapping it annoyingly.

Elochian's wings chatter as he speaks in low tones to Tobias, whose own wings are present and mimic his counterpart's anxiety. His feathers are quieter than Elochian's scales as they tremble, like a soft rustling of blankets.

Silas sits in Arlo's spot on the big couch, feet tucked beneath him and eyes closed, body utterly still. His aura betrays him, a tight orb of shadows barely kept in check.

And then there's Michael standing in the space between hallway and den, stoic and silent. They watch us, and the door.

"There they are," Lindsey says, sighing with relief.

Caspian inhales sharply when Arlo and Kitt come into view, and my heart drops. Despite the frost on the outside of the glass and the distance, the bruises marring the left side of his face are plain as day. Arlo and Kitt hold hands, eyes cast down as they walk the frozen path to the cottage together.

"His face, his *face,* what—" Felix groans, curling in on himself as if in pain.

Arche is there quicker than I can recognize what's happening. He steers Felix away from the window, leading him to sit beside Silas. He murmurs soft words like *breathe* and *let it out,* and Felix does as he says, closing his eyes. He exhales fear and magick, and I can *feel* it now, not just see it. The way magick pours off him in waves, bathing my skin and soul in unsettled power.

I take off my glasses and rub at my eyes, wincing against the oncoming headache. Lindsey throws me a concerned look. "You alright?"

I smile weakly, putting my glasses back on. "Yeah, I'm fine."

She studies me, clearly not believing me. Elochian slips an arm around my shoulder, pulling me close. I lean against his side, sighing in relief.

"Here they come," Caspian says quietly, wheeling away from the window and out of the den, towards the foyer. Like an unspoken code, the rest of us wait while Arlo, Kitt, and Caspian have their moment together. It's always been that way, the three of them sharing a special bond that the rest of us can never hope to achieve. It doesn't bother me anymore, not like it used to.

But I'm still surprised when moments later, Arlo comes rushing into the room. He cups Felix's face, bringing their foreheads together, then does the same with Silas. After, he comes straight for me. His arms wrap around my ribcage, neatly extricating me from Elochian's hold. He lifts me off the ground and hugs me tighter than he ever has. His nose buries into the crook of my neck, and he says, muffled, "You're okay."

I hug him back, clueless as to why tears are welling in my eyes. "*You're* okay."

"I was so worried about you."

"Arlo, *you're* the one who was in trouble."

He puts me down, then cups my cheeks. He gives me a small, firm shake. "And you're the one who put a target on your back to get me out."

"I only told the truth, well. Mostly."

Arlo smiles, but it's forced.

"What are the rest of us, chopped liver?" Gowan mutters, breaking the tension. Arlo hugs her, kissing the top of her head before moving onto the next, and the next, and the next. He moves to shake Arche's hand in thanks, but the vampire quickly hugs Arlo too.

Our family has grown.

We all settle together at the dining room table where Caspian's breakfast buffet waits, long since turned cold. Felix and Silas sit on either side of Arlo, while the rest of us fan out. No one eats, quiet and tense as we wait for Arlo to explain the events of last night. Elochian makes me a small plate of fruit and crescent rolls before sitting down at my left side. I don't really feel like eating, but if the stern look on his face is anything to go by, I don't have much choice.

We compromise. Every bite he takes, I match.

Michael seems pleased by this, quiet as they sit at my right. They have been quieter and quieter these days, no longer playful but more serious. Calculating. Vigilant. My deal with Elochian has tweaked their lips upwards a little bit though, and I take pride in it.

Us eating seems to break the dam. Caspian makes Tobias a plate, and Lindsey does the same for Kitt and Gowan. The boys fuss as Arlo serves them food, but it's superficial complaining. Arche doesn't eat, but he does pour himself a cup of coffee from the carafe waiting in the middle of the table, as does Arlo.

Only after everyone has begun eating or drinking does Caspian's calm finally recede. He gruffly asks, "So, what happened?"

Arlo takes a sip of his coffee, wincing. He sets Thatch's mug down, focusing only on it as he speaks. "Julianna called me as I was headed home, said she had an emergency that she needed my help with and asked me to come by her office straightaway. I did."

"Why the hell would the mayor be in the office at eleven o'clock at night?" Arche asks.

Arlo smiles at his mug, no humor behind it. "It's not uncommon. I was with her for about an hour, then I left. She had evidence of dirty council members, and these old maps of Min Isle turned up in her desk, she wanted to give them to me. She was fine when I left." Arlo sniffs, and I wonder how many times he has said this. I don't know Julianna personally, but I know that Arlo was always fond of her.

Arlo says, "I was halfway home when they came."

"The cops?" Lindsey asks.

"If you can call them that. They started screaming at me, and they—" Arlo leans ahead, resting his elbows on the table. He rubs at his temple, sighing heavily. "They arrested me."

"But what about your—" Cas gestures to his face, but Arlo cuts him off.

"I was *resisting* arrest, according to them. It's fine, I'm just roughed up."

"Arlo, it's *not* fine."

"I'm alive."

"That's not—"

"Julie's dead, Caspian. We have bigger things to worry about."

Nobody disagrees.

"But why?" Gowan asks, small and unsure. "You didn't do it."

"They want to cast doubt. If they could get Quentin to forgo his alibi, then arresting Arlo would be a bonus. As it is, Arlo was the last person Julianna saw, so those who aren't on our side will latch onto," Kitt says, picking at her food. "And if the AWO has people in the police department, city council, and Gods knows where else, they're probably planning something huge. Something permanent."

"So things are about to get ugly," Arche says plainly.

"Indeed," Arlo agrees.

"What can we do?" Lindsey asks.

"Nothing. Nothing but what we've been doing. Standing by the truth, showing people who we really are."

"It could be retaliation," Elochian says finally. "We embarrassed Kavelli."

Silence follows, and I hold Elochian's hand beneath the table. Quietly, I say, "But I saw *him*, Lochian, and after what the deputy said—"

"I *know*, but I'm telling you. Kavelli is involved in this, I'm sure of it."

Arlo says, "I'm sure he is."

Elochian frowns, but says nothing.

Tobias addresses the group, more commanding than I've ever heard him. "I agree with Arlo, that we need to continue as we have been. But no one goes off alone anymore. *No one.* Elochian and I can arrange security if need be. And we need to keep our minds open.

"Just because Leon isn't possessing Kavelli, doesn't mean the demon isn't a threat. He's creating a divide in the celestials, and funding the NOJ. This we know for sure. The ascension ball is our best shot at showing the world we are a united front, something to be proud of, not afraid of. But it will also be the other side's best shot to come at *us*. We'll be exposed."

"No one will be hurt on Adrastus soil," Elochian says. "The Manor is safe."

"Can you say that for sure?" Tobias gently adds, "You would have said the same two days ago about the Magpie, right?"

Elochian nods, jaw tense.

"And what about the witches in the End?" Silas asks, surprising the table. When no one answers, he continues, looking between Tobias and Elochian. "You going to provide security for them too?"

"They will be taken care of," Arlo mutters.

"What does *that* mean?" Cas asks, affronted. "Last I knew you only had room for a few, not an entire neighborhood."

Arlo mumbles something and takes off his hat, glancing at Finnegan who smiles fondly at him.

"Say *what* now?" Cas prods.

"I bought the old apartment complex!"

Absolute, dead silence rules the table for five seconds.

Then Caspian laughs.

Lindsey is next, and then Gowan. Tobias chuckles, and I find myself giggling. Elochian smiles, and Arche does too. In mere moments, the atmosphere has been transformed from rotten dread, to manic hope.

Caspian says, "Of course you did, Lo. Of course you did."

NORTHERN ISLE WEEKLY

From Harmless Potions & Useful Spells to Brewing Chaos & Anarchy: An Overview of the Levena Uprising

It's more expensive than ever to live as a Witch in Levena, and strict regulations are tightening the noose on their way of life. Despite the fact they number less than a few hundred and only a select few are allowed to be business owners, local groups such as Normal for Justice are worried they are dominating the playing field, leaving nothing left for those who have to do things 'the hard way.' Let's take an in-depth look at the upcoming proposals on deck for next quarter, and the reactions of those they affect. (cont. on pg. 2)

The Adrastus Masquerade

Elochian ben Adrastus is opening the doors to Adrastus Manor for one weekend, playing host to a masquerade ball held in honor in the newly ascended archangel, Tobias xir Daemarrel.

It is predicted to be the event of the century, before the Adrastus Clan withdrew into a more private state of being, they were widely known for their frivolous and wild parties.

Not to mention the long-awaited event of a newly ascended archangel in the Northern Region. The archcelestials are already making waves, despite the fact the ball isn't slated until Artune.

(con't on pg. 12)

March

Extravagant

Elochian

All I want is to hide away from the world under some blankets with Quentin.

Instead of that, I'm dealing with *this*. Everything melted at once today, and the ground is a curse. Boot sucking mud. Standing puddles of water. My socks are damp from sweating in boots that are perfect for a *usual* March day. Admittedly the sun feels nice, and my wings soak up the abnormally bright afternoon. It's all about balance. Beautiful sky, shitty ground.

Arlo's roadway is treacherous, and I curse him the entire time. "He's a witch for Gods' sake, surely he could find a way to dry the road. Someone's going to break something."

"You're awfully cheery today, Sir."

"Oh, fuck off."

"Point made."

I sigh, glancing sideways at Michael, having to squint at the sun setting behind him. "I'm sorry. I'm just worried."

"I know, Sir. But everything has gone according to plan, and after tomorrow, you'll be freed from societal expectations for fifty more years."

I laugh. "Is that it? I throw one ball and I can go back into hiding?"

Michael shrugs, grinning. "Sounds like a plan to me."

The house is riotous the moment we walk in the door. Most of the witches that helped us with the river accepted Arlo's invitation for *Yom Tov Ogmes* dinner, which easily doubles those who normally gather here for the holidays. My skin immediately crawls, the sensation heightened by every noise. I freeze in the doorway, just for a second, but Michael stands close to my back, a reminder that he's here for me, no matter what.

I walk inside, and search for Quentin.

Easier said than done. I say hello to Lindsey and Kitt hanging out in the hallway with Gaia and ... Eleanor? I think that's her name, she was with us at the river. Further inside I run into Caspian and Tobias, taking a moment to observe the joyous moment that is Charles seated cross-legged on the big couch, a toddler on either side of him, little fingers swimming through his feathers.

I overlay the memory of him taking down a fierce adversary in less than a second with what's before my eyes now. I whisper to Tobias, "Have I mentioned that you chose well?"

Tobias smiles at me, practically twinkling beneath the warm lighting. "Maybe a time or two."

"He's settling in well, then?"

"Oh yes. He's incredibly serious about his work, and he loves the kids. You would never know he was a supposed troublemaker."

I nod. "Good. It's a wonder what people will do when you're not constantly telling them they're a failure."

Caspian tilts his head. "What do you mean?"

I shrug. "He's sixth generation, and to those elitist pricks, he would never amount to anything. I don't think Charlie ever *expected* to be chosen, but that doesn't mean he didn't want to be. Like I said, it's amazing the way people change when you actually treat them with respect. You both gave him a chance, and I believe Charlie will spend the rest of his life thanking you for it."

"You realize you're an elitist prick as well?" Caspian asks, full of mischief.

"I never claimed not to be. But at least I can admit my shortcomings."

After chatting with them for a few more minutes I continue on my search, heeding Tobias' suggestion to check in the kitchen. Instead of Quentin, I find Finnegan and Arlo standing close together, talking passionately. When Arlo sees me coming, he smiles. "Loch, you're here. Michael, good to see you."

Michael nods. "And you as well."

"Arlo, Finnegan. How did the tree planting excursion go? Looks like the day was good for it."

Arlo chuckles. "Yeah, it went great, actually. Ground's still frozen, but we got a few cuttings into pots. Probably be a few years before we see anything out of them, but Felix was happier than a pig in shit."

"That's an understatement," Finnegan says. "I've never been to a tree planting ceremony before, but I think the kid nailed it."

"Hopefully next year I won't miss it," I mutter, feeling oddly left out. Most of those gathered have been here all day, celebrating the new growth and life coming to the island. "Do you know where Quentin is?"

Arlo nods to the ceiling. "Upstairs with Silas and Arche. Felix too, I think. Go on up, they need an audience. Dinner will be ready in about twenty minutes."

"What'd Caspian make?" I ask, perking up.

Finnegan laughs. "You're the tenth person to ask that."

"It's like you all think I'm incapable of cooking," Arlo says, feigning hurt.

I stare at him.

He stares at me.

He breaks first. "Fine. He didn't cook, but I didn't either. Bunch of the girls are picking up pizza."

I laugh. "Extravagant."

"Easy is what it is."

After giving him shit for a couple more minutes, I take off again in search of Quentin. When Michael follows me, shadowing my footsteps, I turn to them and say, "I think I'll be okay now."

They raise a brow. "Sir."

I smile. "Please, don't 'Sir' me here. We're safe, and you should enjoy yourself while you can. Tomorrow's going to be busy."

And possibly change everything.

Michael hesitates, eyes wandering over my shoulder. I look behind me, seeing Bud. He gives us a little wave, then hurries back towards the den. "Go on. Say hi."

Michael sighs. "You're just trying to get rid of me."

I smile. "Yeah."

They tap their temple. "You'll call if you need me?"

"Yes."

"Promise?"

"*Yes.*"

"Fine. Go find your boy."

I take a step towards Michael. Then another.

I hug them.

It takes a second, then he hugs me back. "It's going to be okay," they say.

I nod. "I know."

I'm only stopped by Demeter, Dimitri, then Gaia, and finally, Rain, along the way to find Quentin. Rain approaches me at the foot of the stairs, her *mayim* features hidden away. She says, "Lord Adrastus. Have a moment?"

I withhold a sigh. "Of course. What can I help you with?"

"I was told that you might have a problem with me."

"I can assure you that I do not."

Rain tilts her head down, reminding me of the way Quentin glares at me over the top of his glasses. Except, she's not wearing any.

"I promise you, there is no bad blood between us. I'm unaccustomed to being around demons not affiliated by the Clan. It's an old rule, one I'm glad we no longer have, but as an archdemon, it's ... it's hard to explain. You're an errant bee."

Rain laughs, a hearty and surprising sound. "A bee, I like that. They do say I have some sting to my sun runs. Well, as long as you don't mind me being in my hive and you in yours, then there's nothing else to say." She claps me on the shoulder, her hand as wide as my entire clavicle is long. "Blessings, Lord Adrastus."

When she moves past me I quickly say, "Elochian. I'd like it if you called me Elochian. And blessings to you, Rain."

Rain smiles, taking off down the hallway without another word. Lindsey's squeal follows moments later, and her high pitched excitement intermingles with Rain's deep laughter. It belatedly hits me what she meant by *sun runs*. She's a solar surfer, I bet that's how she knows Lindsey. I chuckle to myself, amused by the weight lifted off my shoulders, a weight I didn't know was crushing me.

Once again, I search for Quentin, and thankfully, no one stops me this time. I ascend the stairs, running my hand over the smooth, polished handrail. I pass by Arlo's paintings on the walls, closed doors and a few potted plants, some of which hang from macrame like nets from the ceiling. I pause, reaching out to brush my fingers along the bottom of a gilded frame. The painting Arlo created of Thatch, months ago when the man was still in this world. It's realistic, with a whimsical twist.

His eyes are arresting, full of mischief and sunny skies. A halo of sunset curls frames his face, accentuating his freckles and wide grin. I smile back at the ghost of a man, wondering what he would think of this, his house full of love and life. Of Arlo, bringing everyone together. Despite the fact my person is only in the next room, I find myself rushing there.

I open the door, assaulted by a cacophony of sounds that don't process into music until precious seconds later, after it fades. I stand in the doorway, blinking rapidly in attempts to adjust to the dim, colorful atmosphere in the music room. Numerous light strips occupy the edges between ceiling and wall, currently illuminated a color that's between red and pink.

Quentin grins, abandoning the drum set he had been wailing upon. Silas grumbles, acoustic guitar in hand, but waves to me. Felix smiles up at him from his place on the floor, cross-legged and swaddled in a blanket, then says hello to me too. Archeon simply nods, leaning against a length of wall like he'd been there the whole time. The gently swaying microphone stand begs to differ.

I hold my arms out to Quentin and he falls into place, where he belongs. His chest against mine, my arms around him and his around me. His hair tickles my nose, and I breathe him in. "I missed you," I whisper.

He looks up at me, pupils wide in the dark atmosphere. He smiles a little, because I shouldn't miss him. I saw him last night, and stayed as long as I could before I had to leave. We've texted back and forth all day, too. Regardless of all of this, he says, "I missed you too."

Silas very pointedly clears his throat. "Is it still hell down there?"

I smile down at Quentin for another moment before turning my attention to Silas, and Felix who now stands beside him. I say, "Yes, but there's pizza now."

Felix and Silas exchange a look. "Hell warriors?" Felix asks.

Silas laughs, and I don't think I've ever heard the sound. It's rough and brittle, but unrestrained and genuine. "Hell warriors." He puts up a fist, and Felix bumps it with his own. Archeon nods, answering an unasked question.

"Do I even want to know?" I ask, folding Quentin against my side.

Silas stares at me blankly. "Really? You're like, the original hell warrior."

"Quentin, help."

He laughs, wrapping a length of my hair around his finger. "I think what they're saying is it's more fun to conquer big social gatherings if you're pretending to be a hell warrior."

"Oh," I say. "That makes sense."

I hold up my free hand, making a fist.

They all stare at me.

I roll my eyes and start to lower my hand, but Felix bumps my fist with his before I do. Silas follows suit, and Quentin does too. We all look at Archeon, who finally relents with an eyeroll. He straightens from the wall and slinks over like a cat, then gently bumps our hands with his. Through a giggle, Quentin says, "Introverts, unite!"

And I swear, I've never been more thankful for having my person here, with me, than I am right now.

We end up having to dig out the old dining room table that came with the cottage, and it's clear Arlo has some feelings about it. He doesn't say anything, but he looks at anywhere but the table while Tobias helps him carry it out of the big storage room in the back of the house. During dinner, he glares at it now and again like it's about to bite him in the ass. Between that table, the big new one, the coffee table and end stands, everyone finds a place to eat. We're all spread out between the dining room, hallway, and den, but it's nice. I sit with Quentin, Silas, Felix, and Arche, near Arlo at the head of the new table, quiet hell warriors while Arlo does the entertaining.

I didn't know he could talk so much.

He tells Rain about the date he took Thatch on, and how he was a natural at flying through the sunset.

He tells Gaia about Thatch's disbelief in how to release the *Dybbuk*, and his windblown hair.

He tells Josse about Bob's foiled plan to harass Ren, and how Thatch said over and over that Floyd had such *life* in his eyes.

He talks, and talks, and talks.

But the original gang has heard it all before. At one point, Lindsey tosses a crisped piece of cheese at Quentin. "Sooo, any special plans for tomorrow?"

If looks could kill, the one Quentin shoots Lindsey would be annihilating. "Yeah, the ascension and *ball*."

Lindsey scowls at me.

I'm simply lost.

"Am I missing something?" I ask, dabbing my lips with a napkin. Three slices of cheese pizza later, and I'm stuffed.

"Quentin!" Lindsey chides, throwing another piece of food at him.

"*Lindsey*, shut up."

Over a mouthful of despicable pepperoni and pineapple, Kitt says, "It's his birthday." She grins impishly at Quentin, and red sauce stains her lips.

He sighs, taking his glasses off to rub at his forehead.

I stare at him. "Is it really?"

"Yes," he grumbles.

"Even I knew that," Silas says, unnecessarily. "It's on the Day of Artune, how fitting."

"He's a love child," Kitty sings, enjoying this way too much.

"And you?" I gesture to Felix, who responds in typical Felix fashion.

A noncommittal shrug, followed by, "Yes."

I lean closer to Quentin and quietly ask, "Why didn't you tell me? Humans celebrate birthdays, don't they?"

He replaces his glasses and smiles at me. "Yeah, they do. There's just so much going on this year, and besides I'm not one for big parties."

"Me either, and look what happened," Arlo chimes in, like he'd been part of the conversation all along. "I got one anyways."

I shake my head. "You too?"

He shrugs, so like Felix. "Yeah."

"What'd he do last year?"

"I'm *right* here."

"You're an unreliable source," Michael says.

"Correct," I say, gesturing to Kitt. "What'd he do last year?"

Kitt hums, tapping her chin. "Breakfast, thrift store, and movie night at our place."

Lindsey nods seriously. "Mm, that's when he brought home that Gods awful television set and stuffed a plant in it."

Quentin gasps, placing a hand over his heart. "Hey! It's a piece on media and—"

Lindsey winks at him. "Yeah, yeah. I'm just glad you brought it with you."

Quentin shakes his head through a smile, then glances at me. "Seriously, it's not a big deal. Do demons celebrate birthdays? Wait ... when's yours?"

"Oh, and I'm supposed to just tell you now, after I went through all that?"

"*Yes.*"

"Why?"

He grins. "I'm cute."

I say nothing, and our friends *ooh* and *ahh* like we're children. Arche, nearly as helpful as Silas, says, "He's got you there."

"Fine. It's in the summer."

"*When?*"

I smile at Quentin. Quentin, who stares at me with those big green eyes full of delight, lips parted on the edge of a laugh. I say, "You'll have to figure it out."

When the plates start to clear and the towers constructed of pizza boxes dwindle down, the main conversation shifts from theories about magick to theories about the enemy. Once one question hits Arlo about Leon, three more follow in its wake. One stands out from the rest, as does its answer.

"You two were friends once, weren't you?"

Arlo nods, quiet for a moment before answering. "We were more than that. For a long time, my life revolved around him. We lived together. We were happy, or pretended to be. I thought it was normal that he monitored my every move. Every person I talked to, until I didn't talk to anyone. And magick? I could never, ever do it in front of him."

Quentin takes my hand in his, bringing them to rest on his thigh. He doesn't meet my eye when he does so, and I don't stare.

"Why?" Rain asks, one of the few witches untouched by the Taking.

Arlo sighs. He taps the table with a finger, then drags it back and forth like he's making a pattern. "His family was murdered by a very sick, very deranged man, who just so happened to be a witch. His mother hid him beneath a floorboard, where he heard everything. Saw the aftermath. It scarred him, changed him. He became absolutely terrified of witches, and when he grew older, becoming one himself, I think it ... I don't know. Broke him.

"It's taken me a long time to stop making excuses for him, but to this day, I still pity him. When he found out what I was, that was the final straw. He tried to kill me, and Thatch saved my life. It was the beginning and end of everything. Love is why we fought, and I imagine why he fixates on me. To him, it will never be over until one of us is dead. Truly, and honestly, dead."

He stands up, pushing away from the table. "Excuse me."

Arlo escapes for the kitchen, and silence follows in his wake.

Caspian kisses Tobias on the cheek, then wheels after his friend. Kitt isn't far behind him, gently rubbing her horn against Lindsey's temple before she does. For once, I don't feel jealous over their kinship. I'm glad Arlo has people who were there, and are *still* here for him.

Quentin leans over and whispers in my ear, awakening my wings and nerves. "I think I'm ready to go home."

"Me too. Let's go."

Love Without Reason

Quentin

"Today is not about you. No one cares about what you look like. Not your bloodshot eyes, or the damned spot that won't lay down on the back of your head no matter what you do. Today is about Tobias, and Elochian. Be the man they need you to be, and leave everything else behind."

My reflection isn't convinced.

I sigh, running my hands through my hair because *fuck it*, it won't stay where's it supposed to be anyway. I stare down at the black points of my boots, repeatedly trying to assure myself everything is going to be okay. Nothing bad is going to happen, I'll be spending my day in two of the most secure places in Levena. I'll be with Arlo during the ascension, then I'll be with Elochian.

I'll be with Elochian.

I shut the bathroom light off, leaving before I can get one last glimpse of myself in the mirror. My phone rings and I immediately answer it. "I'm coming."

"Do you need help?" Lindsey genuinely asks, and it's her lack of teasing that motivates me. I'm not the only one nervous about today.

"No, I'm coming." I storm into my bedroom, forcing myself to slow down once I cross the threshold. I squeeze my phone between my cheek and shoulder, exhaling heavily into the speaker, and slip my jacket on.

"Okay. Good."

"How many times did Kitt curse the driver?" I ask, turning off the lights in the kitchen and living room.

A laugh spills out of her, riding on the afterthought of a sigh. "I gave serious thought to feeding her mimosas before we left. It's crazy out there, I've never seen the streets so packed."

I pick up my keys, then stop and stare at them for a moment. I run my thumb over the beaded owl keychain Felix gifted me early, and the crystal caged in guitar string, from Silas. Quietly, I ask, "The footroads too?"

"Fucking Typhine, it's like pushing a herd of cows."

I smile, and step out into the hall. "I forget that you were a farm girl."

"Q, you can take the girl off the farm, but you can never take the farm out of the girl," she says, full of sass. I chuckle, locking my apartment. I listen to her as she talks about Kitt's impatience, and rants about Arlo's anxious quiet. I wonder where she's hiding, because I don't hear either of them complaining about her in the background.

We're all riding together, Arlo and the boys, Lindsey and Kitt, Gowan and Iris. Then there's Finnegan and myself, the dateless. At least for me it will be temporary, just until the ball. Caspian is already at the Palace with Tobias, Elochian too. The limousine is Elochian's doing, a favor that the control freaks aren't doing well with.

When I grasp the doorknob at the end of the hall, I look over my shoulder at the two doors opposite each other. My apartment, and the other one which has been nothing but a temporary haven. For Thatch, for Arlo and the boys. For Michael. At the head of the hall between the doors is the hearth which hasn't been lit in some time, and I miss curling up on those old couches with Arlo and the boys.

Doubt takes hold of me, if only for a second. Long enough to wonder, will I ever open my apartment door again?

I square up with what's ahead of me, and turn the knob. I open the door, revealing Lindsey on the other side, down just a couple of steps from the top. She innocently smiles up at me, ending our phone call with the click of a wicked sharp nail, the ends tinged in gold and black glitter.

"You look good, birthday boy. Now give me a hug already."

I open my arms to my best friend, and hold her with all I've got.

It's going to be okay.

It's eerily like attending church, but entirely different.

On both sides of a narrow dirt road, in ten rows of pews, each row a hundred benches deep, thousands of people wait for the ascension to begin. The entire affair takes place in the main courtyard of Haniel Palace, which isn't a courtyard so much as a mini-world. We wait in a field of wildflowers, and at the fringes are giant azalea bushes the size of maple trees, their flowerheads larger than mine and in every color of the rainbow. The distinct citrus of freesia carries on a soft breeze, the artificial wind borders on cool.

The outside world is barely separated from us, the fatal cold kept at bay by marble, stone and glass. Glass covers the entire ceiling, a special kind that transforms according to what the atrium needs. Today, the expansive courtyard calls for an unobstructed view of the heartbreakingly blue sky, bright and near unnatural for mid-March, so the glass is crystal clear, near indiscernible except for the metal framework supporting the panes.

On hexagonal slabs of gravity defying stone, angels and demons perch on the edges and watch the spectacle from above. The hexagons encircle the altar on the ground which the rest of us face as well, the lofts extend outwards and upwards in concentric circles. Harmonious string music drifts all around us, small bands of angels are stationed throughout the wildflowers and on a few of the lofty stones above us. They all play the same songs, in perfect time with each other despite the distance.

I've been to concerts, solar surfing championships, lectures. But nothing I've ever attended has been like this, never with this many people.

Sitting in a front row with my friends on either side of me, I can almost forget about the thousands of people that River could be. I hold Lindsey's hand, and Arlo sits on my other side. He sits completely still, but his gaze wanders constantly. I ask, "Have you ever been to anything like this?"

He glances over at me. "No."

"Your award ceremony was pretty serious," Kitt says, holding Lindsey's other hand.

Arlo turns his attention ahead once more. "That was different."

Kitt shrugs, but says nothing.

I remember it. Through thousands of miles and a television screen, the power of that moment sunk into my bones. Defender of Levena, head bowed and cupped hands outstretched to receive tokens of gratitude and medals for bravery. He was so quiet, humble and modest. I think that was the first moment my feelings sparked for him. I mistook it as romantic affection, when in reality it was recognition. Kinship. Here was someone I could follow, someone who was truly good in this dark world.

Our world dims as the transformative panes of glass darken, and soon we're left with an ethereal nightscape, complete with pinpricks of golden stars. The music reaches a crescendo before crashing into silence, and the murmur of the crowd receives a quick death. Arlo takes my other hand, holding on tight to me. I return the pressure, my attention fixed on a beam of daylight. It emanates from a circle of unchanged panes, beating down upon the stone altar we've all gathered before.

For a tenuous moment, there is nothing. Nothing but a crowd all paused on the same bated breath, nothing but a shaft of light in the darkness.

And then they separate from the surrounding abyss, becoming one with the light. Elochian and Tobias meet at the highest point, wingtips nearly touching the glass ceiling as they face off. They reach for the other, but just before their fingertips touch, their wings stop beating. My heart pounds in frantic anticipation for what's to come.

Elochian gracefully falls backwards, as does Tobias. They plummet nearly two hundred feet towards the ground, head first. Between one blink of the eye and the next they pull out of the dive, skimming the air above our heads with great speed. A powerful gust of wind follows their maneuver, drying out my eyes. I gently pull out of Lindsey's grip, scrubbing at my eyes with the heel of my palm. My hand comes away wet, and I don't know if it's from the air shot into my eyes or the beauty of the moment. Maybe both.

Elochian and Tobias do laps around the atrium, ascending each time they do. Tobias' rose pink feathers practically glow in the dark, luminous and exquisite. The eyes hidden in his wingspan blink against the dark, the irises a creepy pale blue. Elochian's wings look the same as they always do, a lovely mosaic of green, purple, blue and black. The gold is there too, but I'm the only one that can—

"Arlo," I whisper.

"Hm?"

"Can you see the gold in Elochian's wings?"

He watches Elochian and Tobias touch down in front of the altar, hands clasped. Then, he looks over at me. He studies me for a moment, then smiles for the first time this morning. "What do you think?"

"Yes."

"Does he know?"

I shake my head. "No. I—I—I haven't been sure. But I think I'm going to tell him tonight."

Arlo dips his head. "Good."

I open my mouth, but Tobias begins to speak, so I save my question for later.

Voice booming and sure, he says, "In the beginning, there was Ulena, Typhine, Ogmes, and Hizoh. They were the sun, the moons, flora, and fauna. They were day and night, dawn and dusk. They were everything, in a world of nothing. And so they created the first era of humanity, and the caretakers who would look after them. Each caretaker was allowed one creation, one contribution to fill a hole in the universe."

Strained but no less confident, Elochian says, "There was a need for love and companionship, for kindness and purpose beyond oneself. The Goddess of Love said, 'I shall make a being that will outlive all the rest, a being that will guide others, and provide love and aid where none can be found.'"

Tobias adds, "But there was also a need for logic and reason, for fair judgment and accountability. The Goddess of Logic said, 'I too shall make a being that will outlive all the rest, a being that will guide others, and provide safety and shelter where none can be found.'"

"And so, they conspired to entwine their beings, for surely you cannot have love without reason, judgment without kindness, or a desire to serve without the knowledge to do so. Together, they created the celestials, but something was missing. The celestials were fractured, divided and unruly. And so, they granted a fraction of their godly power to families of their choosing, creating the Archdemons and Archangels." Elochian's last words seem to take all the air out of the room, a reminder that the beings before us something other, something *more*.

Increasing in passion, Tobias says, "But in exchange for this, the Arches were bound to their counterpart, their people, their God. *Malakim* and *Shedim* were created for humanity, and for each other. Today, I accept my place at my *bashert's* side, at *your* side. Today, I become your Archangel. What say you?"

And by Gods, the sound that follows is deafening, life changing and full of promise. There is not a single objection, only praise. Only *'yes.'*

Tobias turns to Elochian, extending his hand. The atrium falls silent once again when Elochian carefully cradles Tobias' hand in one of his. Tobias' palm is upturned, a soft and vital offering. Air catches in my throat and Arlo squeezes my hand. Last night comes rushing back to me, and I find it hard to breathe.

"But why do you have *to bite him?"*

Elochian's french fry pauses midway to his mouth, and I do my best not to search for evidence of elongated fangs. I certainly don't need another muffin incident. The pizza at Arlo's was good, but we got hungry a few hours later, well into the time we should be sleeping. Especially given tomorrow's agenda, but neither of us seem too ready for bed.

Elochian says, "It has always been this way. We are to be bound in blood, it is why we have … well, it's one of the reasons why celestials have fangs."

"Right. Okay, I get that, but what about a knife or something less intim—wait, are you saying Tobias has fangs too? I thought it was just a demon mating thing."

Elochian laughs abruptly, one his rare ones that crop up when I've especially pleased or surprised him. My cheeks warm with pride, and then with something more when he reaches across my coffee table and takes my hand. Staring at our joined fingers, he says, "Yes, he does, but they're different from mine. I have to bite him because I was here first, and in doing so I'm accepting what he is offering. I know it seems odd, but this is what it means to be a demon, Dot. We are old, and bizarre, slow to evolve. I'm doing my best to change things, but …"

His eyes lift to mine, full of trepidation and something else, something veiled, but just barely. "Are you sure that you want to do this? I'm not easy. I'm boring, and tired, always so tired. Given my way, I would do only this with you, all the time. Eat good food, play with your hair while you read, sleep until noon, watch old movies and that furrow between your brow when you're trying to work out a scene. My family is manipulative, and so especially demon." He spits out the last word like it's poison.

I release his hand and shuffle on my knees around the table, then settle into his lap. I rest my legs on either side of him, and cup his face in my hands, tilting his head back. His fingers come to rest on my hips, fanning out over my pajamas. He blinks up at me, long and slow. The words are there, right there on the tip of my tongue.

But it's taken so long to get to this point, where we comfortably touch each other without hesitation, without it having to mean anything other than comfort. If I tell him how I feel, will it ruin everything? Will he think I need more because of it?

I dance away from the whole truth, choosing to reveal another side of it. "I am proud to be with you, Elochian ben Adrastus. I choose you, and everything that you entail. Please, believe me when I say that you are it for me. You are mine."

Elochian's breath catches, eyes brimming with wet relief. He lifts his chin a smidge, a silent plea. I oblige him, softly bringing my lips to his. He surprises me by opening his mouth, deepening the kiss. A whisper of a moan escapes me, and his fingers tighten on my sides. My arousal becomes a known entity between us, semi-hard as it presses against Elochian's stomach.

It's happened before, during times we've laid and cuddled together in bed. The first few times were embarrassing, but Elochian wasn't bothered by it, if not a little panicked because he felt guilty. But we talked, agreeing to let the silent elephant in the room just be, as long as it didn't bother me. 'It's a natural reaction,' he had said. Then I laughed, because it sounded so cocky, and he laughed a little too.

But now, Elochian doesn't ignore it. Without breaking from the kiss, he pulls me forward by the hips, then rocks me back, grinding against me. It's so subtle and small that if it was anyone else I would call it an unconscious action, but everything is intentional with Elochian. I pull out of the kiss, resting my forehead against his. "Lochian," I gasp. "What're you doing?"

He breathes against my lips, fast and labored. "I—I don't know. I just—I have to—"

"No, it's okay, I—"

He shakes his head. "No, you don't understand. I—I want to make you feel good, Quentin. I want to do this." He leans in, kissing me gentler than before. "Please."

"Okay," I whisper against his lips. "If you really want to."

"I do."

"Okay. Just—you lead, okay?"

He nods, wings shivering. "Okay."

For a second, nothing happens. We hold each other, lips a breath apart. Nervousness threatens to split the moment in two, and I wonder if we're doing the right thing. Then Elochian's right hand rises, skimming over ribs and nipple until reaching my throat. When he kisses me again, it's more sure, like before. His fingers spread out, settling underneath my jaw. The pressure is unyielding, but soft.

We continue to kiss, opening ourselves to the other once again. He invites my tongue into his mouth, and the joy I feel at nearly slicing myself open on the tip of a budding fang is astronomically stupid. He groans at the friction between tooth and tongue, and pulls me forward by the hip. This time I'm expecting the motion, and I work with him. Despite the clothes between us, the sensation of my cock thrusting against his stomach is overwhelming, bordering on forbidden.

"Lochian," I moan into his mouth.

"Yes?" He sighs breathily in response, fingers tightening everywhere. He guides me ahead for another thrust, and another, kissing the words out of me.

"Ah—I'm too sensitive, I'll—oh fuck. I'll come like this."

His hand moves from my throat to the back of my neck, pulling me into him. My forehead meets his collar bone, and I wrap my arms around his neck. He whispers into my ear, "That means I'm doing good, yes?"

"Y—ah!" I cry out in response to his hips rising to meet my own. He's not hard, and I do my best not to let the thought linger. That's what natural for him, it has nothing to do with me. "Oh, Elochian, fuck. Yes, you're doing good. So fucking good."

"You swear so much like this," He murmurs, like I'm something to be studied. That should not turn me on as much as it does. His hand leaves my hip, skating over the fabric of my pajamas, towards the tent in them. He asks, "Can I touch you here?"

I don't know what makes me say it, or where the sudden bunch of nerves comes from. I whisper, "Yes, but ... over my clothes?"

He nods, and a few seconds pass before his hand closes the distance. He doesn't grab me like I thought he would, simply rubs his open palm over my length, exploring me as much as my pajamas will allow. When his hand settles against the underside of my shaft, trapped between me and his stomach, his lip twists.

"Dot, are you ... is this a piercing?"

"Oh," I gasp as his finger slides over the place where the metal bar resides beneath my skin, exploring the balls securing it on either side. "Yes."

I thrust forward and rub against his hand, moaning at the sensation. Elochian whimpers in response. I pause, until he whispers, "You sound so beautiful Quentin, it hurts."

Well, fuck. If I wasn't in love with him before, I certainly am now.

Embarrassingly, it doesn't take long to finish. We continue our push and pull for perhaps another minute or two, Elochian moaning softly into the crook of my neck and shoulder while I whine pathetically against the same place on him. Then I tense up, body coiling like a spring until Elochian grants me release. Fingers twisted into his shirt, a groan escapes me as pleasure is wrung from my body in powerful spurts.

He holds me through it all, breathing heavily against the bare skin of my throat, his lips and teeth a promise and threat all at once. After a few moments he starts to stand up, still holding me in his arms, and I squawk out a protest. "Lochian! What're you doing?"

"Carrying you to the bathroom."

"I—oh fine," I say, doing my best to hide my face. He sets me down on the counter in the bathroom, then turns on the light. He takes a washcloth out of the drawer, and the action makes me smile. He knows where everything is. He turns the warm water on, then offers me the washcloth.

Hesitantly, he says, "I'll go find some new pajamas for you."

"Okay."

He leaves the bathroom, shutting the door behind him. I sigh, looking down at my lap. "What a mess you've made, Quentin Matsdotter."

I hop down onto the floor and unzip my pajamas, kicking them off, then carefully peel off my boxers. I delicately roll them into a ball and toss them into the same corner as my pajamas, then clean myself up. When I dip the washcloth into the warm water, I find myself smiling. He's always so thoughtful.

By the time Elochian knocks on the door, I've dried off and wrapped a towel around my hips. "I have clothes. Do you want me to—um, should I put my hand through?"

I chuckle, shaking my head. "Go on, I'm decent."

The door creaks open, and Elochian stands on the other side with a bundle of neatly folded clothes in his hands. He certainly didn't find them that way. I carefully take the pile from him, noticing how the fabric trembles in his hand. "Thanks. I'll be just a sec, if you don't mind waiting."

He wrings his hands. "I—I don't mind."

I shut the door, leaving it open a crack to allow sound to easily pass through. I drop my towel and pull on my boxers, waiting for him to break the silence between us. It comes after I've tied my joggers in place, when I'm slipping a white shirt over my head. He says, "Quentin, I'm sorry."

I open the door, not entirely free from my shirt's clutches yet. "What?"

He covers his mouth, but not quick enough to hide the transformation of nervousness to amusement. I finally conquer my shirt and pull the cropped hem down, then reach for Elochian. His hands lower from his wobbly smile, and he takes what I offer. I pull him closer to me and his wings shake, sounding like a rattle. I bump his forehead with mine.

"Lochian, there's nothing to be sorry for."

His lips push thin, and his eyes escape mine, darting off to the side. "This shouldn't be so hard."

I smile. "Pun intended?"

He smacks my chest. "Oh, fuck off. I'm trying to be serious right now!"

I chuckle. "That's the problem." I kiss him and he sighs, releasing his worries into me. "Lochian, I'm not disappointed, if that's what you're worried about. I'm not—I'm not egotistical enough to think that I've got a magic dick that changes everything. You told me before what it would be like, and I accept that. Are you ... are you upset?"

"That I didn't come with you? A little. Yes."

"Oh. I thought ..." I trail off, unsure what I thought. That he was okay with not getting hard? He never really said if it bothered him, only that he couldn't.

After a moment, he says, "I thought too."

"We don't have to do it again, sunshine."

Elochian looks up at me through his lashes, the fine black hairs partially illuminated by the fluorescent lights of my bathroom. "Quentin."

"Yes?" I squeak, and the archdemon smiles.

He stares up at me for a moment, his hair mussed and clothes wrinkled, lip quirked. "I adore you, you know."

I laugh nervously. "Adore me? Is that so?"

He nods, then pulls me towards the bedroom. "Come, I'll tuck you in."

"Will you stay with me until I fall asleep?" I ask, already dreading him leaving.

"Of course."

He keeps his promise. I fall into a world of dreams and nightmares, and he kisses me on the cheek, whispering, "Happy Birthday, my love," against my skin.

Murmuring from the crowd brings me back to the present. Elochian reaches back, pulling a decorative pin from one of the many plaits secured at the nape of his neck. He holds it in his fingers like a pen, and lowers it to Tobias' palm.

"What's he doing?" Arlo asks.

I sit up, leaning over Arlo's way a little bit to get a better view. When I do, my blood freezes.

"Oh no."

Elochian's hand jerks quickly, and Tobias winces in response. Then Elochian gives the pin to Tobias, who gently stabs Elochian's hand in turn. When blood drips from both their palms, they join hands, melding the blood between them. At first, nothing happens, and I wonder if I've fucked this whole thing up by getting into Elochian's head.

They raise their joined hands high in the air between them, or as much as Elochian's arm will allow. Together, with voices empowered by the land, their people, and each other, they say, "We are the Archcelestials of Levena, and we are One."

Pink and gold sparks erupt from their hands, shooting high into the air and exploding like tiny fireworks. They pop off one after another, each one followed by a whistling *fizz* sound. The celestials around us scream and shout their approval, taking to the sky or stomping their feet against the earth. Cohesive motion surrounds us, the world is a frenzy of joy and acceptance.

And through it all, Elochian only has eyes for me.

Very Few Chances

Elochian

"You're ready," Tobias murmurs, securing a slim ribbon at the back of my head.

I search prominent golden ridges cresting over sharp cheekbones for hints of self, but I don't find any there. I reach up, tracing my fingers down the curved slope of my nose. It's smooth, the rainbow scales of my Godly ancestor are buried deep beneath layers of glass, but they shine and throw off color as easily as if they were free.

I've been told all my life I am of a God, that Mithys runs in my veins, but I've never fully absorbed the fact that I am *related* to this person. The Adrastus Mask was one of Mithys' personal possessions, crafted by his own hands and with parts of his own corporate body. The scales once covered his wings in the same fashion my own do, and the intricate carvings on the fringes of the mask are bone from his fingertips, and gold from his eyes.

The last person to wear this mask was my father.

"I'm not," I whisper, hands falling to my lap.

Tobias rests his hands on my shoulders, watching me through the main mirror of my personal vanity. There are three mirrors, with the two outside ones angled towards the center, but all three are framed by a series of candle bulbs, the glass illuminated by golden algae. The wood is painted black, and golden paisleys hide in the detail work. It's my mother's, a place I hardly sit at due to my complicated relationship with mirrors, but Tobias insisted that I sit here while he fastened my mask. An odd thought crosses my mind then, that this is what it would've been like to have a mother.

Someone to fuss over you and fix up your hair, someone to hold you by the shoulders, grounding you to the earth while they listen to your troubles.

And like a crack in a dam, the thought widens, fracturing into other thoughts. Would she be proud of me? Would my father have been? Are they rolling in their graves now, cursing me for breaking tradition? Or would they be proud? Do they find me worthy to wear the mask?

I like to think they'd approve, that my father would've asked Quentin to dance, and that my mother would've stolen him away from the ball, to the library. We'd all meet there, taking our shoes off and sitting together on the floor, and we'd compare our disasters and hilarites of the night, exchanging gossip like fine wine. And as the night faded into dawn, we'd live to see another day. Together.

I bow my head, and cry. I move to scrub at my eyes, trying to force the tears to stop, because we don't have *time* for this, but then I remember the mask is in the way, and my lungs seize.

Tobias' thin fingers deftly undo the ribbon, and he removes the mask before I claw it off. He sets the mask down on the vanity and kneels before me. He says, "Don't try to hold it in, let it out. If you don't know where to put it, give it to me. Give it to me, Elochian."

I do, and Tobias quietly sits with me until I have nothing left to give. "When the lung crushing sobs give way to hiccup interrupted cries, I manage to say, "H—how can you m—miss someone you never k—knew?"

"Your parents?"

I nod, sniffing.

Tobias hums softly, contemplating. "Because you do know them. You know them from the stories your family tells, from the feelings your heart remembers, but your mind forgot. You know them by the space they should occupy, but don't."

I sigh, exhaling the last of my frayed nerves. "I'm sorry. There's so much going on—" I gesture to my head. "I think I'm going to sleep for a week after this."

Tobias smiles. "I know what you mean. No offense, but going home will be the highlight of my night."

I think about the apartment, about Quentin falling apart in my arms. I say, "Don't worry, it'll be mine too."

We stare at the other for a long moment. Tobias opens his arms to me. "I heard you give these out sometimes. Is this one of those times?"

I chuckle, getting down onto the floor with him. We hold each other tight, our hearts in permanent synchronization since our blood became one. I say, "There will be some drama, dancing, and good food. Everything will go according to plan."

Tobias' hand runs up and down between my shoulder blades once before he pulls back, smiling. "I highly doubt that last bit, but we'll be ready for when it does."

A knock sounds from the door connecting Michael's room to my own, and seconds later the door opens to reveal both Michael and Charlie. They step inside the room and stand side by side, then pause, evaluating us for a second. In full *esh shedim* form, Michael asks, "Sir, is everything alright?"

I get off the floor and offer Tobias a hand up, which he takes. "Yes, fine, we're fine. Is it time? Are they here?"

Michael nods. "Yes, Sir. It's time. Mr. Matsdotter and Lord Daemarrel are waiting for both of you."

"Good. Okay. One moment." I turn to Tobias, lips parted on a request, but he already has the mask in his hands. "Thank you."

"Of course." He offers it to me and I carefully take the relic, staring down at it for a moment. I glance at Tobias, who gives me a little nod. I smile at him, then shift my attention to Michael.

"Michael, would you?"

For a moment, Michael doesn't move. As in, at all. His chest doesn't rise, and he doesn't blink. Charlie gives him a little shove, breaking Michael out of his trance. He glares at Charlie over his shoulder, then takes an unsteady step forward, and another. Michael stands before me, fingers twitching at their sides. "Sir, I don't know if this is appropriate," they whisper.

"Please." I hold the mask out to them, and after another brief hesitation, they take it. I turn around, facing Tobias. The cool glass passes over my eyes until settling into place, against my cheeks. I stare at Tobias through the narrow eye holes, and he grins. I had helped him with his own mask first.

The Mask of Haniel was made for the first Archangel of Levena, Juniper Haniel, and it suits Tobias. Smooth white plaster covers his eyes and nose, leaving his cheeks free, unlike my own mask. A myriad of feathers decorate the left side of the piece, a variety of soft downy white and silver flight feathers, the largest of which could cover my arm from wrist to elbow and is situated at the highest point of the mask. Instead of intricate bone carvings, needle-like teeth are embedded at the corner of his eyes in three points. They point outwards, reminding me of elaborate crow's feet.

His outfit is a flowing combination of dress and suit, all white trimmed in silver, and ornamented to match his mask. Tiny crystals that remind me of waterfalls hang from his ears and throat, brushing his shoulders and sternum respectively. Even smaller diamonds have been pasted onto his cheeks, throat, and the exposed part of his upper chest. His luminous pink hair is braided a million different ways to Sunday, like my own.

I've been trying not to take myself in, but I'm pleased that we are complimentary of each other while remaining unique. My suit is tight, all black except for my waistcoat, which has a velvet foundation of black with golden brocade detailing. The symbols and designs pay homage to not only angels and demons, but the witches. Gold studs line the shells of my ears, the right more complete than the left, and a gilded coin rests beside my heart, dangling from a leather cord. The same cloak that I wore on my date with Quentin rests across my shoulders.

Michael securely ties the ribbon and says, "You're ready, sir."

I turn, and Michael immediately bows at the waist upon coming face to face with me. I don't chastise him for it, allowing him to have his piety. Charlie bows as well, but I don't know if it's to me or his own lord. I say, "Thank you. We're ready now."

Michael and Charlie lead us into the hall, where a small security squad composed of angels and demons waits to escort us to the main floor. I recognize Annie and John before everyone bows at the waist, committing one of two marks over their heart. The mark of Daemarrel is new, but simple. It's a '*D*', with a dot inside it. Tobias glances sideways at me, and I nod.

He asks our team, "Are we all ready?"

As one, they say, "Yes, Mx."

We pass through empty halls as a single unit. Tobias walks by my side, our personal *shomer* are at our backs, while everyone else surrounds us in a simple rectangle formation. Our shoes squeak against the polished floor, and winter peonies efficiently placed throughout the halls perfume our journey. If I didn't know better, I'd say the place was empty. There are no servants in this wing, not tonight. The ballroom and its accompanying social areas take up the entire northern end of the main house, an area that otherwise remains empty and unattended to.

After some twisting and turning, one of the *shedim* in the lead unlocks a door, ushering us inside a narrow, private hall reserved for situations such as this, or clever escape. Technically we are *inside* the walls now, but the space is wide enough for the formation to remain as it was, if not a little more pushed together. There are doors every once in a while, offering alternate routes for servants or spies.

Tobias whispers, "Are there secret passages in the Palace too?"

"Oh, I'm sure there are. Demons are considered the less shifty of the celestials, you know."

"I see." Tobias chuckles, but it fades quickly.

"Are you nervous?"

"Of course I am."

"We're almost there."

"Well, that's reassuring."

"I *meant* we're almost there. To our people. They'll get us through."

Tobias nods, smiling. "Yes. You're right. Gods, can you believe it? The day is finally here, and nearly over."

"Don't jinx us yet, angel."

We finally come to our destination, a nondescript door that I probably would've walked right past. It's been awhile since I've been in the walls, or through this particular door. When one of the guards cracks it open, laughter and bickering meets us at the threshold.

What remains of the Adrastus Family waits in a private antechamber that serves as a staging area. When we enter the room, arms linked, most everyone bows at the waist. Tisha, Edward, and Annette conspire together near a hearth, while Mabel and Roque occupy the area closest to the ballroom doors, clearly impatient. Annette smiles at me, one of the few who do.

Edward throws back his drink, then tips his glass in my direction. With the calm of a predator, he says, "You're lucky that stunt of yours worked. What were you thinking, improvising the ceremony?"

I stare at him. My wings are still. Tobias' hold on me is strong. Chin held high, I look down my nose at Edward like he's done to me so many times before. "I was thinking that we are still enacting romantic aspects of a ceremony that has long since become a platonic affair, and there was no need for it."

He laughs, but it's devoid of any actual humor. "That's not for you to decide, is it? It was a matter that should have been brought before the council, I—"

Tobias primly says, "Pardon me, but I believe there is a ball being held in my honor, and you're delaying it with your bullshit." His wings spread, and the left one slides over my own span, nearly curling around my body.

Mabel laughs, the sound patronizing and melodic. Edward's jaw slackens, and Tobias makes a dismissive shoo gesture, then tugs me along. I toss a fleeting glance my aunt's way and find a wry smile there, the corners of which disappear beneath a beautiful ceramic mask painted in a violent ombre pink scheme.

I quietly ask Tobias, "Are you having fun?"

"I have very few chances to be an asshole, let me have this."

"Oh, by all means."

We face doors that are taller than we are, perhaps tall enough for giants. Michael and Charlie stand behind us, talking into their earpieces. After a moment, Michael gives the all clear. "They're ready."

Tobias and I exchange a look. I whisper, "I'm proud of you, Tobias. I don't think I've told you that."

Tobias smiles. "Thank you, Elochian. Let's go find our men. It's a certain someone's birthday, don't forget."

Heat rises to my cheeks as I remember leaving him in bed last night, hair all mussed and skin flush with remnants of pleasure and joy. I chuckle nervously, then nod to Michael. They order the attendants to open the doors, and it takes four on each side to push them outwards. The guards around us have parted, allowing my aunt to stand not much more than an arm's length behind me. My cousins stand behind her in single file, utilizing about the same distance. Not close enough to be stabbed in the back, not unless the person behind you lunged.

When the doors finally swing all the way open, Tobias and I walk past the threshold and into Adrastus Hall, our arms linked and heads held high. Our announcement echoes through the space, originating from a stage situated at the eastern side of the chamber, its exact source hidden by the crowd trained on us. The ballroom is more reminiscent of a cathedral than anything else, the ceilings are so distant you have to squint in order to properly appreciate the colored glass for what it is. Murals depicting our history full of love and loss, of war and peace. A cycle of humanity that goes on, and on, attended to by celestials as they are slowly eroded by time and duty.

There is no tile here, only an endless ocean of starwood. The polished and smooth grain is naturally black, flecked with white that glows in complete darkness. Algae globes hang by thin strands of near invisible kelp cord at various heights throughout the ballroom, and they remind me of enormous bubbles with tiny suns trapped inside them.

The walls are cobblestone, if you can call rocks larger than cars that, but the original architects wanted to keep the natural state of the stones as much as possible. Any gaps in the walls are neatly filled in by smaller chunks, and all of it is mortared together using a mix which includes black sand imported from Jaqul.

I'm enthralled by it all nearly as much as Tobias is, but not enough to distract me from my mission. The sea of people parts, forming a clear path to the other side of the ballroom, where Quentin is. He and Caspian wait on a dais marked only by a semi-circle of crystals emerging from the floor, not entirely separate from everyone else but removed enough, and not higher than anyone else.

Upon seeing me he smiles wide, giving me a little wave before abruptly clasping his hands together behind his back again. He quickly glances around to see if anyone saw him, and I fight a smile. He's wearing the red coat I love, and the shirt beneath it is a beautiful combination of black silk and lace. Black stones hang from his ears, along with tiny golden chains. Layers of matching delicate chains hang around neck at various lengths, and the moonshell buttons of his shirt are undone enough to reveal a generous part of his tree tattoo, and chest.

His mask is elegant, simple and beautiful, just like him. It's a half face style, the black ceramic covers his entire forehead, right eye, right cheek, and down to his jaw. Tiny opal crystals trim the edges of the mask and decorate the flat areas like constellations. Exactly five of my scales fan out from the corner of the eye, shed pieces that I asked the craftsman to include into the piece.

Caspian stares fondly at Tobias, lips quirked just enough to make it look like he's planning trouble. As we get closer I notice

Arlo standing close by, accompanied by our friends. Lindsey, Kitt, Gowan, Iris, Dusan, Idina, and Finnegan. A group of people stand close to them, but I only recognize some due to the masks. Evangeline is easy to pick out, and from there I can guess it's Bud and Rain by her side. Gaia stands close to Arlo and Finnegan, as does Arche. Even Eleanor has braved the crowd.

I've never felt prouder.

Two thirds of the way there, a ghost of a memory crosses our path. I freeze, and Tobias nearly stumbles in response to my jarring stop. I watch as an archdemon and his *shomer* cross the dance floor hand in hand, heart falling out of rhythm when laughter rocks the *shomer's* head back. He twirls the archdemon, then dips him low. Later that night we made love for the first time. I gave all of myself to him, and it was so easy, so unlike last night. Was it because I was young? More carefree? Less traumatized?

Last night wasn't easy, but it was just as beautiful, if not more *because* of it.

Tobias whispers, "Are you okay?"

I blink away the memory, and focus on what's in front of me. I nod without looking at him, keeping my eyes on Quentin. "Yes. I'm fine."

I take a step forward, and Tobias follows where I lead. We step past the ring of crystals and take our place with Caspian and Tobias. Before disentangling entirely, I kiss the back of Tobias' hand and bow at the waist to him, which causes those gathered to cheer. He bows in return with a bit more flourish than I, and the applause doubles.

Tobias leaves me for Caspian, and I fight the urge to take Quentin into my arms and hold him close to my chest for the rest of the night. Instead, I stand by his side and entwine my fingers with his, waiting for the rest of the clan to be announced and join us. Cameras flash and the noise intensifies, but I hold on tight to Quentin.

He smiles shyly at me. "You're a vision tonight, Lochian."

"As are you, Dot." I smile back, running my thumb over the back of his hand. "Regretting your life decisions yet?"

He laughs, oblivious to how beautiful it is, how everyone can hear him, how everyone can see that I'm the one holding his hand. "Not at all. The ceremony was beautiful, I—" He shakes his head, unable to get rid of his smile. "I can't believe you did that for me."

"I didn't have time to get you a proper birthday gift, I hope that was good enough."

He laughs again, softening the edges of everything else into something bearable. "More than good, and I think the outfit definitely counts as a gift, by the way."

I give him a dry look, and he smiles. Then he looks around discreetly, lingering on Tisha before returning to me. "Everything alright, then?"

I shrug. "So far. No problems on your end?"

"None. No one seems to care that witches are here en mass, besides being curious and nosy about it."

"Mm. We'll see how things go after a few hours."

"Okay." Quentin looks down at our joined hands, chewing on his cheek as he does. "You know ...."

"Hm?"

"Well, it's just—you never said if *we* would be dancing."

"I did too."

"When?"

"I—I'm sure that I did."

"Right, okay. So. Yes?"

I smile at him. "Quentin, you were one of the biggest reasons why I wanted to throw a ball in the first place."

"Wh—*me*? Why?"

"I love it when you dance, and I want everyone in the world to know that you are mine. Seemed to be a two birds with one stone kind of thing."

"I—*Elochian*," Quentin says, exasperated.

"What?"

He tugs at his collar. "You can't just *say* stuff like that."

"Why?"

"Because it makes me want to kiss you," he mutters.

I lean over and kiss his cheek. He startles a little, then smiles. He nods to the crowd. "They're waiting on you, I think."

"Well, we can't have that, can we?"

Unwilling to leave him behind for even a second, I lead Quentin towards the single microphone on the dais. The algae bulbs above our heads brighten, while those over the crowd dim a few shades. I run the numbers in my head all day, every day. There are two thousand and eighty-six *shedim* in the Clan Adrastus, the largest of all the clans in the Nether Isles, and our estimations were that fifty percent would be attending. Not to mention the visiting Arches and their inner circles.

According to Xenith, approximately thirty percent of the two thousand, five hundred and ten *malakim* in the newly minted Clan Daemarrel will be attending tonight's ball. I'm unsure if any of our original numbers are still accurate, it feels like there are well over three thousand people out there, waiting. Watching. Panic claws at my throat, strangling my vocal cords.

Quentin gently knocks his shoulder against mine, smiling when he catches my attention. He whispers, "Come on sunshine, show 'em what you're made of." Each word pries the claws from my throat, and I smile back. I nod, then turn back towards the crowd. I close my eyes and fill my lungs, summoning every ounce of power from my ancient blood, and every shred of pride from the fibers of my heart.

Without opening my eyes I can feel it, like an electrical storm has rolled overhead. My wings elongate, comfortably warming my shoulder muscles as they do, and my fangs descend. Murmurs and gasps roll throughout the room, and my braids begin to lift from my shoulders as if weightless. I open my eyes, surprised by what I see. My periphery has widened, and it's now tinged in translucent, bright gold. A visible gilded aura surrounds me, sparking and crackling. My Godliness, visible for the world to see.

And Quentin. It surrounds him, too. He giggles, delighted by the way it feels, then his expression shutters into something more serious. He winks at me, then gives my hand a little shake as if to say, *'get on with it.'*

I do. Speaking into the microphone, I say, "Welcome to the first Adrastus Masquerade to have been thrown in decades. Today I shared blood with my counterpart, Tobias *xir* Daemarrel, cementing the foundations of what will be an eternal and prosperous partnership, one that will serve Levena and her people for millennia to come, long after we've gone. I am blessed to have been paired with such a kind *bashert*, a steadfast man, and a clever witch.

"I am sure by now you've noticed that tradition and I have never been good friends. Most are important, crucial to who we are as a people, but others ... they call for separation, for placing others below ourselves. And I will not tolerate that. As of today, Adrastus Manor will be open. It will be open to common folk, to magical creatures and witches. If you are in need, Clan Adrastus will help, as will Clan Daemarrel. Aid should not be limited to those of certain blood or ability, especially when we have the resources. Tradition is all fine and well, but we must not be afraid to call for change when it is needed. To inspect the way we've been living, and what we're living for. Or who."

I glance over at Quentin and he squeezes my hand, smiling softly. He nods.

I turn back to the crowd. "I have never been more grateful, and proud, to be the head of Clan Adrastus than I am right now. This is the beginning of a new era, and history will make not only us, but all of *you*, into legends for daring to do what is right. Let us dance, and be merry. Embrace your neighbor, and break bread with one another. *L'chaim!*"

Chaos falls. Howls of approval from the demons rise with chattering hoots from the angels, and the band joins in with a great crash of quick and feverish strings. The lights above us fade, shifting focus to the main dance floor. Quentin hugs my arm, grinning. "I don't think I've ever heard you say so much at once."

"A simple job well done would have sufficed, you know."

Caspian claps me on the opposite arm, accompanied by Tobias. "Job well done."

"Oh fuck off."

Caspian laughs, and Tobias smiles. He says, "That was beautiful. Thank you."

"You helped me write it!"

"Yes, I know, but hearing it was ... well you put a certain emotion into things." Tobias shrugs.

I sigh. "Right. Well. Where's Witch and Company?"

"Right here," Arlo says, materializing on the other side of Quentin with most of the original group I saw him with earlier. "That was pretty fucking epic, Loch."

I smile. "Thanks, Arlo."

Dante breaks from Arche's side, wrapping up Quentin in another one of those bone crushing hugs which tears his hand out of mine. I frown, but say nothing as Quentin laughs and says hello to the angel. Dante bows to Tobias, then me. He says, "Never thought I'd be here. That was one hell of a speech."

I bow my head. "I'm glad you came," I say, trying to be sincere, and shift my attention to Arche. "Both of you."

Arche shrugs. "It's not bad."

"I'm glad we meet your expectations," I say, trying to tease.

Arche smiles, a shadow of a thing, but I consider my night complete.

Before we can dance, we have to endure everything I originally promised Quentin. Proper and polite society root around for information on my beloved as they make their way to us, paying their respects to my group before floating over to the rest of my family. Arlo ends up fielding a majority of questions and attention, which I greatly appreciate.

Eventually, our friends begin to disperse, drawn away by other acquaintances, food, or dancing. The initial ordeal takes longer than I thought it would, but Quentin smiles through each obnoxiously placed, *'You must be a special human to catch our Lord's eye,'* and *'Welcome to the Clan, tchotchke.'*

In between our latest round of interrogations, he grumbles, "I am *literally* the same size as you."

I smile, quietly pleased that so far everyone is as enamored by him as I am. "It's not about size. They think of you as a newborn."

"Was that supposed to be helpful?"

"I mean—you're new. To the clan. It's like that."

"Oh, that makes—" Quentin's remark dies as a couple approaches us, and I can practically feel him turn to stone beneath my touch.

On the right is Delilah Sheleg, the Archshedim of Agia Province. We don't interact very often, except for in missives.

It's not a personal thing, I don't see any of the other Arches more than once a year, if I can help it. I am the last Descendant of Mithys, however, which does cause some friction.

In full *esh shedim* form, she wears a tight suit that covers her from wrist to ankle, with a high collar buttoned all the way up her throat, complete with white lace that frames her jaw. The silk fabric of her suit is all black, even the trim, and her heels are sharper than the point of a knife. Last, but not least, is a black ceramic mask with a long nose and white snowflakes across the cheeks.

"Lord Adrastus," she says, unbothered and if I'm being honest, apathetic. "Congratulations on your bond. May I introduce Lady Avina Dow of Agia."

The woman on the left is tiny, but her disposition is fierce. With dark hair cropped close to her head, her eyes gleam like polished jade. A white fur is draped over her bare shoulders, and her dress is blacker than the abyss, simple and without extravagant detailing, but somehow she still screams money. A string of black pearls encircles her throat, tight against her skin.

Her mask is incredibly minimal, the style similar to her companion's, but there is no nose or cheekbones, simply the part that covers her eyes, and the brow plate is finished with snowflakes. Her nostrils flare as she raises her chin, her black painted lips curled in a way that reminds me of Mabel before she delivers a particularly cruel jab.

Lady Avina Dow of Agia says, "Hello, Simon."

Quentin shivers, and his hold on my hand turns brutal.

Despite this, he calmly says, "Mother." He nods to the other woman. "Lady Sheleg."

Delilah simply looks him up and down once before turning her attention elsewhere, clearly bored.

I seem to be rendered invisible, and I'm not as happy about the concept as I thought I'd be. I say, "Good evening, I'm—"

Quentin's mother scoffs, holding up a hand as if to ward me off. "Yes, indeed. I'm afraid you have been duped, Lord Adrastus." She shifts her attention to Quentin. "And I thought you could stoop no lower. Your father would be—"

"He'd be happy for me, don't you think?" Quentin asks, releasing a hollow chuckle. "To finally be with someone who gives a damn about me?"

"Don't be daft. Was sleeping your way to the top of the underworld not good enough? You had to infiltrate an aristocracy as well? You can have all of this at home." She waves to the room, lip curled.

"How dare you," Quentin says, shaking with anger. "What are you even doing here? You exiled *me*, remember?"

"Well I had to, didn't I? You gave me no other choice." She tuts dismissively. "But now, it's time for you to come home. You can't keep running from your duties, Simon."

"I wasn't running from my duties, I was running from *you*. And how can I do anything? You took my title, left me out in the cold when I needed you most, and—and—my name's not Simon!"

I fold Quentin against my side and my wings rise, curling around us. His arms cinch around my waist, but he doesn't break from his furious stare down with his mother.

Her eyes flick from him, to me. Then she laughs, quiet and menacing. She says, "You have no idea who he is, do you?"

I reach for Michael in the space between our minds, sending out red flags. Chest brimming with anger, I say, "You are no longer welcome here. Please, leave."

Her laughter dies. "You're making a mistake, Lord Adrastus. Allow me to explain—"

"Leave." The algae bulbs overhead flicker as I speak. "Now."

She shakes her head. "Have it your way, then. Consider your-self warned."

I stare at her until she walks away, and even then I watch her go, not satisfied until I see a few guardians from Michael's team escorting her out. I bring my lips to Quentin's ear. "Are you alright?"

"No."

"Let's dance, then. I'm tired of this."

He looks up at me, lashes wet with unshed tears. He stares at me, searching for something, then nods. "Okay. Okay. Where—where should we go?"

"Follow me."

Isn't It A Sight?

Quentin

Of course.

Of course Avina would make tonight about her. Of course she would decide that she finally wants me home, but only because she needs me. Of course she would—

"You with me, Dot?"

I inhale, reminding myself to breathe, and nod. It's just so much. I don't know how we got here, and I don't just mean how we slipped through the crowd to this relatively private section of the ballroom. Elochian and Tobias have claimed their places, both separately and together. Elochian held my hand as he did so, and his heart reached out to mine in a beautiful cloud of gold. Again, I nearly told him, with thousands of people as our witness, that I love him.

It's coming, I can feel it. Even so, to be able to say that Elochian is mine, and I am his? I never thought that would happen. I never thought we would get here.

"Me either," Elochian murmurs, ever so patiently leading me through the motions. One hand rests on my waist, while the other gently cups my own hand.

I frown. "Did I say that out loud?"

"Yes."

"What did I say?"

"That you never thought we'd get here."

"Oh. I think I'm losing it."

"That's okay. I'll help you find it."

I laugh breathlessly, resting my head on his shoulder. Elochian sways in place and I allow him to guide the push and pull of our bodies, melting in his arms. It's a different type of push and pull than what we did last night, a different form of coming together to become one.

I say, "I could do this forever, I think."

He hums. "I like the sound of that."

"You don't mind that it's slow?"

"No. Not at all."

The song changes, but we keep on the way we are. After a little while, I say, "I'm the Second Prince of Agia. I—I assume my brother's dead, or something's happened. That's got to be why she came for me."

Elochian's wings flutter once, then go still. After we slowly rock into our third revolution since the word 'prince,' he chuckles. "Okay."

"*Okay*?"

"It doesn't change anything."

I straighten, glaring at him. He lifts a brow, accelerating our dance a touch. I say, "It doesn't change anything."

"No, that's what *I* said."

"Lochian—that's—if anything were to happen between us, we'd be—well, there would be a lot of red tape, formal ties between Agia and the clan—" Elochian laughs, sending me out for a spin. Upon returning, I slap his chest. "What are you laughing at!"

"Only you would describe a potential marriage as a mess of red tape."

My cheeks flush, and not from the dance. "It's true."

"You're not a Prince anymore, Quentin. You don't have to go back."

"I don't want to."

He pulls me close, dropping his voice to a whisper. "Stay."

"In Levena, or with you?"

Elochian's hands abandon their posts in favor of cupping my cheeks. He stares into my eyes, thumbs sweeping over my face. "With me. Your soulmate."

Tears sting my eyes, and my lungs stutter. "Y—you knew?"

He smiles, broad and instant. "*You* knew?"

I laugh. "Yes. Your wingmarks glow whenever I'm around." I fidget with my glasses. "I can see it with these, but I didn't know what it was. But then I saw my own, and I—I didn't know whether to tell you, I didn't want to ...."

He shakes his head. "Of course you did. You didn't want to what?"

I drop my gaze. "I didn't want to scare you."

Elochian's hand leaves my waist and takes a gentle hold of my chin. He tilts my head back, and kisses me. It's like our first kiss, soft and slow. Like us. He kisses me like we have all the time in the world, and we're completely alone. Both sentiments are complete and total lies, but for a moment, I choose to believe in them. I kiss him back, indulging in my soulmate.

After a moment, he breaks away. "Ask me to move in with you."

"What—*really*? You would?"

"Yes, I think I would. I might run away a couple days a week, crawl into a hole and panic, but I'll be back. I promise."

I laugh. "Okay. Lochian, will you move in with me?"

"Of course I will, what took you so long?"

I kiss him through a smile, and we dance together for a little bit longer.

It's Arche who finds us first. He slinks through the crowd, his eyes a dull red that comes with not feeding properly. He sidles up to me, and nods to Elochian. "Hello."

"Hey, are you ready?" I ask, lifting my head off Elochian's shoulder.

"That's what I was coming to ask you. I'll be heading out soon."

"Ready? For what?" Elochian asks, eyes widening.

I smile at him. "I've planned a small surprise for you."

His face falls. "No."

I try not to laugh. "Yes."

"What—how." He states more than asks. "It's *your* birthday."

I kiss his cheek. "You'll see. Michael knows what's going on, ask them." I pull out of his embrace and straighten my clothes, smoothing out any wrinkles.

"Quentin, I don't like this," he says, wings shivering.

"Hey, I'll just be at the stage, okay?"

"Take—"

"I'm taking Annie with me, per Michael's instruction." I nod to the space behind Elochian, where both guardians wait. Annie is all business, but Michael wears a wry smile.

Elochian turns, then sighs and rubs his temple. "Fine. Be careful. Please." He stares at Michael for a moment, then says, "You go with him. Annie, you're with me."

Michael's smile fades. "Sir."

"*Don't* 'Sir' me, if you're going to plan surprises behind my back, then you'll suffer the consequences. Now go on." He makes a shooing gesture, pretending to be haughty. "Annie and the twenty other guardians surrounding me right now will do just fine."

Michael scowls at Elochian. "Sir, with all due respect, no. Annie, go."

Annie nods, crossing the small distance without so much as a backwards glance at Elochian. When she joins my side I say, "Listen to Michael, he knows best. 'Kay?"

"You both realize *I* am the one in charge here?"

"We know, sunshine. We know."

Elochian shakes his head, frowning. "Be quick about it."

I smile. "I will."

Annie ushers us towards the stage, and I follow her lead. Keeping close to my side, Arche mutters, "Well, that wasn't dramatic or anything."

"He's just worried."

"Enough to want his personal bodyguard *and* a witch to escort you across the room?"

"If *he's* here," I whisper, looking at the people we pass by. "He could be anyone."

"I'm dangerous, you know."

"I have no doubts about that."

Arche says nothing. By the time we make it to the stage I'm a little sweaty, thanks to my nerves and the sheer amount of people around us. At first glance the orchestra is composed of traditional instruments like the cello and violin, bass and piano, saxophone and clarinet. An abandoned microphone is at the helm of the stage, and at the back where you have to squint to see it, is a beautiful drum set flanked by two guitars, all quiet. The sight of the drum set spurs me on.

A pair of security guards are situated at both entrances to the raised stage, and I'm sure there are more at the rear of the platform as well. Annie converses with one, quietly announcing our intent. When they allow us to pass through, Annie leads us to the front of the stage, and the music dies. Primo and Silas are already there.

"You made it," I whisper to Primo, who I wasn't sure was going to come.

He smiles. "Wouldn't miss a chance to make music with you for the world, kid."

"Let's get on with it already," Silas signs, figure tense. Since learning I don't know why he insisted on coming, on helping me with this instead of staying behind with Felix at the castle, but I'm glad he's here.

I tell him so, and he blows at a strand of hair draped over one of the eye holes in his mask. I look between Arche, Primo, and Silas. "We all ready?"

They agree in one way or another, severing any chances for me to procrastinate. I've made my bed, time to lie in it. I study the microphone, wondering how the fuck Elochian made this look so easy. I exhale a shaky breath, searching the immediate crowd for Elochian. It doesn't take me long to find him, standing there front and center with Michael at his side, and Arlo too, with Tobias and some of the others. Elochian stares up at me, and I wave a little. He smiles tightly, nerves fraying before my eyes.

I had a whole speech planned, but it's long forgotten, wiped clean by the moment and all it entails. I say, "I've written a song for Lord Adrastus. I hope you like it."

Elochian straightens, the corner of his mouth softening, and I wink at him before turning away. I sit down at my throne, a cushioned stool that spoils me immediately, while Silas and Primo take up the guitars in front of me. Arche gingerly takes the microphone from its stand, holding onto it with both hands. After hearing Arche sing I just knew that it had to be him, no offense to Tobias, but it did take much coercing.

I start us off with a solid, consistent beat on the kick drum that may or may not be based on what I think Elochian's heartbeat sounds like. After ten seconds pass, I add another rhythm using the tom drums, which is Silas' cue.

Silas' tone is warm and strong as he begins to strum. The notes are complex, something he made up on the fly in our first session together, but he makes it look so easy. He deftly alternates between strumming and plucking the strings in what some would consider to be a bizarre way. The piece is organized chaos, strong and relentless. His dexterity is unparalleled, and his nonchalance as he plays could read as smug to some, but I know better.

But then he looks up at Primo, mouth twitching in a way that seems to read, *'try that on,'* and slows his strumming to the original chord which follows the heartbeat.

Primo laughs, easing into his own solo. His notes are a touch more refined, the edges more crisp. He plays like he has all the time in the world, too, fingers lazily dancing up and down the neck of the guitar. It's a gradual thing, the way his notes speed up and become this lyrical masterpiece, something beautiful and truly once in a lifetime. It eventually transforms, becoming one with Silas' chords, and my snare drum hits, marking the beginning of something new.

And then, Archeon sings, revealing the depths of my heart and soul.

"I dream of stones, and the way they skip over the water. I dream of bones, and the way they haunt you. I dream of a day when I'm unafraid, and ready to fight.

Because isn't it a sight, to stand for those you love?

Because isn't it a sight, to say that's enough?

Because isn't it a sight, to sleep in peace beside you?

I dream of stones, and the people they lead us to. I dream of bones, and all they teach us. I dream of a day when I'm terrified, and ready to fight.

Because isn't it a sight, to stand for those you love?

Because isn't it a sight, to say that's enough?

Because isn't it a sight, to sleep in peace beside you?

I dream of stones, and the day you place one on my grave. I dream of bones, and the day yours are laid to rest with mine.

Because isn't it a sight, to stand for those you love?

Because isn't it a sight, to say that's enough?

Because isn't it a sight, to sleep in peace beside you?"

Silas and Primo reach a crescendo with Arche's last line, as do I, and then all of us fade into silence. Five seconds pass, and the ballroom *screams*. Silas drops his guitar, thankfully he's wearing a strap, and squishes his headphones over his ears. Primo laughs again, clearly having the time of his life.

I stand with wobbly knees and Primo thrusts out a hand to me, which causes the applause to double. I join him, Arche, and Silas, and all of us bow at the waist to the crowd. The moment we straighten, Silas makes a beeline for the exit without saying goodbye. I watch him go until I'm sure he's made it off the stage safely, then turn to Primo and Arche.

"Thanks guys, I think it's safe to say it went well," I half-shout over the crowd's continued noise.

Chuckling, Arche loudly says, "I have to admit, we sounded pretty damn good."

Primo extends a hand to Arche, who shakes it firmly. "We really fucking did. Come by the shop sometime, eh?"

Arche nods. "I will. Now if you don't mind, I think I've earned a cigarette."

I laugh. "If you say so."

We watch him go, then Primo offers his hand to me. I shake it, and he says, "Go find your man, and I'll see you around."

"Thank you, Primo. Really."

He winks at me, and I grin. Then we go our separate ways. Instead of using one of the front entrances, Annie opts for exiting the stage using the rear entrance. It was Michael's back up plan in case the crowd became too much, and that seems to be the case. Behind the stage is an empty, narrow hallway that delivers us into a private room for entertaining, reserved for the band. As we go down the stairs connecting the stage to ground level, she says, "Lord Adrastus is waiting for you just this way."

I nod, sticking close to her side. She's always quick and efficient, all business. She—

She doesn't speak, due to a Vow of Silence.

I skid to a stop and bring my hand to my tattoo in attempts to summon the quill, but my fingers pause just short of pushing up my sleeve, as if they've been submerged in mud.

My entire body feels the same way, like I'm immersed in a cold bog. The same feeling I had in the bar. I fight against the invisible force, glaring at Annie as she approaches.

I open my mouth, but her hand is there before I can scream.

"Ah, ah." She quickly jabs at my neck, and it's only after she pulls away do I see the syringe. She tosses it to the ground, then takes a large stone out of her pocket. She squeezes the back of my neck, fingers digging into my scalp, and activates the travel stone. I try to fight, to do *something*. All I manage to do is retain consciousness, even as the ballroom disappears, twisted into somewhere new.

Once warm and full of love, the air is now dank and chilling. The shift of atmosphere seizes my lungs, and I cough against the sulfuric fumes that hit me like an afterthought. My legs give way and I fall to my knees, but Annie doesn't release my hair, simply lowers her arm after the fact. A cry forms on my lips, but dies shortly after its birth. I blink away tears, already struggling to maintain my vision due to the drugs.

"Isn't it a sight," A voice sings, lofty and high. A tall form stands in front of me. "Such a beautiful song could only be made by such a beautiful disaster as you. But there's something missing ..."

The person kneels, then cups my chin and turns my face upwards. I search the person's face, sluggishly clearing the cobwebs from my mind. Curly, shiny horns. Demon. Weird blue mustache, and long hair that tickles my nose and makes me want to sneeze. But it's the eyes that I recognize, cunning and harsh, the irises an unsettling white.

Something cool swipes across my bottom lip. A finger?

"D—Daniel."

"Oh, look at the fight in you." He grins, revealing razor sharp teeth. Every single one of them. The cool sensation goes back and forth across my bottom lip a couple more times. "You really are so pretty like this, what am I to do?"

He lowers his face until we're inches apart, the descent is slow and for lack of a better word, hallucinogenic. His skin fades to a pasty complexion, the pigment ebbing and flowing as it changes. His mustache recedes, and the hairs seem to scream as they disappear. His long hair shortens, flashing wildly between blue, black, white, and red, until it's long enough to reach his jaw, then it remains at black.

His nose crunches, and his cheekbones moan as they smooth out into something human. His horns crumble to dust, and I'm forced to inhale the opal cloud as it passes between our faces. His fingers thin and the nails elongate, piercing the underside of my jaw as his grip tightens. Lastly, his eyes flutter between the familiar toxic blue that I remember, glaring white, and finally, blood red.

Echoed by a murderous ghost, River says, "It's time to pay for your sins, Glimmer."

Sacrilege

Elochian

"Where's Quentin?"

Silas shrugs, glancing over his shoulder at the stage. Primo comes down the stairs on the right side of the stage, and Quentin isn't behind him. Suddenly Arlo staggers towards me, a hand to his head. I put my hands out to catch him, but Michael's there a moment later.

"F—*find* him," Arlo grits out, gripping my sleeve. "He's ... trouble!" He tries, groaning in frustration. His eyes blink to green, then the magick seems to implode and they transform into a cold, dull gold.

"Go! I've got him." Tobias shouts.

It all goes to hell so quickly. Panic spreads like wildfire. Michael and I take off as one for the back of the stage, except I fly over it while he runs.

A feral sound breaks past my lips, clawing out of my chest. The band scatters out of our way, but I don't care. My movements feel like a series of afterimages, occurring in slow motion and hyperspeed all at the same time.

I crash into the hallway hiding behind the stage, and I see them. Annie holds Quentin by the hair, craning his neck back. She looks over her shoulder, and grins at me. My vision shifts to red, and my head feels like it's going to explode. I run towards them, and Michael rushes past me.

Annie disappears, taking my love with her. The world cracks in their absence, the sound deafening. I scream in frustration and rage, coming to a stop in the place they once were. Michael brushes against my side and I snatch him by the front of his suit, slamming his back against the wall.

"Where did they go?"

"I don't know. I'll find him, I promise I will, but we need to move to the safe room." He tries to move me, to take me away.

I shake my head, shoving him back. An exquisite, focusing type of pain shoots up my spine and spreads throughout my wings, a different type of sensation than earlier but one that screams *God* all the same. "This ... this is your fault! I told you to go with him!"

"Loch, stop! You're hurting him," Arlo calls, but it's too far off. Everything is. A shudder wracks my body as it expands, and my nails crack as they lengthen. My teeth sharpen, and thick streams of blood spill past my lips.

Tobias cradles my head in his hands, and I stare up at the ceiling. When—how?

I struggle against the hands holding me down, and a fire builds in my chest.

Tobias firmly says, "Elochian, you have to calm down."

"He—he—"

"Take him out, or he'll take us all with him." Tisha?

I laugh maniacally. "F—fuck you. Let me go!"

"*Elochian*, sleep."

I scream Quentin's name, right until the bitter end.

I wake up alone.

I open my eyes and lose the visage of Quentin disappearing into nothingness. I close them again, but it doesn't return. There is nothing but darkness. I fucked up. I lost Quentin, lost my mind. How long have I been out for? How many hours have I wasted? If I'd marked him, claimed him, made him mine, I would be able to find him. I would be able to feel him, feel what he's going through.

But I didn't.

I get out of bed with great difficulty. My bones are heavy and mind slow, my muscles scream and my joints creak. My wings are limp, folded pathetically against my back. I've been changed into lounge wear, and the sun creeps in at the edges of drawn blinds. My heart clenches, and I brace myself on a corner post of the bed frame. The edges of my vision darken, and a gentle knock sounds on my door.

"Yes," I say, sitting down on the edge of the bed.

Michael steps inside, softly shutting the door behind them. They approach, then kneel within arm's length from me. They bow their head and say, "Sir."

"Report," I order, blinking away dizziness.

"It has been thirteen hours since Quentin was taken. No one was hurt, and no one else was taken. We have since learned that approximately one third of our staff were Kavelli sympathizers, including Annie. Interrogations have been completed, and those involved with Kavelli are currently being detained in the dungeon, awaiting trial. The Manor has been thoroughly searched, but we've found no evidence of foul play involving the building itself.

"We do not know Annie's motives, only that she used a travel stone to take Quentin. Moments before she did so, the wards protecting the Manor broke. We do not know how or by who, but they are in the process of being repaired. The chain of command has been helmed by Lord Daemarrel, and he enacted Code Silver. The press is relentless, and Carina Wells called for an emergency meeting which started one hour ago. Mr. Rook suspects that she is working with the enemy, given how quickly her statement came, and with details the press was lacking."

"And where's Quentin?"

Michael bows their head further. "We don't know."

I sigh and run a hand through my hair, pulling harshly when I encounter tangles. "And you?"

"Sir?"

"Are you okay?"

"Yes, Sir."

"Be honest with me. I—I hurt you very badly, didn't I?"

Michael looks up. "I'm fine, Sir."

I shake my head. "I shouldn't have laid my hands on you, Michael. I am so, so sorry."

Michael's lip trembles. It's the first time I've ever seen him break, if only a little. He says, "You didn't hurt me, Sir, I assure you. But you were right. It was my fault, you are my Lord, and I disobeyed you. I fully accept the consequences of my actions, and I lay my punishment at your feet."

Michael leans forward, bracing his palms and forehead against the carpet. I sit there, staring down at him. "Get up," I say, voice breaking. "Get up."

"I can't."

"Yes, you can. I need you to."

Michael doesn't move.

I slide down onto the floor, and push him back by his shoulders. I take his face in my hands, wet with tears. I say, "Get off the damn floor, and help me find him."

"I can't—"

"You can, and you *will*. Now get up."

"Okay. Okay."

Together, we rise.

"What do we know?"

Arlo sits across from me in my office, looking absolutely exhausted. He says, "Nightingale and Fin have been looking in the End and reaching out to their contacts, but so far there's been no leads. Daniel's office has been searched, and his personal residences are empty."

"What about disturbances in the magickal field?"

"Besides the initial ... severing that I felt when Quentin disappeared, and the storm, there's been nothing. I can't find traces of Leon's energy anywhere."

I rub my temple. "And you can't go looking for him in the Veil," I say, but it's a statement overshadowed by an unasked question. I can't *actually* ask him to risk—

"I tried," he whispers. "I tried last night, I can't. It's like someone's boarded up the door, and not just to me. There were a few deaths in the city, and their spirits are trapped here."

At first I say nothing, coming up to the wall everyone else has been up against since I passed out. I shift in my chair, wincing at the pain in my back. "How is everyone else?"

"Fucked. Tobias and them are at the Palace, Cas' pants are all in a twist because the kids won't sleep, or Tobias. Lindsey is ... not good. Kitt finally had to drag her home this afternoon. Gowan's worried sick, which isn't good for the seedling, they're so hard to grow." He sighs heavily, raking a hand through his hair.

"And you?"

"Fuck off."

"Arlo."

"Don't. Just don't."

"Fine."

Arlo tips his head back, staring up at the ceiling. He swallows tears and says, "He could have had me ten times over. Why take Quentin?"

"Because this story isn't about you."

He looks at me.

"Have you ever seen an archdemon transform?"

He stares at me for a moment before answering. "Nearly did last night."

"Nearly, but the point was for me to lose it entirely. You saw ..." I glance over my shoulder at Michael, then back to Arlo. "I wouldn't have stopped. I'm not ... I'm not myself. I would've torn apart anyone who I thought was in my way. Could you imagine the field day fucking Wells would've had? Edward, or Kavelli even, could've usurped me in the name of public safety. But that prospect was only a bonus."

"And why's that?"

"I have a feeling that Quentin is what he's wanted all along."

"But he doesn't even know Quentin."

"Michael, the—thank you."

I watch as Arlo goes through the paper folder provided by Michael. His brows furrow, and he says, "Fuck."

I relay the information permanently engraved into my brain since reading it. "River Parish attended Agian Academy for the Gifted for three years, which occurred during the same time that Daniel Kavelli went on sabbatical, his whereabouts unknown. Posing as a young human, he flunked out and was arrested multiple times on drug charges, promoting prostitution, and assault. He was released every single time, both in Agia and Levena. Six months after Quentin moves in with Lindsey, the human River Parish isn't heard from again."

Arlo closes the folder and slides it across the desk to me. The corner of a photograph peeks out. Bandages and broken bones. He quietly says, "Tell me what to do. Help me, Elochian. Tell me what to do."

"When you don't know what to do, start at the beginning. Come on."

When I take my key out of my pocket, Arlo smiles.

"You have a key to his place, too," I snap.

"Yes, but I'm his landlord."

"Focus."

The apartment is slightly cleaner than the last time I saw it, which makes me pause. It's not so far-fetched that Quentin cleaned bright and early this morning, but my paranoid brain wonders if someone wiped the place of evidence. But of what?

"I'll start in the living room," I say, avoiding looking directly at the couch. Was it only a couple days ago that I wrung such beautiful music from Quentin?

"I'll take the bedroom," Arlo says, and I wish I thought of that first.

"Sir, should I check the cafe?" Michael asks.

I nod, and they leave without another word. I start to rummage through the things on Quentin's desk. It feels like sacrilege, and I don't even know what I'm looking for. There's character sheets and newspaper clippings, pencils with the rubbers chewed off and tealights burned down to the wick. It's like he simply stepped away. Arlo bangs around in the bedroom, probably being less careful than I am. I look through the garbage, but there's only the greasy, paper bags from the other night.

Everything else is clean, but the bags are still in the garbage.

"Arlo, wait."

I sprint into the bedroom, finding him kneeling beside the mattress, his hands between it and the box spring. The blankets are all messed up. I point to them. "Was that like that?"

"What?"

"The bed. Was it made?"

"Um … yes."

"Someone's been here."

Arlo stills. "Are you sure? I don't feel anything."

"Quit—you need to start acting like the rest of us. Go off what you see, not what you feel. Quentin doesn't make the bed. We—we have a nest. He wouldn't have straightened it out."

Arlo stares at the bed. "Okay, but why? What were they looking for?"

"I don't know."

Arlo's phone starts to go off, and he lets the mattress fall back down. He checks it, frowning. "Primo wants to see me, he says he's found something."

"Something as in Quentin?"

"He doesn't say, only that it's important, and it needs to be now."

"All right, let's go."

He looks up. "You're coming?"

"Yes, we'll be quicker if Michael drives."

He nods, then dials a number. "Okay. Let me call Dusan real quick, then we'll go."

I cast one last glance at the bed, then step out of the room. I move towards the front door, thinking about Michael, but something catches my eye. Quentin's corkboard, above his desk. There's an empty space, in between scrap papers and photocopies of old architecture. There was a map here.

Miracle

Quentin

"You're making this much harder than it needs to be. Then again, you always did."

I sit in a corner, knees pulled up to my chest. Hands tucked into my armpits, I lean against a cold wall, staring at the smooth cement ahead of me. A pile of blankets, *my* blankets, have been thrown into a nearby pile. Once neatly folded piles of clothes, also mine, are in the mess too, and an untouched food tray rests beside it. Along with a bed, the room has other furnishings like rugs, a dresser and desk, a hearth and sitting area. The hearth is dead, and curtains hang over windowless frames. It all reminds me of a noble's room in an abandoned castle. It's all rich and high quality, but time and disuse has dusted the room, eaten at the corners of the bedding and curtains.

Wherever we are, it's certainly not Levena.

River stands over me in the form I knew him as, arms crossed with a hand cupping his chin. "No one is coming for you,

Quentin. Even if they wanted to, they wouldn't be able to find you." He squats, reaching for me. I turn my face away and he sighs. "You don't want to make me angry, baby."

"Get angry all you like, it's not going to change anything. I left you for a reason, River. I. Don't. Want. You."

His hand snaps for my head, and he slams it against the wall. I bite back a cry, drawing blood from my lip. He looms over me, body pressing against my side. Gods, he's fucking hard. Of course.

He brings his lips to my ear, and I slowly wiggle my right hand out of my left armpit. "You don't know what you want. That damn *witch* ruined you, got inside your head and lured you away from me. But don't worry, after I'm done with you, no one will be able to take you away from me again. I—"

I swing up and back with all my might, catching him in the cheek with my boot knife. It lodges with a sick sound and River cackles, releasing me to lean back on his heels. I scramble to my feet and he reaches up, fingers curling around the hilt. I tap into my tattoo, trying to call upon Arlo's magick, but it's as dead as it was when I was first thrown into this room. My knife was my last resort, good ol' human ingenuity.

River yanks the knife from his face, and blood flows freely from the wound. He stands, unbothered by the pain or his morality. He says, "I thought you didn't like knife play, baby, but it seems to me you're doing just fine." He holds up the knife, studying it. As he does, the skin over his wound begins to knit together, and the blood seeping out congeals until stopping completely. River glances up at me, and grins. "He says that I can play with you, as long as I don't hurt you too much. You remember how it goes, don't you? You were always so good at playing bait."

Something about the way River says 'He' makes me wonder if I'm talking to River at all. Is this Leon, and River says it's okay?

I don't have time to dwell on it. He takes a step towards me, and I retreat a step. It goes on like this for three more steps, then I run directly at him, screaming my fool head off. I've got nowhere else to go, nowhere to run, and I'll be damned if he touches me. I'd rather die than be touched by him ever again. I drive my shoulder into his chest, and he doesn't try to stop me. He goes down laughing, even when his back hits the floor.

I draw my arm back, and he smiles up at me as my fist makes its descent towards his face. Then he disappears, like he was never there at all. I end up punching the stone floor instead, and scream as bones shatter into pieces. River's behind me now, his hand closes over my mouth. He says, "My turn."

I throw my head back, knocking my skull into his. He doesn't budge, and all I earn for my efforts is a knife poking through my jacket and into my side, and blood pouring down my neck from what I assume is a broken nose on his part. He grinds against my back, tracing the knife over my ribs.

He whispers, "Do you have any idea how lonely I was? When my father died, my first thought was Simon—ah, Quentin, yes, you like that now, don't you? Quentin would know how to make this better. You cried so much when your daddy died, and that's all I wanted. To cry on your shoulder. But then they took you from me. That fucking *witch*, and *Elochian*."

He spits out Elochian's name in a different way than when he says witch, and it highlights the presence of Leon within him, poisoning his mind like a parasite. River was always psychotic, but never like this. This is next level fucked up. Warmth blooms along my side, followed by sharp pain. I stiffen, trying not to flinch against the pain.

I try to speak but can't, so he spreads his fingers, keeping his hand firmly in place over my mouth. I say, "You're such a sore fucking loser, Leon. Pathetic is what it is, needing to use a sick man's body and his delusions to hurt Arlo. Well guess what? Arlo won't come for me, he's smarter than that. You've fucked up. You won't win."

The knife travels to my chest and slices through the front of my shirt, the buttons tink on stone as they fall. When he begins to speak, I know I've caught Leon's attention. Voices overlap each other, one angry, and the other amused. They say, "You're right. You are nothing. No one is coming for you. But that's not why I brought you here. Not entirely. You see, I made a promise to my host, and I always deliver. Can you say the same for your friends?"

"You're lying."

"I never lie," they say, resting the tip of the knife against the hollow of my throat. "I can't. It was the price I paid for truth. Would you like some?"

"N—" The knife pierces my skin, and I try not to swallow, to do anything. For the first time, I feel afraid. Not of dying, but of the mess I'll be leaving behind. Will Elochian be able to survive this? Will Arlo ever forgive himself? Will Lindsey be okay?

"The truth is, love *always* makes mistakes. I loved Arlo, and look where it got me. You loved this beast, and look where it got you. You think you love that demon, but you are no more a pet to him, the same as you were to this one. You are a human, a plaything that everyone will outlive, outgrow. But if you let me into your heart, you can live forever. I'll even make *you* a promise. I won't touch a single one of your friends, even Arlo, if you do this for me. This meat suit was never strong enough to withstand me, but *you*—you are something special."

I want to scream 'liar,' and scream, and scream.

"Wh—" Blood trickles down my throat and the tip of the blade withdraws from my skin, but remains pressed to it. A threat. "Why me?"

"You underestimate yourself, little Quentin." Leon chuckles, dipping his fingers into my mouth. "You aren't supposed to exist. You can wield magick that isn't yours. You are bound to a witch, and alive to tell the tale. You know how many people I've tried to make like you? It's a miracle. *You* are a miracle, and I'll treat you like one. We could do great things together, all you have to do is let me in."

"It's not—it's just a tattoo," I say over his fingers, nauseated at his invasion, at the drool dripping down my chin. He could hurt Arlo so easily with this body. I never thought about it that way before, how easy it would be to hurt Arlo, if I wanted to.

"Oh baby, lying doesn't suit you," River says, his voice stronger than Leon's at the moment. "We can be together forever. We'll put your mother in her place, and we can rule. He knows what he's doing, okay? Now open your heart, and let him in."

This is my chance. I close my eyes, and think of Elochian.

I think, *'I'm sorry,'* and, *'I love you. I love you, I should've told you that I love you.'*

I think, *'I hope to hell this works.'*

I lurch ahead and twist my body to the side, impaling myself on the blade in order to cut my own throat. River screams, and I smile through the pain and darkness taking me under. You can't possess someone who's already dead.

Holy Ground

Elochian
One Hour Ago

"There was a map here."

"What?" Arlo asks, coming to my side. He puts his phone away, glancing between me and the overloaded corkboard.

"There was a copy of a map here, he scribbled all over it. It looked like Levena, but … different."

Arlo considers the empty space for a moment, eyes drifting to the timeline. Then they flare with emerald magick and he snaps his fingers. "I got a book a couple of months ago, it was—" He starts looking around, scanning through the squat bookshelves, the whole affair much smaller than you think a library of Quentin's would be.

"It was what?"

"Uh–architecture, it was about architecture, and it had street plans dating back to the sixth millennia. I let him borrow it, he said he wanted to research how the town changed in the time after the fire, compare it to Thatch's notes of before."

At this point I've started looking too, but we find nothing. In this case, nothing turns out to be a clue. His shelves are small but fully packed, with no gaps except for the bottom shelf. "There's no dust on the shelves, but if you look on top of the books." I run my finger over the upper edge of a book, disturbing tiny dust bunnies. "Quentin takes all the books off when he dusts, moves them around."

"Fuck," Arlo says. "It has to mean something. How was Levena different back then?"

"How wasn't it?"

"True."

I sigh, looking around one more time. "What did Dusan say?"

"Ah, kids are fine, she said they can stay as long as they need to. Come on, Primo's waiting on us. We'll call Kitt on the way, she might know something." He quickly makes for the door and I follow him, unable to do anything else.

Michael is silent while they drive, and the streets are full of people. We have to pass town hall on the way to Primo's, which is a nightmare. There are signs condemning Carina's impromptu promotion to mayor, and signs condemning those people. Carina's AWO followers are easy to spot, they all wear white lilies pinned to their coats. There are NOJ supporters there too, but they are more reserved, acting as the backup for the more vocal

AWO. I still don't understand why they're two organizations instead of one, but as far as I can see, the NOJ is for the elite, the rich and wealthy. In my mind, the AWO are their peons, cannon fodder and propaganda machines all in one.

There are signs with my name on them, too. Calling for my resignation in favor of Kavelli.

"Don't they know what he's done?" I ask Arlo, my hands curling into fists in my lap.

"No. They're blaming it on us," he says, staring out the window. "Annie was a witch. Did you know that?"

"No, I didn't."

He's quiet for a minute before saying, "You need to create support for demons who happen to be witches. Someone they can talk to. I'm not saying it was your fault that Annie flipped, but she felt the need to hide her magick. Repressing it like that isn't good."

"I know."

Arlo shifts his gaze to me.

"I *know*, Arlo. I'm working on it, I really am. When Quentin's back, I can—" The words die on my tongue when I realize we've flipped places. This story began with me telling Arlo he needed to buck up, to deal with Thatch being gone and do his job.

And now it's me who needs to hear it.

"I know," I say, because that's all I can do right now.

He reaches over, taking my hand in his. He squeezes once, then looks back out the window. Minutes stretch by, and when Arlo's phone rings it startles both of us. "Kitt," he says to me, then answers and puts her on speaker. "What've you got?"

"The book Quentin borrowed was Ancient Architecture of the Northern Region, and I was next on the list to read it. I only looked at it a couple of times, not enough to remember what the maps looked like, but I do remember that Levena was much smaller back in the day. It was more of a fishing village, with the castle being the center of town.

"Funguy Park and the surrounding area was a swamp, and *Etz Hayim*'s roots made building impossible until the celestials came into the picture. Then they drained the northern end of Levena, and found a way to build over the roots. Before that, the landscape was entirely different."

Complete silence follows after Lindsey's history lesson. Eventually, I ask the question we're all thinking. "And how does any of that lead us to Quentin?"

She sighs, exhaling into the phone. "I don't know."

"So—wait. Why is the cemetery so far away from Old Town? That's original, the dates—Thatch's grave is ... it's there," Arlo asks, becoming distressed.

"It was common for people of that era to follow the tenets of Nicen, which called for any cemeteries to be separate from the main village. Something to do with zombies. I don't know why they chose that area *specifically*, other than it's nicer ground once you get around the tree and swamp. Maybe it was considered holy ground?"

"Maybe," I say. "But most holy places have churches or temples accompanying them, a shrine at least. The Cromaeris is all the way across town from the Netherspring, near the End. That's original, why not build the cemetery there?"

"True ..." Kitt trails off.

Arlo asks, "Kitt, the mausoleum goes underground there, doesn't it?"

"You're the Hedge Witch here, not me. I haven't been there in ages."

"I think it does," Arlo says slowly. "Underground would be a good place to hide, but the mausoleum is public. Unless there's a private level."

"Are you onto something?" Kitt asks.

"Not sure. See if you can find out how many levels are there, and if there's anywhere else in Levena that has underground access."

"Arlo, really?" I say.

"What?"

"There is a public extensive network of underground tunnels beneath Levena, most are residential, while others are used for travel. There are service tunnels too, but nothing private. Most of the technicians are demons who live in River Street."

"I've already been in contact with them, there is no evidence of foreign activity in the tunnels thus far," Michael says, speaking up for the first time since we left the cafe. The car rolls to a cautious stop outside Primo's. "We're here, Sir."

"It was worth a shot," Kitt says. "I'll do some digging, keep me posted."

"You do the same. Love you, Kitt."

Kitt pauses, then says, "I love you too, Lo. Loch, make sure he doesn't do anything stupid."

I chuckle, despite everything. "Okay. Be careful."

After she hangs up, we get out of the car without sharing any sentiment between us. The lights are off and the curtains are drawn, which is eerie enough in the evening. The empty streets and howling wind doesn't help. Arlo and I exchange a look that says, *'trap, right?'*

Michael takes the lead, and we follow him down the foot path. Arlo keeps an eye on what's behind us, and I focus on the small alleys separating Primo's from the businesses, waiting for someone to jump out at us. But Michael pushes the door open, and we make it inside with incident. Primo stands by a front window, peeking through the curtain.

"Better lock that," he says.

Arlo does so, while Michael asks, "Where are they?"

"'Cross the street in Tinnie's, then there's two who've been patrolling. Not sure who they are, only that they have a great interest in this place but never stop in. Ones over in Tinnie's were gawking through the window 'till you pulled up. We better be quick."

"Put up some shields, Arlo," Michael says, then communicates a set of orders through the earpiece, suggesting backup may be needed. Arlo goes into Hedge Witch mode, tapping the tattoos on his neck with glow to life in time with his eyes.

While Arlo does his thing, Primo watches him with barely veiled curiosity. He says, "Quentin came 'round a few weeks ago with your lads. We made some music, and he asked me some questions. Wanted to know if the building had always been here, or if it was new. I had no clue, all I knew is it was a failed diner when I bought it, took me ages to get the grease smell out of here.

"After he left, I did some digging. Turns out it used to be a dry cleaners before that, and then a dentist's. It goes on and on until the sixth millennia, when it was first built as a temple dedicated to Da'haut. Imagine that? Once a shrine to the God of Knowledge, now a music shop. Made a vow then and there to never let it become a diner again."

Arlo finishes, hands dropping to his sides like they're lead weights. "It's like casting through water here," he says, panting a little.

"Come on," Primo says, taking off for the back of the store. He leads us down a small hallway, then unlocks a door to the left. We all start to pile into the room, but he shakes his head and gestures for Michael to help him. Arlo and I squeeze together on the threshold, and my wings won't stop their fucking chattering. In the back right corner of the room, Primo and Michael shuffle some storage containers off to the opposite side, then they roll up a large rug. Primo removes a slab of plywood and rests it up against the wall, and underneath that is a hole in the floor.

More specifically, a square where the old hardwood planking has been roughly cut away. And underneath, embedded into the stone foundations of the place, is a fucking trapdoor, complete with a big rusty knocker.

Primo wipes the sweat from his brow and says, "All temples, even the small ones, have an emergency exit." He reaches down and takes hold of the old ring, and it creaks as he pulls the trapdoor open. Cold, dead air wafts past us, lifting my hair as it goes.

"Holy shit," Arlo murmurs.

"Well said," I add.

We all peek into it at once, finding only darkness.

Michael is the only one with any sense. They ask, "Where does it go?"

Primo throws him a look, eyebrows raising. "No idea. Found it and called you. I did drop a rock down there, but didn't hear it land. So, figured the young and spry would mix better with this sort of thing."

"Thanks," I say, having a disturbingly good feeling about this. I look over at Arlo. "Feel anything?"

"Absolutely nothing." He squats down and extends a hand over the empty space, wiggling his fingers. "Can't even summon a light."

"Which means there's a good chance he's down there."

Michael puts a hand out to stop me from jumping in. "Sir, I cannot allow you to jump into pits of darkness without a plan. We have no idea how far down it goes, or what's on the other side."

"The plan is I won't jump, I'll fly, and I'll be careful."

"You're not going down without me."

Hesitantly, Arlo says, "Elochian's our best shot. If this place is being watched, this would explain why. If Quentin is down there, and we leave and come back ... maybe they'll move him, and we blow our one lead."

"Can you feel him?" Michael asks quietly. "Through your link?"

"I think so, but I don't know ..." Arlo says, glancing at me. "But we can't always rely on magick. My gut's telling me this is important, if that counts for anything."

Michael sighs, scrubbing both hands over their scalp. They exhale a gust of frustration, then reach into a cargo pocket. They take out a set of small two-way radios, and offer one to me. "I want to know what you're doing every second that you're doing it. If you can't talk, you tap the speaker three times to let us know. Go slow, and let us know what you see."

I take the radio, then stand on my tip-toes and hug Michael, wrapping my arms around his neck. He holds me tight and I whisper, "I'll be careful."

We pull apart, and Michael visibly puts himself back together, face pulling into cold calculation. He says, "We've got your back."

"I know."

I square up with the trapdoor, and Arlo claps my shoulder before moving out of the way. He says, "Come on, old man. We haven't got all day."

I smile at him. "Try to keep up, witch."

He smiles too, and I ignore the lines of worry pinching his eyes, choosing to float into the darkness instead. I hold onto the radio for dear life, slowly lowering myself into who the fuck knows what. As the dark overtakes me, my heart catches up with the sheer idiocy of my brain. I pump all of my anxious energy to my wings, and do my best to focus. Quentin.

I'm doing this for Quentin.

That helps, and my eyes adjust to the dark, allowing me to get an idea of my surroundings. Cement. I'm in a tube of cement, wide enough for my wingspan and then some. I can't see the bottom clearly, but I whisper my findings to Michael. He says nothing, and I continue. After nearly a minute, my boots scuff on cement.

I immediately crouch down, tucking my wings tight against my back. I remain completely still, scanning the area in front of me. A cavernous hallway, constructed similar to the tube itself. Smooth, dark gray cement studded with moss. Just cement by itself shouldn't be strong enough to hold a construction like this for so long, it'd crack all to hell without the larger bits that concrete has, but here it is. The air isn't humid, and it doesn't smell like anything in particular, except for maybe the sterile cool of a morgue.

"There's no one down here," I say quietly. "Michael?"

The shaft of light from above isn't much, but when it disappears I immediately notice. A scream echoes from the other side of the tunnel ahead of me, full of anguish and fear. Cold skitters down my spine and my heart spasms, causing me to stagger and brace myself against the wall.

"We have a problem," Primo says, huffing into the speaker. He lowers his voice, and it's rough with exertion. "The way's shut. Arlo says the link broke, you have to hurry."

My stomach drops to my feet. "What—"

He shouts, and a great crash follows the sound. Static, then nothing.

I'm alone, in an unknown place. There's a fight above me, and the link is broken.

Which means ... oh.

No.

No.

I fall to my knees, gritting my teeth in an attempt to hold back a wail. Pain ushers in a world of power, and none of the humanity. My vision whites out like I've been hit with a flashbang and something hot runs down my cheeks, hotter than blood or tears. As if understanding the need for stealth, my metamorphosis is silent and excruciating.

My wings snap backwards, thickening as they extend in size, and spikes grow in succession along the outer ridges. Poison seeps from every point, dripping onto the floor around me with a betraying, acidic sizzle.

My limbs and hands elongate, and my nails transform into hooked talons. My legs bend backwards, snapping brutally into place. A second set of shoulder blades disrupts my spine, and another set of wings fit with even sharper spikes erupt from the new sockets in a bloody mess.

I open my mouth, testing this new jaw of mine, and run a forked tongue over each new tooth. Poison drips from them too, but a different kind, one that's flammable. As the transformation completes, I regain my vision, which cuts through the darkness like a knife. I'm twice the size of my usual form, and four times as conspicuous.

In the distant part of my brain that carries consciousness and morality, I realize how terrified Quentin is going to be of me.

But then that's swept away by one thing and one thing only. Bringing him home. Alive.

I prowl into the cavern ahead, leaving behind shreds of my clothes and the flesh and blood of my old body. I don't have a map, but my ancient blood sings to me here. It's familiar with the place in a way I can't describe, but I don't need to. I simply need to listen. After a few minutes, dim light marks the end of the corridor, where it spills into something larger. I keep close to the wall, counting voices.

Then again, it doesn't matter how many there are, does it?

I step into a cement chasm untouched by time, a place that shouldn't exist, should have crumbled millennia ago, but here it is. There is nothing to hide my arrival, the place is open and full of people, generators, and portable light stands. I briefly scan the prison-like cells surrounding the perimeter of the first, second, and third level, supported by metal scaffolding and walkways.

A bullet pierces my shoulder, rocking it backwards.

I look down at the hole oozing blood, then at the person who fired it. A demon. Traitors. All of them.

I launch forward, faster than the shot that went through me. When the screaming starts, I lose all sense of mind. There's nothing but slash, bite, rip, tear, kill. Blood splashes into my mouth and I spit it out, spraying venom on those trying to take me down at close range. Magick spurts onto my tongue, bitter and electrifying. One witch tastes like fire, while another tastes like ice. The snipers on the upper levels spray me with bullets, but they pass through my wretched body with little effort, and I feel no pain.

I feel no pain until one of my wings is clipped, and a ground shaking roar tears out of my chest. I inhale, filling my lungs with oxygen, then exhale harshly, lighting the spark in the back of my throat which ignites the venom dripping from my mouth, and all that was spilled. The black fire is immediate and explosive, inflicting serious damage before dying out within seconds.

I don't recognize those I kill, except for two. Annie fights me to the death, and by Gods do I make her fight. The other person is Tina, and she walks towards me with open arms. She says, "Please. End it. It hurts."

I do, and I make it quick. I can taste her relief, her memories before death and after. She never wanted this. She never wanted any of this.

It doesn't take much longer to eliminate those on the ground. I brace myself for takeoff, but a harsh cry distracts me. I tilt my head, shifting my attention to the head of the space, on the ground floor. There's a door made of wood, not bars, and it's cracked open. Dim and violent sobs escape from it, and I make my way closer. Quentin's scent tainted by blood hits me, and I rush for it. I have to crouch down to fit through the doorway, and even then it's difficult.

A familiar demon—Daniel, River—sits with his back to me, hunched over a body. When he hears me scraping against cement, his eyes widen. He stands with Quentin in his arms, both of them covered in blood. He stumbles towards me and says, "Take him. Take him. I can't—" His face screws up and he groans in pain. "I can't hold him back much longer."

My talons scrape against the demon's skin when he rolls Quentin into my arms, and the thought crosses my mind to tear his head off. But the wound across Quentin's throat, his absent heartbeat and white face, all of it turns me away from revenge, and towards home.

When I do, the demon—Daniel, River—cries out, "Wait! You have to stop him."

A man skids to a stop on the other side of the door and I bare my teeth at him, holding Quentin close to me. I inhale, summoning oxygen. His gaze skitters between me, Quentin, and the demon. He swallows and puts up his hands, then shakily says, "Loch. It's me, Arlo."

I whine, holding Quentin closer to my heart.

"I know. Can you—can you turn back?"

I stare at him, trying to relay that I don't know how. Quentin's not safe yet.

"I—I can make him better, but you have to give him to me. Trust me, okay?"

I bend down and rub my hot, bloody cheek against Quentin's cold, also bloody one. I shift my attention to the witch—no. *Arlo*. Ever so gently, I pass over my world to him. He takes Quentin with great care, then says, "I can't bring you with me, but you'll know where to find me. You *know* where he'll be, okay?"

A guttural sound escapes my throat, and Arlo smiles tightly before disappearing.

The demon behind me cries out for help, and I turn to it with hunger in my heart.

He Loves You

Quentin

Death isn't what I thought it would be.

I follow a winding path, and iron lamplights keep me company. It's cold, but my coat keeps me warm. Fat snowflakes tumble downwards, and the sun comes out from behind the clouds every now and then. There's no people around, and I don't recognize the land, but I swear I've been here before. There's a frozen lake on one side of the path, stretching as far as the meadows on the other side do. After a while, I start to wonder where I'm going.

"That depends. Where do you want to go?"

I glance over at the person beside me, unsurprised by his sudden arrival. I find myself unable to stop walking, so I give him a smile instead of a hug. I say, "Hey, Arlo."

He smiles back, but it's sad. "Hey, Q."

I turn my smile to Bosko riding on his shoulder, the bird surrounded by a vague black cloud. Hesitantly, I ask, "Is home an option?"

"It is."

"But?"

He doesn't say anything for a minute, opting to stroke Bosko's feathers instead of answering me. Eventually, he says, "You won't be human anymore, but you won't be a golem either. You—your soul was damaged, Quentin. We don't know how, but it was. The only way to bring you back is to tether you to your soulmate. You will share a spirit."

"Oh. Does ... what does Elochian say about that?"

"Elochian isn't awake right now, and he probably won't be for ... well, for some time."

"What? Why? Is he okay?" I try to stop walking, and I can't. It freaks me out this time, and Arlo rests a hand on my shoulder, shaking his head.

"He's okay, just recovering. He came and got you, you know."

"He did?"

"Of course he did, Q. He loves you."

I nod, wiping at my eyes, which is when I notice I'm not wearing my glasses. "How much longer can you wait to ... do whatever it is you need to? I can't do something like that without asking him."

Arlo hesitates, and he squeezes my shoulder once before letting go. "You don't have much time." He nods to the path. "You're almost there. It has to be now, if you're going to stay. Gaia's here with me, and we can do it."

"Oh." I steal a glance towards what lays ahead, and there is something on the horizon. A glimmering outline of ... buildings? No, trees. Maybe. We walk in silence for a little while longer, and I wrestle with my conscience the entire time.

Arlo says, "If I were in Loch's place, and Thatch was you ... well, there'd be no question. I'd want him to. And I think if Elochian finds out that I let you go when there was a way to bring you back, well. He might kill me."

I laugh wetly. "No, he wouldn't."

Arlo lifts a shoulder and says nothing.

Bosko takes flight, going on ahead of us. We watch him disappear into the vague horizon, and my heart settles on a decision.

My muscles jerk with recognition, and my eyelids part with great reluctance. I'm confused by how normal my surroundings are. I lay on my back, scanning the room with great difficulty.

There's the scuff in the paint where I once laid on my bed with Lindsey, we had our feet up on the wall.

There's the scrollwork baseboards which haven't been dusted since I moved in, and it shows.

And there, laying right beside me, is Elochian. Eyes closed, chest slowly rising and falling.

I want to scream.

I try to reach for him, but the movement won't come. My breathing quickens, and a soft voice says, "Your body is becoming reacquainted with your mind, and you are under the influence of many pain medications. In addition to your lacerations, your hand was broken, and your trachea was damaged. You're stable, thanks to your witches, but healing."

I shift my gaze, straining to see the source of the voice. His aunt sits in one of my kitchen chairs, dressed in loose, fluffy clothing. She runs a comb carved from bone through Elochian's hair, returning to the humming my panic had interrupted. Heart numb, I close my eyes, falling back into the warm ruminating from Elochian's side. We're both tucked beneath the blankets, and he's close against the wall, which is normally my spot in bed.

Tisha says, "I never wanted children, or a partner."

I open my eyes, staring at her.

She doesn't look at me, simply continues to brush Elochian's hair. "I don't have a motherly bone in my body, and bonds are ... they're dangerous for celestials. But as a descendant of a dying royal house, I wasn't given much choice. The bond between his parents was extraordinary, the type of love you find once in a lifetime. Do you know what it was his mother died of?"

I blink at her.

"Heartbreak."

Tisha falls quiet for a little while after that.

I open my mouth, and my tongue rasps against my lips like sandpaper. Tisha sets the comb down upon my nightstand beside my glasses with a quiet clack, then picks up a cup with something sticking out of it. She says, "You can't speak, or drink. But I can give you this. Open."

She brings the cup close to my face, taking out what looks like a sponge on a stick. I do as she says, and my jaw cracks. She gently swabs the inside of my mouth, and whatever the sponge has been soaking in is cool and fresh, not really tasting like anything but clean.

After Tisha finishes, she sits back down. She doesn't pick up the comb again, instead she stares at Elochian's face. He looks so peaceful like this, to the point of being eerie. She whispers, "Well, if someone has to break his heart, I'm glad that it's you." She glances over at me, and a wry smile plays at her lips. "Get some sleep, chick. He has a way to go."

The next time I wake up, we're alone.

I'm able to move a little this time, but it's slow going. Everything hurts and my bones are tired, like the day after having the worst flu of my life. Elochian has been turned onto his other side, facing the wall. A pillow is wedged between his knees. I have no sense of time, only that it's currently nighttime, evident by my open curtains.

I rest a hand on his back, between his upper and lower wings, over his spine. I ache to whisper his name, call him from the depths of wherever he is. What happened to him?

The door creaks open, and I look over my shoulder to see Michael sneaking into the room. When they see that I'm awake, a cascade of emotions crosses their face. Relief. Hesitation. Sadness. Michael sits down in the chair at our bedside, the same one Tisha was in before. They stare at me, and I stare at them. I try to smile, and it ends up being a small, wobbly thing.

Michael bows their head, and cries. They say, "Don't. Don't smile at me."

I want to ask what's wrong, why are they so sad. Michael pinches the bridge of their nose, shaking their head. Their tears are quiet, but their shoulders heave with the force of sobbing nonetheless.

Michael says, "I am so, so sorry, Quentin."

I scrape energy from the dregs of my being, and reach out to Michael. He takes my hand, his grip firm. He presses his forehead to my knuckles, exhaling a shaky breath. Michael begins to transform, and the change is less horrifying than the type of shifting I witnessed ... before. Gods, what even happened? Where is—

My spiraling thoughts are brought to a halt as I realize what's happening.

The form that Michael takes is one I've never seen before, but I know it for what it is immediately. Their head is still shaved, but the short hairs are black. Black crystalline-like horns protrude from their head in a circular fashion, like a crown, and some grow beneath my hand, gently pressing against my skin. Upward curving lines crease the corners of their eyes, which are big and full of color. Literally, his irises are kaleidoscopes of colors that never settle. Their wings are similar to Elochian's in the sense that they're covered in scales, but the shape is different, and Michael's scales are black and red. Finally, a tail not dissimilar to a scorpion's extends behind him, curving forward to hug his back.

I bump Michael's forehead with my hand, and he looks up. I pull my hand back, then point to my eye. I point to my heart, and finally, I point at him.

Michael's thick brows furrow for a moment, then he smiles.

"Me too, Quentin. Me too."

Three days later, and I'm able to get out of bed with help. I should be happy about it, but Elochian's still asleep. Not to mention my best friend washes my ass crack like her life depends on it. From my shower chair I swat at her, face burning with embarrassment. Lindsey rolls her eyes, straightening up from her squat. She's fully in the tub with me, on the opposite end from the shower head, dressed in shorts and a ratty t-shirt. She wipes loose hair away from her eyes with her upper arm, hands occupied with a soapy washcloth.

"This is true fucking love right here," she huffs. "Not sure why you're complaining."

I laugh, and it hurts, but it hurts so fucking good.

She laughs too, and that feels even better (worse).

My laughter shifts to sobbing, and I bury my face in my hands. The steam surrounds us, providing a false sense of security and soundproofing. Lindsey presses her forehead to mine, unbothered by the water pouring down on our heads. She hums an old elvish lullaby, a rock in my storm. It hurts to cry, like my throat is being sliced apart all over again. Instead of reminding me of dying, the pain reminds me that I'm alive.

A knock sounds on the door. "Is everything okay in there? Do you need help?"

Lindsey rolls her eyes, giving me a teasing smile before calling, "We're fine, Mom!"

A moment passes before Michael answers, the exasperation clear in their voice. "Yes, dear."

Lindsey rubs her nose against mine, and I manage a smile. "There he is," she says. "Alright, come on. You can do this."

I nod, telling myself over and over that she's right. I can do this.

Lindsey helps me out of the shower, settling me onto the closed toilet covered in towels. She towel dries my hair, then brushes it away from my face. Despite my protests, she covers my face, upper body, and calves, in lotion. She doesn't apply it to my throat, reserving that tender area for the healing balm from Arlo. She applies it carefully, and it numbs the pain from crying.

When it's all said and done, I'm dressed in my favorite pajama suit and smell better than I have in Gods knows how long. I lean on Lindsey, looping my arm around hers, and glance at myself in the mirror. I look better, and worse, than before.

Lindsey had shaved me in the shower, and I almost wish she didn't. My hood is pulled up, and it casts shadows on my hollow cheeks. The stubble had hidden the weight I've lost, which is now highlighted. My eyes are bloodshot and bruised, all I do is stay up and stare at Elochian, waiting for him to wake up. If I do sleep, my world is full of nightmares.

And then there's that angry incision across my throat, the scarring rough and pink. The balm is supposed to help smooth the skin too, but I don't think it will ever fully fade. I reach up and touch the thick beginning of the scar, the first place that the blade sunk in. In a way, I'm glad that it won't fade. My story has been painful, but I'm still here. And without River, without my mother, without every bad thing that has ever happened to me, I would never have met Elochian.

"Quentin?"

My hand falls to my chest, fingers spread wide. I tap my thumb against my sternum, letting Lindsey know I'm okay. She glares at me in disbelief. I gesture for her to open the door, and she sighs.

She peeks down the hallway. "Michael's with him, sure you don't want to come hang out in the living room for a bit?"

I stare at her.

"Men. Impossible."

The moment we step inside, I look at Elochian. He's on my former side of the bed, facing the room instead of the wall. Still asleep. Michael sits by his side, reading one of my books despite my protests. He claims to actually like them, but I'm not convinced he's not doing it just to tease me. I can't be too mad, Michael has been nothing but dutiful to Elochian, and me.

They change Elochian's position every two hours, making sure all pressure points are cushioned. They make sure I eat, my diet won't be normal for another week but thanks to him, liquidized food tastes somewhat good. He changes Elochian's clothes everyday, and washes him in bed. I nearly offered, but it felt wrong. We've been intimate, but Elochian hasn't exposed himself to me entirely.

The only thing Michael will *let* me do anyway is keep Elochian company, keep him warm. Michael hardly leaves the apartment, the living room has temporarily become his, but he doesn't stay in my room all the time, thankfully. I know he means well, but I'm starting to go stir crazy. My students have been taken care of for the rest of the semester, and I'm oddly sad about the fact I never got to read their final papers. There has been nothing to do, but wait.

Lindsey says, "One grumpy Quentin, ready for momma bird."

Michael sets his book aside. "Too grumpy for visitors?"

I sigh, glancing at Lindsey. She smiles, somewhat bashfully, which isn't a very Lindsey look. She says, "He's been wanting to see you, and it might do you some good to get out of the room."

Channeling frustration I point to the bed, and Lindsey helps me into it without another word. I curl up close to Elochian, linking my fingers with his, and Michael covers me with layers of blankets. I listen to him and Linds leave the room, and only once the door shuts am I able to breathe normally. I lay there for a long time, trying to sleep. I'm so fucking tired, but it won't come.

What if he wakes up, and I miss it?

What if he never wakes up?

What if he never wakes up, and it's my fault?

I've only been given the bare bones of that day, something else that pisses me off. I know that an old prison was discovered beneath Primo's, which is where Elochian broke into his true form, and found me. Arlo and Michael were delayed by assailants, but aid arrived in the form of Tobias, our witches, and a fuck ton of demons and angels. But according to Michael, by the time everyone caught up with Elochian, there was nothing to do but deal with a subdued River, a dead me, and the aftermath.

No one will elaborate on that last part.

How did a small army become unneeded? How many people did Elochian … kill? I still can't wrap my head around that part. Elochian killing anyone, even bad guys, just seems … impossible. But he must have, I'm not as naive as my friends like to think. Not only did he change into his true form, something most Arches *never* do, but he transformed and survived. There's a reason that they don't, it's a last resort. There has only been a handful of recordings of Arches surviving the change, and they're never the same after. Researching everything there is to know about celestials, specifically archdemons, is another thing that keeps me up at night.

Idina tried to warn me, and I didn't listen.

A familiar pattern raps on the door, and before I can say anything, Arlo steps into my room. Once upon a time I dreamed of this moment, but now all I want is for him to leave. I roll over in bed, reluctantly letting go of Elochian, and glare at Arlo as he takes a seat.

He takes off his hat and rests it on his knee. He says, "I wanted to talk to you before I left, it'll only take a minute, okay?"

I gesture for him to go on, by all means.

Arlo takes a deep breath. Quietly, he says, "I know you're angry with me. I know you're frustrated. I know you're sad, and tired. I know what it's like to want to stay in bed and not see anyone, and wish everyone would leave you the fuck alone. With that being said, I'm not going to do that. I'm going to be here for you, by your side, until Elochian wakes and beyond, because I love you. You are my brother, my best friend, and I fucking love you. I don't regret what I did, and I would do it again."

And just like that, I'm crying again.

I open my arms to him, scowling the entire time so he knows this isn't over. He crawls into bed beside me, and I hold him close. His head rests against my chest, and his boots hang off the mattress. I wonder if Arlo's ever been the little spoon in his life, but I can imagine Thatch making it happen a time or two. Then again, did they ever spend the night together more than once?

April

Empty Shell

Quentin

Two weeks after I rise from the dead, which is three weeks after the masquerade ball, my apartment is packed to the brim. Caspian works in the kitchen, accompanied by Silas and Felix who act as his errand boys. Arlo talks with Finnegan and Arche in hushed tones, squished close to my desk which has been abandoned, to say the least. Gowan and Iris sit on the floor to the right of the couch, while Lindsey and Kitt sit opposite them. They talk about mundane things like nurseries and fundraisers, and it digs under my skin. Charlie and Michael sit on the couch, playing with the Daemarrel children situated between them.

I didn't invite a single one of them here. They all just showed up. I suspect the culprit is Arlo, who's kept his promise and visits every other day or so, keeping me in the loop on the latest happenings. Lindsey and Kitt visit too, but I'm able to wash my own ass now, thank you very much.

The bathroom door creaks behind me, and I look over my shoulder to see Tobias. I've only seen him a few times, and Cas even less. It's not their fault, and I remind myself of this now. He comes up beside me and we stand at the mouth of the hallway together, overlooking our irrational family. He glances over at me, and I give him a tight smile.

"I suppose this is nice," I say, my voice is still rough, but I'm no longer in pain.

Tobias nods. "It is." He smiles a little, watching his kids play with the guardians. It fades when he quietly says, "Everything is going well with the Clan."

"Tisha still being weird?"

"If by weird you mean helpful, then yes."

I take a moment, trying to find the right words. I say, "I'm just waiting for something to go wrong. She's been adamant against witches living in the Manor for … ever? And now it's okay that Elochian's temporarily out of the picture?"

Tobias considers me, looking like he's aged a decade in the past month. He gained not one, but two clans after his ascension, acting as the temporary Arch for the demons like Elochian had been doing for the angels all these years. Finally, he lifts a shoulder. "Perhaps she felt moved by his speech, and is tired of fighting."

Well, if someone has to break his heart, I'm glad that it's you.
"Maybe."

Tobias looks behind us, stealing a look at my bedroom door. I follow his gaze, hoping that his angel senses are tingling. He doesn't say anything though, at least, not about that. He turns towards me, dropping his voice. "I thought you would like to know that River's fate has been decided."

I hold my breath and run a hand through my hair, which has gotten longer. To be honest, I was surprised to hear that he wasn't killed on sight. Tobias was the one who brought River into celestial custody, where he's awaited trial ever since. Apparently, if you are affiliated with a clan and commit a big enough crime, the local authorities allow it to be handled 'in house.'

Which was lucky for us, considering the mayor is still Carina, her husband is the new Chief of Police, and the city is tearing itself apart.

I thought I would cry in relief, or rage, or something. But I've only felt the brutal cold of apathy, like I buried and grieved for River long ago. The only time I'm warm anymore is when I'm laying next to Elochian.

"And?"

Tobias' lips press thin, and he glances at Arlo. I track the movement, finding Arlo watching us with a blank expression. He shakes his head a little. Tobias looks back at me and quickly, but quietly, says, "Before I tell you, I want you to know something. It doesn't change anything, it certainly doesn't change the fact that River was a monster. But his last act was giving you up, and keeping Leon inside his body."

My blood runs cold. "What? I thought—I thought ghosts couldn't possess the dead."

Tobias stares at me, bewildered. "They usually can't, but Leon isn't a normal ghost, Quentin, we don't know what it is exactly he's become. Is that—oh, Quentin."

He embraces me, pulling us deeper into the privacy of the hallway, and I allow him. But I don't hug him back. I shake in his arms, unable to stop the hot tears burning my cheeks. "I d–didn't w–want him t–to use me to h–hurt Arlo."

Tobias whispers, "It's okay. You're okay. You—you were very brave, Quentin."

Eventually, I hug Tobias back. No one bothers us, and bit by bit I start to feel better, or at least able to mildly function. I wipe at my eyes, and Tobias fixes my hair with a sad smile. I exhale a shaky breath. "Bastard always had to get the last word in. River, I mean. Is it … is it ungrateful to hate him for it? I'm—I'm glad that he didn't let that happen, but fuck. I don't want to be indebted to him."

"Don't think of it like that. Think of it as reparations for all the pain he caused you."

"I … I guess you're right. Okay, tell me. What will happen to him?"

Tobias studies me for a moment before saying, "Arlo's team has divined all they can from River, he's … he's dying. He's an empty shell, and Leon's influence was like a disease that will continue to destroy his body even though he's abandoned it. He will be admitted to an asylum in Aeris Rook that specializes in cases like his."

I wait for something like pity or relief, maybe anger to surface, but nothing comes. I say, "Oh. Okay. Thank you."

"Are you …" Tobias trails off, fidgeting.

I give him a small smile. "Okay? No. But I will be."

Salvation

Elochian

I turn to the demon crying for help with hunger in my heart, and I raise my hand to strike. He closes his eyes and whispers, "Thank you."

I hesitate.

An angel—my angel— rests a hand on my shoulder and says, "I'll take it from here, my friend. My love, my bashert. Come here. Please, Elochian. Come here."

Quentin is all I see.

Quentin extending his hand across the bar, firmly shaking mine despite the nervous tremor in his voice.

Quentin playing the drums, head thrown back and eyes closed in ecstasy.

Quentin waiting for me at our booth with warm drinks and a sleepy smile.

Quentin telling me about stepping stones, and his fingers brushing against mine.

Quentin in the snow, Quentin on the trolley, Quentin in bed.

Quentin in bed beside me, wearing that damn unicorn pajama suit and reading a book. His knees drawn up to his chest, glasses slid down his nose, tangled hair grazing his shoulders. He quietly recites words about Uriel and Haniel. The blankets are warm and—wait—his hair …?

Quentin glances over at me, then back to his book. He inhales sharply and does a double take, tossing the book aside. He slides down his mound of pillows until coming face to face with me. He whispers, "Lochian?"

I reach out to touch his face, but stop just short of doing so. "Are you … is this real?"

Tears and a small whimper escape him and he sucks in a breath, trying to steel himself. "Yes. I'm real, and so are you. We're okay. Everything's okay."

Carefully, I rest my hand on his cheek. "Oh, Dot."

He laughs wetly. "Hey, sunshine. I'm going to hug you now."

"Please."

He wraps his arms around me and pulls me close to his heart. One of my arms squishes between us, while the other wraps around his lower back. Our legs entangle, ankles hooking around calves. I close my eyes and breathe him in, listening to his heart. I run my hand up and down his spine, and he holds onto me for dear life, fingers digging hard enough to bruise.

After a few moments I lift my head, aligning our gazes.

I bring my lips to his, and kiss him. He kisses me back, smiling against my lips, and the feeling that crashes over me then is enough to make everything worth it. I will not wait another second.

"I love you, Quentin."

He laughs quietly, but bright all the same. "You have no idea how happy that makes me. I love you too, Lochian. I was going to tell you ... before."

I cup his cheek, running my thumb across his warm skin. "You did, *isa*. With your song."

He makes a face. "*Isa?* What does that mean?"

I smile. "Salvation."

Quentin softens, but his flush doesn't disappear. He whispers, "Oh. Well, that's alright then."

"What ... what day is it?"

Quentin winces, subtle but there all the same. "April ... third?"

I swallow, blinking rapidly. "Oh. I—oh."

"Yeah ... do you—do you want to talk, or do you want to be held?"

"I don't know," I say, then am assaulted by images—*memories*—of blood in my mouth and flesh between my teeth, magick flowing down my throat. Of Quentin, lifeless, throat slashed—

"Hey," Quentin says, and air lodges in my chest. "It's okay. We're okay."

"But how? I—I saw you."

Quentin smiles tightly. "You saved me."

"No, I was too late. I was too late, and you—"

"Listen to me, Lochian. You saved me. I—I did die, a little bit, but Arlo brought me back. But there's a catch. I—Okay, so. This doesn't have to change anything between us, and if someday you change your mind and we don't … *happen*, I—I won't use it against you. The thing is, my soul was … damaged."

Quentin starts to cry, but he doesn't stop talking.

"They couldn't resurrect me into a *golem* because of that. Arlo said they could bring me back if I tethered my soul to my soulmate's, to you. But you weren't able to say yes, and I never would have forgiven myself for taking that choice away from you, so I told him no. I told him no, and he did it anyway. I—I've been so mad at him. I—I'm really sorry, Elochian, and I understand if you don't—"

I kiss him.

And I kiss him.

And I kiss him.

I say, "Stop."

I say, "I love you."

I say, "I'm thankful you are here, with me."

He asks, "You are?"

"Life without you is not worth living, Quentin."

He sniffs, wiping away fat tears and snot. "Really?"

I smile, gently taking hold of his chin. "Yes."

"Well, that's good, because I'll be around as long as you are." He tries on a trembling, but genuine, smile. "So … get used to it."

I kiss him once more, and that smile widens. "Sounds like a life well spent to me."

November

The End

Elochian

"We're going to be late," Quentin mutters, searching our bedroom frantically. I sit on the edge of the bed, yawning. My wings stretch out, shaking with the release that follows. He pulls out the drawer of the nightstand, then opens the closet and rummages around for a second before giving up with a dramatic groan. He gets down on his knees beside me, searching beneath the relatively new bed frame.

"*Isa*," I call, holding up a leather bound binder stuffed full of papers. Kind of hard to miss, honestly. Quentin blinks up at me, glasses tilted and damp hair tousled. He sighs, burying his face in his hands.

"I'm losing my mind," he says, muffled.

"Good thing you have me to find it."

His hands fall into his lap, and he smiles. "True."

I set the binder down beside me, then offer him a hand. I pull him into my lap, and he wraps his legs around me. His arms encircle my neck, and mine settle around his waist. He rests his head on my shoulder, lips brushing against my neck. I rock him back and forth, humming his song. With a gentle finger, he strokes the spine of my upper right wing. I shiver beneath him, and he pulls back.

Alarmed, he says, "I'm sorry, I wasn't thinking."

I blink, unable to get rid of the haze that's fallen over my eyes. My heart races, and my fangs tingle in a way they haven't in months. "No, it's ... okay. Try it again."

Eyes locked onto mine, he does it again, but with more pressure this time, using three fingers instead of one. He whispers, "Like that?"

I shudder, hands gripping his hips. I drop my head, pressing my forehead to his collarbone where his soulmark resides. My fangs slowly drop, and it's a pleasure pain that awakens a side of me we haven't revisited since my rampage. I haven't been ready, and Quentin hasn't either. That night left its mark on both of us.

But here, now, I feel ready. I want him, for no apparent reason at all. It's just another day in our hectic but beautiful life. The question is, does he want me?

"Did I break you, sunshine?"

I lift my head, leveling our gazes. "Quentin, I'm asking you."

He tilts his head. "Asking me ... what?"

"That day in the woods, when we first kissed. I ... I told you that one day I would want you to ask me. I'm ready."

"Oh." Quentin smiles, then shakes his head. "You know, you could always ask me."

I laugh a little. "I could, couldn't I?"

He kisses me softly, stealing my laughter. "You could."

"Quentin, would you like to have sex with me?"

"Yes," he whispers against my lips. "Yes I would. Do you ... do you want me to take the lead?"

"Please."

"Say it again."

"Please."

He reaches for my hands, guiding them to the hem of his shirt. I've seen his naked body and he's seen mine, we've showered together and slept in nothing at all, but this feels different. My fingertips float over his skin, and within moments his shirt is tossed to the floor. A great heat rushes me through at the idea that *I'm* the reason he's covered in goosebumps. *I'm* the reason he's becoming hard between us.

Quentin takes my shirt off, slow and careful of my wings. His fingers graze the scarred remnants of bullet holes. A total of five scars were left behind, scattered across my chest. He blinks rapidly, hand falling to my heart. Then he gives me a small smile, and pushes. I shift back onto the mattress and he takes my pants off, then I do his. We do each other the kindness of leaving our socks on.

Quentin trembles when he lays back against our pillows, nipples hard against the chill. He's fully erect now, and I'm halfway there, something I try not to think about in fear of scaring the moment away. I brace myself over him, staring into his wide eyes. He reaches up, tracing my lips with his fingers. "You're so gorgeous."

"As are you, lovely. As are you."

He swallows, drawing attention to his throat. Instead of fixating on his scar, I study his pulse, how it rapidly thrums beneath his skin. But he knows me, knows what I'm thinking, what I'm feeling. He's my person. He says, "I'd be honored to wear your mark, you know."

Slowly, I bring my lips to his throat. I kiss him there carefully, but the tips of my fangs scratch his skin anyway. A breathy moan escapes him, and his hips rise to meet mine. I whisper, "It will hurt."

"Some of the best things do."

"Mm." I travel downwards, leaving kisses in my wake. His stomach quivers, and I chuckle against his skin. The fingers of my free hand skims through the dark hair on his thigh, then curl around the heart of him.

"Oh, Lochian." He whimpers, an echo of how he sounded all those months ago in the living room. He thrusts into my hand and I press my thumb along the underside of him, teasing the piercing there. I'm enraptured by the sight of him in my hand, him undone beneath me by such a simple touch. He stares down at me, eyes glazed over with love and lust.

He reaches for me, ever so gently touching my cheek. "I'd like to touch you, too. Come here."

I align our faces once more, sliding my arm beneath his head so I can hold him close to me. We breathe each other in, air leaving us in shaky bursts. As his hand lowers between us, I bring my lips to his and kiss him through the moment. It is soft and sweet, unhurried, like us.

He takes us both in hand, stroking tenderly. Firm and unrelenting, but gentle. The sensation of my uncut shaft sliding against his, my tongue delving into his mouth, his hand sliding up and down, our nipples rubbing together every so often. It's almost enough to push me over the edge immediately.

But then Quentin gently wraps his fingers around the base of my left wing, and squeezes. I groan, curling into Quentin as my release takes me by surprise. My lips slide past his and I sink my fangs into the soft flesh beyond his ear. Venom drains from them, pumping into Quentin's body with a singular purpose. To make him feel nothing but pleasure while I make him mine.

The bite will scar, faintly, and from now on, he will always smell like me.

Everyone will know that our *khawbar* has awakened. I am bonded to him, and he is bonded to me. It is a connection that goes deeper than *bashert*.

Maybe now, he will finally realize how much I treasure him.

"Lochian," he cries out, coming seconds after I do. His hand stutters to a stop, squeezing tight. His warmth spills, melding with the mess I made on his hand and stomach. His entire body stiffens with the force of his orgasm, and only after he's completely finished do I retract my fangs and lick the mark. There's a minimal amount of blood, but I make sure it's all gone so he doesn't have to see it. Even the tiniest drop makes him sick.

I kiss the underside of his jaw, then his cheek, and his lips. I whisper, "Are you okay?"

He nods slowly. "Yes. Just ... need a minute. Am I ... high?"

"It'll wear off in a few minutes. Don't move, I'll get some towels."

"Ngh," he says eloquently, pulling me back down. "Be gross with me. We can shower after, don't leave."

"Okay, *isa*. Okay."

"Lochian?"

"Yes?"

"I love you."

"And I you."

"Lochian?"

"Yes?"

"We're going to be late."

I laugh, and hold him close. "Fashionably."

We are late, but that's alright because our feast is delayed.

Not the celebrations, though.

There is no Game this year, and no festival held in the Scarlet Illusionist's honor. Levena is dressed in her best, all oranges and reds, decorated with the year's bounty. Lights and banners are strung from lamppost to lamppost, criss-crossing over the streets. Giant posters no longer depict a mystery illusionist, instead they proclaim the celebrations to be '*The First Annual Min Festival.*' You can find out all you need to know about the festival, what the fuck Min is, or was, and the people who founded Levena, at the museum, which is lit up brighter than a chandelier and no doubt full of people.

Our feast, however, is on a tiny island. The trees pay homage to Thatch in their own way, shedding leaves in vibrant sunset hues. There's hardly an inch of ground not covered in them, and I don't think I've ever seen the cottage more beautiful.

Red and orange banners hang from every bit of trim and spiral around the posts of the porch. Candles burn in every window, all reds and oranges and yellows. Gourds and pumpkins litter the backyard, some painted, others carved. Products of the garden that Felix started in the spring. Long tables riddled with crockpots and random dishes are scattered in the backyard too, keeping a big bonfire company.

Everyone is loosely organized into groups. The chit-chatters, parents and their feral children, the 'I'm going to rip someone's head off if we don't eat soon,' the musicians and dancers, and the hell warriors. Of course we fall into the latter, keeping Felix company while he waits for Silas to come back. He asked Silas to check on Arlo, who disappeared to the river before Quentin and I arrived. Quentin talks with Arche, and Finnegan quietly observes the whole affair.

His place in our family has been cemented firmly this past summer, but he and Arlo have been acting odd this past month, delicately avoiding the other. Quentin seems to think Finnegan has an unrequited crush for Arlo, and while I didn't agree with him at first, seeing him today makes me wonder. He's wearing the eyepatch Arlo crafted for him, and he doesn't squint as much beneath the sunlight filtering in through the waning colors of the canopy. His leather jacket is new, his long brown curls are shiny, and I keep catching whiffs of cologne. But I can't tell if that's him or Arche, who always loads up on it to hide the cigarette smell he carries from home.

Quentin doesn't like to talk about it, but I think he feels the same way I do about the whole thing. Just ... sad, for both of them. Arlo will never love anyone but Thatch, but it's such a lonely thing, to love someone who may never return in your lifetime. And Finnegan is a good man, he deserves to be with someone who can love him back the way he should be. Felix paces as we wait for Silas, and hopefully Arlo, to return.

Finnegan says, "He's okay, Lix. He just needs a minute."

Felix nods, but doesn't say anything. He stops pacing and stands close to Finnegan, who rests his hand on the back of Felix's neck, over the thick collar of his jacket which has grown too small for him. *Arlo* did make it for him a year ago now, but Felix still likes to wear it. Maybe Quentin and I can get him a new one for his birthday, transfer the name tag over.

Silas breaks through the treeline separating Witch House's meadow from the woods, hands in his pockets. Felix stiffens as if struck by lightning, and energy burns behind his eyes in flashes of gold and pink. He remains still, waiting for Silas to approach.

Everyone else watches Silas too, but he avoids them, choosing to focus on Felix.

Humming softly, Silas dips his chin. He quietly says, "He's waiting."

Felix sighs, running a hand through his hair. Finnegan crosses his arms, holding his elbows. Quentin looks up at me, chewing on the inside of his bottom lip. I lean down, kissing his forehead before lowering my lips to his ear. I whisper, "I love you, Dot."

Quentin smiles, eyes a little wet. "And I love you, sunshine."

Felix asks, "What do we do?"

Silas hums again, deeper this time, and his fingers twitch back and forth. He looks around like he's seeing everyone for the first time, eyes catching on our family and friends, on the tables and pumpkins. He turns back to Felix, and with a little smile, he says, "We wait with him."

Felix exhales, the weight of worry tumbling off his shoulders. "Okay. Yeah, you're right."

To the nosy crowd watching us, Silas says, "We're moving this party down to the beach. Witches, you're in charge of moving stuff. Kitt, could you and Lindsey direct them down there?"

Kitt salutes him, her other arm is slung around Lindsey's shoulders. "Sure thing, boss."

"Good job," Finnegan says, winking at Silas before taking off in Caspian's direction. Silas whispers something to Felix, then follows after Finnegan. Felix turns to us, his business face on.

He says, "You two want to take care of the kids? I have a job for Caspian, and Tobias is helping with all that." He waves into the air behind him, where candles, tables, dishes of food, and decorations lift into the air. Doc walks by with a massive pumpkin hauled up onto their shoulder, nodding as they pass since their free hand is holding on tight to their wife's. I note how Arche conveniently slipped away before Felix asked for babysitting help.

"Sure," I say, earning a startled look from Quentin.

"Thanks," Felix says, then takes off into the dispersing crowd.

"Are you scared?" I ask Quentin, teasing.

He huffs. "Kind of."

I laugh, taking his hand in mine and holding on tight. "Come on, surely you can handle a couple of tiny demons?"

A tiny smile escapes him, and he bumps his shoulder against mine. "Are you talking in metaphor here?"

"I might be."

"Well, in that case—"

"Q! Loch!" Felix calls, waving us over to where Marlena and Zeke are running amuck, trying with all their might to trip up the witches focusing on moving things through the air.

We laugh, then herd the tiny demons towards the beach.

When it's all said and done, we sit with Arlo at his table. A sunflower wreath has been laid against the nearby stone pillar overlooking the river, along with a bouquet of marigolds, carnations, fern leaves, and other flowers and bits of greenery I don't recognize. The beach stinks like low tide, but no one complains. Dusk settles, and the banners hang from low branches, glowing beneath the last rays of sun. Towering candles slowly burn on the tables in their places between dishes and plates, and the gourds and pumpkins surround the tables in a haphazard circle.

Michael sits beside me, and Lindsey sits beside Quentin. The Daemarrel family, including Charlie, occupy the end of the table opposite from Arlo. Gowan and Iris act as a buffer between Arlo and Finnegan who talk in passing, but focus their main attention elsewhere. Finnegan speaks with his mother, while Arlo mostly listens to everyone else.

Doc and Ilisia flirt at the head of our neighboring table, while Dusan and Idina tell stories of old Levena. Arche and Dante, who still remains an unaffiliated angel but is close with Tobias, keep Rain and Bud company. Dimitri and Demeter sit with Gaia and Primo, who has since joined Clan Adrastus.

You would think that would be the end of it, but no. At more tables are Ren and Bob, Josse and Floyd, Quentin's old friend Leroy and his uncle, and the staff from Thitwhistle's. Helena, Rhea, and the bakers who I always get mixed up, Ally and Ollie. And last, but not least, is Janet, who hasn't gone by Chief in quite some time. And of course, Kleo and her family, which require two tables on their own.

Food and warm conversation is passed back and forth. Most of the talk involves Thatch, which means Arlo smiles more often than not during dinner. He seems so incomplete without Bosko, who passed away in his sleep on the last day of October. Quentin's feather faded the moment it happened, and he was cold all night. The link between Arlo and Quentin needed to be reforged, and Arlo insisted that it was old age, but I wonder if it's just another secret that he's hoarding. I hope that one day he will confide in me like he used to, but until then, I'll be here, waiting until he's ready.

Towards the end, when home cooked food has been swapped for warm drinks, Quentin glances at me, eyebrows raised. I tilt my head, resting my hand on the satchel at my side. It was tucked inside the house, Quentin and I had planned on doing this privately, but current events changed our minds. He exhales a heavy breath, then pushes his seat back and stands up. The chatter dies, and all eyes fall on him.

"I have something I would like to say."

I open the satchel while he speaks, retrieving the leather binder inside.

"Given that we don't know how long we'll be waiting for, I thought it might be a good idea to keep a record of all the changes that our family, our friends, and our town, has gone through while Thatch is gone. I ... I initially wrote him a letter, and I know that Elochian and Caspian have too. They're in here, and my accounts of the last year, which are less, um ... personal. There's other stuff too, like copies of the research I've done."

I offer him the binder and he takes it, swallowing nervousness. "So, if anyone wants to read it, or add to it, they can, but I think it should go to you first, Arlo." Quentin comes around the table, hugging the papers and leather close to his chest. He stands before Arlo, who has risen as well. He quietly says, "We miss him too, Arlo. You're not alone."

Arlo pulls Quentin in a hug, squishing the binder between them. He holds him close, and my old sentimental heart bursts at the seams. For a moment, we are okay. We are alright. We are sad, and flawed, and a little messed up, but more than anything else we are happy, because we have each other, until the end.

Character Guide

Clan Adrastus

Annette Adrastus: Member of Clan Adrastus, daughter of Tisha Adrastus and cousin to Elochian Adrastus. Esh Shedim. 155 years old. she/her.

Edward Adrastus: Member of Clan Adrastus, son of Tisha Adrastus and cousin to Elochian Adrastus. Esh Shedim. 173 years old. he/him.

Elochian Adrastus: Archshedim of Northern Region. Archshedim. 170 years old. he/him.

Ember Adrastus: Former Sovereign of Levena Chapter of Clan Adrastus, spouse of Sachiel Adrastus and mother of Elochian Adrastus. Deceased. she/her.

Mabel Adrastus: Member of Clan Adrastus, daughter of Tisha Adrastus and cousin to Elochian Adrastus. Esh Shedim. 170 years old. she/her.

Roque Adrastus: Member of Clan Adrastus, son of Tisha Adrastus and cousin to Elochian Adrastus. Esh Shedim. 157 years old. he/him.

Sachiel Adrastus: Former Archshedim of Levena, son of Uriel Adrastus, spouse of Ember Adrastus and father of Elochian Adrastus. Deceased. he/him.

Tisha Adrastus: Sovereign of Levena Chapter of Clan Adrastus, aunt of Elochian Adrastus, sister of Ember Adrastus. Esh Shedim. 1,906 years old. she/her.

Daniel Kavelli: CEO of Kavelli Solar, known supporter of NOJ, son of Samson Kavelli. Jinni Shedim. 185 years old. he/him.

Samson Kavelli: Former CEO of Kavelli Solar, father of Daniel Kavelli. Esh Shedim. Deceased. he/him.

Michael Nehorai: Shomer of Elochian Adrastus. Jinni Shedim. 151 years old. he/they.

Gilla Priess: Administrative assistant to Tisha and Elochian Adrastus. Mayim Shedim. 200 years old. she/her.

Annie Yakom: Security at Clan Adrastus. Esh Shedim. 69 years old. she/her.

Bartholomew Zadok: Former Shomer and partner of Elochian Adrastus. Malakim. Deceased. he/him.

Clan Haniel

Andromeda Eilweir: Steward of Clan Haniel, descendant of Juniper Haniel, spouse of Xenith Eilweir. Malakim. 201 years old. she/her.

Xenith Eilweir: Shomer and spouse Andromeda Eilweir. Malakim. 201 years old. he/him.

Charlie Crash: Shomer Trainee of Clan Haniel. Malakim. 32 years old. he/him.

Juniper Haniel: First Archmalakim of Levena. Deceased. she/her.

Kita Lansworth: Shomer trainee of Clan Haniel. Malakim. 53 years old. she/her.

Amber Mirthwood: Shomer trainee of Clan Haniel. Malakim. 26 years old. she/her.

Roland Teketo: Shomer trainee of Clan Haniel. Malakim. 97 years old. he/him.

Ichabod Vered: Master of Arms of Clan Haniel. Malakim. 214 years old. he/him.

Garren Family

Dusan Garren: Headmaster of Garren Castle, daughter of Idina Garren. Gold Dragon. 1,609 years old. she/her.

Idina Garren: Former resident of Levena, mother of Dusan Garren, daughter of Henix Garren. Silver Dragon. 3,751 years old. she/her.

Henix Garren: Sun Witch, former resident of Min Isle and Levena. Father of Idina Garren, son of Bailey Garren. Gold Dragon. Deceased. he/him.

Bailey Garren: Former resident of Min Isle and owner of the first bookshop in town. Father of Henix Garren. Silver Dragon. Deceased. he/him.

Misfits

Theodore 'Doc' Atthias: Psychiatrist, spouse of Ilisia Atthias. Behema. 75 years old. they/them.

Ilisia Atthias: Self-employed artist, spouse of Theodore Atthias. Human. 53 years old. she/her.

Lindsey Carbon: Internal Auditor at Genesis Credit and professional solar surfer, fiance to Kitt Meissa. Elf. 87 years old. she/her.

Caspian Daemarrel: Audio Engineer, spouse of Tobias Daemarrel and father of Marlena and Zeke Daemarrel. Half Elf, Half Katan. 100 years old. he/him.

Marlena Daemarrel: Daughter of Caspian and Tobias. Esh Shedim. 3 years old. she/her.

Tobias Daemarrel: Self-employed bookbinder and Archmalakim of Northern Region, spouse of Caspian Daemarrel and father of Marlena and Zeke Daemarrel. Archmalakim. 130 years old. he/him (they).

Zeke Daemarrel: Son of Caspian and Tobias. Mayim Shedim. 2 years old. he/him.

Quentin Matsdotter: Physics Professor and Erotica Author. Human. 26 years old. he/him.

Katerina 'Kitt' Meissa: Curator of Scarlet Museum and owner of Kitt's tattoo studio, fiance to Lindsey Carbon. Qieren. 90 years old. she/her.

Thatch Phantom: Watcher, founder of Min Isle and former acolyte to the God Da'haut, partner to Arlo Rook. Appears Human. Exact age unknown. he/him.

Arlo Rook: Hedge Witch and owner of many establishments in Levena, partner to Thatch Phantom and father of Felix

Rook, guardian of Silas Uziel. 72% Human, 28% unknown. 102 years old. he/him.

Felix Rook: Undefined Witch with Teleth abilities, son of Arlo Rook. Human. 13 years old. he/him.

Silas Uziel: Chaos Witch, charge of Arlo Rook. Human. 15 years old. he/him.

Gowan Zra: Owner of Phoenix Rising Studio, partner to Iris Tullianna. Dandelion Fae. 140 years old. she/her

New Witches

Demeter Chayat: Organ Witch, solar surfer, nibling of Dimitri Chayat. Elf. 76 years old. ae/aer/aers.

Dimitri Chayat: Tech Witch, self-employed, nibling of Demeter Chayat. Golem, formerly elf. 76 years old. ne/nem/nems.

Josse Exheart: Metallurgy Witch, inventor and clockmaker. Opal Dragon. 1,386 years old. he/him.

Gaia Lichin: Necromancer, self-employed. Krakeni. 39 years old. she/her (they).

Archeon Mochizuki: Teleth Witch, astrophysicist and astronomer at Scarlet University. Vampire. 108 years old. he/him (they).

Rain Pines: Air Witch, professional solar surfer. Mayim Shedim. 51 years old. she/her.

Bud Raff: Kinetic Witch, exotic dancer. Human. 42 years old. he/him (they).

Evangeline 'The Nightingale' Wroughtfern: Crystal Witch, leader of a shadow group which dominates the black market in Levena, mother of Finnegan Wroughtfern. Tzipor. 305 years old. she/her.

Others

Avina Dow: Lady of Agia. Human. 57 years old. she/her.

River Gadot: Ex-boyfriend of Quentin Matsdotter. Young Human, exact age unknown. he/him.

Rhea Hachohen: Barista at Thitwhistle's. Treant. 98 years old. they/them.

Eilae Krisgella: Mother of Kleo Krisgella, partner of Gareth and Niena. Elf. 254 years old. she/her.

Gareth Krisgella: Father of Kleo Krisgella, partner of Eilae and Niena. Elf. 243 years old. she/her.

Niena Krisgella: Mother of Kleo Krisgella, partner of Gareth and Eilae. Elf. 206 years old. she/her.

Kleo Krisgella: Felix's best friend, daughter of Gareth, Niena, and Eilae Krisgella. Elf. 15 years old. she/her.

Tina Lakai: Resurrected Shedim, exact age unknown. she/her.

Julianna Moreland: Mayor of Levena. Behema. 74 years old. she/her.

Helena Nitzani: Barista at Thitwhistle's. Vampire. 67 years old. she/her.

Edward Primo: Owner of the music store Primo's, former famous musician. Mayim Shedim. 73 years old. he/him.

Dante Shar: Physicist at Scarlet University, friend of Quentin Matsdotter. Malakim. 106 years old. he/him.

Delilah Sheleg: Archshedim of Agia Province. Esh Shedim. 195 years old. she/her.

Janet 'Chief' Stone: Police Chief of Station 7. Tannin. 49 years old. she/her.

Lucas Salone: Bartender at The Ethereal Magpie. Esh Shedim. 21 years old. he/him.

Leonidas 'The Witch Killer' Sydon: Shadow Witch, former terrorist of Levena. Malakim. Previously deceased, current state debated. he/him.

Iris Tulliana: Instructor at Levena School for the Deaf, partner of Gowan Zra. Bearded Iris Fae. 109 years old. she/her.

Leroy Tzur: Carpentry Teacher at Levena Central, friend of Quentin Matsdotter. Orc. 46 years old. he/him.

Carina Wells: President of PTA at Levena Central, known NOJ and AWO supporter. Elf. 94 years old. she/her.

Chad Wells: Police Officer at Station 7, spouse of Carina. Elf. 103 years old. he/him.

Finnegan Wroughtfern: Editor of Magickal Radickal Gazette, son of Evangeline Wroughtfern. Half Katan, Half Human. 38 years old. he/him (they).

About the Author

A queer author with endless coffee stains and a craving for adventure. Aelina's work is heavily influenced by their love of the outdoors, fantasy punk, and a desire for more inclusive fiction. Aelina also writes under the pen name Noah Hawthorne. Visit neshamapublishing.com for information on their other books, playlists, and more.

@neshamapublishing on Instagram and Tiktok

Also By

When Witches Sing is a Yuletide novella that takes place after Phantom and Rook, and includes connected short stories from the perspectives of Felix and Silas, and new characters Calen and Lysander. The first half briefly touches on years Thatch was gone, while the second occurs after the ending of Phantom and Rook. Felix and Silas' stories occur at the same time as Matsdotter and Adrastus.

Take me to Iverbourne is a dark steampunk fantasy series, and The Eternal Machine is the first book Aelina wrote.

Acknowledgements

It's been a heck of a year, and I couldn't have gotten through it without my family and friends. The reader, author, and artist communities give me hope and humanity in a time where such a thing is hard to find. I want to especially thank Foxglove Faun for bringing the cover to life, she captured Elochian and Quentin beautifully.

I also want to thank my Crew of Misfits, who are without a doubt my found family. They make me feel grounded, and like I belong in a world that can be less than understanding of anyone who fits outside the boxes we're given. They are the true definition of friends, and I am forever thankful for them. Thank you to Katrin, who helped to make this story into something coherent.

Thank you to my husband for fourteen years of being my person, and always loving me.

Here's to a few more decades, my love.